MURDER

On Big Stony Lonesome

MURDER

On Big Stony Lonesome

Frederick Poss

Mill City Press

Mill City Press, Inc.
555 Winderley Pl, Suite 225
Maitland, FL 32751
407.339.4217
www.millcitypress.net

Paperback ISBN-13: 978-1-66288-533-4
Ebook ISBN-13: 9781—66288-534-1

Endorsements

*"*Murder on Big Stony Lonesome* by Frederick Poss tells the timely tale of a high school boy caught between generational Nazism and his moral compass. The novel opens with the foreboding symbolism of predator and prey as a wolf observes Jack, the carefree protagonist, walking home. With the storytelling of William Kent Krueger, and the passion of Jodi Picoult, Poss dares to expose the raw hatred of white nationalism, and its tyrannizing nature. When Jack's family wreaks havoc on their Northern Wisconsin neighbors, he risks everything and seeks the help of Grey Fox, the Ho-Chunk sheriff. The collocation of a Jewish family, a native police chief, and a German grandfather creates a sobering dichotomy of characters that will haunt the reader long after the novel is finished."

—Bibi Belford is the award-winning author of Crossing the Line, a historical fiction novel set in 1919 during the Chicago race riots

* *"Murder on Big Stony Lonesome* is a raw and honest expose about a crime that horrifies a small rural town in Northern Wisconsin. Contemporary topics such as greed, family dysfunction, and white nationalism permeate these pages. Masterfully crafted scenes that include authentic dialogue move the story forward in a swift manner. Sentences shine off the page while relaying the depth of emotions from lead characters. Ultimately, a young man must save himself—and his family legacy—in this action-filled compelling drama from award-winning writer Frederick Poss."

—Dr. Laurie Scheer, Writing Mentor, Director— UW-Madison Writer's Institute 2010-2021 and Co-founder, New Nature Writers

*"The Proud Boys, Oath Keepers, and various Neo-Nazi groups continue to emerge from the shadows, gaining notoriety in the public forum of political discourse and action. Where did they come from? Who are they? What makes them so angry? Author Frederick Poss's new novel *Murder on Big Stony Lonesome* captures the essence of alienation these groups feel and act upon. This page turning account takes a deep dive into the personalities, ethos, and lifestyle of one such group of Neo-Nazis. It's a timely portrait that should be read by anyone

wanting to understand what makes a person declare themselves a revolutionary and attack anyone who gets in their way."

—Robert Goswitz, author of The Dragon
Soldier's Good Fortune

*(This) "marks the debut of a fantastic thriller writer. Obsessed with a true-crime case for decades, Poss has poured a lifetime of experience into his first novel—and it shows. A dynamic plot, a compassion for his characters, and a foreboding setting all combine to create an unforgettable thriller. Poss is adept at fashioning a rollicking plot and constantly demonstrates his skill at crafting unforgettable characters and vivid settings. This is a writer to cheer for."

—Nick Butler, internationally successful author
of Shotgun Love Songs, Little Faith, Godspeed,
and The Hearts of Men

Acknowledgements for Murder on Big Stony Lonesome

I HAVE SO many individuals who helped me put this story together. First, I must thank my sister Lucy. She was the state crime lab investigator who in real life came to Tomah, Wisconsin and literally dug up the evidence out of a frozen cranberry bog. Lucy was my chief source for the plot. Next is Dr. Mark Attermeier, a physician who kept an open mind about an elusive illness in my gut, and because he did, he saved my sanity and my life. Third, Al Lowry, my friend and retired policeman, not only was a good source for legal information, but he also kicked my butt enough to see me finish the story. Fourth, my novel accidentally bumped into a terrific online writing critique group, and I will be forever indebted to all eight members and the insight and guidance of its leader, Dr. Laurie Scheer of UW-Madison. Special thanks to Bob Goswitz and Bibi Belford and Laurie for their marvelous endorsements.

I was fortunate enough to have my wife Cheryl persuade her reading group to review the first completed draft of the story. They were some of the toughest critics and best helpers I had: Cathy Hoffman, Carol Skutley, Virginia Hilbricht, Sharon Schulte, and Sue Waldusky. In good conscience, I also must acknowledge the entire English Department of UW-Eau Claire for their acceptance and support during my time teaching there, especially Marty Wood, Jack Bushnell, Karen Welch, Max Garland, Jan Stirm, Stephanie Turner, and Blake Westerlund. These folks were incredibly good to me, exceptionally professional, and their interest in what I was about boosted my uncertain self-confidence.

The Good Lord happened to bless my high school English classrooms with some amazing students, and foremost among them is Nick Butler, author of *Shotgun Love Songs*, *The Hearts of Men*, *Beneath the Bonfire*, and *Little Faith*. Nick helped me pick the title; and after reading the story, he even provided a wonderful endorsement for the book. What a guy!

Finally, very few books ever get written without lots of support on the home front . . . and I am blessed to have a great wife, daughter Cheri, son Nick, daughter-in-law Sara, and grandsons Carsten and Oliver.

And I mustn't forget one other contributor: the wolf pack on Big Stony Lonesome.

–EPIGRAPH–

IN **2018,** THE Southern Poverty Law Center identified 1,020 active hate groups in the United States.

o– https://patch.com **(2019)**

o·A new interactive map shows there are 15
hate groups in Wisconsin.

o– https://patch.com **(2019)**

oJewish Americans comprise 2.4% of the population of the United States.

o-www.pewresearch.org

o57% of the religiously motivated hate
crimes committed in the US in 2020 were
against Jews.

o -www.jns.org/fbi-reports

oThe Milwaukee Jewish Federation reports 101 antisemitic incidents in Wisconsin in 2022. There has been a 494% increase in such incidents since 2015.

Table of Contents

Chapter 1

A VOICE WITHIN *him told the alpha wolf it was time to hunt . . . and in the same breath grimly reminded the pack leader there was a basic law of nature which only human animals could occasionally ignore. . . safety!*

Safety! — this and only this he knew was the single most important ingredient in balancing all of life's essential equations. Yes, certainly he felt an irresistible bond to his mate, a Luna wolf who had shared with him their time as the alpha pair of the pack. Yes, he would instantly rush to her defense if things ever came to that. Yes, he would defend his new litter of cubs to the death as well.

But love, if it could ever exist in the natural world of fang and claw, was a pale creature of little consequence unable to justify a reason to die. If the struggle to stay alive was likened to a game, safety trumped the need for food, water, shelter — even sex and companionship. Safety first, foremost, and last.

The voice spoke again, this time with urgency. Time to move. Reluctantly, the sleek, brindle brown, black and white wolf obeyed, realizing he was abandoning the familiar haunts of his spacious granite den on Big Stony Lonesome peak earlier that afternoon than was his custom. While both male and female wolves in living packs all shared the work of raising their young, the aggravations and chaos visited upon him by the squirming black littler of his late season pups was proving too much for his patience to bear this day. Hunting, on the other hand, always restored his leader's dignity and sense of patriarchal purpose. And within an hour, surprisingly enough, with the onset of dusk, after a quiet journey down from the bluff country and an even quieter stalk into the surrounding marsh along Highway 173, he came across familiar prey . . . a human from the von Himmel pack.

With a hunter's passionless logic, he studied his situation with the intent of a predatory creature who had to feed his family by stealth, cunning and ferocity. His ultra-keen senses alerted to the young human approaching out of the obscure black gauze of an autumn Wisconsin night well before he saw his prey was a boy.

His nose, at least 100 times more sensitive than a human's, dictated a rapid and eloquent discourse. Advancing quickly upon his target, all his senses announced ahead on the lonely road was a vacuous target broadcasting the delicious scent of a human who lived near chickens and pigs. If the wolf could have smiled, he would have done so broadly. So typical of its kind, this two-footed adolescent prey, meandering over broken asphalt and potholes, lost to some oblivious and utterly unsafe place.

The young human's disregard for the basic danger of his situation stressed the animal's patience beyond acceptable limits. Seeking relief, the pack leader stretched his lips to their extremities, the open-mouthed, half-grin of a practice bite. Yes! He would take this one. Such careless behavior wasn't something Mother Nature ever rewarded. And the red meat would be so welcomed back at the den where his ravenous sons waited. They almost lost their lives to starvation when a bullet had terminated his brother's ability to help provide.

. . . But something made him pause.

Was all this just too easy? The plan appeared to be beyond reproach. Just belly low along the saw grass ditch until he was even with the prey. Then a short, violent rush. A lunge for the throat. After all, while this was his first human target, it was not his first stalk.

These thoughts made the wolf salivate uncontrollably. Just a chance like this one to avenge the moment a fully-grown von Himmel put a pistol bullet in his sibling's head rekindled a powerful surge of retribution. Settling the score with any of this human pack, even if it was just a young one, made the pack leader's heart sing in exultation.

On the other hand, everything in his experience told him that humans were the most fatal of dangers to his kind. People had guns, poisons, hunting dogs, vehicles, and a deep, abiding hatred reserved especially for wolves . . . and ironically enough, hatred in equal measure for other humans. Human beings, especially the von Himmel clan with their need to kill without any need to eat their prey, presented risks that he could not fully calculate.

Then the voice that told him to hunt warned him there were more humans about to arrive. It wasn't a smell. It wasn't a noise. But there was a dangerous rebalancing of energy in the atmosphere around him. The mathematics of a kill no longer added up. Fight or flight. Better to be safe than sorry.

So maybe another time? Another place? When there was no room for escape? Time to leave the voice commanded.

Chapter 2

MAYBE HE WAS just a fifteen-year-old high school freshman, but Jack von Himmel sensed something was wrong even before he saw the angry faces of his father, his two uncles and finally his grandfather emerging out of the foreboding gloom of the north country's September sunset. Perhaps it was the sudden silence of the northern Wisconsin bog on both sides of Highway 173? One minute earlier, despite the fading autumn light, the roadside marsh had comforted the boy on his walk home with the lyrics and trills of jays, larks, and red-wing blackbirds.

Now not a sound. It was as if a deadly beast of prey had announced its presence to all living things except Jack, and they had taken the hint.

The long, fast strides of the three younger adults in his family hurrying toward him in the middle of the north country's loneliest stretch of this remote Wisconsin highway rapidly announced to Jack trouble lay ahead. Like predators on the hunt, these man-wolves all had their eyes laser focused on Jack.

Why suddenly had he become their target? Yet the biggest threat the boy knew would be his grand-father, Herman, who followed last but inexorably astride the family's only horse. His *opa's* face, Jack realized was a mirror of Odin in perfect wrath.

Just minutes before, the boy had stepped off the school bus with his first girlfriend, Sara Koleski, and walked with her up her family's cranberry marsh dike road. Wiping away a few wispy cobwebs, they nestled into a spacious porch swing on the wide, white veranda of her family's colonial home. They joked about school, shared their small inventory of strange teacher behaviors that day, and after a few minutes of playing Rock, Paper, Scissors, instead sat in blissful silence and held hands. Their together time was suspended momentarily like a Luna moth in a wolf spider's gossamer tube.

But the early autumn smudge of lemon- orange sunlight disappeared. Sara had to go inside. Jack had to face a two-mile hike down a dark road carved out of sphagnum moss and bog water to finish his farm chores before supper.

Then all his assumptions disappeared with the sunset stain over the horizon and the fast approach of the four men . . . his father in the lead, his two brothers alongside, and followed by his grandfather Herman.

Herman von Himmel was a man who simply dominated people, animals, and situations. To stop his horse the old man simply clucked his tongue, and his mount instantly stood stock still as his rider used his only arm to hold onto the saddle horn and dismount.

Yet in the next instant the horse reared up, its nostrils flaring as it seemed to catch and identify a slight but dangerous scent in the night air. Its instincts detected a slinking motion down in the marsh. Something was crawling away. Its potential threat was more than enough to trigger a bucking response.

"Ya—you just stand here now and be good," Herman von Himmel steadied his horse and whispered into the sorrel's twitchy brown ear. With the invisible enemy now retreating into the deep recesses of the bog, the gelding knowingly nodded its head. The man slipped a sugar cube out of his pants pocket and slid it into its mouth. "Ya—*das gut*, big fella," Herman murmured.

This was the *good* grandfather Jack knew and tried to appreciate, the man who had an intuitive communication link with every animal on the von Himmel farm. But the boy braced himself. He knew it was time for the *other* grandfather to announce his presence.

"Jack! I ask you this only once," his grandfather demanded. "Why are you so late coming home?" Despite being in his late fifties with an amputated left arm, Herman von Himmel had fluidly slipped off his mount, stomped down the ditch bank and entered the marsh grass and bog water pool that Jack had backed into for escape. The old man was a timber wolf on the stalk.

His anger rising even higher, the old man accusingly stabbed his only pointer finger at the boy "This is the third night in a row you come home late stomping up this old marsh road. Our farm animals are crazy for food!" He paused to gather his breath and shouted, "Why I got so worried about the cows and pigs, I make all three of my useless sons come help me find you."

Herman's ramrod posture paralleled his rigid shock of grey-white hair, near vertical eyebrows, and a snarl to match the best of any meat-eater. At six feet-four the state leader of Wisconsin's Nazi party looked like a snow-capped volcano about to erupt. Despite the much-too-cold weather for the first week of September in the Midwest, the old man was only wearing a short sleeve t-shirt. His bare right arm rippled with muscles thick as steel cables, his fingers resembled claws. His left sleeve hung empty and limp except for the stump of what a power takeoff couldn't grab, and Herman was losing his hair-trigger temper as fast as he had lost his arm.

"I—ah—I just" . . . Jack stammered, and his grandfather backhanded the boy across the length of his throat, knocking him to his knees. The old man's skull-capped ring tore into the boy's neck.

"Don't lie!" the old man raged. "*Dumme!* You should be home doing your chores. The animals in our barn been making terrible noise waiting for their straw and oats!"

The boy stood, stepped out of the swamp water, and slumped to his knees on the rising edge of the ditch. He looked up at his grandfather and whimpered, "I met a girl, *Opa*. And I thought the horses and pigs could wait just a little."

Then, after a hesitant pause, Jack added— "I thought you would approve of her."

But *Opa* von Himmel had slipped off his leather belt as the boy spoke and doubled it in his hand.

"You are not to think! You are just to answer! Why will I approve?"

"Because her parents are rich, *Opa*!" Jack cried out as he staggered back into the ditch water. "She is their only child." Through his tears and pain, the boy shuddered and said— "You always say to me 'marry a rich woman.'"

The boy struggled to right himself and ward off another blow. "You say it's just as easy to lay with a wife who has a big bank account as to lay with a poor one."

Jack forced himself to convulsively smother his fear and anguish. Any more emotional display on his part was simply an invitation to receive more of a beating.

"And just how do you know her family is rich?' The old man's voice was still electric blue with anger, but its intensity lowered noticeably with the hint of a new income source no matter how many years distant.

Jack had been soaking his hands in the near-freezing ditch water, so he placed them on the side of his throat to cool the welt he knew was forming there. "It was when school started last week just before Labor Day," the boy rushed to explain. "The first day of English class when I saw her sit across from me, I didn't know anything about her family. I just knew as soon as we looked at each other, my head was spinning. And I think hers was too!"

The heavy, leather belt rose.

"Her name is Sara," Jack rushed to add. "The next day we started sharing lunches, and she told me about her family's business. She was worried about coming to a big public school after eight years of being taught at home."

Jack paused to apply more cold water to his neck. "There were so many kids, some of them might

10

pick on her. She didn't know what to do. Then she saw me."

"And why she pick you to like? Why not some other boy?"

"Sara said it was because I am bigger, taller, maybe stronger than the other boys, *Opa*. She thought no one would pick on her if we were together. And today she said she liked my straight blonde hair and blue eyes!" Jack's face brightened momentarily when he thought of Sara—her playful gypsy green eyes flecked with tiny golden shards, the midnight black ringlets of her wavy hair and best of all, the strange necklace suspending a six-pointed golden star just a few inches below her chin.

Grandfather Herman cleared his throat audibly, a signal that he intended to make a speech. Jack knew every word that was to come. Then the old man said something that stunned all four members of his audience.

"Come to your *opa*, Jack," Grandfather von Himmel said gently. "You must forgive my bad temper. I am sorry I hit you," and the old man opened his one serviceable arm and motioned for the boy to come forward for an embrace.

Jack felt trapped. Should he trust the invitation and let the violence of the moment pass, or was this too another means to get him close enough to inflict more pain?

"Come, Grandson. I hurt you no more," and Jack, feeling he had no other choice, reluctantly move close to his grandfather. The old man's mood swings were as unpredictable as they were extreme.

As the boy and old man first touched, Herman sensed hesitation in the boy and spoke to address it.

"Yah, Grandson, I hit you out of anger because I have hope in me at times that you can be something more than the failures what my three grown sons are." The violent mood had evaporated. Old man von Himmel spoke with a sincerity that spontaneously replaced his rage. He looked across his four-member family in a moment of reflection.

"When I was just a *junge* child," he began ponderously, "my *vater* Heinrich would come home wearing his dark brown shirt and tall boots from a secret Nazi rally. It made me want to be just like him in every way. Now all four of you should want to be like me!"

Jack involuntarily sucked in a deep breath. He knew every word of the speech that was about to be delivered.

Von Himmel looked at Jack impassively as the boy dabbed carefully at his throat. "You are just a little *dummkopf*," the old man said temperately and stroked the hair back from the boy's forehead. "Help me buckle my belt."

Then just as swiftly, *Opa* von Himmel changed his topic again. "But our family can always look to get real money," he said and nodded his head in agreement with himself. "Your *vater* and his two brothers just hire out as day labor on the cranberry marshes and local farms." The elderly man switched his gaze to assess his three adult sons. "Most all their pay goes down their gullets in beer, so we must live in a broken-down mobile home."

The old man started climbing up the embankment. Half-turning back toward Jack, he said, "The small amount of cash *Vater* gave me disappears like the Jews in his father's prison camp. With no one here holding down steady work, we still must live on the little bit of savings my grandfather Friedrich salvaged from his prisoners at Nauthausen."

Then, as if prompted to defend the indefensible, Jack watched as his grandfather reached the top of the bank and cleared his throat for another oration. "My *urgroßvaer* . . . my grandfather he was Commandant Friedrich von Himmel! His was the only camp with walkways outside the prison walls so the high command could watch the Jews and gypsies starve as they waited for their turn in the gas chambers."

Herman stopped to thread his belt back into place. " My *vater* Heinrich was *Hitler-Jungen* then. He wore the black, red, and white diamond of the youth corps proudly on my shirt so when he paraded in the camp, his *vater Friedrich* could see he was growing up to be like him." The old man paused to emphasize the question he wanted to pose: "Maybe I can find someone to make uniforms for all four of you?"

Herman von Himmel waited briefly, then spit in the ditch water. "Thank Odin that *Vater* sent me to America. He said to me over and over that if the Jews had been smart, they should have sent the Nazis to the death camps first—but they didn't, so we sent them.

Jack allowed himself a few seconds to quickly touch his throat. Would the wound show when he went to school the next day? If it did, how could he explain it? Why did his grandfather have to be so angry? For Jack the only need he understood was the basic desire to be safe. Safety, first, foremost and last.

Chapter 3

THE THREE ADULT sons—Karl, Gunther, and Ade, had remained intentionally silent, but Jack sensed Herman was expecting someone to validate what he had just said. The young boy wondered if some concluding words might be coming from his uncle Ade. The man was physically the smallest but also the smartest of the three brothers. Jack's own father, Gunther, was a hopeless drunk. Uncle Karl was the community hothead. As Jack had predicted, Ade spoke, timidly advancing a little humor, however dark.

"*Ja, Ja, Vater.* Another couple of years for Jack and who knows?" Ade said, a faint smile tracing a small crescent across his face and up to a small, dark birthmark. "Maybe right out of high school, he marries rich, and we all live off him?" Ade stole a glance at his brothers, searching for approval even if it came in the form of suppressed smirks.

There was a hint of humor in Uncle Ade's voice as he continued, "Maybe even I could try marriage again, eh? Maybe Gunther could force himself away from the twenty gallons of beer he drinks every day and have another Jack with some jolly, fat German woman with big tits?" Seeing the beginning of smiles on the faces of his brothers, Ade turned, tugged on his oldest brother's unruly beard, and patted him on the shoulder— "But we all know for Karl, it's just too damn late!"

As much as his neck wound burned, Jack even had to laugh, especially considering how risky it was to use humor around his grandfather. The boy studied his *opa* for a moment. He couldn't help but notice the old man remained uneasily pensive. Maybe what his grandfather said about the failures of his three adult sons was truly a deep source of discontent? His father and two uncles all had married right out of high school. Within a year all three marriages dissolved, the young women finally disgusted with the crowded life in a double-wide, their husbands' alcohol issues, and constant verbal abuse.

Jack knew it was Herman's wife, Freida, who had the responsibility for raising him as a child until her passing a year earlier. Her silver braids were wound as tightly to her person as her devotion to Catholic marriage vows. But her kindness and patience had made all the difference in the developing Jack's moderate nature.

When his grandfather flew into one of his tirades, she would take the boy aside and say, "Now, Jack, it's just your *opa* making big talk. Hot air coming in to fill up a big balloon, then going out in a whoosh. It makes *Opa* feel important, but it changes nothing. Hitler, he is still very dead, and the Nazis, they still lost the war!" She always finished her little sermon by giving her grandson a sly wink that gave Jack a small measure of comfort.

Then as quickly as the reflective moment had settled on Herman, his demeanor abruptly changed again. He strode back down the bank and dug his right hand into Jack's neck, inching the fingers into the boy's throat.

"And what does my little *dumme* know about why his girlfriend's family has so much money, huh?"

"They grow cranberries, *Opa*!" Jack stammered . . .. "They own a big marsh operation."

"And which one is it?"

"The one just down the road from our trailer only a couple miles," Jack choked out his answer.

"But there are two big marsh operations near us, boy! One north. One south. Which one is it?" and he shook Jack hard to force a reply.

"The south, *Opa*. The south!"

With that information, Herman von Himmel eased his grip on his grandson. Jack finally was able to breathe.

Karl rushed down the bank to speak to the old man. "But, *Vater*, to the south is the Koleski Marsh. Like everybody else around here, I always thought they were Polish. But when I worked there one afternoon this summer, they were having a party. I asked what the occasion was. One of the old women bringing out the plates said they were celebrating a young cousin just turning thirteen. She called the party a *barmitzvah* . . . That means they are *Juden!*

Chapter 4

HERMAN SPAT DOWN the bank into the bog water. "*Juden?* And why, Karl, you not tell me this before, huh?" One look at his grandfather's face made Jack step back into deeper water. The old man had conjured a ferocity about him that Jack had never seen.

The head of the family and state Nazi leader gathered his two fists together and began pounding the knuckles against each other. "We will have to pay the Koleskis a little visit very soon," he rasped. "We will drop by some time after midnight. And we must do it quickly, before the word gets out to my followers that my family are Jew lovers! If we don't strike those Jews first, we will be attacked ourselves!"

With a vicious look at Jack, von Himmel spun around and began barking orders as he forced himself back up the incline and the road home. "Today is Tuesday, September 6. Look all of you to tomorrow night. We will make our practice run then. If all goes as expected, then on Thursday we will get our revenge—*Ja?*" His three sons all simply nodded their heads. Herman was in much too dangerous a mood to interrupt or to question. "We go back to our home now," ordered von Himmel. "Jack feeds the animals. We make our plans!"

The three adult sons vigorously started hiking back up the embankment. Jack, however, hung back a little. He took a minute to press the bottom of his t-shirt into the cuts on his neck and consider what had just happened. His grandfather had just announced an attack on the Koleskis, and that simply terrified the boy.

Sara's family was to be attacked because he shared school lunch with her? Jack felt overcome by panic and fear. "But why?" he asked himself. He struggled to keep his mind clear and composure intact. Until this moment, the boy had simply heard the hate speeches from his grandfather, his two uncles and his dad, but he never saw them do anything serious about it.

Now, in one night's crazy mix of hatred and revenge, everything had changed. His first girlfriend and her family just became the targets of his own Nazi family. Jack knew as certainly as he understood anything in his life, he had to stop the attack—stop it no matter what the cost.

After the hunt earlier that night to locate Jack, all four adult von Himmel family members sat down at the dinner table for pork roast, potatoes, and gravy. When Jack took his place at a little television tray alongside the adult table, he realized things were continuing to go in the wrong direction fast. The boy saw his grandfather emerge from one of the three small bedrooms in the trailer wearing his grandfather Friedrich's best Nazi SS uniform. It fit perfectly.

The teen listened with ever increasing concern when he saw his grandfather Herman stand and begin an all-too familiar speech.

"When my *urgroβvarer* Friedrich, he is your great grandfather, boy, had my *vater* Heinrich come to this country as the war in Germany was coming to an end, the relatives in a nearby town who took him in began teaching him most of what he taught me." Von Himmel paused for a bit of dramatic effect, but since even Jack had heard this same speech many times before, none of the adult sons or the boy himself registered any particular interest.

"As I have said many times—"

"Yes, you have, *Vater*," Karl, the sassiest and least savvy of the sons managed to say. His remark drew a few conspiratorial snickers from his other brothers, but Jack knew enough to remain silent and still.

"Shut up, *das Aas!*" retorted Herman, and Jack found he was unconsciously cringing for the possible blow that could be coming Karl's way.

"As I have said, my grandfather Friedrich, disguised as a common soldier, surrendered to the Americans before the Russians could murder him. But he planned for my father's future just before he turned himself in. Once made a prisoner of war, he was shipped here to Wisconsin because most of the men from here were still in Germany killing us!"

"There was no one to pick the cranberries and work on the farms," Karl added without a prompt, continuing from the script all the brothers and boy knew by heart. That's what German prisoners of war had to do until the war ended."

"*Ja,* that is correct, Karl. Maybe there is still hope for you?" agreed Herman. "Camp McCoy and our nearby town of Hamot was a good place for prisoners of war. Plenty Germans had already settled here. Plenty of farm work to be done. My grandfather Friedrich was even visited by some relatives who lived in Wisconsin Rapids. That's how he got his son Heinrich a place to live."

"Yes, *Vater,*" said Karl again. "But now your three sons are the prisoners of this damn trailer!" Gunther and Ade smothered laughter in their sleeves lest they draw the short straw if Herman grew upset. Karl, however, enjoying his moment of defiance started tugging on his thick, blackish-blonde beard. Even Jack had to admit to himself his uncle's antics added to his comedy, no matter how much the cost might be.

"Shut it!" ordered Herman. "Wisconsin is a good place for us. Plenty of pig to eat, strong beer to drink, and some who still support the Nazi cause. Most important, the state back then needed farm hands and cranberry workers because in 1944 the marsh owners still had most of the work done by hand."

"*Ja!* Hand labor all right!" shouted Karl. "The three of us know all this too well. Even today, it is always us what do it . . . hard labor with our hands!" and he held up the calloused palms of both hands, then tugged on his beard again. "Hand labor it is! Our labor, our hands!" and this time all three sons burst out in belly laughs.

Karl had gone to the well one too many times, however. Herman lunged across the dinner table and backhanded his mouthy son. "Shut up, *Schweinehund*! When I want some smart comment from you, I will say so!"

Jack knew the blow was bound to be delivered. Like almost every night the boy could remember, he saw Karl or his dad or Ade slump over, drooping their head in a gesture of defeat.

"Now my sons, your great grandfather Friedrich only stayed a short time in this country because the Jews were still hunting men like him," continued Herman. "You know he tried to get away to Argentina but died just before arriving." The old man was so engrossed in his harangue that he failed to notice the rest of the von Himmels had simply refocused on eating dinner.

"Yet he saved Heinrich, his son, just like a proper papa should do. Just like I expect all my sons and my grandson to do for me too!" The old Nazi used his right eye, the best of his pair, to scan for any dissension in the ranks. Not finding any, he continued. "And Heinrich done his *vater* proud. In 1968 he not only had me, his son, but he also founded the Wisconsin Nazi Party." Herman paused; a light veil of sadness dressed his features. "Ya, my *vater* done so much good. Then he drives to a celebration of the first year of the Wisconsin Nazis, drinks too much, and gets killed when he falls asleep at the wheel and crashes into a telephone pole coming home."

From behind a cloud of cigarette smoke and a bottle of beer, Gunther asked, "But, *Vater*, how does this help us get back at the *Juden* who own the cranberry marsh?"

"You tell me, Mister Smartass!" Herman retorted.

Perhaps out of a desire to spare a brother another beating or possibly to curry favor for himself, Ade spoke up instead. "The cranberry operations themselves will give us the means to destroy them."

Herman thrust his face within millimeters of his usually quiet son. "*Ja?* Just how they do that, Adolf?" Jack could see his grandfather ready both of his massive fists if he had to punish his smallest son for his pale skin, weak frame, and expression-less face. The boy had always sensed a simmering tension between father and son. Herman called his youngest son Adolf, but the man himself always insisted on being called Ade.

"The growers all have dynamite," Ade cooly replied. Save for the small, dark red birthmark on his left temple that darkened as he answered, his uncle's face barely registered emotion.

"*Danke!*" thundered von Himmel as he rubbed his hands together in obvious pleasure.

Striding over to stand behind Ade, Jack watched as his grandfather began to strenuously massage his son's shoulders. "We steal the dynamite from the same kikes we attack! *Ja das gut!*" Herman was warming to his subject now, and that intensity pushed itself down through his arms into the pow-erful fingers he used to knead his youngest son's narrow shoulders.

Things had gone too far decided Jack. He had to speak up. "But, *Opa*, you shouldn't hurt the Koleskis. They have done nothing to us. Sara is my friend!" he pleaded.

Herman grabbed for the boy from the other side of the kitchen table but came up just short. "*Verdammt!*" he shouted. "*Juden*, are *schwein*! Say anything more and you will be pig food for our animals!"

"Oh hell, Dad. He's just a kid! He doesn't know any better," growled Gunther. At the same time, his uncle Ade gave Jack a swift little kick under the table. When the boy looked over in surprise, he saw his uncle's face writing an essay on danger. One more hard stare from his uncle convinced Jack to be silent for his own protection. Safety first.

"Forgive me, *Opa*," Jack said. "I was daydreaming about fishing at the Granite River dam and spoke foolishly without thinking."

Von Himmel's face gleamed with a stormy sheen of oily sweat. His one massive hand mopped the perspiration up his wide forehead and into the frosty forest of white hair sprouting out at all angles from his head. For almost a minute, Herman von Himmel simply stood in the middle of the trailer's kitchen, saying nothing, thinking of a direct reply. Then he backhanded Gunther across his right ear.

"That's for screwing a sixteen-year-old girl child and bringing this half-wit grandson into my world!" he snapped at Jack's father. While Gunther fumbled at his chair, Jack tried to shrink away from the kitchen table and bury himself in the darkness of the little bedroom he shared with his father.

Herman glared at Jack. "Then again maybe my grandson can learn from his father's mistakes?"

Returning to his topic for the evening, the old man plowed ahead with the details of his plan. "It is nearly the night for harvesting the cranberries, *ja*?" No one dared to reply.

"We know the growers got to wait until the coldest early September night when the temperatures drop to almost freezing. The closer to thirty-two degrees without freezing the fresh fruit crop, the redder the berries get and the more money the marsh owners make. Right?" The old man turned slightly and focused hard on Gunther.

Jack felt a moment of panic for his father. The boy knew this was the moment Gunther needed to redeem himself or face another blow.

"The growers have to open each of the little sluice gates on their big dike, *Vater*," Gunther said. "First, they turn on big sprinklers to put a little water on the crop to protect it from the frost for a short time fix, then they have the time it takes to open the sluice gates along the dam. The lake water slowly covers the berry beds to completely protect them from freezing and then floats up the crop to begin harvesting."

"*Ja, gut!*" beamed Herman. Then the old man turned his attention to his sassy son Karl. "And so,

Mister Long Beard, when the lake water is needed at the critical moment, what do we do next, huh?"

Karl understood he had never been thought of as the brains of the family, but it was impossible not to realize his father would come around to him with a test question. He brushed back an unruly lock of dark blonde hair, scratched his neck where the ragged beard began and said," We blow the whole frickin' dike and wipe out their entire crop! The reservoir lake rushes down and sweeps away a hundred years of groomed vines and buries their crop in floodwater and mud."

Then in a rare flash of imagination, Karl added— "And we leave a little souvenir behind so others with our beliefs know it was us, know that the von Himmels still make war on the inferior races and that they should leave us in peace."

Using his right pointer finger, Karl swirled two large, imaginary letters across the tabletop. "*Ja!*" he said. "SS! We leave these letters on the back of their mailbox. Our message will get out, and we will be safe."

Herman von Himmel clapped his hands in surprise and glee. Maybe his rigid discipline was finally going to start paying off with his brood of adult sons? "Tomorrow night, Wednesday, we practice. Thursday night we attack. Together we can all watch and enjoy!"

Jack winced as he heard his grandfather revel in the family plan. What about the Koleskis? They would lose their entire marsh just because their daughter happened to like a boy who lived with Jew haters. Jack's gut twisted tight as a fresh spot weld on a bridge girder. How could he warn Sara but remain anonymous . . . and safe?

Chapter 5

IT WAS JACK'S desperate need and faint hope he could prevent the bombing that led him to risk a conversation with his grandfather the next morning at breakfast time.

"*Opa*," he said gingerly. "I finished the chores up good this morning. It's only 6:00 am, so I have plenty of time to eat the nice hot meal you make for me."

Von Himmel made a small grunt to acknowledge Jack's presence, eyed him suspiciously for a moment, then returned to frying bacon and eggs.

"Grandfather," Jack continued. "I have a question for you."

A single malevolent eye swiveled in the boy's direction.

"I don't understand why cranberry growers need dynamite. Can you tell me?"

"Why should I tell you anything?" and the old man turned up the heat on the frying pan.

"Please, *Opa*. I want to learn from you," said the boy trying to put just the right amount of respect and pleading into his voice to get past the wall of hostility the grandfather still carried from the night before. Of course, if Herman von Himmel was to sense Jack's real intent—to somehow intervene—Jack would face the beating of his life.

"So suddenly your grandfather is not such a *dummkopf*?"

"As I said, *Opa*, I hardly knew what was coming out of my mouth last night at the dinner table."

"Hmmm!" said the old man and he briefly returned to poking at the bacon and eggs. Then after a few seconds of reflection, he decided in the boy's favor.

"*Ja*, I will tell you. It is the only way you will learn." Then to emphasize his intent, von Himmel lifted the spatula up from the pan and pointed it directly at his grandson. "But mind that you listen carefully. I have no intention of repeating myself. Understood?"

"Oh, of course, *Opa*. Thank you so much!"

"Tell me, Grandson, do you know where cranberries originally were found?"

"No. Please tell me."

"The berries were found growing wild in marsh places like Massachusetts. Near the sand dune beaches along the ocean. People who settled there learned from the Indians that the bitter red berries were one of the few good fruit crops that could be grown so far north."

"So how did the sand help the fruit grow? Don't you need fertile soil to grow a crop like fruit, *Opa?*"

"One should think so," agreed the grandfather as he warmed to the conversation. "But cranberries are like Nazis, Jack," and he laughed at his own simile.

"How so?"

"They are hard on the outside, bitter on first taste but full of pure goodness when allowed to ripen."

"And sand—it helps the cranberries grow?"

"*Ja!* But it took a long time to figure that out. The berries were also native to Wisconsin in swampy areas of the state like Hamot and Wisconsin Rapids. The Indians used them for hundreds of years before our superior race of whites arrived. But here we got no ocean, no sandy beaches."

"The cranberries need something sand has in it, something like fertilizer?"

"No, not really, boy," and von Himmel turned off the gas stove and covered the eggs to finish cooking under the steam. Motioning for Jack to come close, the old man rested his one good arm on the boy and spoke with surprising affection.

"In the middle of the 1900's, the state government set up a test station near here to figure out how to fight bugs that ate the berries. There they made a

32

big discovery. Europeans like us, not some redskins living in teepees, discovered that you had to have sand to grow the best cranberries."

"What did they find out about sand, *Opa?*"

"They found the best cranberries grew in the marshes closest to the sand beaches by the Atlantic Ocean. But the sand was not a fertilizer at all. The sand was blown onto the beds close by in the howling windstorms of winter when the beds were covered with ice. When spring came and the ice melted, the sand did the one thing every fruit crop has to have happen."

"What was that?"

"It pruned the cranberry vines taking away all the dead leaves. You see, sand is just a small knife with very sharp edges. By cutting out all the weak parts of the berry crop, the healthy vines were able to grow big. This is the same thing that Adolf Hitler was doing with the Jews in Germany!"

Jack thought it was safest to nod his head, but what his grandfather was saying didn't make any sense. Pruning fruit is not the same thing as murdering millions of people.

Herman continued, "You could say that sand is like a good Nazi. We remove the weak, and we allow the strong to succeed."

The idea of pruning away people disgusted Jack, but he needed a connection to Herman if there was to be any chance of preventing the Koleski bombing. "Maybe we take some cranberries up the Externstein hill by Monroe if we ever go there again and sacrifice some of that blood-red fruit to Odin? Maybe that would be enough to make up for what I did, *Opa*? Maybe there's no need for an attack?"

"*Nein*! Odin is a god of blood, not fruit, and I do not intend to sacrifice you on the Nazi Irminsul shrine close to where we fish at the Granite River dam. The bomb attack must take place, or we will be attacked instead." Von Himmel moved away to check the food he had on the stove.

"Wisconsin, boy, has no ocean with sand beaches," he said as he poked at the eggs and returned to a more comfortable topic. "But we do have the best sand in the entire country. Pure sand, white as sugar and hard with very sharp edges. Perfect for pruning as it sinks into the beds once the winter ice melts."

Jack realized he had missed his mark but decided there was still a chance to win his grandfather over to an alternate plan. "That must be why the growers have dynamite. They go to the big mounds around here and blow up enough sand to truck over to the frozen beds in winter, *Ja?*"

"*Ja, Ja! Das gut!*" replied the old man. "They drive the trucks right over the ice covering the vines and spread the sand evenly across the beds. Then all they have to do is wait for spring to come, and the warming temperatures release the sand to cut away the useless and the weak. Good Nazi sand!" and both laughed . . . a hearty one from von Himmel's belly, a forced one and a weak smile from Jack. The moment would prove to be the zenith of their relationship.

Chapter 6

A RARE HERMAN von Himmel chuckle brought the other three adult sons out of their beds and into the double-wide's small dining area. Huge clouds of steam billowed up out of the coffee mugs Jack had distributed and now moved from seat-to-seat filling.

Gunther slurped the blistering brew down in one voracious glug. "Gimme some more of that nigger coffee, son!" he exclaimed smiling at his own little metaphor. "Black and nasty! —that's how I like it. Gimme some more quick!"

Jack was beaming with an unaccustomed happiness as he poured the coffee for his father, and the man picked up on the changed expression.

"What makes you so perky this morning?" he growled.

"Just feeling good, *Vater*. I dreamt of us walleye fishing at the Granite River dam by that rocky hill that *Opa* calls the Nazi Externstein. On top is where the Third Reich's Irminsul shrine is." Then Jack,

sensing the upcoming agenda item for the breakfast table, ducked out of the conversation circle.

Herman von Himmel, in an automatic man-
nerism, roughly cleared his throat. "*Ja!* So now we
talk about the details of our attack," and began to
rub his hands together with furious friction.

Looking at Gunther first, old von Himmel said,
"Now according to my plan, you will be ready to
cause a distraction if needed."

"How am I gonna do that?"

"You will take some of those old, worthless tires
we have out back by our storage shed.

Go to the south end of their marsh property
along the county road and set them on fire with
some gasoline if you see someone come out of the
house to sneak up on us."

"Ok," Gunther assented. "But when are we
gonna do this?"

"Tonight is for practice, tomorrow night for real,"
von Himmel said. "It has been getting colder and
colder this past week. Tonight will be the right time.
We sneak over and check out everything. The radio
weatherman says cold front tomorrow. None of the
growers can take a chance on losing their crops
to frost, so that will be the perfect night to blow
the dike!"

"Speaking of time," said Ade, "what time of night
do we do this?"

"1:00 in the morning exactly. It should be the coldest part of the night!" von Himmel said, nodding his head as if in agreement with himself. "We will set our watches to be all together in our efforts."

"And what about me?" asked Karl.

"You will get in close to the house, but not so close as to alert any dogs. Any sign of trouble, and you shoot off the pistol I give you. Any real threat to you or us, and you will use the pistol to remove the threat—any threat," he said ominously. Understand?"

Karl's wide grin announced his understanding and agreement. He was excited to be able to handle one of his father's Lugers again. He loved the idea of impending violence. The last time he was allowed to use the pistol, he proved his marksmanship to his father when a pack of wolves tried to get at their farm animals. One of the predators lingered just a little longer at the fence than the others, and Karl nailed it with a head shot his first try.

Jack ran to his bedroom and cried when the wolf was killed. The pack had found the little barn and the family's small collection of cows, pigs, and horses a few months earlier. Instead of trying to shoot them, Jack had secretly saved table scraps and put them out in six dishes. He reasoned that a predator with a full belly was no longer a threat to the family livestock, and an occasional bowl of meat was easier to provide than the constant vigilance it would take to try to hunt and shoot a creature as wild and cunning as a timber wolf. The pack leader had witnessed Jack filling the bowls and seemed to silently assent to the arrangement, that is until his brother wolf lingered too long.

Herman turned to Ade next. "And you, Adolf," he explained, "will go with me to their warehouse and pick the lock tonight so when we break in the tomorrow night, we can find and remove enough dynamite sticks to do the job."

"How many sluice gates do we have to blow up on their dike?" Ade asked.

"Ah," smiled his father, "that is where Jack comes in," and he turned suddenly to focus on the grandson who had inched away from the table to lean against the stove.

"Jack," von Himmel announced, "you been riding that school bus and playing patty cake with that little Jew girlfriend of yours. Today you will put that to some use!"

Jack found himself ready to back away from this conversation, but he was tight to the stove with nowhere to move. The boy hesitated, then asked, "How will I do that, *Opa*?"

"Ride the bus, hold her hand, walk to the house and when you get there ask her to show you their marsh. Just a little walk down the dike road. And, of course, as you walk, you will count how many sluice gates there are for flooding their berry beds. Then, come straight home, and tell us tonight! That way tomorrow night we will know precisely how many sticks of explosives we need."

Jack was staggered by the fact he was to be involved in what his grandfather called "the attack." However, he quickly realized the fact that nothing would happen until the next evening. Today or tomorrow would provide him a chance to somehow warn Sara and her parents to be on guard.

His grandfather finished the meeting with quick review. "You all know your jobs. Don't none of you come home drunk tonight, or you will regret it! Adolf, from what I remember seeing from the road, it looks like they got maybe twenty bog beds for their cranberries. We will be certain from the number Jack gives us tonight. But if I am close, then you and I will each be carrying bags of about twenty sticks of dynamite, two sticks for each sluice gate. It can be something easily done."

Von Himmel cast a surly glance around the table, then back at Jack. There would be no more talk. His sons turned to finish their breakfasts before getting in the family pickup and heading out for ditching work. Jack quietly went back to his little bedroom, picked up his schoolbooks, put on a jacket and headed out to wait for the bus.

"What can I possibly say to Sara?" Jack feverishly asked himself. Soon he would be sitting next to her all the way to Hamot High.

Chapter 7

JACK DECIDED THAT sitting on the bus or next to Sara in class was just not going to give him the time and privacy he needed to give her a warning. And as he thought about it, what kind of message could he give without implicating his own family or himself? The idea of a secret note on her school desk seemed to make some sense at first. But as he thought more about it, the boy realized only a few kids in school lived on cranberry marshes. It wouldn't take very long to figure out he likely was the author.

Then Jack thought about sticking a warning note in her purse or school bag. That seemed like a better idea because it would be anonymous if he picked the right time and place. For the better part of the day Jack felt that would be the best plan. He even used some of his lunch time to slide off to a remote corner of the auditorium where he sat alone and composed it.

Things changed, however, when he and Sara were sitting together on the bus going back home after school. Her long, black hair was curled, and she wore a bright, kelly green dress that perfectly matched her eyes. The six-pointed star on her necklace perfectly matched the aspen leaves along the road coloring gold from the sudden cold.

"Oh Jack," Sara bubbled, "I just have to tell you about our substitute teacher in world history class today." She turned herself to square up with Jack as they sat on the bench seat of the bus, thus providing no hidden moment to slip a note into her school bag or purse.

Listening to her relate the substitute teacher story made Jack wince with the knowledge his family intended to destroy her family's livelihood just because they were Jewish. "What did it matter they are Jews?" Jack thought to himself. "What is so wrong about that?" With the certainty of a sledgehammer stroke, his grandfather had literally beaten into Jack that Jews were the scum of the earth. But the old man never explained why. Why were they so bad? How was Sara's family posing any kind of threat or harm to his family or, for that matter, anyone else's family in Hamot?

And it felt like the more that Grandfather raged about the Jews, the less convincing all his accusations became. Wasn't it just as likely that other peoples of the world had bad individuals too—even Germans? And for everything that Jack had witnessed growing up in a rundown old mobile home filled with swastikas, what was so good about being a Nazi? It seemed like all they did was to hate everyone else and beat each other up. Grandma Frieda had no time to hate anybody, and she made it clear to Jack he shouldn't either.

As the bus slowed down to let them out, Jack realized he absolutely must find a way to put Sara's family on their guard, but not involve himself or his own family. If his dad, his uncles, or his grandfather ever discovered he had tipped off the Koleskis, Jack was certain he would get a terrible beating . . . or worse.

A redwing blackbird flushed from the cattails along the ditch road as Jack and Sara slowly strolled the gravel road leading up to the Koleski farmhouse. Cackling as it rose, the small bird suddenly pivoted mid-air and dove at the two teenagers. "Probably protecting its nest, even in early fall," said Jack as he and Sara ducked.

The bird and its protective action instantly raised another concern for the boy. "What would the Koleskis do to me if they found out my family blew up their dike and emptied their lake?" he worried. "What would happen to me at school? What would the Hamot police do if they discovered I was part of

44

a crime?" Jack's head reeled with so much anxiety he almost didn't hear Sara speaking again.

"Yeah," she giggled, "Talk about getting protection. Tommy Traber was carted off to the office by no less than the principal himself!" Sara had to stop and hug herself to contain her laughter.

"Miss Schrunager, the substitute, was talking about unrestricted submarine warfare in World War Two, and Tommy was in the back of the class making fun of her. He was talking to the kids around his desk, and he said how funny an old, dried-up granny like her would look in a black bikini as she stood on top of the conning tower commanding a U-boat." The retelling of this made Sara double over again in laughter. Her emerald eyes were precious gems sparkling in the Indian summer crown of autumn sunshine.

"Huh? —Oh ya, right, real funny," muttered Jack, trying to appear he had been listening the whole time.

"Anyway, Tommy got so wrapped up in describing the black bikini that he failed to notice the substitute teacher was listening and coming down the aisle toward him," Sara chuckled. "Before he knew it, Miss Schrunager reached out and speared his left ear like she had eagle talons for fingers. Then she pulled up so hard that Tommy tipped over his desk as he struggled to his feet. I thought he would lose a perfectly good ear lobe!" Remembering the scene made Sara nearly explode. "Then his ear hurt so bad," she said, "he made a big mistake and called her Screw Knocker!"

Her laughter was infectious enough to even make Jack smile for a few seconds. Then in a sudden, earnest voice he found himself lecturing his girlfriend.

"Sara, needing protection isn't funny," he said.

"What do you mean, Jack?" she asked.

"Well, your substitute was just a really old lady doing everyone a favor by standing in for the absent teacher, right?"

"Well, yes, I suppose so," she replied.

"And a kid who is known for his mean pranks starts making fun of her for doing her job. I think she deserved some protection and respect. I sure know what it's like to be afraid and needing a protector."

Sara paused as they ambled up the driveway to the Koleski home. "Jack," she asked with sincere concern, "what are you afraid of? Who are you afraid of?"

Jack squirmed. He did not want the track of the conversation to lead anywhere near his own home situation.

"I believe you and your family should think about real protection," he replied. "Hey, I live in a wrecked up old double-wide just up the road. You folks live in a great big, beautiful house with a bunch of garages and all kinds of warehouses and stuff that could be robbed."

"What does that prove?" Sara asked a bit defensively.

"It just proves that I really care about you, Sara. That's all."

Sara blushed. The intensity of feeling in Jack's declaration confirmed that he was still being the good protector which originally attracted her to him. She reached up to grasp his hand and hold it in hers.

"Oh, Jack. That is so really nice of you to say! I told you how worried I was going from home school to a public high school. You were there then when I needed someone, and now I see you are just continuing to do your job!" she gushed. "And you are right. With me being a new kid, Tommy Traber could have easily decided to pick on me instead of the sub."

Jack felt like the momentum had made a favorable switch, so he plunged ahead. "That's right! And I am not only going to protect you, but I want your whole family and your entire marsh business to be safe too. There are always people who are jealous of success."

Sara's face registered a little bewilderment.

"And how are you going to protect all this?" and she gestured with a wide swing of her hands that encompassed the entire landscape of buildings, lake, and cranberry beds. Remembering his assignment, Jack quickly counted twenty-two berry beds.

"I can't literally protect all this," admitted Jack. "But I can remind you and your family not to take what you have for granted. I can point out that this week is harvest time, and your parents should be careful about what goes on around the house and marsh."

The blackbird came diving down again and nearly tangled itself in Jack's scruffy head of blonde hair. It was perfect timing. They both ducked again at the same time and came up laughing together. Jack was certain he had hit his mark . . . not too little, not too much. Hopefully, the Koleskis would be extra vigilant the next night and would flood their crop with protective lake water to insulate the berries from frost. He had done all he could. At the very worst, someone else's cranberry marsh would be dynamited soon.

Jack gave Sara his best smile, put his arm around her waist, and tentatively kissed her on the lips. To his surprise, she kissed him back firmly . . . then again. Someone was showing Jack real affection, someone other than Grandma Frieda. The first kiss felt, well, strange, an awkward pressing of the flesh.

But certainly not the second kiss. . ..

Chapter 8

THAT NIGHT JACK was careful to leave Sara's front porch with more than enough time to get home before the light started to fail. All the way home he kept repeating the number twenty-two out loud just to make sure he didn't forget. And as he approached the trailer, there was his grandfather standing on the stoop waiting for him.

"How many cranberry beds do those filthy Jew *drecksaus* have?' Gone was any trace of affection. His grandfather's face was a mask of malevolence. He had just called the Koleski family "dirty pigs," and he spat out the words like they were big game bullets.

"Twenty-two, *Opa*," Jack responded instantly.

"*Gut!* Now go do your chores." Clearly, Old Man von Himmel had his mind focused on preparations for the bombing and didn't want to trifle with idle chatter.

The three von Himmel sons were noisily slopping down bratwurst and beans when Jack came in

from taking care of their farm animals. Jack unob-
trusively collected his plate from the pantry shelf,
filled it and sat down in a corner to eat.

"So, men," announced the old man. "Tonight, at
one in the morning we are going to do a practice
run." Von Himmel's left eye always cast a slightly
off target, blind directional stare, especially noticeable when he was worked up with emotion. With
this practice test announcement, the frozen-in-place
eye shone brightly but aimed up and away from
its audience. Intentionally or not, it gave observers
a sense of unease and discomfort for not truly
knowing who it meant to confront.

Karl looked up from his plate and cleared his
throat to protest a late-night excursion into bog
country in near-freezing temps. Ade's right foot
came down hard on Karl's near in-step and a brief
but intense glare stopped the man from lodging a
protest. It also saved him from a quick, savage blow
to the part of his face nearest his father.

Instead, Karl coughed and simply threw his
head back to move his long blonde bangs out of his
eyes and over his forehead. Then he attacked his
food instead, burying his face in his plate.

The more carefully he listened, Jack found he
had lost any appetite for supper that night. "What
if my count of the bog beds isn't right?" he worried.
"What if they are discovered sneaking around the

property?" Then Jack remembered the earnestness of establishing protection he had passed on to Sara and her family. "What if they are out there tonight and Karl pulls out the pistol?" The suddenness of the concerns gave Jack a sharp pain in his gut. He didn't even realize he automatically reached for his stomach and held it tight.

The eye was swiveled toward Jack. It seemed to swell to twice its size. "And what is wrong with you?" von Himmel asked.

"I have a stomachache, *Opa*. Can I be excused to go to bed please?"

The grandfather made a gargling sound deep in his throat to show his irritation. Then he agreed. "*Ya*, go to bed. You are not needed tonight and would probably get in the way or make some noise." With a dismissive gesture toward the little cubicle that they called Jack's bedroom, the old man turned to re-establish contact with his three adult sons.

"It is now 8:30 pm," he said as he glanced at his wristwatch. "All of you line up your heavy coats and thick boots so there is no fuss later on when we need to leave." He passed his gaze over each of the men making sure they were watching him exclusively. "We leave here at precisely 12:15 am and walk to the marsh so there is no sign of our vehicle if someone drives past."

His three sons nodded dutifully in agreement and went back to their meal. Jack lay on his bed with his knees curled up almost to his chin. Fear clawed at his heart and mind. He cried softly and roughly wiped away any sign of tears lest they were noticed.

Just a few minutes past midnight, there was a great deal of clumping about in the dimly lit trailer. Right on time, the four men threw on their heavy woolen coats and trudged out into a frosty-sharp, September night in Wisconsin.

Chapter 9

"**ARSCHGEIGE!**" **THE WORDS** exploded from the front door of the trailer, jerking Jack out of a restless sleep. Lights snapped on; heavy boots pounded the floor. Someone other than himself was obviously in deep trouble. Jack immediately recognized it was his grandfather doing the shouting.

"*Arschgeige!* I say it again! You are worthless!" and the heavy thud which followed the curse told Jack that one of his two uncles or his father had just been knocked to the floor. Jack turned over on his bed and stared into the garishly lit kitchen. He saw it was his father who was down.

"How many times did I tell you we had to remain hidden, huh? And all you had to do was to watch the house!"

"But *Vater*," Gunther pleaded. "I was doing my job. I was hiding in the bushes and watching. The house looked all dark. I thought they were all

53

asleep." Gunther tried to get to his feet but a swift kick to the ribs stopped that effort entirely.

"Oh, I thought the house was dark and they were all asleep!" the old man sarcastically mimicked. "What were you thinking—that those Jews would turn on all their lights and sit on the front porch as they stood on guard?"

"I thought they would be out on the marsh watching the thermometer to see if they needed to open the sluice gates tonight. Why would they guard their house?" Gunther von Himmel made no second attempt to rise from the floor, but his father kicked him again anyway. "But I never expected them to be watching for intruders!"

"*Scheisse!* You have turds for brains!" von Himmel raged. "I don't know why they were guarding their house either. They should have been out on the dike checking the temperature. But the point is that they weren't out on the marsh. Someone was sitting in their darkened house, watching. When you used your lighter, the man came outside and called 'Who's there?'"

The grandfather strode across the body of Gunther, knelt beside him, backhanded his son's woolen cap off and grabbed a handful of hair.

"And what do they see, huh? They see the orange light of your cigarette coming from the bushes in front of their house!" —and with that outburst, von

Himmel smashed Gunther's head into the heating grate on the floor.

Two strikes later, Gunther's forehead was a messy tangle of blood and shoulder-length, greasy light brown hair. When Himmel raised the man's unconscious head again and smashed down, it was obvious he had no intention of stopping. Ade coughed loudly and stepped toward his father to intervene. He couldn't simply stand by and watch his brother beaten to death, but the old Nazi unleashed a furious snarl toward Ade before returning to his work. Gunther was going to pay the ultimate price for the botched practice raid.

"*Opa!*" It was Jack's voice and then the boy himself, dressed in tousled pajamas, slowly advancing into the light from his corner bedroom. The same crazy snarl from the old man clawed out at Jack as he approached.

"*Opa*—you are beating my *vater* to death. You must stop!"

Karl and Ade instantly leaned back and away from the confrontation lest they too would be victims of their father's insane anger. Von Himmel did pause for an instant, but he still held up Gunther's bloody head like it was John the Baptist's.

No one ever dared to talk to the old man as Jack was doing. The sheer audacity of being told to stop briefly confused von Himmel. "Who is this who tells me what to do in my own home? What are you anyway? —just a *dumme* who got us all in trouble in the first place!" and as the grandfather rose to move toward Jack, he released Gunther, letting his face hit the grate with a metallic crunch.

Jack did not step back. Instead, he took a small step forward to meet his grandfather.

"*Opa*," he said in a strong, steady voice, "you must not kill my father."

"And why not?" he thundered. "I brought him into life. I have the absolute right to take life away from him." The enraged grandfather reached for Jack.

"Yes, *Opa*," Jack agreed. This affirmation stopped von Himmel cold. What was this the boy was saying? What he was doing seemingly made no sense, and he did not back away.

"So maybe I kill you too?"

"Yes, *Opa*," the boy agreed, then with a significant pause he added—" but then you would not have enough of us to complete your attack tomorrow night. Without our attack, you will be at risk."

This undisputable logic and obvious courage caught the old man off guard. He could think of nothing to say in return.

Sensing a shift in the argument, Jack stiffened his resolve and continued, "Yes, *Opa*. I am saying we should still attack a marsh tomorrow night. But since this one is on such alert, let's hit another cranberry operation. Five miles up the road to the north is the Einhoffer marsh. They are even bigger than the Koleskis. It would make even more news if they were hit."

"And—" he added with subtle emphasis, "they are not on guard."

Von Himmel stepped back from the impact of Jack's words. He was utterly dumbfounded. Nothing in his experience, little as it was with the boy, had prepared him for the daring and intelligence before him.

"All right," von Himmel hesitated as his audience audibly gasped. His mind tumbled in on itself. "We will do it as you say. Tomorrow night it is."

"Yes," the old man continued the more he considered the idea. "Yes!" He could get the attack he wanted and with the proper number of people to make it work! "The Einhoffer marsh," he ordered—"no practice test necessary. We have all worked on that property and know it well. They keep the dynamite in a little shed far from the farmhouse. Yes, that will be the plan."

"But they're Germans, not Jews!" exclaimed Ade.

"No matter," retorted von Himmel. "We still leave our little SS call sign on the mailbox."

What Herman von Himmel had just said and done because of Jack transfixed the others in the room. In fact, the old man was amazed as anyone in what he had just agreed to do. No one ever stood up to him when he was seething with hostility.

He turned away and ever so slowly moved toward his own bedroom, lost in a world of new thought and new plans. What kind of grandson did he have?

Just as he reached the bedroom door, however, the old man turned back toward the others who were now bending over Gunther and beginning to provide first aid.

"But make no mistake—tomorrow night there can be no excuses!" he snarled, his reincarnated expression a fierce combination of anger and hate. "If someone does anything wrong, what Gunther looks like now will be a tiny scratch compared to what I do next!" Then the grandfather entered his bedroom and closed the door. No one needed to ask what he meant.

Chapter 10

SOMETHING NEW WAS going on with Sara. The next morning when she flounced down on the bus bench seat next to Jack, the boy was taken aback. His girlfriend had been transformed—a touch of rouge on her cheeks, a dab of cranberry red lipstick, a pink bow to tie back her wavy, black hair, and a splash of perfume that whispered of honey and lemon. The only old and familiar item about Sara was her necklace suspending a gold star with six points.

"Good morning, Jack von Himmel!" she bubbled.

"Good morning to you! Wow! I love the new Sara Koleski I am seeing. Who is this girl?"

"Oh, I'm not such a much, Jack" she said, the wide smile on her face betraying how much the compliment truly meant. "Just a little girl stuff here and there," and then she laughed so hard she had to cover her mouth with her hand. When Sara Koleski found something funny, her mirth broadcast itself across the near world.

Jack had to laugh too. Her happiness was too contagious not to infect Jack, and a moment of mirth was a rare commodity in the von Himmel family.

Then Sara's deep green eyes and entire expression narrowed tightly with intent. "But Jack," she said, "my whole family wants me to thank you."

"For what, Sara? I haven't even met them beyond just saying hello."

"They want to thank you for alerting us to possible danger."

Jack suddenly found it difficult to breathe. "So something happened, Sara?"

"Well, yes and no. Something sort of happened."

"What do you mean 'sort of'?'

"Dad's two brothers checked the bog temperatures outside like always, but my dad sat in the living room with the lights turned off. Looking out our picture window, he thought he saw someone light a cigarette in the dark by our bushes near the driveway ditch."

"But nothing harmful really happened? Just someone maybe smoking out by the road?" Jack mind was scrambling, but he felt he had to make the incident as small and meaningless as he could.

"Yes," she paused a moment then agreed. "I suppose you are right. It was likely just somebody having a cigarette."

"If that even happened," said Jack pressing down to make the episode smaller yet.

"Yes," Sara agreed. Then she turned and snuggled herself tightly into Jack's right arm. "But I know you keep us safe," and with the exuberance of the moment, impulsively she raised her face to Jack and kissed his cheek. She was about to giggle but something stopped her: a fresh, angry welt on the near side of Jack's neck with parallel black and purple blotches above and below. Sensing something unknown and unwelcome, Sara quickly looked away. What could she say? What had happened to her Jack?

Jack couldn't decide whether to shout for joy or slump over in utter relief. The moment of testing had come and gone, he realized. Hopefully, something else would go wrong tonight, but even if didn't, Jack knew Sara would have what she needed— safety.

No person, in Jack's way of thinking, could live without safety. It was far more important than love he believed. Being safe meant staying alive, no matter how bad the situation. Jack felt an emerging hope for his future with Sara and the unexpected joy she conjured within him.

"How is safety different than having someone say they love you?" Jack would ask himself. His constant conclusion was simple and always the same. He could taste safety in the hot food his grandmother cooked. He could feel it in the firm but rare hugs she offered. Love, on the other hand, would have to remain nebulous, undefined, if it existed at all.

When times were dangerously crazy in the trailer, the boy would whisper, "Odin, protect me!" whether he fully understood his grandfather's religion or not. Four large, angry drunken men, muscles hardened and honed every day from the backbreaking day labor picking strawberries and cranberries generated tremendous tension when conflict broke out among them in the narrow confines of their old mobile home. And for a young teenage boy, there was literally no place to hide.

One finger tap on each on the two Viking wolves, Freki and Geri, who hung on a gold chain around Jack's neck had sufficed for an appeal for his safety. His necklace icons and his grandmother's arms provided the only actual refuge in the constant moments of family drama and drunken tumult. Whatever love might or might not be, there was something concrete about being safe. Unlike the complex tangle of feelings welling up inside him as he sat next to his first girlfriend, Jack knew safety was something he could touch, taste, even smell in the comforting essence of fresh baked bread on his grandma's apron.

Then he met Sara on that fateful first day of school. Now nothing was the same.

Chapter 11

JACK MADE SURE to come home early again from Sara's front porch. He didn't want to bring any undue attention to himself. He quietly went about feeding the animals, doing farm chores, and laying out plates, cups, and silverware for supper. During dinner, very little was said around the table, but the boy did notice the heavy coats and boots were all laid out in preparation for the night attack. After cleaning up and doing his homework, Jack suppressed his desire to stay up and see the others leave.

"Good night, *Opa*," he said, looking back into the kitchen from his bed. "Good night, Dad, Uncle Karl, Uncle Ade." Maybe pulling the covers up over his head would help control the waves of anxiety he felt breaking against conscience. If there was any safety in sleep. Perhaps tonight the *dream wolf* would not pay him a visit?

After a long pause from the other room, his uncle Ade said softly, "Good night, Jack," and when the others turned away, his uncle made a pushing down gesture with his left hand to indicate Jack should stay in bed the whole night. "Sleep well," he whispered, and he made the gesture again to reinforce his message.

Jack understood. Uncle Ade had kept him safe occasionally before and now was doing it again. Safety, ironically, was the single most valued element in the lives of everyone—Sara, Jack, Gunther, Karl, and Ade—everyone except for Herman von Himmel. They all needed to be safe from him. When the men returned from their mission, his grandfather might prove dangerous on contact, and with that thought Jack shut his eyes and tried to sleep.

The wolf pack on Big Stony Lonesome slept well that night, too.

The boy was sound asleep when the four men strode out the door and down the rickety front steps. They wore their usual woolen jackets and boots, but von Himmel had obviously been thinking about how to improve their chances. Each man now had his face smeared with charcoal ash and soot, and the old man had taken the extra step of searching through Gunther's pockets and removing his cigarettes and lighter. Herman also distributed insulated gloves to protect against the cold and to avoid fingerprints.

"Adolf, I have decided we will use the pickup truck," the grandfather explained. "It will carry some gear I want to use, and we can park it hidden off on an old logging trail near the Jew's driveway. Two of you will load up the back end and then sit in the bed."

Pointing nervously toward the small barn they referred to as the shed, von Himmel continued, "Karl, you and Adolf go back there and get the big waterproof bag I keep in the shed. Fill it with the bolt cutter, two trenching shovels, electric cord, a battery, and the flashlights I have covered with red cloth." Despite the solemn authority in his voice, Von Himmel's hands trembled noticeably as he gave the orders.

No one dared disappoint the old man this night, so the two brothers quickly returned with the supplies. As they loaded their gear into the bed of the truck, all three of the sons could see their father was acting strangely giddy. The reason now became apparent.

"I have a little surprise for all of you—and that grandson too," crowed the old man. "What's that? He's just a dumb kid who you should leave alone," Gunther replied gruffly, beginning to show a glimmer of concern for his son.

"The surprise is that we are still going to blow up the Koleski Marsh . . . despite what that bossy high school brat of yours said to me last night, Gunther!" The glee and bitterness in von Himmel's voice was viscous as cold sludge in a sewer pipe.

"But I thought it was agreed we would attack the Einhoffers?" Karl took the risk to respond. "We all know they are the largest cranberry operation around here. It would make the biggest news, just like Jack said."

The old man couldn't contain his defiance and temper. "*Ja*, ain't nobody going to tell me what to do, especially some idiot high school kid. We will blow up those Koleskis because that's the family that Jack got us all in trouble. Not with nobody else's marsh. We got to blow up the Koleskis so that others like us understand it is the von Himmels who made this insult to every Nazi in the county go away."

With one swift wave of his good arm, the grand-father indicated everyone should take their places in the pickup. Since in the end it didn't really matter to any of the the adult sons whose marsh was dyna-mited, they all shrugged. Karl drove with Herman beside him. Gunther and Ade had drawn short straws and suffered the frigid night air as they rode in the pickup's open bed behind.

It only took five minutes to drive to the Koleski's marsh even without using headlights. Karl swung the truck off the highway far enough to hide it on the logging trail.

"We use this truck for another reason," explained Herman as everyone climbed out. "In case something goes wrong, in case someone doesn't do their job," and the old man looked precisely at Gunther, "we can get away fast in this," and he patted the hood of the old rust and red Ford 150.

"Now," he said, "I have seen three Koleski men working on the marsh. All look alike. Keep in mind that those Jews are likely walking around between the house and the marsh. Someone might even be up on the dike itself," and the old Nazi pulled out a well-worn Luger to brandish in the moonlight. "This will take care of any troublemakers!" he said emphatically and handed it to Karl as he was the son posted closest to the house.

His words, however, were not as reassuring as he meant them to be. All three sons instantly remembered their father's brutal beating of Gunther the night before, and they couldn't avoid thinking about the dire warning their father made at that time for anyone making a mistake. The Luger only made them even more unsure and unsteady as they stepped out of the pickup and went to work.

Gunther smeared the letters SS on the mailbox by the road then, after rolling two spare tires into it, hid in the ditch. Karl, acting as a scout to sound an alarm if needed, settled in close to the warehouse. No sign of alert, however, registered in the nearly freezing September night. Ade, carrying the large, waterproof bag with the tools inside, followed his father to the explosives' shed.

"Stupid Jews," Herman von Himmel sneered. "They must think they scared off the intruders last night. Now they are all watching the temperature gauges in that out building where they keep the power switches for their marsh lights." His father was in an agitated state of nervous fear mixed with ecstasy Ade decided. There was nothing for the son to say in reply except to grunt agreement.

Moving with the alacrity of a bull snake on a frog hunt, Ade picked the lock on the Koleski's tool shed door, went inside, and rapidly filled his carry sack with two dozen sticks of explosive. He had decided ahead of time to take a couple extra sticks of dynamite against the chance there was an unexpected need for them. Out of an abundance of caution, he put the two extra sticks in a separate bag. If nothing else, the explosives could be stored in their family barn and kept for some other attack.

Using his covered flashlight, Ade searched for and found the necessary blasting caps. He also grabbed two crimping tools and a long spool of wire to connect to the battery he brought from their farm. Just before closing the Koleski's shed, he pocketed an equally long spool of fuse cord in the event the charges couldn't be set off electronically.

When he emerged, he simply nodded that all the supplies were now in his possession. Herman blinked in agreement and silently started a slow walk in a tight crouch toward the dike. The marsh was as still as it was bitter cold, and as the two men approached the dike, they could hear snippets of conversation drifting their way from the electric supply that held the controls for the spray system building across on the other side of the reservoir. The von Himmels slowed their approach to remain undiscovered.

Keeping low and avoiding talk, Ade and his father each went to a sluice gate where a series of wooden slats were stacked in vertical fashion to hold back lake water used for watering the cranberry beds. Moving from one gate to another, they efficiently dug out small holes, buried the sticks of explosives, inserted a blasting cap into each, and attached the electric wire which would detonate the charges. After tamping down the earth around the explosives, both men continued down the line to the next pair of gates.

Ade was silently cursing the icy temperatures, cranberry marshes, the state of Wisconsin, and most of all, his father, by the time all twenty-two sluice gates were primed to blow. He tried to slide his hands inside his pants to warm them up, but the shock of the cold was too much for that sensitive area. Out of sheer desperation, he chose to vigorously rub his fingers together so he could keep his hands flexible.

Carefully following the wire back to the first gate they worked on, both men paused for a moment, their mouths pumping long shards of frozen breath. Moving back from the lake margin as far he judged was safe, Ade cut the wire just long enough to reach both battery terminals, peeled off the insulation from both ends and fastened one exposed wire to the negative terminal of the battery. He took a deep breath and handed the other exposed wire to his grandfather who sat on the rim of the end of the dike.

"Danke!" the old Nazi whispered. Calmly, he rose to a squatting position, winked at Ade and in a normal tone of voice said, "Heil Hitler!" Then the old man touched the remaining wire to the positive terminal.

Chapter 12

THE BLAST WAVE smashed into the two men every bit as hard as it smashed the twenty-two sluice gates. Like a tidal wave of solid concrete, the lake rose to twice its size at the dike before spewing its entire volume in one mad rush out across the cranberry beds and nearly a half-mile north into the bogs.

Unprepared for such overpowering force, both Adolf and his father were lifted from the safety of hiding above the dike and thrown down below it instead. Before they could recover their footing, the massive wave of black water and debris hurled them across the marsh. In an instant, Ade and his father were fighting for the lives, desperately struggling to keep their heads above water long enough to grab an occasional breath. Ade managed to keep hold of the bag with their tools, but the impact was so sudden and severe, all of the tools spilled out the open top. Metal screening and pieces of dike gate careened around the two men and into them from every angle.

But it was the bag that saved them. Ade, thinking fast, kicked his body high above the water, flipped the bag upside down to fill it with air and using it as a life preserver, splashed across the rolling tide of water to grab his father. Dark water whirlpools sucked at all their limbs. Thick clumps of marsh grass and finely-ground shards of sand littered the air like confetti on a New Year's Day parade.

"*Vater!* Here!" was all Ade could manage to shout as he extended his arms and the bag toward the old man. They both attached themselves to the make-shift life jacket and held on like death itself. The tidal surge from the reservoir carried the men well past the end of the beds and deep into the bog country beyond. Fortunately for them, the power of the initial surge had spent most of its energy before the wave took them into the bushes, pines and marsh grass that lay beyond the cultivated beds.

Then, just like it had roared into life, the wave crested and died. Both men found themselves lying in knee-deep muck and brush. "Luck was a lady this night for us, *Vater!*" coughed Ade, and he smiled while humming a few bars of Sinatra's famous song.

"A smart thing you did with the tool bag," the old Nazi panted as he rose to his knees in swamp water. "It saved us!" and von Himmel laughed despite himself. "But I think my damn ears never gonna stop ringing!" Both men shook their heads at the truth of what he said.

Ade didn't know whether to laugh or cuss. There remained a shrill roaring sound in his own ears, too, and he noticed neither his father nor he had fully regained their balance. Ade decided that no amount of anticipation could have prepared the two men for the thunderous power of the dynamite. On one hand, both men nearly drowned; on the other hand, the attack had been wildly successful. The only bitter taste that remained alive and well from the event was a mixture of swamp water and blood recycling itself through their mouths.

He decided the last few moments were insanely comic and started to laugh. But just as he began to chuckle, he heard voices shouting in the distance.

"Come, *Vater*," he coarsely whispered. "We have to get out of here before they catch us!"

Herman von Himmel could only wheeze in reply as he was still choking out water he had swallowed. They clambered to their feet, and dragging the empty tool bag in one hand, Ade led his father eastward out of the bog in the direction of Highway 173 and the escape Karl and Gunther hopefully could offer.

Chapter 13

For Karl and Gunther von Himmel, it seemed like a small atomic bomb erupted when the dynamite blew. A huge ball of cranberry red flame rocketed up beyond their shelters of buckbrush and cattails as they faced the lake. The shockwave hit next. With the fury of the Passover's Angel of Death, the blast spilled both to the ground, sucking their breath away. A tsunami of sound hurled outward from the explosion, momentarily deafening both men.

Karl recovered first, pulling himself to his feet and shaking the thunder from his head. He understood once the explosives touched off, his brother and he needed to get back to the road fast. Together they stumbled forward in a shuffling run, the dim red light from the covered flashlight vaguely showing the trail. No sounds from the house emerged to pose the threat of discovery.

"Gunther! Gunther! Where are you?" he hissed as he moved closer to the road and where he believed his brother to be. "Gunther?"

"I'm here! I'm here, Karl." finally responded Gunther. Then they nearly collided as Gunther jumped up out of his hiding spot.

"My God! How much dynamite did those guys use?" Karl complained. "It sounded like the second coming of Christ when they detonated it."

"We've never used more than a couple sticks before, but they had to make sure they had enough," Gunther explained. Then he quickly added, "We must get to the truck and drive up the road right away. Ade and Father should be climbing up out of the bog and looking for us."

"Yeah, providing they're still in one piece," Karl muttered as he removed the red cloth cover on the flashlight and used its full beam to allow them to hurry back to the truck. They rapidly crossed the highway, and as they started the pickup and put it in gear, the Koleski house and yard came alive with light.

"Go! Go!" Karl hissed at Gunther, but his brother had sense enough to quietly roll down the logging trail with the headlights off, turn onto the road, and ease the truck toward their anticipated rendezvous. Desperately needing a strong drink, Gunther von Himmel steered the old truck a hundred yards up the highway, then stopped just for a few seconds, dug a can of Old Milwaukee out of his right jacket pocket, and before Karl could complain, he chugged the beer in two swallows. It steadied him.

After crawling along in the battered F-150 using the moonlight and the covered flashlights for several minutes to find their way, both driver and passenger were relieved to see two figures staggering up from the bog ditch and onto the road.

"Get in quick!" snarled Gunther, and Ade put his arm under his father and helped him into the pickup. Then Karl and Ade jumped into the truck bed and Gunther drove away, slowly increasing his speed over the last mile to the trailer.

Once they arrived, it took both Karl and Ade to assist their father up the steps and into the door. Gunther put the vehicle inside their small barn. Then, his concern mounting, he hurried back inside the home. There he found quite a scene.

"*Ein furze!*" shouted the old man as he reclined in a rocking chair, and laughing hard and loud, he farted. "Kaboom!" he shouted and passed gas again just as loudly. His antics came as desperately needed comic relief. The high tension of the bombing suddenly was replaced by farce.

Amid the uproar, von Himmel kept muttering something in German. Standing next to him, Ade thought he heard the old man say something about "pipe" and "flame," but he couldn't understand the whole statement.

"*Pfeife*? *Pflaume*? What are you saying, *Vater?*"

"I am saying that bomb damn near turned my dick into an asshole!" and they all roared with again, laughing so hard they started choking. A few shared slaps on the back and all was well. "My sons," continued their father on a more serious note, "you have heard me talk of the Spear of Destiny at times, yes?"

Their nods to the affirmative assured the old man he could continue. "*Der Speer* was in danger tonight, and I'm not talking about Hitler's gold-wrapped spear point neither!" he explained.

The questioning looks from his audience told von Himmel to finish his thought. "When Adolf and me set off all that dynamite, another big spear was blown backwards and almost destroyed!"

"But *Vater, Der Speer des Shicksals* you tell us about you said came from Odin himself. It was used by the Roman soldier who stabbed Christ on the cross. Are you really talking about that?" asked Gunther.

"No, not that one—" and the old man reached down, unzipped his fly and dug into his underwear. "The big spear that almost got blown to pieces…is mine right here! – *Der Beidl!*" An avalanche of belly laughs poured out across the entire trailer as the old man shouted, "*Der Speer des von Himmels!*"

"*Pille Palle, easy-peasy!*" Ade cried out. "Let's get out the brandy, boys! We've got a real raid to celebrate!" and he headed for the shelf where the liquor was stored while Karl opened the cabinet doors to find some glasses.

"Brandy?" their father shouted. "Brandy *geh zum Teufel!* These Wisconsin *schwein* drink nothing but brandy! It's only spoiled fruit juice. No! We are gonna drink real German liquor tonight."

"But we don't have any, *Vater*," Karl responded.

"To hell we don't! You get your ass into my bedroom and look in the far, right corner," commanded the old man.

Karl was shocked. His father never let anyone near his bedroom, much less actually go inside and dig around. Pushing back a long, brown-blonde curl from his forehead, he entered. From glimpses he had seen before when their father opened the door, Karl wasn't entirely surprised to see the walls adorned with a menagerie of swastikas in various sizes and a few pictures entitled "DER FÜHRER" speaking to the masses.

But sticking out from under the bed was a photo album. When Karl knelt to pull the liquor bottle out from low shelf next to the bed with his right hand, he used his left to fkiss quickly through the pictures inside. What Karl saw momentarily made him gag.

In the album were candid photos of prisoners in a Nazi concentration camp. All of the prisoners were dead, lying in grotesque ones and twos in front of a large, gated door. Stamped in engraved steel lettering was the single word "NAUTHAUSEN." Standing over the dead, like Bavarian royalty posing with their trophies from a stag hunt, were two unmistakable people: Heinrich von Himmel, at the time a laughing, carefree child of five and his father, Commander Friedrich, left hand on his son's shoulder, right hand holding a Luger. Scrawled across the bottom of the photograph were the hand-written words— *"Guten Appetit!"* Karl was simply appalled. For the first time in his adult life, his father's depravity crossed some kind of line, went just too far. Scattered among the pile of bodies were several small children—all shot to pieces.

"Hey there, Mister Bearded Man," his father Herman bellowed. "Hurry up! We are thirsty out here!" and with another short glance at the photo, his son refocused on his errand, grabbed two clear glass bottles of some unknown drink, and returned to the kitchen. Karl would reflect on the prison camp photos at another and more solitary time, but dissension's seed now was firmly planted and ready to grow.

"Ahhh," said the old man. "That is more like it!" as he took charge of both bottles.

"What exactly do you have in these?" asked Gunther. "There are no labels."

"I took the labels off on purpose, *Dummkopf*. I don't want none of you boys sneaking into my room and drinking up my best German booze!"

By now the camaraderie of the initial return home was fading. Ade lost his patience and burst out—"So what you got in those frickin' bottles, Dad?"

"Frickin' Peppermint Schnapps, *dummer Arsch!*" barked von Himmel. "And it will grow that little sausage you carry between your legs into a real man's dick!" The room once again erupted with guffaws and laughter, or rather most of the room erupted. Three of the von Himmels howled in glee. Ade, on the other hand, only smiled the wan smile of a man who realized he had just been labeled the dumb ass of the family on its most momentous night, and the label-maker was his father.

Before three of the men stumbled off to bed, Karl had to make two more schnapps' runs to the bedroom. Ade, however, sat apart simply sipping a bottle of beer. An hour ago, he had been the son who saved his father's life as well as his own by creating a makeshift life preserver out of a tool bag. Now, just sixty minutes later, he was a target for his father's crude jokes. Unaware of his brother Karl's feelings of dissension, Ade decided before the final curtain came down on this latest family drama, he would have to be the one to have the last laugh.

The sonic shock waves from the marsh bombing had to travel more than twenty miles to reach Big Stony Lonesome's bluffs. But when they did, the alpha wolf and his mate sprang from their sleep, bristling with fangs and fight. Much later, when the noise and the distant and very brief cloud of fire in the sky disappeared, the pack leader continued to pace restlessly outside his cave. The disturbance had to come from only one source, and it was his duty to protect his family and pack . . . especially from the most unpredictable and deadly predators in his world: humans.

Chapter 14

AMAZINGLY ENOUGH, AN extra pillow pulled tightly enough around his ears ensured that Jack slept fitfully through most of the drinking orgy in the house during the night and early morning hours. When he woke up, no one else was stirring. He concluded that something must have gone right with the attack. Must be they blew up the Einhoffer dike and got away safely, he concluded.

To start his chores, the boy grabbed his wool coat and thick gloves. The last few mornings were colder, maybe freezing, he decided as he stepped outside to feed the farm animals. A brutal east wind was blowing hard this morning, stroking his face with the frosty embrace of wind chill in God's country.

Chores done and a quick, solitary breakfast finished in a trailer resounding with heavy snores, Jack jumped on the school bus as it pulled over to stop. He was eagerly waiting for the Koleski stop. He wanted to enjoy Sara's happiness without any pressure. After all, the attack must have either been thwarted or moved up the road.

When the bus slowed, Jack looked out to see Sara where she always stood. Oddly enough, she wasn't there. Just as Jack was concluding that she must be ill, the entire bus population rose to their feet and crowded to his side of the bus. Two kids clambered over Jack to get a good look outside at something in the marsh.

"What?" Jack complained. Then he turned to look for himself.

There across acres and acres of what used to be a large, prosperous cranberry marsh operation, was only one thing: 100% destruction. The flat, water-ravaged scene carried north of the outbuildings as far as the boy could see. Only dismal little mud humps of what had been the marsh's reservoir dike remained, protruding like irreverent thumbs from an almost empty bowl of chocolate pudding.

And before Jack could turn to his left and take in the entire picture, his brain froze. Standing on the near edge of what used to be a huge reservoir lake was Sara's dad and his two brothers. Alongside of them and across the landscape of the home and warehouse were at least a dozen police officers.

Unexpectedly for Jack, the bus lurched forward to continue its run. "Everybody sit down!" ordered the driver, but the boy couldn't look away from the devastation. Hadn't he convinced his grandfather to move the attack to another marsh? Then, in what Jack was certain was the worst moment of his life, Jack looked toward the family's house. Sara stood there looking in horror at what used to be the Koleski Cranberry Marsh.

Chapter 15

"DADDY, OH PLEASE tell me this hasn't really happened!" Sara was pleading for this waking nightmare to dissolve like mud in the wash. She hadn't even thought to watch for the school bus and her Jack. It was just 6:30 in the morning and freezing cold, but a flood of white-hot tears cascaded down the girl's face and onto her father's arms as he held her. Peter Koleski's heart broke and broke again as he tried his best to comfort his sobbing daughter, now near to hysterics.

His grip on her tightened. He swiped his green and gold, sweat-stained Packer's cap from his sunburnt, balding head. "Sara," he said, "go ahead and cry. I am crying too inside. This has been a marsh producing cranberries since they were first farmed in Wisconsin."

Sara tried to comfort herself. A quality in her father's voice told her she needed to get a grip on her emotions. He had something vital to say.

"Listen, honey," he said. "The Nazis tried to wipe out our family line with the Koleskis who stayed in Germany in the 1940's. And the SS failed!" He dropped to a knee to look her straight in the eyes. His voice carried reassurance and safety. "Sara, I promise you that my brothers and I will not be defeated by this, by whoever did this terrible thing."

He had to look away for a brief instant to center his emotions. "As sure as the sun rises in the east and sets in the west, Sara, we will rebuild. I have already sent my brothers to bring in hired help today from the Ho-Chunk reservation. The tribe has always helped us before, and there is plenty of berry crop on the ground that isn't frozen."

He straightened and laughed. "Yup! Our berries are even washed and ready for market!" and he laughed again even louder. His confidence and strength washed over Sara like rain in the desert, restoring her faltering sense of hope.

"Oh, Daddy," she reached out and hugged him fiercely. "I believe we will too!"

Then there was motion behind her father. "Peter—ah, I mean Mr. Koleski. Could I just have you for one more minute to review what you and your brothers have reported to the first officers on the scene?" It was Dewey Lassiter, a family friend and easily recognized visitor to their marsh. Most importantly, he was the Hamot Chief of Police.

Dewey wore his uniform pretty much like his fifty-nine-year-old body had slept in it for the past week. A dab of black-grey hair untucked itself from under his weather-faded Stetson.

"Sure thing, Dewey." Peter Koleski turned back to Sara. "It all will be OK, honey," he said in the best fatherly voice he could muster. "You are staying home from school today, but since we all are fighters around here, go ahead and pick up a bucket and fill it with all the berries you can find." With that and a broad smile that he did not completely own, Pete Koleski turned back to wrap up his interview with the police.

"Hey, you there!" a second Hamot police officer angrily shouted at another man who approached the two men. "You can't see anybody here. This is a police investigation—not an Indian reservation."

Both Koleski and Lassiter spun around to see who was approaching. Then the police chief said in a loud, commanding voice, "It's OK, Mike. He is police too!"

"Huh?" the officer said. "He's just an Indian!"

"And you're just a prickly Irishman, Michael Flaherty!" retorted Lassiter. Then in his well-rehearsed chief of police voice, the police chief said, "Let him go wherever he wants. The man whose arm you are trying to grab is Josiah Grey Fox, Sheriff of the Ho-Chunk Nation's tribal police. And what's more—if you don't quickly let go, he's likely to break your arm and a few other body parts too!"

Flaherty gave Lassiter a dirty look, shared it with Grey Fox, and tried to storm off in an angry huff. Deep inside, however, the Irish cop was relieved to get away from the red man. Grey Fox stood six-three, with wide shoulders and forearms thick as cord wood. His red-brown face had the thick cheekbones of his race and chiseled jaw of a boxer.

Lassiter watched and sighed slightly as he shook his head. "Sorry about that, Jo. Mike is actually a pretty good cop, once you get past his attitude toward natives."

"Ho-Chunk natives," replied Grey Fox with a smile. "We are Ho-Chunk."

"Right, Jo. Sorry. We all should know better," apologized Lassiter. "I suppose you are here to investigate?" he inquired as he fumbled to remove the grey Stetson he perpetually wore.'

"Yep, Dewey. The lake flooded ceded-territory land. Our treaty rights go all the way to Black River Falls and down through Monroe County. Besides, the Koleskis have always welcomed men and women of our tribe as regular workers to pick and package the cranberries. This was a crime against our land, our water, and the men and women of our tribe as well as yours."

"Right," agreed Lassiter. The police chief tried to restart the conversation with an officer of the law every bit his equal. "You know, Josiah, this old cowboy cap of mine is the last and only connection to my original home in Amarillo. And like the Koleski marsh here, if somebody tore it up, I would be taking very particular exception!"

In the background, Sara watched the meeting of the two men develop. She observed a sudden, hard edge to the otherwise gentle features of the Hamot police chief. It provided her a brief snapshot into the surprisingly sharp mettle of his interior.

Sara decided Dewey Lassiter was a man of the law.

"What do you have, Dewey?" asked Sheriff Grey Fox.

"Not much to be honest." He frowned into the morning sunshine as his gaze followed the margins of the now devastated dike and cranberry beds. "I have all my men and officers from Black River's PD looking. Don't have to try too hard to see from the footprints it took more than one person to blow up the dike."

"Sure," Josiah agreed. "But why blow up a dike?'

"For the life of me," Lassiter pondered, "I really can't see why the Billy hell somebody wanted to do something like this?"

"Whoever did this to us," Sara chimed in and stepped closer to the men, "they timed it just right."

Chief Lassiter realized an introduction was in order. "This is Sara Koleski, Sheriff. Sara, this is Sheriff of Police for the Ho-Chunk Nation, Josiah Grey Fox."

"Just call me Jo," he said. His friendly grin and a big hand reached out to greet the girl. "Please know all Ho-Chunk people are sorry for your loss." He shook her hand solemnly. "Now, Sara," he continued, "what makes you say this was perfectly timed?"

"Because it almost froze last night," she explained. "See, we need real cold temps to turn the berries as bright red as possible in order that people will want to buy them. We are paid based on how red the berries are, providing they don't freeze. Last night it got down to 33°."

"I see," said the sheriff as he reached into his shirt pocket, removed a notepad, and started writing. "And tell me, Sara, has any police officer interviewed you yet?"

"Nope. But I am ready, willing, and able. My dad just told me that the Nazis tried to kill off our family in World War II, and they failed because Koleskis are fighters." The grit and determination in the girl's voice gave certainty to her words.

Dewey Lassiter coughed uncomfortably. "Well," he said to Grey Fox, "we are just launching our investigation. I am sure we would have gotten around to talking to Sara here sometime soon."

"I am sure too," said the sheriff. "But as Sara is right in front of us, I think I will take a short stroll down the driveway with her for a little chat."

He shifted his body toward the girl, and she nodded in agreement. "Let's go, Sheriff Jo!"

"And, thanks, Chief Lassiter. I'll catch you later today to hear any updates, and—" Grey Fox glanced at Sara, "share whatever my assistant can provide in information or ideas."

"It appears she already has," grinned the Hamot police chief, and with a slight dip of his Stetson, Lassiter walked toward a group of his officers huddled at the other end of the lake.

"Ok, young lady," Sheriff Grey Fox said. "Let's head out, and you tell me whatever you think someone who doesn't know much about cranberry marshes ought to know."

"Sure thing, Sheriff Jo," Sara said as they began walking down the gravel driveway and out toward the county road.

"But first thing, Sara. Tell me about anything that has seemed strange or different or out of place lately," Grey Fox asked.

"Well," the girl paused for a few seconds before continuing the walk, "it's been getting cold faster than normal around this area, Sheriff. And like I said, that has meant all the growers have had to be out at their dikes and pumping stations watching the temperature."

"Uh-huh," agreed the sheriff. "But why is it so critical that the bog temp stays above freezing for even a few hours?"

"Oh, that's because any fruit is damaged even by a little frost," the girl explained. "The berries are worth less money if they freeze. Then growers like us have to sell them for canned sauce to a big processor like Ocean Spray. Where growers make their best profit is by spraying water on the cranberries just before they freeze. The sprayed water protects them so we have time to open the sluice gates on the reservoir dikes, flood the beds, and let the water float up the fresh fruit for harvest."

"My goodness! That's quite an explanation," said Sheriff Jo. "But let's go back to what I started asking you first. Anything different around here for you?"

"Well, I have my first boyfriend." Sara added shyly, "He rides the bus with me and lives just a little way down the road." She leaned just a bit toward Grey Fox and whispered, "We sit on the porch for a little while before he walks home."

The sheriff had a broad smile. "And who is your new guy?"

Sara blushed a little. She wasn't sure she wanted to discuss her first boyfriend with an adult she didn't really know, but there was something very comfortable with Sheriff Jo, something very safe about him.

They were finishing their walk to the end of the driveway when the girl decided she would share. "He's Jack von Himmel, Sheriff." Then she hurried to add, "And he's really nice. He protects me from kids who might want to bully someone like me who is new to public school."

Grey Fox winced. He knew all about how some kids harassed his friends from the reservation, especially when they went to high school. The sheriff looked back at the girl and suddenly understood the true significance of the six-pointed star she wore as a necklace.

"That is a real good quality for your boyfriend to have," agreed the sheriff. Then as a little follow-up, his police officer nature led him to ask, "And just how does Jack keep you safe?"

Sara hesitated. To her, having a tall, caring boyfriend at school and sitting next to her on the bus was all the protecting she needed. Then she remembered something.

"The other day for example," the girl said, "when we were riding the bus, Jack told me that our family had property to protect during this important time and that we should be on the watch to keep it safe."

Grey Fox felt something ckiss. He wasn't exactly sure of what he just learned, but somehow it didn't seem like a usual thing a high school boyfriend would say.

"So your family— did they increase watching for trouble?"

"Oh yes, they sure did, Sheriff! And I give Jack all the credit too."

"Credit for what, Sara?"

"That very night after I told my dad and his two brothers about what Jack said, they didn't all go out to watch the bog temperature gauges."

"What happened instead?"

"My dad's two brothers went to the gauges, but my dad turned off all the house lights and sat in the living room by the big picture window just to see if there were any people sneaking around."

"And were there? Did he see anyone?"

"Not exactly, Sheriff," said Sara, and she paused to recenter the six-pointed star she wore on a gold chain as a necklace.

"What *exactly* did he see?" Grey Fox's curiosity spiked.

"He saw an orange light."

"That's all? He saw a light?

"Well, what he told me he saw was a flash out in the bushes in the ditch by our house, and then a little orange dot, maybe a cigarette being smoked. That's what he thought he saw."

"So perhaps the flash was from a cigarette lighter being used?" asked the sheriff.

"Yes, sir. It's funny though."

"What's funny, Sara?"

"Jack said the same thing you just did when I told him about it the next morning on the bus. He asked me what happened too."

"Hmmm. And did he say anything else?"

"Jack said I shouldn't be really concerned. It was maybe someone just smoking a cigarette out there by the road," the girl said. "To be honest, just like Jack said, it maybe wasn't for sure that it happened at all," and Sara stopped the walk for they reached the end of the driveway, and it was time to turn back.

The sheriff stopped too. But it wasn't just to turn the walk around. He couldn't help thinking, "People don't crawl down into water-filled bog ditches in the middle of a September night just to smoke a cigarette, especially when it's freezing cold." Besides, in the police and crime business, there were no such things as convenient coincidences. None.

The freshman girl bounced over to the mailbox. "I forgot to pick up the mail last night. Jack usually reminds me when we get off the bus together."

"Yes, I am sure he is helpful," Grey Fox agreed.

Then, swiftly, in an entirely different sheriff's voice, he shouted— "Stop! My God, girl, don't move! Listen to me carefully, Sara. Do exactly what I say!"

Sara heard the dire tone of his voice. Suddenly she was terrified . . . but why she couldn't understand. "Yes, Sheriff," she murmured and froze in place just in front of the mailbox.

"Move very slowly away from the mailbox. Do not touch it. Step softly. Just keep slowly walking past me and when you get up the driveway call Chief Lassiter to come here right away— but tell him to walk softly too and not bring any vehicles near that mailbox."

Sara's entire body was trembling, but she gathered her wits together, gingerly walked past the sheriff and headed for her house to call other policemen. What she didn't understand was why she had to do this. She and Sheriff Jo were just having a little chat, just walking down the driveway.

Josiah Grey Fox's guard, however, was instantly on high alert. Something out of place had caught his eye as the young girl reached to get the mail. What he saw made his gut wrench tight. Most rural residents don't smear the letters SS on the back end of their mailboxes.

Chapter 16

"**WELL, SHUT MY** front door!" Chief of Police Lassiter said in amazement as he studied the Nazi symbol smeared across the mailbox. He had approached with great caution, not sure of just what all was going down.

Then Lassiter pushed back the Stetson which was now even more sweat-stained and ran his left hand through his thin, greying hair. "Jo, do you think there is a bomb in there too?"

"Better not take any chances, Dewey," the Ho-Chunk sheriff said. "Have one of your guys get on the radio and call the national guard boys over at Fort McCoy. It's likely they have bomb removal equipment and training on what to do."

"Yep, good idea," agreed the Hamot chief as he stepped toward the house to head back up the driveway.

"And two other things, Chief," said Grey Fox. "Have someone walk down here softly to rope off the driveway with crime scene tape. And we'll need a fingerprint guy to work on the mailbox on the outside while we are waiting for the bomb squad. After the squad is done checking for explosives, maybe we can brush the inside of the box for prints too."

"Yes, Jo. You're absolutely right," Lassiter said. "Sure am glad to have you part of the investigation,"

"Tell that to Flaherty," chided the sheriff. Then as the Chief of Hamot Police hurried back up the drive, Sara reappeared, moving uncertainly toward Grey Fox.

"Sara, you've got to stay back. There might be explosives in the mailbox," warned the sheriff.

"Oh my gosh!" she exclaimed and took a step back. Then summoning up her willpower Sara said in a determined voice, "but there is something else I have to tell you, Sheriff Jo."

"Ok. Just don't come any closer to tell me. Now what do you need to say?"

"Well, it is something else about Jack von Himmel."

"What else?"

"I think someone is hurting him!" The girl blurted this out.

"Why do you think so, Sara?" Now Grey Fox's suspicions were on full alert.

"Because the other day on the bus when Jack was warning me, I saw a long red mark on his neck. It looked fresh, partly bright red and partly black-and-blue. I'm sure it really hurt."

"Did you ask him about the mark?"

"No, I'm sorry, Sheriff. I was shocked when I saw it. I really didn't know what to say or how to ask him."

"And Jack didn't ever say anything about them, did he?"

"Not really. But I do remember he was telling me about how not everyone is protected and safe in their home," the girl said. She waited just a second, then added— "You don't think someone in his house is hurting him, do you?"

"If they are, you can believe I will put an instant stop to it and see that the person goes to jail. I'll make it a point to stop by there real soon." Then Grey Fox motioned to the girl toward the house. "Now it's best if you go on back up the driveway, ok?" he said. "If you think of anything more, just write a note about it or keep it in your memory for when we talk again."

"Sure thing, Sheriff Jo," she agreed, and the young girl began retreating to her house. About halfway back, she came to an abrupt halt. "Oh, and I just want you to know that I think you are the best investigator we could have!"

"Thanks!" the sheriff said and gave her a reassuring glance. "I promise we'll figure out who did this, and I am going to be checking on Jack to make sure he is safe too."

In another minute, Chief of Police Lassiter and another officer returned with crime scene tape and began to tie it to seal off the driveway to stop any incoming or outgoing traffic.

"Hey, Dewey," called Grey Fox as the two policemen finished their taping work. "We need to talk for just a minute."

"You bet," answered Lassiter. He tied the last knot to secure the tape to a small tree and strode over to the sheriff in typical, cowboy bow-legged fashion.

"What's up, Jo?"

"Well, in talking with Sara, she mentioned her boyfriend gave her a vague warning there might be trouble."

Lassiter forehead crinkled. "And who is her friend?"

"Sara said it was Jack von Himmel. You know anything about him or his family?"

"Hamot is a small town. So, yes, I do know a bit about the von Himmels," and the chief's eyes narrowed. His expression revealed deep concern.

"Jo, I know there are four adult men and the boy living in an old, beat-up mobile home just a couple miles from here," he said. "And I know the oldest is Jack's grandfather. He's maybe in his mid to late fifties and looks like he lives on battery acid and cow manure. Haven't actually talked to the man, but I saw him come to the station to pick up a couple of his worthless adult sons when we put them in the drunk tank. The old man keeps away from the public."

Lassiter shifted his balance, spit a wad of tobacco chew, and continued. "He looks like a real rough piece of real estate. Big man, big gut, and a perpetual scowl like he had to live eating nothing but cranberries. The first time he came by to pick up his sons I thought he looked like death warmed over. And his sons are just a mean-mouthed bunch who drink too much and start bar fights. One of them carved a swastika in a cell they used to sleep off a night's drunk."

"A swastika? That's interesting, Dewey. Something along the lines of the SS painted on this mailbox maybe?" Grey Fox considered what he had just heard. "I have to say I am more than a little suspicious. Sara told me that her boyfriend Jack not only warned her the day of the bombing about protecting their marsh, but he had a red welt on his neck as well. Like someone had hurt or maybe punished him, Sara said."

"Whoah! I don't like the sound of any of that, Jo. You think it's possible the kid knew some trouble was coming down the pike and suffered some abuse?"

"Maybe yes. How about you leave your second in command here, Dewey. He can supervise the bomb squad and fingerprint work, while together we go to the high school to pay Jack a quick visit?"

"Done and done, Jo!" and Chief of Police Lassiter instantly stepped away to get the plan in motion.

Chapter 17

LASSITER AND GREY Fox found Jack in study hall just at
the 8:45 am bell for second period. The Ho-Chunk
sheriff thought the boy's eyes would explode
from their sockets when he saw the police uniforms coming.

"You are Jack von Himmel, right? asked Lassiter.

The boy nodded dumbly, fear of discovery par-
alyzing his body.

"Jack, this is Sheriff Josiah Grey Fox of the
Ho-Chunk Nation," explained the chief, "and I'm
Chief of Hamot Police Lassiter. We need for you to
come to the station with us now. There are some
questions we want to ask you." Josiah Grey Fox
noted that the police chief was playing his cards
tight to the vest by not telling the boy anything
about the explosions on the marsh.

The ride back to the police station was silent.
Jack sat by himself in the back seat of the squad car

as Chief Lassiter drove. Sheriff Grey Fox followed them in his own vehicle.

As they arrived at the station, Jack couldn't avoid noticing the unique look of the PD's building material. The exterior of the station was built with large rectangles of an unusual rock called Lannon stone. From a distance the building's surface looked like a soft, inviting creamy white with streaks of tan and brown in it. But as the vehicle drove up close and drove inside the garage, the entire color scheme changed drastically. The Lannon stone up close morphed into a harsh grey-colored rock with rusty orange scars instead. A sense of foreboding settled over the boy as Jack tried to prepare himself for interrogation.

After they entered the station, Lassiter showed Jack down a corridor and into a small, sparsely decorated, windowless room that had a strong antiseptic odor to it. Just a few chairs and a small table populated the space. There was a large mirror on the wall in front of Jack. The police chief took a chair with his back to the mirror and said, "Please sit down, Jack. I don't want you to be afraid of anyone here. Nothing will happen to hurt you in anyway, and we will tape record our talk if you don't mind."

Then Chief Lassiter pulled himself closer to the table and nearer to Jack. He turned on the tape recorder and looked the boy directly in the eyes.

"Jack, I want to know if you are aware that the Koleski marsh dike was blown up last night?"

"I could see that the dike was gone," the boy admitted. "All the kids on the bus could see the destruction when we stopped to pick up Sara Koleski. She's my friend, but she didn't go to school this morning."

"Why do you think she stayed home today, Jack?"

"Well, I didn't know the dike was blown up" ventured Jack. "From the bus, it looked like it just gave way."

"No, the dike didn't just give way. It was dynamited in the middle of last night, and it's my job to find out who did it and why," said the chief. He continued, "I hear you are friends with Sara. Is that true?"

Jack flinched a bit, then decided it was best for him to be honest at least about things that didn't seem to matter much. "Yes," he agreed. "She and I usually sit together on the bus."

"Jack," explained Chief Lassiter, "I want you to know you can end this interview at any time. You are not being accused of any crime or wrongdoing, and if you wish, you can ask for your dad to be present. Ok?"

Jack considered inviting his father to be there in the room, and in the same instant decided against it. He wanted to keep the fact of this interview away from all the men in his trailer home. "I don't need my dad here," the boy said. "I didn't do anything wrong."

"We didn't say you have done anything wrong, son," Lassiter replied.

Then after a moment of wait time, the chief went on. "You see, police officers are out at the scene of the crime right now, and one of them happened to talk to Sara. She mentioned you two are friends, so that's why you are here. We just want to hear anything you might know."

"Gosh, sir. I really don't know anything," the boy said.

"Are you really sure about that, Jack?" Lassiter moved even a little closer. "You haven't seen anything different or unusual around the Koleski marsh lately?"

"No sir," replied Jack. "I don't spend my time there."

"Oh, but you do spend some time there, at least according to Sara," the police chief insisted. "She told us when the bus lets her off at the driveway after school, you walk up the drive with her and you both sit on the big sofa on their porch. Right?"

Jack flinched hard this time. He mentally kicked himself for his mistake. "Oh, uhuh. I just didn't think that was very important," he said lamely.

Lassiter came down a bit harder on the boy. "Jack," he said in his best police chief voice, "you must understand that a crime has been committed. Millions of dollars have been lost for your good friend's family, the Koleskis."

The chief's voice added a sharper tone next. "And not telling the truth, the whole truth, to the police is a serious crime.

Jack's face reddened and he squirmed in his seat. "Yes, sir," he said.

"So even if some little bit of information you have doesn't seem important to you, I want you to understand you need to tell me about it. Tell me right here, right now!" Lassiter backed off just a bit and allowed his body to relax visibly before continuing.

"Now, Jack. I want you to think hard for a few moments. After all, we are talking about Sara and her family. They are facing financial ruin, son," and Lassiter moved himself closer to the boy again. Lassiter could see the red welt on the boy's neck which Sara had described.

As much as Jack tried to keep the consequences of the bombing for the Koleski family out of his mind, what the police chief was saying ate into the boy. He hardly could imagine what the Koleskis were going to do now that their business was gone.

"Jack," the police chief asked, "do you like Sara Koleski?

"Oh, sure I do," the boy answered. The tension in his body relaxed a bit. Talking about a safe subject was much easier, he thought.

"You wouldn't want to see her and her family lose their home and business, would you?"

"No, sir," said Jack, and the tension came rushing back into him.

"So, you understand what can happen to a family that has no money or no home, right?" Lassiter asked, his voice rising a notch.

"Well, not exactly. I guess they wind up being poor like our family. We live in a crummy trailer, my grandfather, my dad, his two brothers and me."

"Wrong," said Lassiter. "They won't live in a trailer because it takes money to buy one, even a banged-up trailer. What they do is lose their home and property because they can't pay their mortgage each month." The police chief's voice and manner rose with intensity.

"They have to sell off all their possessions and leave their home." Lassiter's statements were on automatic fire now, and he burrowed into Jack's credulous ignorance. "They must find a cheap public assistance apartment and crowd into it, kid. Sara's dad and his two brothers will have to find low-paying, part-time jobs. The whole family will have to go on welfare."

Jack's eyes began to well up with hot tears and his brain pounded with guilt.

"Is that what you want for her? You want Sara to suffer like that, kid? I thought you said you were her friend?"

It was too much. Jack broke down and sobbed into his folded arms as they rested on the table. Great shuddering sighs punctuated bursts of tears from the boy. He was crying for Sara. He was crying for her marsh. He was crying for himself and for what his family had done.

Chapter 18

HAMOT POLICE CHIEF Lassiter waited and watched. Softly sobbing, the boy kept his head buried in his arms. He was showing no sign of regaining emotional balance. "Good time to leave him be for a bit," the police chief decided, and he quietly pulled back from the table, nodded to the mirror behind him, then stood up silently and left the interrogation room.

Josiah Grey Fox had waited and watched from behind a glass partition. A part of him ached for Jack while Lassiter had turned up the heat in the questions, but another part of him knew the hard interrogation was a necessary element in discovering the truth. "Bad Cop first," thought the Ho-Chunk sheriff, "now it's time for Good Cop," and with that, he walked away from the one-way mirror, strode to the door of the interview room and entered. The room's stark emptiness pushed back on his senses. Three folding chairs, one small wooden table, and the artificial gleam of a row of fluorescent lights, all demanding justice. The bittersweet pine scent of disinfectant hung in the air so heavily, Grey Fox could taste it.

Jack had not fully recovered himself yet, but Grey Fox's instincts told him it was best to seize the situation. He walked quietly over to the young boy, patted him lightly on his near shoulder, and when Jack looked up, the sheriff passed him a white handkerchief.

"Here, Jack. Go ahead and wipe your eyes."

Jack complied. The sheriff waited some more. After the boy sat up and blew his nose, the man sensed he could start his interview. He began with a faint smile and said gently, "You know Jack is a good first name. Mine starts with the same first letter. I'm Josiah Grey Fox, Sheriff of the Ho-Chunk Nation's Tribal Police." The boy blinked but said nothing.

"Jack, I can see that you really do care about Sara, don't you?" the sheriff said.

"Uh, yes sir," replied Jack, his voice, and nerves still shaky. The boy sat up a bit and tried to smooth out his rumpled t-shirt, but the effort only managed to spread tear stains across the length of his forearms.

"You shouldn't feel bad about that, son," Grey Fox counseled. "You did what good friends do for one another. They care. They help. They do what you were doing . . . trying to keep Sara and her family safe."

Jack nodded. There was that "safe" word again. Then he wondered when the hard question was coming.

"Ever notice how birds, even little ones, fight to protect their nest and their young?" asked the sheriff.

The question surprised the boy entirely. He was not prepared for talking about birds in a police station. "Yes sir," Jack replied. Then he ventured to add, "When Sara and I walked up her driveway the other day, a red-winged blackbird came diving down from a tree limb to chase us away. Must have thought we were too close and posed some kind of danger."

Grey Fox nodded with approval. "Exactly," he agreed. "Tell me, Jack . . . have you ever seen them go after bigger, predatory birds who come too close?"

"Oh, you bet I have," Jack said. "I've seen them even go after an eagle way up in the sky. The little birds keep attacking the eagle's tail. I think they try to pull out tail feathers, so the big bird finds it hard to fly. They chase the eagle away from their nest and chicks."

"Right!" confirmed the sheriff. "They risk everything against a threat much larger than themselves in order to protect what they care about."

"Blackbirds are really awesome that way," agreed Jack, and he felt himself warming to the sheriff. The man's wide shoulders, chiseled brow and jaw, and gentle voice spoke of reassurance the boy needed. "They don't care about themselves at all. They just dive in and fight for all they're worth."

"And that is what you were doing, Jack, when you got this— right!" and Grey Fox eased his hand up to the boy's neck and bent back his shirt collar. With great care and a sensitive touch, the sheriff lightly stroked the base of Jack's wound. "You gave up caring about yourself to protect someone important to you, son. And you paid the price."

Jack collapsed into his own arms again and began a low moan that built to a crescendo of wails. His entire body shuddered under torrents of fear. Josiah Grey Fox's eyes swelled with tears too. He quickly brushed them away. This entire situation was an outrage to decency, and he had to stop it.

Chapter 19

"**IT'S TIME TO** tell the truth, Jack. The whole truth and nothing but the truth," and as he concluded, Sheriff Grey Fox stood, crossed to Jack's side of the table and lightly gave the boy a reassuring pat on his near shoulder.

The words tumbled out of the boy like a flash flood in a tight gully. "It was my grandpa who decided to blow up the dike. He made my dad, and his brothers help him. I couldn't stop them no matter how hard I tried!"

"What did you try to do, Jack?"

"My grandfather was beating my father's head into the floor. I told him he had to stop, so he got up and started to come at me instead."

"Why was your grandfather beating your dad?"

"Because it was my dad who lit the cigarette that someone in the Koleski house saw," the boy explained. "My grandfather did a practice run two nights ago. My dad was smoking a cigarette that almost gave them away. *Opa* was punishing my dad for his mistake."

"Wait a minute, Jack. I am getting this story backwards in time," said the sheriff. "How about we start at the beginning instead. I know you started spending time on the porch with Sara before walking home, right?"

The boy nodded agreement. "Yes, and I got in trouble with *Opa* and everyone at home because I stayed with her too long. I was late to get home and do my chores. The horse and pigs and chickens, they all needed to be cared for."

"Ok. When you came home late what happened?"

"They didn't wait for me to come home, Sheriff. They came down the road looking for me. They were all mad because of the noise the animals were making wanting their food."

"Ok, Jack," the sheriff said. "They came down the road looking for you. Then what?"

"My grandfather climbed down the bank first and hit me hard with his belt. He was shouting at me. He wanted to know what I was doing."

"They figured out you were visiting Sara. How did they do that, son?"

"My grandpa whipped me. That's how I got this cut, sir," and the boy pointed to his wounded neck. "I told him I was seeing my girlfriend, and then they realized the Koleskis were Jews. *Opa* hates Jews. He

made my dad and his brothers all hate Jews, too."
Jack revealed this as if it was all self-explanatory.
But to Josiah Grey Fox, very little made any sense.

"All right, son. The four men of your family
hate Jews. But why did that lead them to decide to
blow up the Koleski cranberry dike and flood their
marsh beds?"

"Because Grandpa Herman said we had to.
Otherwise, he said, eventually the word would get
around that I was a Jewish girl's boyfriend. When
the other Nazis in this area learned his grandson
was dating a Jew, they would come and punish our
family for betraying the cause."

"Jack, you did just say your grandfather is a Nazi,
and there are other Nazis right here in Hamot?" To
put it mildly, the sheriff was incredulous.

The boy nodded his head.

"Let's find the station's first aid kit and put a
little medicine and bandage on where you're hurt,"
said Grey Fox.

Jack could only nod again.

Chapter 20

IN THE VIEWING room, behind the one-way mirror, Chief Lassiter nodded in grim agreement. He, for one, was not surprised. There had been rumors and drunken bragging about how Nazi Germany was still alive and well in Wisconsin. In fact, he had heard the KKK had some connections too because of the common hatreds the two groups shared.

Unprompted now, the rest of the story gushed out of the boy as Grey Fox bandaged the boy's throat. "Grandpa Herman said we had to attack the Koleskis in such a way that they were really hurt, and it was decided to leave some kind of sign or symbol that would tell others like us we took care of our own problem. That way no one else would get revenge on us."

"And you decided to go along with this?" asked Grey Fox.

"No," Jack protested. "I decided not to go along."

"So what did you do, Jack?"

"Two nights ago, Grandpa had my dad, and my two uncles go to the Koleskis to practice blowing up the dike. All of us von Himmels have worked on the marshes, so we knew growers keep dynamite around to blast sand hills and get material to spread on the beds."

"And something must have gone wrong in the test run?"

"Yes, Sheriff," the boy agreed. "When Grandfather talked about the practice run at breakfast, I gave Sara the best warning I could after school. That night her dad and brothers were on their guard. When my dad lit up a cigarette from his hiding spot to watch the house, Mr. Koleski saw the flash, turned on the lights and came outside."

"I take it your grandfather was not real happy with your dad," the sheriff said following the logic of the boy's story.

"Yes, right When they all got back to our trailer, my grandpa was so mad at my dad he started smashing his head into the floor." Jack paused briefly and heaved a ponderously heavy sigh. "I couldn't let him kill my father," he said in a voice much older than his fifteen years should produce.

"You tried to protect your dad?"

"Yes, Sheriff. I came out of my bed and told Grandfather Herman he had to stop."

"Weren't you afraid you would be beaten too?"

"Sure, I was. But I've been beaten many times before. Even if it killed me, I couldn't let my grandpa beat my father to death."

"Jack, what you did was incredibly brave. How did you stop your grandfather from going back to hurting your dad or you?

Jack's face grew immobile as a cliff face. "To tell you the truth, I don't think of myself as all that important, Sheriff." The boy paused to gather the little inner resources he still possessed. "I told him if he killed Dad and me, he wouldn't have enough people to do his attack. Without our attack, the other Nazis in the area would come gunning for him instead. Right now, they think of him as their leader."

"My goodness, son. Most high school freshmen wouldn't have the brains to think of that, much less the guts to do it."

"Thanks, Sheriff," the boy said humbly. "I don't know... but my life in the trailer with four angry men hasn't meant that much to me. When my grandmother was alive, I didn't mind it so much. But she died more than a year ago." He went on: "It wasn't until I met Sara that I found myself caring about things." Then the boy's head dropped noticeably to rest at a sharp angle on his chest.

Jack's chest heaved solemnly, but he did not look up. "And I told him he should attack somebody else, some other marsh like the Einhoffer's that was bigger and was not going to be on the watch for trouble." Jack stopped for just a moment.

"Yes, Sheriff Jo," the boy continued, "I thought I had stopped one attack by aiming their anger at another target." The boy stopped briefly and sat up straight. "I realize now that what I did was wrong. No one should ever be attacked. But it was the only thing I could think of right there in the moment." The boy's dropped even further on his chest.

"But they didn't change their target after all, Jack. What do think happened?"

"I don't know. My guess is that Grandpa Herman didn't like me standing up to him, and after I went to school yesterday morning, he went back to bombing the Koleskis." Jack coughed then added— "My uncle Ade still has two dynamite sticks in our shed he stole from the Koleskis."

Chief Lassiter took that moment to rap on the mirror. It was time to end the interview and get search warrants as fast as possible, he decided. He didn't want the adult von Himmels to realize that Jack wasn't in school and start hiding evidence.

Sheriff Grey Fox understood the cue to bring things to a quick conclusion. "Jack," he said, "what you have told me and what you've done took great courage. In my tribe, you would be moved from child to manhood for what you have risked to say and do." A thin smile graced the boy's face, then evaporated.

The Sheriff had to pause for just a second to keep his voice in a calm, even tone. "Telling the truth, especially when you do it to protect a friend, is an act of courage. And we won't let you down. I'll talk with Chief Lassiter and get you moved today to a foster home so you can live in protective custody. The chief and his officers will keep you safe."

The words "keep you safe" reassured Jack somewhat. He had no idea what would happen next, but he was sure he could trust Sheriff Grey Fox. Hopefully, he could trust the Hamot force to keep him safe too.

Chief Lassiter entered and showed Jack out of the room. He took the boy to his private office, reached into a small refrigerator, pulled out a bottle of the only soda pop he allowed in the station. He popped the top, smiled, and gave it to the boy.

"Here you go, son," the chief said as he offered the beverage to the boy." He winked at Jack and added, "Dr. Pepper—it's the only pop that puts lead in a man's pencil!" The boy was happy to have something to drink. His mouth was bone dry.

"One of my officers," Lassiter gently explained, "will come back to check on you, Jack. I have to make a few arrangements," and the Hamot Police Chief quickly walked out the door.

It was the last time the two would see each other alive.

Chapter 21

CHIEF LASSITER MOVED with the alacrity of a man leading a crusade. First, he poked his head into the break room and explained the situation to Officer Flaherty because he had been out to the marsh, was second in command, and for better and worse, had met Josiah Grey Fox. "Get the boy into a foster home and be damn sure you set up strong protective custody, Mike," he ordered. "That young kid has more nerve than a lot of grown men I've known. He just admitted the adults in his family did the bombing, so he is at risk. And I want this done yesterday!"

Next, the chief called the court office of Judge Terrence Windsill, the county magistrate. "Judge? This is Dewey Lassiter. I need search and arrest warrants for the home, out buildings, vehicles, and property of Herman von Himmel, and his sons Gunther, Karl, and Adolf."

"What's your reason, Dewey?" Windsill asked as he sneezed into the phone from his perpetual allergies.

"We have reason to believe they blew up the Koleski dike and flooded their cranberry marsh last night, Judge." Then he added as an afterthought, "And I'll be coming back to you for further charges of child abuse, too, later on."

"What's your evidence, Chief?'

"I have an eyewitness to the planning, and he knows where the dynamite they used is stored."

"And just who is your witness?"

"Their fifteen-year-old, Jack. He's the son of Gunther von Himmel. We interviewed him because he is friends with Sara, Peter Koleski's daughter. That boy is a real gutsy young man, sir—he admitted that the adults in his family did it out of hatred."

"Hatred of what?'

"Jews! It turns out they secretly are Nazis, and they felt that Gunther's boy, Jack, was getting them in trouble with other local haters by flirting with a Jewish girl. The boy said the men decided to show they were still good Nazis by attacking the marsh. Josiah Grey Fox from the Ho-Chunk PD found the letters SS smeared on the Koleski's mailbox."

"Sounds like you have solid evidence, Chief. Come on over in about an hour. I'll have the search warrants ready for you when you arrive." Judge Windsill cleared his throat over the phone to give himself a minute before his next statement. "And, Dewey, make sure the proper steps were taken and documented regarding the interview of the minor, all right?"

"Not a problem, sir. On tape we gave the boy the proper caution he wasn't a suspect, and he could have his father present. The boy voluntarily declined to have his dad there."

"There is no current law requiring parents or an attorney to be present when questioning a minor, but don't be surprised if the interview is an issue if this goes to trial, Chief."

"Right. We taped the interview and Sheriff Grey Fox witnessed it too. Thanks, Judge! I guess if worst actually came to worst, there is also the possibility of having the Ho-Chunk Nation put these bad guys on trial!" Then Lassiter put the phone down to move on to his next task—preparing a strike force to serve the warrants.

If the von Himmels were big-time haters, he reasoned it was likely they would have a large stockpile of weapons and ammunition. Just coming onto their property could easily spark a shoot-out. Lassiter considered his options and decided to recall most of the crime scene investigative team and contact the State Patrol. He wanted to lay out the best plan he could for approaching the von Himmel property, go over the details with each team member... then arm each of them to the teeth.

Chapter 22

As he was driving Jack to a safe house and foster care in a distant town, Officer Michael Flaherty of the Hamot Police Department let his eyes shift off the highway toward the boy for just for a second. He wanted to confirm something. "So, Jack," he asked as he briefly glanced at the boy—"your dad and his brothers actually have been long-time Nazis?"

"Yes, sir. For as long as I can remember," and Jack shifted uncomfortably in his seat in the squad car. Simply being in the cruiser made Jack uneasy. He couldn't decide whether all the electronic gear and weapons made him feel more fearful or more fascinated. The long dagger tattooed on Flaherty's right forearm generated the same mixed effect.

Flaherty's eyes returned to the highway. "My gosh, kid! Who would have thought that we would have real Nazis in our little town of Hamot?"

"Yes, sir."

"Do they dress up in Nazi uniforms and practice saluting Adolf Hitler with outstretched arms?"

Jack squirmed in his seat some more. It felt to him like Officer Flaherty was talking like the adults in his family were highly regarded movie stars.

Jack finally decided it was best he answer all questions police officers asked him. "Yes, sir," he replied, then added— "my *opa*, my grandfather Herman, has a real one from World War Two. My grandpa's grandfather, Friedrich von Himmel, was an SS Commander in charge of a concentration camp, so my *Opa* has his grandfather's uniform as well as one he somehow got for himself."

"I take it your grandfather kind of raised up his three sons to be real haters too?"

Jack didn't understand the question. To Jack, no one could be *kind of* committed to hating Jews and believing the white race was superior to all others. He decided on a safe response—

"Yes, sir. But my grandma Freida told me to ignore all that. 'Just hot air' she would say."

"You ever get a chance to put on one of the outfits yourself? You know, dress up and goose step around and shout 'Heil Hitler!'" Flaherty was getting more excited as he was drove.

"No, sir. I never dressed up in any Nazi clothes. When Grandfather, my dad and his two brothers start waving Nazi stuff around our trailer, they usually are drinking too much. It makes them act rough and loud. I get afraid when they are like that, so I go outside and pet the horse."

"Jack, my lad, you are missing out on a lot of fun! When I was a kid, I loved playing soldier, and I didn't even have a real uniform to wear like you do."

"I don't see how being a Nazi even for a little while is any fun," said Jack. Then he added, "Besides, like I said, being around my family when they are being rough and drunk in their Nazi stuff makes me afraid." Jack paused and took a deep enough sigh that Flaherty should understand the boy wanted to end the topic of conversation.

And to underscore it was time to change the subject, Jack leaned forward in his seat and pointed to the town welcome sign they were approaching.

Flaherty repressed a sigh of disappointment. "Fine how-do-you-do," he thought. "Just trying to make a little conversation with a goofed-up high school kid. Screw him!"

"Yup, Jack," the cop remarked when the boy leaned back in his car seat. "This city probably will be your new home until the trial is over." Then he continued, "And you will like it here, I am sure."

"Why, Officer?"

"Because you will be living with my mother and dad in the house where I grew up."

127

As they slowed down to enter the beginning of the south end of the town, Jack decided to risk asking a question of Flaherty. After all, the boy was still very afraid of what his grandfather might do if the old man ever found him.

"Officer," Jack asked putting all the smile he could into his voice to hide his misgivings, "what makes you so sure I will like this city and be safe with your parents?"

Flaherty chuckled. "Oh, I'm sure you're gonna like my mom. After all, she put up with me for eighteen years before I headed out on my own."

Jack flashed a big smile at Flaherty to show he understood the officer's attempt at a bit of levity.

"Sure thing, Officer Flaherty! I bet you were a real tough kid growing up in this paper mill town."

Flaherty didn't seem to understand. Was this little punk trying to mock him? "I was a tough kid for a while. Then my mom made me behave and act right, just like your grandma. After that I decided I would clean up this place single-handed. And I did, too, as a policeman! Then I came to Hamot for a better job. I'm already second in command and just a heartbeat away from being chief of police. Just a couple more years and Dewey Lassiter will have to retire due to old age if nothing else."

They were approaching the downtown area now. A few little shops and restaurants were fitting in between family homes and apartment buildings. Flaherty turned the squad car into a narrow, broken concrete driveway leading to a dainty, red brick, vine-covered home. A cheery little old lady rose from a lawn chair to welcome them.

Flaherty stopped the vehicle, gave a little wave to his mother, then turned and winked at the boy. "Yes, Jack," he said in a confident tone of voice. "There's no place on earth where you could be more protected. You're safe and sound—here in Wisconsin Rapids!"

Chapter 23

LASSITER'S STETSON WAS getting a real work out. With his nervous energy and tension at fever pitch, he prepared for serving the search and arrest warrants. The more that he did, the hat came off and went back on his head like the lever of a fast action repeating rifle.

"Right, Commander. We'll need a team of your best state patrol officers, and we need them fast. They will need to be wearing protective armor and carry automatic weapons. I have every reason to believe these Nazis will not want to submit to arrest without a gun fight."

Lassiter looked up from his phone to see Officer Flaherty enter the PD. The chief of police gave the patrolman a little hand gesture indicating he should just wait for a minute, and after arranging for the raid to take place in three hours—1 pm, Lassiter put down the phone and started strapping on his body armor vest.

"I take it you have the boy safely settled in a safe house the Rapids PD provided and approved. Right, Mike? And they agreed to provide round-the-clock protection?"

"Yup. All taken care of Chief." Flaherty scratched at his tattoo trying to release some of his eagerness and tension. Finally, he couldn't postpone the obvious any longer and blurted out, "How do we take down the Nazis, Dewey? Should I break out the riot gear and tear gas?"

"We," replied Chief Lassiter in a tightly controlled tone of voice, "are only going to provide back-up, Mike. I am letting a team of real pros from the State Patrol come in and hit the place first. We will be there too, of course, along with the county police and Ho-Chunk Nation Tribal Police, but only to provide support."

"But Chief—" and Flaherty stepped nearer to Lassiter's desk, "this should be our bust!"

"Not really, Mike. We share jurisdiction with the Ho-Chunk tribe, the county, and the state, but we are only a city police force. The State Patrol has the most manpower, training, and tactical gear to do the capture, but we will be there to put on the handcuffs." Then Lassiter's wait-a-minute hand gesture turned into a stop sign. "But I will not take any unnecessary chances with a hate group that likely has dynamite and may have automatic weapons. Period. End of story!"

"Dammit, Chief! Moments like this only come once-in-a career," and Flaherty's neck veins indicated his temper was getting the better of him. "You gotta let me get in on the action. You gotta—"

"I don't have to do a damn thing you want, Mike," snarled Lassiter. "I'm the Chief of Police here, not you. If you don't like it, run against me in the next election. But for now, the answer is no!"

"Well, screw you, Dewey!" and Flaherty slammed both of his fists hard into Lassiter's desktop.

"Whoa there, bucko," retorted the chief. "You just took one step over an important line. I am ordering you to stay here and mind the jail. No shoot 'em up stuff for you, Mike. You're out of control, and I don't like your attitude. You can sit your ass down at the front desk until we have made the captures!" And to punctuate the order, Lassiter added— "Now get the hell out of my office!"

Mike Flaherty didn't move. He simply stared down at Chief Lassiter. But Lassiter stared back, and his eyes shone with greater intensity than the policeman could muster. Flaherty snorted in disgust, turned, and stormed out of the room, slamming the door as he left.

Chapter 24

A PHONE CALL to the von Himmel trailer was so rare that when it came even Herman himself nearly jumped out of his skin. Due to major league hangovers, this particular Friday no one felt up to going to work. After finishing lunch, all four men were dozing on the worn-out recliners scattered around the trailer's combination living room / dining room. Of course, no one dared to answer the call save von Grandfather Himmel. That was his job exclusively and to violate that protocol meant an instant beating.

"*Ja*? This is Herman. Who are you? rasped the old man."

The caller must have given his name because the old man nodded and said, "*Ja*" again. Then von Himmel's voice changed. "What do you mean where is my grandson, Jack? He should be coming home from school now, or maybe he is hanging around a girlfriend's house too long again."

The caller passed more information and bewilderment registered on the old man's face. It quickly passed and turned into a bitter scowl. "Wisconsin Rapids, you say? What in hell is he doing there?" More talk from the other end of the line.

"You saw him walking into the Flaherty house there with a Hamot police officer, eh?" Von Himmel's gaze passed around the room, announcing his growing anger to each of his sons.

"*Himmeldonnerwetter!*" shouted the old man into the phone. "Damn it all!" Then he thanked the anonymous caller and slammed down the phone.

"What's up with Jack, *Vater?*" Ade asked as he rose from his chair and moved nearer his father.

"We have some people who keep a close watch on most police in this state," the old Nazi explained as he began rubbing his fists against each other. "Our source in Wisconsin Rapids happens to live across the street from the Flaherty house. They're old people whose son Mike is a cop here in Hamot. Mike was well-known in the Rapids for running his mouth and acting like a big shot. Our source knows Jack from seeing him at some of the meetings I've held. Our spy said he was sure he saw our Jack get out of a squad car and be led inside."

Ade rolled his eyes, then spun around. "Quick! We got to hide the Luger. We got to empty out the shed of the two sticks of dynamite I kept! The cops have to be coming for us!"

Karl was up and moving first. Stamping out his cigar with one hand, he pushed himself erect with the other and bumped past his father, a man still dumbfounded by the caller's information.

"Where you got the Luger, *Vater?*" shouted Karl. "You know—the one I shot that damn wolf with when it came around our barn? Where in your room do you keep it?" Then without waiting for a reply, he shoved the door to the old man's room open and began a hasty search. To hell with his crazy old man's revenge on some pathetic cranberry marsh! No more orders from the top of the family. Karl would look to protect his own hide, and if that included using an automatic pistol to stay the hell out of jail—so be it!

In the meantime, Ade was moving. He jumped for the front door to run to the shed and hide the dynamite. The door had always been a little off center, so once there he started to shove it open.

Then he stopped.

"Freeze!" and a man in camo and heavy battle gear reared up out of thick grass in front of the trailer. He leveled what looked like a small machine gun at Ade, and as he did so four more armed men just like him raised up from under the trailer. The lead man jumped up the steps, kicked the front door wide open and stepped inside the mobile home.

"Everybody freeze!" The automatic rifle and the command forced Ade to step to his right, putting the policeman between him and his family. A blur of action to his left forced Ade even farther back. Then the officer shouted, "Hold it or I'll—!"

A pistol shot exploded through the entryway followed instantly by Karl von Himmel hurling himself over the body of the state patrolman. Karl's leap carried him out and away from the trailer door. As he hit the ground and rolled onto his left shoulder to break his fall, Dewey Lassiter stood up from behind a rusted old tractor, his pistol leveled at the fugitive.

"Stop!—" Lassiter managed to shout before Karl shot him through the neck. The police chief grabbed at his throat, blood erupting through his clenched fingers.

A fusillade of lead from nearly all sides caught Karl von Himmel as he came erect, lifted him briefly from his feet, then dropped him to the ground like a concrete block down a well hole. His pistol hand twitched and another salvo of bullets tore through him from top to bottom. The trigger finger that had taken the life of a wolf with pups to feed and a police chief with the law to enforce wouldn't move again.

Karl's bloody blonde locks had just begun to paint the ground where he lay when a state trooper kicked away his pistol. At the same time two other troopers rushed to assist Chief Lassiter.

The Hamot police chief clawed at his throat as patrolmen tried to stem its fountain of blood and fluid.

"Tell my wife—" Lassiter struggled to say. He kicked convulsively once. Then as suddenly as the gunfire birthed life-taking lead, he was gone.

Karl von Himmel died too, wordless, and now utterly still—a bully, a drunk, and a bar fighter no longer. A camo-garbed officer knelt beside him and checked for a pulse. Finding none, he simply stood and shook his head. No need to say a thing.

A noise at the trailer door turned everyone's attention back to the living. Two state patrolmen were helping a third officer down the steps. The injured officer was tightly clutching the center of his right forearm, pushing down on a hastily wrapped gauze bandage.

"Just nicked me," the wounded patrolman grunted through his teeth.

"Nicked you, like hell, Al!" a squat, thick-bodied, officer with a commander's star on his helmet and a take charge voice stepped forward. "Trooper Lowry," he said, "this is no time to play hero. You did that already when you were the first one in the door. Sit down now and keep pressure on that wound."

"Right, Sir," replied the injured trooper. "Guess I just didn't duck in time!"

"Nothing to apologize about, Trooper. I want you to know I am proud of you . . ." then sweeping his eyes across the entire scene of armed officers, State Patrol Commander Frederick Post reached inside himself for his biggest voice. "I am damn proud of all of you, men!"

Post surveyed the horrific scene before him. He strode across the scruffy front yard and knelt beside the body of Dewey Lassiter. Post's lips moved in silent prayer before he stood, making sure he caught everyone's attention.

"Take a good, hard look at what you see," he said. "Here lies my friend and a great police chief. He is dead because he was an officer of the peace, not an officer of violence."

The brittle warmth of an early September sun dappled the bloody scene with long, thick rays of light fighting through small alleyways among cumulous clouds swollen and grey.

"Peace officers like us die sometimes because we pledge our lives to uphold law and order," Post said. "In the most basic terms that means we just don't shoot first. We shoot second. We wait until we are attacked or fired on. We say, 'Stop or I'll shoot,' and once every so often that obedience to the law costs an officer his life because the bad guys of this world don't always stop. My father was the first black sheriff of Dane County, here in Wisconsin. He lost his life this way too."

Post moved slowly to the body of Karl von Himmel. "This sumbitch fired first. And although that action took the life of Chief Lassiter . . . all of you upheld the law. You waited to shoot second. And when you did . . . nobody missed!"

Commander Post returned to his friend, slowly moved Lassiter's hands from around his throat and composed them cross-armed across his chest. With great care Post reached to his left, picked up the chief's blood-stained Stetson and then placed it gently over the slain officer's face. "Goodbye, Dewey. God speed," he whispered.

Then Post crossed the yard, walked up the steps, and barked orders to bring out the remaining von Himmels in handcuffs. Soon the somber siren of an oncoming ambulance creased the edge of onrushing night. The sonorous wail of a police van leaving with its load of prisoners played a shrill counter melody to an arriving ambulance. The dissonant duet of competing vehicles lamented their tasks to carry away the criminal and the dead alike. Together they made an off-tempo concert meant to escort the respective occupants to their next destination, but certainly not to offer comfort.

"Cover the chief's body with a plastic tarp from our assault vehicle," the state patrol commander explained to the officers standing next to him after the von Himmel clan was whisked away. "I hope the rest of those suckers get life without parole!"

Trooper Lowry looked up at his leader and smiled. "Right, sir. And given all the Heil Hitler stuff inside their trailer, maybe they will be housed in the Jewish Black American wing?"

Chapter 25

HAMOT POLICE CHIEF Michael Flaherty glared at Herman von Himmel and spit through the bars of the jail cell at the old man's feet. "Yup," he sneered, "you do have a right to one phone call. And one day next century I'm gonna let you make it!" Flaherty punctuated his comment by snapping to attention and snapping off a Nazi salute Hitler himself would have enjoyed.

Ade rushed to the cell gate and sneered back at Chief Flaherty. "Hey, *dummkopf*! We know our rights! Tell the chief of police to come in here instead. We want to deal with him, not some dumbass like you."

"You *are* dealing with the chief of police, d-u-m-b-a-s-s!" retorted Flaherty. "Or maybe you bright boys forgot you killed the last one we had about an hour ago."

"Stupid mick! No one in this cell killed anybody," Ade snarled, his lips curling back over his front teeth. "Karl did it while we sat on our sofa chairs following police orders to raise our hands. You can't charge us with a crime we didn't commit!" He shifted his tone of voice to one laced with amiable sarcasm. "So—let us have our one call. If you don't, you're going to be the one the town blames when we all get off on a technicality."

Chief Flaherty seethed inwardly. "Ya, right. I'll get you a phone. Just make it quick!" and he sauntered off to his new office to get a phone he could plug into the cell's receptacle.

When the new police chief returned with the portable phone, it was Herman von Himmel standing at the cell gate to take delivery and make the call. The two men eyed each other contemptuously, and Flaherty headed for the door to give the caller some privacy.

"*Ja!* Just hold on there, Officer," requested the old man. "I want to make this call in private, alone. It is my right because I am the head of our family. I have to choose an attorney to represent all three of us."

"I know exactly who to call," Herman von Himmel said turning to his sons. "He is the best defense attorney we can get for people like we are. And I pay his organization, the KKK, plenty dues money and donations, so he must come to us."

"Who is this lawyer guy? Ade asked.

"He is called Forrester. He lives in Madison and is the director of the KKK for most of the north country in America," explained von Himmel. "He is a good hater, just like us SS men. And most importantly, he likes to live in luxury. I know this from a visit last year."

"Ok," said Gunther dismissively. "He lives in luxury. Why should that matter to us?"

"It means everything, Gunther!" hissed Ade, turning to face his brother. In a nursery school voice suitable for an ignorant child, Ade went on to say, "It means he likes money and the things it can buy. And Father is going to offer him more money than he can shake a burning cross at, by God!"

"Oh, uh, sounds good," offered Gunther and with a trace of embarrassment he returned to sit on his bunk. After easing himself down on the edge of his mattress, Gunther muttered— "but we don't have enough money to shake at anybody . . . do we?" – but no one paid him any attention.

Ade smiled a bit, winked at his father, and said, "Go ahead and make the call, *Vater*. Offer him some incentive money if he can win our case and get us off the hook."

Chief Flaherty stepped out of the jail briefly and returned with another officer armed with a shotgun. "No funny business, gents," he said, "or Officer Stone and his double barrel twelve gauge here will save the county and the state the cost of any trial. Now you, old man, turn around and stick your hands out the slot so we can cuff you up!"

Chapter 26

ONCE THE DOOR to the phone room closed, Herman quickly checked his wristwatch. After he confirmed to himself it was only 3:30 pm and law offices were still open, he dialed a number in Madison that he had memorized just for occasions like this.

"Law office of N. B. Forrester," replied a female secretary whose syrupy voice oozed over the phone line like molasses in Mississippi mud. "How can we help y'all today?"

"I need to talk to Forrester," the old man said. "Tell him Herman von Himmel is calling, and it is very important I speak to him right now."

"Yes, Mr. von Himmel. He is in the office today. Please just wait one moment while I connect your call."

A few frustrating seconds later, a voice with a hint of a chuckle answered. "This is Forrester," then added with a laugh, "what trouble did your boys get you into now, Herman?"

"*Ja.* Plenty of trouble," replied von Himmel. "I don't trust the phone because I am calling from the Hamot Police Department. Me and my two sons are in jail here. We are charged with bombing a cranberry operation. How quick can you come? We need to get out on bail!"

"Of course, Herman. Forrester's voice was now that of a sharp defense attorney on alert. "You have been a longtime member and supporter of our cause. Has bail been set yet?"

"No, we have been told that will be done Monday morning at 10:00 am at the courthouse in Sparta."

"Then I will see you at 8:30 tomorrow morning so we can talk about the details of what happened. I have a new assistant attorney in the office, so he'll take care of our other cases for the time being. Now if you and your three sons are in the slammer, where is Jack? You said you and two sons were in jail. Can number three take care of your grandson?"

"Not to worry about Jack. Just be here tomorrow for our talk, and I promise you we will pay you very, very well. My third son Karl is now with the Valkyries who are taking him to Valhalla. He died with a weapon in his hand defending me from the cops."

"I had no idea your problems were this serious, Herman. I'll see you and your two sons tomorrow morning," and with that the phone conversation ended. Von Himmel's rap on the door summoned Chief Flaherty, and the old man was quickly returned to the cell.

After Flaherty left, Gunther rushed to his father. "What's gonna happen, *Vater*? Is the lawyer taking our case?" Ade just stood silently where he was, watching the expressions on his father's face for any extra clues about what might be going on.

"His name is Forrester, and he will be here tomorrow for a meeting and our bail hearing on Monday. Like I said, he is the best lawyer we could get for people such as us," Herman replied. "Now leave me alone. All is taken care of, Gunther." Herman von Himmel wasn't a man used to being interrogated for anything, and much to both of his sons' disappointment, he shuffled over to his cot for a nap.

As he lay down, the old man smiled to himself. Yes, he had a complete plan—a plan to take care of the bombing charges, a plan to pay Forrester, and even a plan to take Jack for a visit to the Externstein once he could be located. "The boy's final visit to our Nazi shrine—one last time," thought Herman von Himmel. "Odin be praised!" and he smiled again before he closed his eyes and slept in less than eternal rest.

Chapter 27

THE NEXT MORNING neither Gunther nor Ade were happy about the fact their father was meeting with their defense attorney alone. Von Himmel did not sympathize with them about it. He just abruptly left the cell when the deputy came.

"So, Herman," Forrester began as the two men sat down in the small, windowless conference room. "What's this about bombing a cranberry marsh?" The lawyer's razor cut hairdo, his artsy, three-piece seer sucker suit, his peach-scented cologne and his flint grey eyes behind Foster Grant sunglasses were a sharply-etched contrast to the rumpled old man who had slept in a prison jump suit.

"*Ja*, we did it," affirmed von Himmel. "But we had no other choice."

"No other choice because—?"

"Because my grandson Jack was snuggling up to a Jew girl from the high school, and if we did not do something to her kike family real fast, other

Nazis around here would come to pay us a visit with dynamite instead."

"How on earth do you blow up a cranberry marsh, Herman?"

"It is simple, Mister Big City Lawyer." The old Nazi was getting nauseous from inhaling the fruity aftershave fumes filling the tiny atmosphere of the conference room. "We used their own dynamite to blow up the dike that holds the lake reservoir they use for a water source to irrigate the beds and spray the berries against the cold." Von Himmel never spared anyone his annoyances. "The dam burst, and the rush of water tore out the crop beds below," he sneered.

"Look, buddy. I am your best and likely your only chance to beat this, so spare me your frickin' attitude," Forrester jabbed his finger into von Himmel's chest to emphasize his point. He jabbed hard enough to make the old man's head snap back and collapse his silver-white shock of hair down onto his forehead.

"*Ja*, all right then," replied the old man, throwing his head back to reinstate his hairdo. "Me and my three sons snuck over two nights ago and blew up the dam. We got away clean. Everything seemed fine yesterday right up until I get this phone call from Wisconsin Rapids," and von Himmel had to pause. He just wasn't made for long explanations, and the emotions of the events rushed to his throat.

"Us Nazis, we got our people watching around the police stations and homes all over the state. A friend of mine who watches in the Rapids called and said he just saw our Jack being taken into a house there, and he wanted to know why this was happening."

"What did you think then?"

"I didn't think anything, *Dumme*! I knew right away that since the cops had Jack, they would make him talk about our attack. And soon after that, they would come for us!"

"Don't call me dumb again, if you want an attorney of my caliber." The warning tone in Forrester's voice made it clear von Himmel had to calm himself or lose his lawyer.

"*Ja*, sorry. I just get too worked up about all this. And you haven't heard the worst part yet," the old Nazi explained. He ran his thick fingers across the top of his forehead in a vain attempt to improve his disheveled appearance and settle his nerves.

Despite von Himmel's obnoxious rant, Forrester was taken aback in this recounting of events. "You mean there is something worse than having a family eyewitness to your planning a felony crime like dynamiting a business, then spill it all to the police?"

"The cops had our trailer surrounded even as I finished the phone call." The Nazi coughed, then nearly dropped his head low enough to hit the tabletop. "They shot Karl when he used a pistol to try to get away." Von Himmel paused to cover his face with his massive hand. He shook with silent emotion. "My son Karl is dead! So, *ja*, there is something worse! The undertaker comes today for me to make funeral arrangements. But we won't have none."

"My god, Herman. I had no idea it was this bad." Forrester offered. "And you figure that they have Jack stashed in Wisconsin Rapids as a prime witness. That's a major problem!"

"*Nein*! Not a problem if you can get me and my sons out on bail, Forrester!"

"Herman, getting you all out on bail is going to come down to paying a small fortune for bond money. How much do you have?"

"I got some savings my *vater* Karl sent here from Germany," conceded von Himmel as he dabbed at his eyes. Ever cautious in discussing wealth, the old man whispered into Forrester's ear, "You just go out to the trailer and look in our little barn," he said.

"You will find some small lead weights and little building bricks in the near left-hand corner as you enter. Rub off their cobwebs and wash the color off with paint thinner. They are gold. It is all the savings that I was given. But it is enough to pay up to a half-million in bail for us and a retainer of $100,000 for you!"

The old man's eyes were alive with fire and ferocity as he continued. "But if you need anymore, that will be a problem." With a strange, emphatic tone, von Himmel added, "My gold has supported our entire family." Then Herman drew himself close to Forrester and using his only arm held him by the shirt collar.

"But don't go looking for more than I just explained if you know what's good for you, Mister Lawyer Man. The little bit still left exists only because I do what my *vater* Heinrich always says—keep your wealth as close as your own skin! That's why I not spend his savings on a fancy house and big cars. We live small to not attract no notice. And I save what I was given for maybe a time like this."

Von Himmel let go of Forrester's shirt, as if he was releasing a soap bubble, not a high ranking official in the Ku Klux Klan. The old Nazi stood, moved to the door, rapped for the guard, and left for his cell when the door was unlocked. He was instantly relieved to get out of that cologne-soaked environment.

However, in his abrupt leave-taking, as sharp a character as Herman von Himmel was, he failed to notice one significant thing about his defense attorney. After mentioning there was at least a half-million in gold available, Forrester's eyes came alive with fire too—the fire that comes from greed.

Chapter 28

"**If Your Honor** please, my clients request the opportunity to make bail," Forrester said in a tone of voice that sounded as full of peach syrup as his Georgia secretary. It was 10:00 am, Monday morning, and the bail bond hearing was now in session. Forrester turned to extend an eloquent smile to a courtroom entirely packed with locals who had heard of the case. The century old tiger oak floorboards occasionally creaked as the audience shifted their weight on church pews that had been repurposed rather than discarded, a behavior typical of a thrifty, agricultural county.

"So they can blow up some more cranberry marshes?" asked the county's district attorney, Tamara Blake. "In case defense counsel has forgotten, setting off a bomb brings the felony charges we've made." As a prosecutor, she was known as a fiery, red-haired Scot who wasn't afraid to mix it up in court even if her sarcasm caused a little trouble now and again.

"The People, Your Honor, do not want any bail offered to these three felons," she argued. They blew up the Koleski Marsh dike, ruining the entire cranberry operation and causing about ten million dollars in damages—at least half or more of it uninsured costs for money the family does not have. Moreover, one of them, Karl von Himmel, shot it out with state patrol officers when search and arrest warrants were served. He's at the mortuary right now."

"And so is your case against these innocent men, Madame Prosecutor!" Forrester shot back. "They are alive because they raised their hands and followed police orders. The only lawbreaker was shot full of holes. What's more, your honor should be aware that the basis for the search and arrests was an illegal interview of one of the adults' fifteen-year-old son.

"Which he can argue at trial!" the D.A. retorted. "No bail for these dangerous men. During a search of their property, police officers discovered two sticks of dynamite in a little barn next to their mobile home, dynamite with the Koleski name printed on each stick. It's likely the FBI will be taking an interest in this case."

"Dangerous to whom?" replied Forrester. "Judge Windshill, other than a couple misdemeanor drunk and disorderly charges, these men represent no threat to anyone. They have a small farm with animals that need feeding and care, and it's not against the law to own a little dynamite. Both the father, Herman, and the son Adolf, have no criminal records. They live in a broken-down trailer and simply do not have the financial resources to make them a possible flight risk."

"But the dynamite sticks had Koleski Marsh as a label, and one of the family whipped Herman's grandson, Jack," Blake retorted. "A wide belt mark was found on the boy's neck when we took him into protective custody, Judge. The mark perfectly illustrates these felons are capable of both brutality and violence."

"But we are not here today for speculation about child abuse," Forrester instantly responded. "The people's request for no bail is an over-reaching denial of any citizen's basic legal rights."

Judge Terrence Windshill put up his hand as a stop sign to both attorneys. "I've heard more than enough. The defense is correct that defendants have the right to bail in most cases. The prosecution is correct that these men are accused of a heinous, violent crime."

"So what do you want to do?" Forrester interrupted.

"Silence out of you is all that I want, Mr. Forrester!" snapped the judge. "In this particular case, I am going to use the wisdom of Solomon and split the baby in half." Windshill coughed his allergic cough, adjusted his glasses down his nose, and announced his ruling.

"The defendants are eligible to apply for bail in this case," the judge said, and before District Attorney Blake could object, he further explained, "providing they each can post one hundred thousand bucks, and I am not talking about male white-tail deer!" The judge shot a fierce look at the three defendants. "Don't any of you forget that here in Wisconsin, defendants have to come up with the full amount for their bail money, not ten percent like in other states." And with that admonition and a sharp rap of his gavel, the magistrate stood up, everyone rose, and he left the room.

Immediately after the ruling, Forrester sidled over to Tamara Blake's table. "And my clients will be posting the $100,000 a piece for bail," he sneered. Then he winked, smiled, and added, "Just thought you might want to know."

"But you just said they didn't have any money!" Blake responded angrily.

"Oh no, I didn't, Miss Prosecutor. What I said was they didn't have the finances to represent a flight risk. I didn't say anything about covering the cost of bail." Forrester felt he was in his element now, successfully fencing with an authority figure. "They'll be going home to their trailer by tomorrow afternoon." His smile was as wide as it was insincere.

The KKK attorney gave Blake another wink and an exaggerated smile, then turning to his clients he said, "See, I am worth the price of admission for you boys. I'll have you out right after I make a little trip to the bank and the bail bondsman tomorrow."

"Damn, you're smart!" Gunther burst out. "I never thought we would get out of jail!"

Herman von Himmel just snorted and said, "*Ja,* you did good. But then again, that's what we are paying you to do. Just remember what I said about the money, Mister Lawyer."

Forrester lavished the three men with one more gorgeous smile. He closed his black leather briefcase, made a sharp turn in perfect military fashion, and marched out of the courtroom.

Gunther and Herman simply followed Forrester's parade out the door. It took a nudge, a shove, and Patrolman Stone's tight grasp of his forearm for Ade to budge. His movements were slower, resistant, more deliberate. Had any of the departing crowd bothered to look, his face announced he was a man suddenly suspicious and absorbed in re-calibrations. There were at least two other men now wondering how much Herman von Himmel's horde was worth and where he had it stashed.

Chapter 29

N.B. FORRESTER USUALLY was a man of exceptionally fast thinking. That trait had served him well in all his cases at trial. In fact, Forrester was always quick to tell his clients as well as the boys and bosses at headquarters down south that he had never lost a major case; never even had to plea bargain a case down for a reduced sentence. He was just faster and smarter and bolder than any chump city or county D.A.

Of course, the net effect of all this success pumped mega quantities of helium into his dirigible-sized ego, but now more chips were on the table than he had ever dreamed of. Gold chips, he realized, and he was certain there was more than the half-million-dollar horde which von Himmel had reluctantly admitted to possessing. Maybe enough to make his own escape to a warmer climate. After all, he thought, it isn't just old Nazis who can disappear in a South American country with no extradition treaty with the United States.

The image of the agitated rabbit from *Alice in Wonderland* reared up in Forrester's imagination. The repetitive words from the Disney movie he had taken in as a child rolled through his brain. "I'm late. I'm late. For a very important date!" the nervous critter kept repeating as it scurried to its next appointment in the story's world of bizarre animals and insane rulers. The rhyme stuck in his mind, irritating the lawyer as much as it seemed to propel him to action.

"First things first," he told himself as he unlocked the driver's side door of his white Mercedes coup. "Got to rent a motel room, buy some good work clothes and mud boots, but most of all, purchase a big old draw-string bag to carry whatever loot is out there at the von Himmel place."

As soon as Forrester finished that thought, he had another. "And if by any good fortune I should actually discover the entire treasure horde of gold no doubt liberated from Jews only steps from the gas chamber, I have to find a way to destroy any chances of bail for the von Himmel crew. Then I have to destroy any chances of them being found innocent!" That happy thought removed any trace of Walt Disney's rapid rabbit, the attorned realized.

"Yes sir, and I have just the right answer to this puzzle in protective custody," Forrester realized, "and his name is Jack von Himmel." His thought process now was now moving at something approaching the speed of light. "And . . . I'll have to beat it out of the country the day sentences are delivered, lest any of those Nazis get the idea to have me exterminated real sudden like for selling them down the river."

Another scene announced itself in Forrester's mind. As he sat down in his Mercedes and put his briefcase in the passenger seat, he vividly recalled a moment on the UW Madison campus as he sat in Poetry 101. Maybe the professor's name was Fitzpatrick? The obese, desperately near-sighted man was always in a rush, much like a bunny down Alice's rabbit hole. He charged into the ancient classroom one spring day just before the ten-minute limit when students could leave, stumbled over one of the thousands of warped wood floorboards in Bascom Hall, and accidentally spilled his lesson plans across the desks and laps of every student sitting in the front row.

Without missing a single beat, Fitzpatrick glanced at the lesson plan disaster, looked every student briefly in the eye and announced— "Somebody give me a poetic line or two that fits this moment, and I will give him or her an A for the semester!"

A swift and audible gasp proclaimed the surprise and befuddlement of almost every one of his classmates. But never slow on the draw, Forrester shot up from his seat and using his best rhetorical impression of Scottish burr he recited— "The best laid schemes 'o Mice and Men, Gang aft agley!" And in the next instant he explained, "The poet is Scotland's Bobby Burns, and the American English version of the last line is 'often go awry.'"

"Bravo, Mr. Forrester!" responded his instructor. "And you not only correctly cited the last line, which many people cite incorrectly, but you also added context to your quotation in case any of the unsophisticated members of this class did not understand 'Gang aft agley.'" Then Fitzpatrick waved his arm across the span of the entire student body and said," Forrester gets an A for the semester. The rest of you can go home now and study classic poems for the next time my briefcase spills my lesson plans. Class dismissed!"

Returning from the daydream, the attorney caught himself smiling a rare, truly authentic smile. "Yes," he said aloud to himself as he studied the fine features of his aristocratic face in his rearview mirror, "Winner, winner, chicken dinner!"

The luxury car growled to life, and Forrester whipped out into the slow streets of tractor and diesel truck town of Hamot, Wisconsin. He was certain there had to be at least one motel, however small, poorly furnished and cheap it would be, somewhere in this land of swamps and buried treasure.

Chapter 30

IT WASN'T NAMED "The Lonely Arms Motel," Forrester decided, but it should have been. Rick's Motel consisted of five little Quonset huts all cut out of the same barracks-looking army brown siding with barn red trim set near the marshy end of Lake Hamot. And he was fortunate to get the last room. As luck would have it there were four long-haul semis whose drivers would let their engines rattle and cough all night occupying the other rooms. But where and how Nathan Bedford Forrester slept that night mattered nothing.

Once a motel room was secured, his Mercedes 280 was once again in gear, searching for a clothing store downtown. Aptly enough, the only place with blue jeans, flannel shirts and L.L. Bean muck boots was named "The Cash and Carry Store." While picking out his rural attire, Forrester briefly considered buying a rifle or handgun, just in case something "gang agley." As a general merchandise store, the place had virtually everything a rural person would need—guns, chainsaws, red flannel jackets, and a wide selection of industrial-sized brassieres.

In the end the attorney decided he didn't need a weapon. After all, he *was* a player in and of the legal system engaged in appropriate defense work on the behalf of three clients, entitled to the presumption of innocence. It would be a bad look for him to be found packing a .38 without a concealed weapons permit if in some unpredictable event, he was stopped and searched.

Following the directions of newly anointed, much less appointed Chief of Police Flaherty, the defense attorney sped down one rural road after another, weaving his way to the von Himmel property and crime scene.

As he approached the trailer from the narrow country road, no doubt could exist about the violence which had erupted there several hours before. Pulling into the sand and gravel driveway, Forrester had to swerve to avoid the crime scene tape surrounding two dark red patches of ground next to each other where Dewey Lassiter and Karl von Himmel convulsively gulped their final breath.

Walking around the trailer and out to what the von Himmels called their shed, Forrester decided he didn't mind wearing his new country garb at all.

The land behind the home pointed downwards, not yet a bog but also not entirely firm soil either.

"Just happen to have these shitkickers!" the lawyer proudly announced to the marsh country, and he lifted his right foot to admire his new muck boot. Then he strode over to the small double-door shed, untied the crime scene tape, entered, and looked to his left. Just as Herman von Himmel had described, there in the corner, covered in dried mud and broken stems from hay bales, were small lead weights that were the size of giant popsicle sticks and small muck-covered building bricks only a fifth of their normal dimensions.

"Gotcha!" laughed Forrester, and he unclasped the heavy canvas bag he had hooked to his belt. "This shouldn't be all that difficult for a 'Cash and Carry' man like me."

But it was more difficult. The weights and bricks had been covered with so much dirt and fodder that the stuff had congealed to form a concrete-like glue. The gold was stuck to the wooden floor in one solid mass too heavy to lift or separate.

A quick search of the entire barn revealed several items of interest and one big issue. The issue was the animals were thirsty and starving, and that made them intolerably loud. If Forrester were to continue to work in and around the barn, he decided he needed to take care of them. Besides, he decided his clients likely would be happy to know he had done this unexpected favor, a favor which might cement their trust as tightly as the gold was attached to the barn. "A treasure that I am going to relieve them of as soon as possible!" Forrester reflected.

Filling the water troughs, spreading a couple of hay bales around for the cow and horse, and pouring out five bags of oats and corn to renew the grain supply for the sheep, goats and pigs silenced them.

The next task was to look for a way to dissolve the caked-on muck. Hadn't the old man referred to using some paint thinner? And, like always, his mind came through for him again. By climbing up a ladder to the second floor, Forrester quickly located several large tin cans labeled Acid Wash.

Then he discovered something else. Back in the dark recesses of the east end of the shed, the lawyer was attracted to what appeared to be wooden cases covered with old gunny sacks. D.B. Forrester's instinctive curiosity about anything covered up in a corner led him to pull back the gunny sacks and inspect the cases.

"Hot damn!" the attorney shouted. "If I'm not as crazy as a pet raccoon, these are the way Herman's father got the gold out of Germany and delivered it here!" And bending down to brush away the cobwebs, Forrester gleefully examined heavy wooden shipping crates stamped **U.S. Army Priority**

Building Supplies. "Sure as hell!" Forrester said out loud. "What better way to smuggle the stolen loot out of Germany than to put a military label on the boxes!"

Sweeping more dust and debris away near the bottom of a crate revealed even more of the Friedrich von Himmel's ingenuity. "**Deliver to Supply Depot, Fort McCoy, Hamot, Wisconsin**," read Forrester. "And the fix was in with the Quarter master's office. Some poor slob running a forklift got a few extra bucks to load the back end of a haul truck with what he thought were boxes of building bricks some cheapskate would rather steal than pay for."

Returning to his work, the Midwest Director of the KKK, carried down some tins of acid, carefully poured the wash over the bricks, pried them loose, wiped them off on rags in the shed, and filled his sack with the little bricks and bars of pure, blessed gold. Going back and forth from the barn to the vehicle, Forrester had to make three trips. The precious metal happened to be heavy he learned, and there was no need to risk damage to anything inside the bag.

Once he was finished with the gold he had been told about, the lawyer instantly began a feverish search for the rest of the horde. "*In Xanadu did Kubla Khan, A stately pleasure dome decree!*" he chortled. "First, I'm going to go through the rest of this barn with a fine-tooth comb, just in case." But hours later, all the combs in the world could not produce another weight or bar. No Xanadu on the near horizon. No stately pleasure domes either.

Forrester retied the tape around the barn doors and turned his attention to the trailer next. The suppertime sun of northern Wisconsin was already painting the western horizon with smoldering streaks of burnt sienna and canary yellow. "Gotta get to gold digging"'," he said to himself. "Not much sunshine left, and I better not turn on any lights in the trailer."

Moving quickly to his vehicle, the lawyer also realized he needed to move it to a less conspicuous spot. He pulled the Mercedes behind the home, slid over the leather front seat to dig out a flashlight from his glove compartment, and opened the passenger side door to get out.

He had one foot on the ground and was twisting himself around to put down the other when something made him freeze in place. With the greatest patience and slowest of motions, Forrester returned his leg to the car and gently but quite firmly closed the door.

"Nice damn doggie," he cursed as a brindle brown, black and white wolf, much larger than pictures on television showed, padded its way along the margin of the marsh only forty steps away. It had huge paws, stood waist high if Forrester would have been standing up, and most interesting of all, its lusterless eyes were focused everywhere but on the lawyer. The animal seemed so intent on sniffing the reedy edge of the bog that Forrester considered leaving his car on the driver's side and entering the trailer.

He sat with his hand on the doorknob, unsure of what to do. In compulsive fascination, the lawyer watched the wolf hunt and sniff. The animal never moved out of sight, but never spared a single glance in Forrester's direction either. And after thoroughly checking all he could, the attorney concluded no other meat-eaters were skulking nearby, although he couldn't understand why all the farm animals in the pen kept stomping and bellering inside their high wire fencing.

"Must be you've been drawn here by the smell of the blood," the lawyer spoke to the animal. "But you're a sorry ass excuse for a killer," he said as he spat out the window.

"Wee, sleekit, cowran, tim'rous beastie..." he drawled contemptuously, quoting Bobby Burns' poetry to the animal. Forrester concluded if he ever saw a wolf again, there was no reason to feel any fear.

"You cowards have to kill in a pack; no guts to do it one-on-one!" he sneered. But the evening shadows had extended themselves in long, narrow red pine stilettos which stabbed the von Himmel trailer with deep, black wounds. The attorney realized it was time to leave.

"Catch you later, Wiley Coyote!" the Forrester jeered at the disinterested predator. . . then added—"now eat my dust!" Turning on his headlights and easing his sports car out from hiding, the next multi-millionaire of the world spun out of the von Himmel driveway and headed back to Hamot with the first down payment of what he was certain would be his ticket to a life of leisure.

If the spirit gods of the north country were in a playful mood, they might have decided to temporarily grant the alpha wolf and each of the other five members of his pack the power of speech. The wolves then could have explained to the defense attorney in detail how it is customary hunting behavior for them to appear not to notice their target until it is entirely too late for their prey to escape.

But the gods apparently were in a mood as sullen as the sudden onset of nightime upnorth. Instead, the pack leader glanced at his companions, half-yawned, half-smiled, kissed his fangs with an incredibly long, pink tongue but said nothing in reply to the departing attorney. At least nothing for the present. For the time being, court was adjourned.

Chapter 31

IT WASN'T UNTIL one in the afternoon on Monday that Forrester showed up at the Hamot P.D. and Courthouse. Chief Flaherty happened to be at the desk, and the attorney graced him with a grin flashy as it was fraudulent and plunked down the $100,000 bail bonds for his each of his three clients.

"There ye be, Matey!" the lawyer jibed in a good rendition of Long John Silver. And just to irritate the cop, Forrester leaned across the desk and barked out "Aaargghh."

"Up yours!" snorted Flaherty.

"Oh, come on, Chief! Can't you enjoy a little humor in this occasion? After all, it can't be very often that the pile of loot this size crosses the humble Hamot Clerk of Court's desk," and to emphasize his point Forrester mimicked cleaning spots from the top of the quarter-sawn oak desktop.

"Uh huh," Flaherty said. "I'd just like to know where those lowlifes found the money to get their freedom." And the chief added as he leaned forward toward Forrester, "But if I ever find out you had anything to do with some funny business to come up with this amount of dough, I'd be happy to find you a nice little cot in our slammer, buddy!"

"Well, as we all know, Officer, to get bail, some states make people pay only a partial payment for their bond, but in Wisconsin they must provide the entire amount. Fortunately, old man von Himmel has some serious money laid away. Don't get your hopes up too high that he'll be spending time in your lockup. Remember, he has me for his attorney." Forrester straightened up, changed his mood, and spoke roughly to Flaherty. "Now let my clients out!"

After collecting their belongings at the desk, the men silently walked out the door, down the steps and followed Forrester to his car. Herman von Himmel could contain himself no longer. Stopping in the middle of the otherwise empty sidewalk, the old Nazi pushed his face into Forrester's and bellered, "Lech mich in Arsch!"

Forrester understood he was being verbally assaulted but maintained his court room cold neutrality. "Sorry, Herman," he smiled, "but I don't speak German."

He said, "Bite me," wheezed Gunther in between a smoker's cough.

Forrester regarded Herman with a very cold smile. "Now why would you want me to do that?"

"Because you need to make up for letting us sit all morning in this damn jail, you shyster!" and von Himmel's face bulged like a birthday balloon hooked to a helium factory pipeline.

Forrester just smiled again. "Well, for your information, Herman, there is no bail bondsmen here in Tomah. I had to drive all the way to the Twin Cities to find a place that could handle the king's ransom in gold bars it took to get you three out of the clink." Then with an even wider grin, Forrester shoved von Himmel backwards. If not for the attorney's Mercedes, the old man would have gone down hard. "See, not every bondsman will take gold in the place of money. So back off!"

As it is with so many bullies, Herman von Himmel did not do very well when someone stood up to him, not even with a high school boy like his grandson. Fussing and fuming, he pointed his two sons to the back seat and climbed into the front himself.

"I want to go to a telephone booth now," von Himmel announced. "So, boys, pass me up all your spare change." Mystified by the request, both Gunther and Ade dutifully dug coins out of their pockets and handed it up to their father.

Then the old Nazi turned his focus to his attorney. "And did you cash in all what we discussed, or did you use just enough to pay the bail, Mister Lawyer Man?

"Oh, Wisconsin law requires payment in full for bond money. They put the gold in an escrow account as evidence you were all good for the bond if you happen to flee prosecution."

"What's a escrow?' asked Gunther, his voice echoing up from the back seat along with an acrid blast of cigarette smoke.

"It's a bank account held by a third party, like your attorney, as a guarantee," explained Forrester, in his finest scholarly manner. "Now throw that damn cigarette out of my Benz!"

"Just you be careful to leave what's left of my little treasure alone. Do not try to steal my money!" warned von Himmel.

"Fine with me, Herman," said Forrester, his smile a finely cut example of Northwoods ice sculpture.

Two blocks later, the lawyer pulled up to a public phone booth near the city library, pointed at it and chuckled, "Help yourself—but you better have plenty of quarters!"

The old Nazi struggled out of the low slung, tight fit of the car seat and, as if shaking off the rust from a jail cell, stretched, dug the pile of coins out of his pocket, entered the booth and dialed. As he waited for the connection, he made sure the door of the booth was tightly shut so nothing he said could escape.

"*Ja*, this is Herman von Himmel. I got a job for two of our best Nazi men which must be done tonight, and I will pay each ten thousand dollars to do it."

The person on the other end of the line said something, then von Himmel replied, "*Ja!* — the job is to break into a safe house tonight in Wisconsin Rapids when everyone is asleep. Knock my grandson Jack out but leave the two old people alone if possible. Keep Jack tied up in the trunk. You know where I live. Tomorrow, I need them to drive to my trailer and deliver him to me. But they must not arrive until after nine in the morning. Got it?"

Apparently, the other party did not get it. The hired help had to come from St. Paul, and it wasn't until the old man agreed to pony up twenty-five grand each did the deal go through. The three passengers watched von Himmel nod approvingly as he hung up and returned to the vehicle.

"And what was that all about, Herman? Anything your lawyer should know you are doing?" Forrester lost much of his grin as he said this. His suspicions were strong that the old man was up to something.

"None of your damn business, Lawyer Man," the old Nazi replied. "Take me to White's Funeral home two blocks down to pick up my son's ashes. Then just drive us home. Gunther, you can still get some work at a marsh this afternoon. Adolf, I need you to help me clean up the trailer." The tone which von Himmel used to deliver these orders left no room for question or comment. Forrester dropped off Gunther at the Raezan Marsh about eight miles short of the von Himmel trailer with the understanding that Ade would come back to pick him up at 6:00 p.m.

Later, as Forrester rolled up the driveway to the von Himmel's place, he couldn't help but do a quick scan for any wolves, not that he would mention his encounter to his clients. They could fend for themselves he decided. The two von Himmels poured themselves out of the limo and began to stretch out the kinks from the ride as Forrester put the car in reverse and backed out to the road to leave.

"Now, Adolf," Herman von Himmel began in an abnormally gracious voice, "I have a plan which I want you to help me with."

"Yea, sure, *Vater*" and Ade paused to push back the mop of dark hair that covered his forehead and birthmark. "Whatever you need."

"I need you to be a grown-up man tomorrow morning, that's what I need!" and to emphasize the serious nature of his request, Herman von Himmel set down the wooden box with Karl's ashes and put both of his heavy hands on Adolf's shoulders.

Ade was confused by this. "What do you mean, 'be a grown-up man'?" he asked.

"The situation is this. Gunther may be my son, but he is a drunk and a *dummkopf* who cannot be trusted. You, Adolf, are the opposite—sober, smart, and worthy of my trust!" Von Himmel patted his son on the shoulders to affirm this compliment.

Ade was cautious. Yes, he felt good about his father finally recognizing he was the smart son of the family, but he also was convinced his father Herman had been maneuvering events and people the last few crazy days as he formulated some kind of master scheme.

"What do you want your smart son to do tomorrow?"

Ade saw tiny slivers of fire start to dance in his father's eyes. "I found out where the cops are hiding Jack," he said. And before Adolf could express any reaction, von Himmel carried on. "My phone call in town was to arrange for Jack to be brought here tomorrow morning, *ja?* But my two helpers do not show up until Gunther is gone."

"Why should it be important that Gunther not be here?"

"Because I do not trust him to do what has to be done with the only witness to our attack plans, that's why!" Von Himmel's eyes were now simmering orbs of fire and smoke.

Ade instantly understood. "You are saying both of us have to wait for Gunther to be gone and for Jack to arrive so we can kill him, aren't you?"

"*Ja!*"

There was a moment of sustained and very pregnant silence. Ade was jolted by this insight into his father's mind. As a son, he also realized he was about to be offered what amounted to the keys to the kingdom if he played his cards right. "I had no idea you had the connections to have some people kidnap Jack," he said in the most complimentary tone he could muster, but the darkening of his forehead birthmark underscored the suspicion he felt.

"Us old Nazis," von Himmel beamed, "we don't get by without watching all the cop stations and places they use in this state—even safe houses. It is a matter of self-preservation, Adolf, something you will learn as I lead you into the core of knowledge about the Nazi network of contacts as well as our Nazi religion."

Ade was shocked. "I figured you had contacts, but you mean there actually is a Nazi religion? I had no idea of such a thing."

"We worship the oldest and most powerful of gods, the Viking god Odin. I will show you at the Externstein hill tomorrow night when we bury Karl and Jack beside the Irminsul shrine. But tell me now to my face—will you join me in this plan and embrace the life of a true believer? Understand if you accept, I will pass something on to you I have at the shrine which should make you invulnerable unless you drop it!"

Ade took just a few seconds to regard his father. He knew there was really no choice. If he said no, then his father likely would kill him too—very possibly right on the spot. He would use his enormous hand to choke Ade as easily as he smashed Gunther to the floor. Besides, while Jack was a good kid who he felt a little affection for, the boy was really the only evidence the prosecutor had to prove her case against them. Jack had to die. Just simple math.

It was all agreed to with a nod from Adolf and a pat on his shoulder from his father.

Chapter 32

"**DON'T WORK TOO** hard, Gunther!" yelled Adolf the next morning as his brother revved up their old blue-white-and rust Ford pickup. Gunther laughed and returned the favor by popping the clutch on the truck, spewing gravel around, then turning out of the driveway for a day's labor at the Raezan Marsh. And it was good for him to leave in a hurry judging by the scowl on his father's face.

"*Das Gut!* He ruins our truck, but at least he is gone," Herman von Himmel announced as he came down the trailer steps to meet Adolf.

"Now, Adolf, I want you to get us ready. It's quarter past eight already, so go to the shed, get the army backpack I have hung up on the right-hand door. Fill it with two hammers, two saws and two knives. Then go inside the trailer, take out an empty tin can from the trash and roll up the red-and-white plastic tablecloth from the kitchen. Put both inside the pack too."

Adolf swallowed hard. He did not have to use his imagination to understand the tools were for disposing of Jack. But the tin can, and the tablecloth didn't figure to him.

Von Himmel read the questions he could see expressed on Adolf's face. "Adolf, my son. I will cut Jack's ropes with this," and he flashed a long folding buck knife from his right pants pocket. "I tell him we must go to a lonely place to get money for our trial. It is nearly two miles straight back where the Goodyear Marsh turns into a deep bog lake."

"Ok. I know the place." Adolf said. "It's way the hell back in the boondocks. Nobody would look there because nobody would ever want to fight their way through the swamp, snakes, and bugs. We're lucky it's so cold now! Then what?"

"When we get to the spot and I am talking to Jack, you slowly get around behind him. After I give him this knife, you hit him in the head with a hammer. That's what!"

"Hmmm. Well sure. I can do that, *Vater*. Not sure why you want him to be armed, but what do we need the tin can and tablecloth for?"

"The tablecloth holds the blood until we wash it off in the water, Adolf. Then we burn it."

It was a strange sensation to hear his gruff, at times violent father start using his first name in a respectful manner, Adolf thought. "And why the tin can?" he asked.

"That is for religious purposes—to hold his heart. I will show you when we make the visit to Monroe tonight, climb the Externstein and release Jack and Karl to Odin's Valhalla at our Nazi shrine there. We call our shrine the Irminsul, my son. It is a place where blood sacrifices are made to Odin, our god."

Externstein? Irminsul? Adolf's mind was a whirl-a-gig ride at a county fair. But he swiftly decided it was best not to ask too many questions. Herman von Himmel did not suffer fools lightly, and among his various fanatic traits, Teutonic religious beliefs topped the chart.

"Now get going!" and Adolf did not linger to ponder any more of the tasks. It was the shed first, the garbage second, and the kitchen table third.

Chapter 33

AT FIVE MINUTES past nine Herman and Adolf von Himmel were gob-struck in amazement when a dark green Pontiac sedan pulled into their driveway with two men in sunglasses and grey, three-piece pin stripe suits sitting in the front seats and Jack in the back seat smiling out the open car window.

"Your bag of tools out of sight?" von Himmel hissed at his son.

"Uh-huh!" was all that Adolf could manage. How on earth did these two men get Jack away from the safe house without a struggle? Were they the cops?

"Hello, Mr. von Himmel!" the first grey suit and sunglasses said to him as he exited the car. "I am Lester Reig, State Patrol, and this is Detective Harold Gier." Reig explained pointing to his darker complexioned, shorter companion. Reig flashed a wallet with a badge and credential. He put out his hand for a friendly handshake and continued, "We are here to carefully deliver Jack back to your custody from the safe house in Wisconsin Rapids."

Then without a pause, he went on— "I explained to Jack and to the old couple who took him in that all the charges were dropped against your family, and it was time to return home." He gave the old man a conspiratorial wink. "I told them we could not reveal his next destination."

Then to make sure von Himmel understood, Reig explained, "Just so you understand, we left Rapids about an hour ago, so you would have time to properly welcome your grandson." Then rotating toward the boy, he said with an engaging chuckle, "After all, Jack, it wouldn't be the end of the world for you to skip school just for today, right?"

Jack chuckled too. He had been completely surprised by the officers' arrival, just as his caretakers were. But the men were so pleasant, and when they pulled out impressive badges and paperwork, everyone relaxed. It looked to the boy that despite telling his story to the Hamot PD, his father, uncles, and grandfather were off the hook and life could go back to normal.

The man who was introduced as Harold Gier nodded to Adolf to come over around behind the sedan so they could have a private talk. Adolf got the hint, and so did Jack's grandfather. Old man von Himmel assumed a happy tone of voice and said,

"*Ja*, our little Jack played quite a trick on us with the local cops, but we got all that straightened out with them. No more problem. Right?" And with that, von Himmel walked to the front passenger door and pulled out a small bag which he assumed contained a few items which Jack was given during his stay.

Returning to the grey suit named Reig and his grandson, the old man tapped Jack on his shoulder and smiling his best smile said, "Now you little trickster, come inside and I cook you some bacon and eggs."

Jack was all too happy to accommodate the man he thought would be raging with anger. He turned and said thanks to Reig and Gier, touched both lucky charms around his neck, then bounced up the steps and entered the mobile home.

Lester Reig turned away from the home to shield his appearance and removed his sunglasses. "I know," he said to von Himmel. "You expected us to bring the boy home all tied up. But busting in that home presented way too many risks. We didn't think you'd mind getting the boy the easy way—no police alarms going out for another couple days, plenty of time to do what is needed with the boy and cover your tracks."

Von Himmel was nearly speechless. He could not conceive of such a low-risk strategy.

"Come to our shed for a minute," the old man said. "Just stay outside while I dig out your pay. Almost all of my treasure is gone for bail money. But what's left, I weigh it in front of you. Gold is $135 an ounce right now, so that tells me you each get 185 ounces."

Mr. Reig, and after a few seconds, Mr. Gier followed von Himmel toward the shed. Minutes later the two men returned to the driveway carrying two bags of coins, ingots, and wide grins. In another minute, they were back in the sedan, driving into oblivion. No real identities, just sun-glassed officials in grey suits with papers that looked legal enough to pass the inspection of a gullible kid and two trusting senior citizens.

"So quick change of plans, *Vater,*" Adolf told his father.

"What we do, son?" and the question itself came as joy to Adolf, joy to realize he was now stepping into a newly delegated leadership role.

"You cook Jack breakfast," said Adolf. "Be happy. After the meal, tell him about some help you need to dig up money you have hidden back in the Goodyear Swamp. Tell him it's to pay lawyer fees. I take my bag. We walk to the bog lake and execute him just as you said."

"Zum Donnerwetter!" cackled the old Nazi. "I can't think smart no more like you. You gotta do

that for us now, Adolf! I like your plan. I go now and start cooking for Jack."

"And, Dad—make sure you don't mention anything about Karl's disappearance or funeral."

Adolf watched his father hike up the stairs as best as his arthritic legs could manage. The sight made the young man shake his head in tepid disgust. After the door closed, he said, "So you're happy we're about to murder your only grandson, you bastard!"

"You would sell me out in a New York minute too if necessary! Well, fine! But if I can ever figure out where the rest of your father's treasure chest is hidden, old man, you better frickin' look out! If it was me, I would have killed those two phony cops just to play it safe."

Adolf shot a wad of spit and phlegm out between his two front teeth, and for luck, rubbed the engraved names of two ravens on a chain around his neck, Hugin and Munin. Not that he really listened much when old Herman would get lathered up about the mythology of the long ships and their raiders. He dismissed the memory, walked over behind the trailer to pick up his tool bag and came back to the front steps. After a minute's thought, he decided some bacon and eggs would taste pretty good.

Chapter 34

IF N.B. FORRESTER had a seat at the von Himmel breakfast table, he likely would have made some sarcastic pun about Jack "wolfing" down his food. But the lawyer wasn't at the table. Herman, the old Nazi sat there instead, and he was determined to use this opportunity to do some religious education.

The idea somehow made von Himmel feel more comfortable about what he planned...Odin be praised! Yes, he knew his grandson Jack had to die. Yes, he and Adolf had to kill him. But the code of Norse warriors and their supernatural beings could not just be mechanical routine. It was essential that his son and grandson had an understanding, even if incomplete, of a centuries old belief and ritual system if the offering of his grandson was to be accepted.

It was not enough, he knew, to offer blood sacrifice to Odin, King of all gods, Fierce and Terrible in Thought and Memory. Hugin and Munin—ravens who represented both mental qualities—had to accept it. Acceptance was possible only when the necessary rites were observed for captive and captor. Without the proper ceremony and prayer, Jack would never enter Valhalla, the sacrifice would be for nothing, and Odin himself would be put at risk if he lost his intelligence and memories all because of a clumsy warrior servant on earth.

"And how are the bacon and eggs, Grandson?"

"Oh, they are delicious, *Opa*! They are so good they must have been made in heaven!"

"Ha!" roared his grandfather, and the old man brought his massive hands together with a thunderclap of power.

"Do you know what your von Himmel name actually means, Jack?"

"No, *Opa,* I don't. Tell me, please."

"Von Himmel in German means 'in Heaven.' You should be proud to know that!"

"Oh, I am. I am!"

Then squaring around to include Adolf in the conversation, von Himmel continued, "And do either of you know where our Heaven is, and what it is like when you go there?"

"I know you call it Valhalla," shrugged Adolf as he strolled into the kitchen.

"And what else do you know about it, Mister Adolf Know-It-All?"

Adolf ignored the hint. "Oh, it is a beautiful place, Father. Lots of sunshine and fluffy Grey Foxs." Then he looked at Jack with a furtive grin and added— "And plenty of pretty girls too!"

Jack was about to laugh, but his senses read the darkening furrows around his grandfather's face. This was no laughing matter to Herman von Himmel.

"Silence, *Arschgeige*! Valhalla is not what you say. Valhalla is a death house that honors all Norse warriors like your brother Karl who died in battle with a weapon in his hand. It is a hallowed hall in Asgard where Lord of all gods, Odin, rules. It is a home for our noble dead who left the earth, blade in hand, fighting to the last." And after a second to gather himself, von Himmel reached under his collar, pulled out a gold necklace with a wide, thick thunderbolt at its base, and whispered, "Odin be praised."

Jack shivered. From some far away corner of the sky, came a strange, pounding rumble.

"For heaven's sakes, Herman," Adolf said dismissively, "you almost got me believing that sonic boom from an army jet over Fort McCoy was Odin himself shaking his hammer or shooting lightning bolts out of his ass!"

Herman von Himmel said nothing. In a cat-quick lunge, he had Adolf by the throat. "Now what's so funny, you *Rotzlöffel* brat!" and with his one hand he simply held his adult son high enough off the trailer's grimy brown carpet that Adolf couldn't breathe or move.

Suspended and his airway locked in a crushing grip, Adolf only managed to bubble spit.

"You will not waste my time, *bananenbieger* clod!" and with that, the old Nazi threw his son down to the floor. Adolf rolled about, gagging, and slobbering for several minutes. Jack sat perfectly still.

"Now both of you will see something no one here has ever seen before!" announced the grandfather. "Look at me now!" he commanded, and with a single sweep of his right hand, Herman von Himmel removed his left eyeball. "Like Odin himself, I am blind in this one!" he shouted and held up the glass orb for his audience to admire.

For more than an hour after von Himmel's ghastly revelation the only sounds around the trailer were the bruising gusts of autumn wind promising a frosty death from due north. The early Wisconsin fall rushed fast and full of itself this cold day, the purple cone and red bee balm flowers bent under its weight, bruising the sandy patches around the property like scattered, scarlet remains from a Teutonic struggle. Patchy grey clouds with ominous black bottoms swept across the skyline.

Herman von Himmel roused himself from deep meditation and began explaining the details of the pilgrimage he expected Adolf and Jack to make. "*Ja*, Jack, we got to go into the Goodyear and dig up my money bag to pay the lawyer," he said. "And I don't got no intention of going off into the swamp or carrying around a big bag of loot without you two along to keep me and our money safe!"

"Safe!" it was the one word that always registered badly with Jack when he heard it mentioned. Somehow the word "safe" seemed to be a dangerous contradiction coming as it did now from a fanatical Nazi popping out one of his own eyeballs to certify his claim to be God-like.

Chapter 35

"HE'LL BE PLENTY safe with my folks up in Rapids," Flaherty assured Patrolman John Stone.

"How's that, Chief?" the patrolman asked with noticeable concern. "Aren't your folks both in the eighties?" Stone was a young cop built like a sumo wrestler and had a similar straight-ahead approach to finding answers.

"Not a concern, buddy." Flaherty was really enjoying his new status as police chief. "They are both sharp as tacks."

"Uh—yes, but they are eighty-year-old tacks. Right?" Clearly, something about this was not sitting well with Stone. The patrolman noticed the scowl which came over his new commanding officer's face, but his inquiring mind continued to probe the situation.

"Tell me, Chief, who is guarding the couple and the boy? Must be a pretty good cop from the Rapids force? It's a job with some danger to it, and I didn't see you send any of us up there to do the job."

Flaherty's throat tightened, bulging his neck veins out enough for Stone to notice. "Like I said, Patrolman, not an area of your concern."

The remark, the way it was delivered, and the obvious discomfort Flaherty displayed over the question only served to pique Stone's curiosity and basic cop instincts.

"Well, sure it is a concern, Chief. Dewey Lassiter made it clear the kid's protection is a concern. Our concern. I am just asking—who is guarding that teenage kid and your elderly parents?"

Flaherty sense of entitlement overcame his good sense. "Just shut it, Stone! It's none of your frickin' business how I protect them, OK? The chief didn't think it was anybody's business that he was claiming the extra pay for protecting the witness. Hey, his folks lived only a couple blocks from the Rapids PD office. That snot-nosed, punk high school kid would be just fine with his mom and dad, and nobody had to know or object to how the money was handled."

"As long as you **are** providing protection, Chief," and with a poignant hard stare at his commander, Patrolman Stone ambled toward the office door.

It all might have ended there, but Flaherty's fragile ego meant he was a man who had to have the last word. "Get the hell out of my office," he snarled, "and don't let the door hit you in the ass!" The taunt made Chief Flaherty's entire day by providing salve to the wound he had taken when Chief Lassiter ripped into him about not going on the arrest team.

That salve, however, did nothing for John Stone. In fact, predictably it had the opposite effect. People who choose careers in law enforcement do so for a universe of reasons. Some like the idea of helping and protecting their community; some have a natural urge to bring order out of chaos, and a few here and there just like the power they feel from a badge and a gun.

Almost all of them are individuals who are born with a hair trigger bullshit detector. Once the detector goes off, the alarm just gets louder with every evasive answer. And in the case of John Stone, there were full blown, five alarm sirens now shrieking in his mind.

"Hello, is this Wisconsin Rapids PD?"

"Yes. I am Officer Tellen. What is the nature of your call, sir?"

Adjusting his considerable weight on the small chair the phone room provided, the Hamot patrolman explained, "I am Officer John Stone of the Hamot Police Department. Our new chief Mike Flaherty placed a teenage boy in protective custody with you. I am just making a wellness call to check on him."

"You say you are Patrolman Stone of the Hamot PD?"

"Yes. I am. My badge number is 235698. The phone I am using is 608-372-1296. And I really do want to know about the protection for the boy. Our chief said he placed the boy—Jack von Himmel— with Flaherty's own parents who run the safe house in your city. Will you please check on his welfare?"

"Well, just a minute, sir. I have to confirm that you are who you say you are."

"Fine. But when you get finished checking on me, you better start checking on the boy." Stone was building up some steam himself now, but another voice on the phone interrupted his thoughts.

"Hello. This is Chief of Police Ted Gibczjek. I am looking at a list of officers in Hamot, and I am seeing your name. What kind of hat did Chief Lassiter wear?"

"He covered his balding head with a worn-out old Stetson. He grew up in Amarillo, Texas, and it's time to stop playing games about who I am. What's the status of Jack von Himmel in your safe house?"

"All right, Patrolman. I believe who you say you are. And at this moment, I am worried to death because we have no knowledge of anyone in protective custody here. Why don't you let me talk to your new chief, Mike Flaherty?"

"Oh, you'll get a chance to talk to him once he is handcuffs! The boy tipped us off that his father, two uncles and grandfather blew up a cranberry marsh. When we went out to arrest the adults, one of them shot and killed Dewey Lassiter. Flaherty has been telling us he placed the kid in Rapids with his parents and under your protection. Now you are saying that can't be true. You are telling me that no one is protecting two elderly folks who are hiding a witness to a major crime."

"My God!" Gibcziek shouted into the receiver, "what kind of cop, what kind of Chief of Police would be doing something like this?"

"An incompetent, maybe even criminal one, sir! With your permission, I'll place Flaherty under arrest and try to get to the bottom of this fast. That kid is at very serious risk!"

"Uh—no, you better not arrest him, Officer. There is a state patrol office at the intersection of I-90 and I-94 just outside of your town. I am sending them to you immediately. Not that I don't believe you couldn't do the job, but Flaherty would challenge your authority."

He paused to just long enough to catch his breath. "The state boys are levels above your chief, and they'll be there in ten minutes. I'll shoot over to the Flaherty house, then let you know what's going on."

"Good. I'll wait for them to make the arrest. It's past time somebody sent in the cavalry!"

Chapter 36

FROM BEHIND THE low angle of the front desk, Chief Flaherty saw a wide-brimmed navy-blue cavalry hat with a badge approaching. "You are Chief of Police Michael Flaherty?" the hat asked.

"Yup, I'm the new chief. What brings the State Patrol's fancy hat to my PD?" Flaherty relaxed back in his office chair and just for the fun of it slung his feet up across his desk. "Hey-why not?" he thought: "Rank does have its privileges."

"I am Commander Frederick Post. Take your feet off the desk. Stand up and turn around. I am placing you under arrest for fraud in the case of false protection for Jack von Himmel!"

Flaherty froze. He couldn't believe what he was hearing. What was happening to him? Things became instantly clearer when Commander Post slapped Flaherty's feet off the desk, yanked him to his feet, spun him around and slapped handcuffs on around his wrists.

"Wha—What? What the hell is going on?" Flaherty stammered.

A maelstrom of uniforms and strange faces instantly surrounded the chief. Then a familiar face emerged to confront him. "They are doing their job, Flaherty! Which is one thing you weren't doing, you liar!" Patrolman John Stone's fierce dark-grey eyes burrowed into the suddenly unemployed chief of police. "Now where is Jack von Himmel?"

Flaherty's expression transitioned from disbelief to complete fear. Without thinking, he snapped back— "I'm not saying nothing to any of you. Get me a lawyer!"

"Oh, you will tell us everything, Flaherty, and you will do it just as soon as we put you in the interrogation room," explained Post in a flat, matter-of-fact way. "And you'll do it to save your sorry butt. Should any harm come to the boy who you were supposed to protect, and you will be facing federal charges. I have already contacted the FBI. They are on their way here as I speak. Abetting a kidnapping, maybe complicity in a bombing. You are now a popular guy!"

"But—" protested Flaherty. "I've got my rights!"

"Yes, you have," agreed Post. Then stepping into Flaherty, the State Patrol Commander whispered inches from his face— "You will have the right to twenty years to life in federal prison. And, knowing what you've done, I wouldn't be surprised if someone in the Department of Corrections accidentally lets it slip out to your jail buddies that you were a cop!"

Flaherty's entire body shook at the impact of Post's words.

"Right, Flaherty. At the very least you have the right to quickly acquire an industrial strength immune system for your new permanent home," Post said.

"Bet you'll have all kinds of friends, Chief." Stone couldn't resist the opportunity to get in one last zinger. "All of them up your ass."

Post let the effect of the patrolman's words reverberate in Flaherty's mind, then turned to the three other state patrolmen he brought along and said, "Put him in jail, gentlemen." Then he turned to Stone. "Right now, Officer, you are the new acting Chief. Give my men a key to a cell, then phone the only criminal law attorney Hamot has and get him down here pronto. I want to interrogate that pathetic excuse for a cop asap!"

Chapter 37

"**OPA, WE'VE BEEN** hiking through this swamp for more than an hour, and my feet are wet and cold—and I am getting tired too!" Jack wasn't sure his complaint would do much, but he decided it would feel good just to say something about what was becoming an ordeal. "How much farther do we have to go?"

Herman von Himmel gave no indication he either heard or cared about his grandson's complaint. The elderly, hard-bitten Nazi just lowered his head a bit more, hunched forward and continued on ahead snapping branches out of the way as he proceeded. Jack found no comfort in the fact they were headed southeast away from the trailer but somewhat parallel to the Koleski Marsh.

From behind the boy, Jack heard his uncle say, "Don't bother your grandpa, kid. He's got a lot on his mind, and I don't want him to get mad at you, ok?" Adolf actually meant every part of what he said. He knew that his father was capable of irrational fits of temper, and this was not the place or the time for one of them. Not here anyway, although the time would come soon enough.

"Ok, Uncle Adolf," conceded Jack. "It's just that this trip is so boring. All we do is stomp through the cattails, climb up banks with sharp prickly brush and wade through mushy spots that look like dry land until you step on them."

"Yup, but it won't get done any faster by complaining about it," said Adolf. "Now try to walk a little faster so you don't get too far back. Your grandpa needs to get the little bit of money he has left that's buried out here so we can pay the lawyer."

But Jack's attention was directed elsewhere. As they climbed up onto a short stretch of higher ground, the teenager bounced off the deer path they were following and headed off in a diagonal to his right.

"Look, Uncle Adolf! It's a crab apple tree." Jack glanced back over his shoulder at his uncle and hearing a rush of wings turned back toward the tree. To his surprise and glee, a large flock of soft brown and grey, medium-sized birds all sprung from the among branches supporting clusters of two-inch apples, the pale yellow and sparkling red fruit painting the subdued, ash brown of the marsh with unexpected, vibrant hues.

"Yikes!" the boy shouted as he was instantly immersed in a frenzy of flapping wings and alarm calls. As the birds spiraled up into the sky, Jack returned his gaze to his uncle. "What kind of birds are those? They blended into the tree so much I couldn't really see them until I was almost on top of them, Uncle."

"Cedar Waxwings, kid," Adolf grumped. "Now please come back to the trail."

"Sure thing! But I just have to get a couple of apples first." And typical of kids given orders they instantly disobey, Jack sprang toward the tree first, grabbed two small fruit from gnarled, twisted branches and then hopped back to the trail.

"Here you go, Uncle!" and the teenager playfully tossed one of the apples to Adolf. He was about to resume the march when something far behind his uncle seemed to be moving in the cattails. Jack watched for a few seconds. He thought he caught a glimpse of two ponderous, grey shapes coming nearer. Did swamp deer look grey in September? It couldn't possibly be people following from behind?

Then more disturbed birds from a distant location rose in a flutter, and their flight satisfied his curiosity. He turned and hopscotched his way forward over patches of dry ground and small holes of muck and bog water to close the distance to his grandfather.

Over his shoulder again, Jack called backwards—"Those chubby waxwings must be good thieves, Uncle Adolf! They had black bank robber masks across their eyes and the back of their heads. They were there to steal the apple tree's treasure."

Adolf nodded assent but said nothing. He followed his father's example and just bent forward and resumed the slog through the Goodyear's mud, spindly jack pine and scrub oak. "And in another hour or so, kid, I am going to steal your sorry life away, and you're not even going to see it coming." That idea and the reassurance he felt from reaching down into his big bag to feel the hefty shank of the hammer's handle carved a tight, cruel smile across his face.

"Jack fall down, go boom!" he thought and the brief chuckle the phrase brought to his lips stiffened his resolve to get this pathetic mess over with as soon as possible.

Chapter 38

"**I am Commander** Frederick Post of the Wisconsin State Patrol. I am in the Hamot Police Department interrogation room with former Police Chief Michael Flaherty and his attorney, Mr. Robbie Maberit. We are recording this interview."

"Has my client been read his rights and agreed he understands them?" the attorney asked immediately.

Flaherty was fortunate to have a man like Maberit there to ask to represent him, Post decided. The lawyer had a solid trial record around the state and a strong reputation despite the fact he was a small-town attorney.

"Yaa, all that shit has been taken care of," said Flaherty, his dismissive tone of voice ignoring the fact he was putting off his own lawyer. "They read me my rights, and I damn sure told them I understood them. And in case you haven't figured it out yet, that's why you're here, Maberit!"

"Enough of that, Flaherty!" snapped Post. "Now let's get down to business, shall we? What did you do with Jack von Himmel who you said to fellow officers here you sent to Wisconsin Rapids for protective custody?"

"Hey, they weren't my fellow officers! Get it right," snarled Flaherty. "I am the Chief here, not them, and I explained to my subordinates my plan was to take care of that mealy-mouthed kid who knew about his family blowing up the cranberry marsh."

"You **were** the chief here, Flaherty," Post retorted. "Now you're just a criminal facing a long list of potential felonies."

"Exactly what felonies will my client be charged with, Commander?" Maberit asked.

"That all depends on what he says to me in this interview," Post responded. Then moving himself a bit closer to Flaherty, the commander said," Now I'm not in the habit of asking twice—what did you do with the boy who you said you were sending to Rapids?"

"I took him there myself. That a crime?" sneered Flaherty.

Before Post could reply, Maberit leaned into his client and spoke in a flat tone of voice— "Drop the sarcasm. Drop it now. It won't get you any favors when it comes to sentence recommendations!"

Flaherty shrugged off the advice initially, but after pausing to reconsider, he seemed to sag lower in his chair. "Ok. I get it. But what I want understood is that I didn't intend any harm to come to that kid. I figured I could drive him up to stay with my folks. The pay for the overtime money could go to me as well as anybody else. And given the fact that I was the new chief . . . I should get to decide things like that." As he paused in mid-sentence, Flaherty began to massage his dagger tattoo with nervous intensity.

"I was just looking to make a little extra dough. The kid should have been fine. My mom and dad—"

"Are in their eighties! And in no condition to understand what you were doing to the boy and to them, much less protect themselves or Jack von Himmel." Post was shaking with rage as he faced down his suspect. "I know they were both uninformed and incapable, Flaherty, because the Rapids police chief talked to them and then to me just before I raced over here to interrogate you! They had no idea what you were doing with them and the boy!"

"Commander, what's in it for my client if he answers your questions and cooperates in the investigation?" Post stopped for a moment to get a read on the attorney. He saw a taller, athletic man with a square jaw, a short crew cut for his light blonde hair, eyes somewhere between dark brown and black, and a demeanor that spoke of integrity.

"Well, Mr. Maberit," explained Commander Post. "Let me put it this way. If the boy is killed because of your client's greed and incompetence, there is a life sentence without parole in it for him. Wisconsin has no death penalty, but maybe the feds do for this."

Post continued, "There has been a bombing of a cranberry marsh, a fatal shootout at the von Himmel trailer, the illegal hiding of an adolescent witness by an officer of the law who has stated he did it for the money and the resulting kidnapping of the witness who now may already be dead."

Post swiveled in his seat to confront Flaherty with startling ferocity. "Now no more damn games! Did you have anything to do with aiding the two men who took Jack away from your parents' home?"

Flaherty sagged even lower in his chair. He dug the fingertips of his opposite hand into the blue ink on his forearm. "No," he answered lamely. "I wish to God I knew what happened, how those two guys figured out where I stashed the kid and where they took him...but I don't know. And that's the God's honest truth. How anybody in Wisconsin Rapids would know and recognize Jack von Himmel seems impossible. And how someone arranged for his abduction is just plain crazy."

"Crazy like a fox," Post concluded. "For now, I am charging you with gross negligence of duty and felony fraud." He looked to the door to the interview room. "Come in, Chief Stone. Escort our ex-Chief of Police to his royal cell."

Chapter 39

FINALLY, AFTER AN exhausting series of sinkholes and briar patches, Jack sensed the von Himmel buried fortune was close at hand. Beyond the figure of his grandfather and the descending landscape spilling from hard ground down to soggy marsh, the boy could see snatches of a good-sized lake peeking out between tag alders and pine boughs. The surface of the bog water looked midnight black against the pastels of the pink, lime, and ochre leaves from oaks, maples and birch trees encircling the lakeshore. The pungent musk of stagnant water and dying vegetation whirled up from the dank grasses at the shoreline's edge like a third flock of startled birds.

Along the north margin of the wilderness lake, the wolf crouched low in the marsh grass and willows, observing this strange three-human parade that seemed

to purposelessly toil its way into his lair. They carried various items, but the mountain wolf could discern no weapons. The hair on the back of his neck bristled as he identified the grey hair who led the expedition and an another, younger adult who was likely a son.

Then the wolf's curiosity piqued when he saw the last human in line. It was the boy who had fed his pack when they came by for a visit. There was something different about this young one that reached out and spoke to the wolf. Could there be something like respect or under-standing between man and beast? Or at least toleration? The pack leader shifted his weight to lower himself among the reeds. He would study this procession into the wilder-ness. He would practice watchful waiting.

Then he sensed a second procession following the same parade route.

His grandfather motioned for Jack to stand a few paces apart from him. It seemed to the boy that he was about to receive another historical narrative about the Vikings and their religion before they dug up the money for the lawyer.

"Now, Jack, I want you to stand in front of me here by me along the shore. I am going to tell you more about Odin and Valhalla," his grandfather said, and he pointed to a spot just in front of a line of tightly packed white pines.

As Jack moved to stand where he was supposed to, Herman von Himmel motioned to Adolf. "And you can take the tools out of the bag that we need to get started. I want you to start digging right there," and the old man indicated a lumpy patch of dry ground behind Jack and slightly to the boy's right.

Adolf did as he was directed. but his movements seemed strangely deliberate to Jack, and somehow the timbre and pitch of his grandfather's voice made the boy feel uncomfortable. It was like he was being placed on a stage of some kind but for no apparent reason.

"Now my grandson, I want you to take this and open it." Old man von Himmel reached down into a pants' pocket and removed a long folding knife. As he handed it to the boy, Jack saw a weird intensity in his grandfather's face that forced him to step back away from the weapon.

"Come now! Take this when I tell you and open it up!"

Reluctantly, Jack accepted the buck knife. It was unexpectedly heavy, awkward in his hand, and why he needed it made absolutely no sense.

"Why are you giving me this, *Opa*?" the boy asked.

Continuing in that strange tone, von Himmel answered, "To teach you about Valhalla. To teach you and your uncle about our warrior religion." And at the mention of his uncle, Jack turned briefly back toward where his uncle Adolf was to begin digging, but the man had moved directly behind the boy and instead of a shovel, he was holding a hammer.

"Now look at me when I talk to you!" von Himmel commanded, and Jack slowly turned back to see what would come next.

"Open up that knife, Jack. Pull the blade out of the handle."

A terrible chill caressed Jack's backbone. Something very wrong was going down he sensed, but he couldn't imagine what on earth it was about. Reluctantly, the boy opened the blade.

"Good boy!" said his grandfather, but there was violence Jack sensed in him as he said it.

"What are you doing, *Opa*? I don't want this knife. It makes me feel afraid!"

"Fear is a wonderful thing. It is something that every warrior has in his heart but overcomes when it his time to go to Asgard and be with Odin!" And with that explanation, Herman von Himmel reached down inside his shirt and pulled out his necklace with its thunderbolt, wide and gleaming.

"Now—attack me! Attack me!" von Himmel thundered, and he pulled out a Browning .45 pistol from his waistband and aimed at Jack.

"Nobody is attacking anyone except us!" A fourth voice entered the dialogue, and two men in sunglasses and wet, mud-covered grey suits, emerged from the stand of white pines behind the three von Himmels. They both held AR 15's. The one with the darker complexion turned to his right to cover Adolf, the taller one doing the speaking raised his rifle toward Jack's grandfather. Jack recognized him as Lester Reig of the State Patrol.

"I don't know what the hell you were about to do with this kid," said the man taking charge, "but you're going to dig up all the money you must be hiding here, and you're going to donate it all to us— if you expect to live." Then pointing the army rifle directly at von Himmel's chest, the man said, "Now drop that Luger if you know what's good for you."

"Ha!" von Himmel spit back contemptuously and only lowered the pistol to his side. "You *dummkopfs* kill me and you kill the only one who knows where all the rest of the money is buried." The old man spit again and said, "So twenty-five thousand wasn't enough for each of you to be satisfied with for sneaking my grandson out of Wisconsin Rapids as phony cops? You had to come back and follow us out into this swamp to satisfy your greed, didn't you!" The old man's words pulled both gunmen closer.

His grandfather's words made Jack gasp. He realized in an instant his grandfather had these bogus cops kidnap him and return him to the trailer. Jack was to be killed by his own family to cover up what he knew and saw. That's why he was given a knife and told to attack—it was necessary for him to die with a blade in his hand to enter Valhalla! All of this was insane!

But Jack wasn't going anywhere without a fight! With a cat-like swipe, Jack turned and drove his knife back and up into the crotch of the man covering his grandfather. Then keeping his momentum, the boy completed his spin by lunging in a desperate dive for the lake.

In milliseconds, the stabbed man reflexively pulled the trigger on his gun, the single bullet striking von Himmel center mass. Adolf swiveled and drove his hammer into the temple of the other gunman before he could turn enough to bring his weapon to bear. A burst of semi-automatic fire spewed straight into the clouds from the rifle, but ended almost as soon as it started when Adolf descended on the man with a flurry of hammer strikes to his head.

The screams and moans of the other man, bent in half at the waist, tore Adolf away from his first target. In two quick steps, he leapt upon the gunman who knelt on the ground, bent in half from the six-inch blade shaft planted in his gut. A torrent of hammer blows crushed any flicker of life remaining in what had been Lester Reig.

When he had poured out all his rage into demolishing the two adversaries, Adolf swung his attention to the crumpled form of his father. To the young man's surprise, Herman von Himmel was moaning, but there was no blood visible anywhere on his body.

The old man suddenly sat upright. "Why am I not dead?" he demanded of Adolf.

His son was as taken aback by the question as much as he was by the fact his father had been shot in the chest but was now sitting up and talking.

"My god, I don't know. Are you sure you're not hit anywhere?"

Herman von Himmel gingerly felt his chest. His right index finger found the answer. Grasping his gold necklace by the base, he held it up to Adolf. "See here, son. See the big dent in the center of Odin's golden thunderbolt. That is what stopped the bullet. I am alive because of his protection." He paused, looked to the sky with rapturous gaze and murmured, "Odin, be praised!"

Both men were temporarily without words or thought from the discovery, but the mental paralysis didn't last long.

"Now, Adolf, take one of those rifles and chase down Jack!" commanded old von Himmel. "Kill him quick before he gets to the cops. I'll stay here with your tools and cut up the bodies into tiny pieces for the fish to eat."

Adolf grabbed a rifle, wiped blood spatter from his face and arms, struggled up the incline of the bank and rushed back along the edge of the bog lake.

The mountain wolf took note of the violence but took no action to get involved. Humans killing other humans with guns. And with no intention of eating what they killed! Such purposeless slaughter offended the wolf's sense of natural behavior. He decided to remain hidden. It was the safest option, of course. Perhaps there would be carcasses available in time?

Chapter 40

JACK FIGURED HE had a decent head start. None of the gunshots he heard hit water were aimed at him. And when his breath ran out and he surfaced, there were no shots coming his way from the shore. While briefly safe, the boy knew at least Uncle Adolf would be racing after him. Jack realized that he could move faster back to the trailer if he continued swimming on top as long as possible. His lanky body allowed him to take deep strokes, surging ever forward with a swimmer's crawl to make his escape. The adrenaline and the cold bog water pumped massive bursts of energy into the boy, carrying him quickly to the end of the lake pointing back to his home.

Then, as if struck by one of Odin's thunderbolts himself, when Jack reached the end of the lake, he lifted himself up onto the bank and decided he would change direction. Instead of running right back to where he was expected to go, the boy realized he knew a better place to reach—one that held the hope of safety and perhaps, even love. If only he could find it before Adolf found him!

Chapter 41

JUST AS SHE finished repainting their mailbox to cover up its crude SS symbols, Sara Koleski saw the bedraggled figure of some person staggering up her driveway in zombie-like exhaustion. Her reaction was revulsion followed by fear. Who was this? Was this someone coming to attack her family and the marsh again? Would her parents working out in the drowned cranberry beds even hear her if she screamed? Then the alien figure gestured toward her and called out, "Sara! Help me please!" and she knew it was her Jack and that something terrible was going on.

"Jack, Jack!" she repeated as she rushed to him and cradled him as he collapsed in her arms. "What is happening to you?"

Jack coughed to clear his lungs and wiped his hair back from a forehead replete with scrapes and scratches from buckthorn bushes he had rushed through headfirst. "Sara," and he coughed again. "My uncles, my dad, my grandfather. They blew up your marsh. I told the police, and now my family is trying to kill me." He coughed again, his chest heaving in desperation to catch his breath. "They are right behind me. Where can I hide?"

"Oh, Jack!" Sara cried. Looking down at his torn clothing and bruises, she shuddered and began to weep. Sara raised her head to look into Jack's eyes, but something stopped her short. The ugly lash mark on the side of her boyfriend's neck, oozing blood now from the brush cuts he had received in his escape, pushed an unexpected idea into her mind.

"You can hide in my room just for a bit," the girl said with grim determination. "My folks are working out there," and she gestured toward the ruined cranberry beds. "If I tell them, my dad and his brothers will grab their guns and shoot it out with your family. If they do that, somebody likely will die, Jack, and I don't want any more harm to come to us."

Jack pushed himself up on one arm, shook off some of the swamp mud and water, and said, "You're right, Sara. And I think I threw them off my trail because when they tried to murder me out by Goodyear Lake, they saw me heading back to our trailer, not to here."

"Quick, Jack, let me help you up. After we get you inside the house where you will be safe at least for a while, I know who can protect you better than anyone else."

"Who's that, Sara?"

"You met him at the Hamot Police Department, I bet," she explained. "His name is Sheriff Josiah Grey Fox, and he gave me his phone number."

Chapter 42

"**WHAT IN ODIN'S** name are you doing back here, Adolf? von Himmel raged. "Did you find Jack and kill him like I said?" Adolf had returned to the site of the shootout with great apprehension, fearing the very reaction from his father he was now witnessing. His father still had a rifle.

"I had to come back, *Vater*. I couldn't find Jack, and there were no keys in their car. It must be disposed of fast!" As he said that, Adolf looked down at the wider scene of the gunfight. He had expected to see some blood on the ground, but nothing in heaven or earth could have prepared him for the butchery and gore that encased his father and the immediate area. He gagged at the shattered bone fragments, yellowing marrow, a thumb, and thick black blood congealing in the middle of the tablecloth.

"I thought the next best thing to do was to come back and help you dispose of all the evidence, get the car keys from a pants' pocket, and drive their car into a bog before anyone discovers it."

"But what happens to us when Jack tells the cops we killed these two?" raged von Himmel, using the clean part of the shirt from his upper arm to wipe away the sweat and ooze of butchering two men.

"He can claim any damn thing he wants to, Father," said Adolf slyly. "But if we get rid of all the evidence, he is just a foolish kid with an empty story. These dead guys never mentioned it was us who sent them to Rapids to get Jack, right? And you need bodies for proof!"

"By Odin and all of his might, Adolf, you are absolutely right! How am I so lucky to have a son who is so smart, that's what I want to know!" Then von Himmel lowered himself to rest on the back of his legs. "Take my Luger and roll up your sleeves. We got to finish cutting up the bodies, smash the bones into bits with the hammers, then wade out and dump the whole mess into the lake. Last, we got to clean ourselves off and burn the tablecloth."

Ade quickly added to the scheme. "I can throw all the tools into the lake farther up. We'll leave nothing for the cops to find on the shore here! No evidence," Adolf bragged, "—no crimes to charge us with." He laughed loudly, triumphantly, then pushed up his sleeves and knelt to help. He was surprised to find he took pleasure in the work.

Chapter 43

JACK'S APPROACH UP the Koleski driveway was inconspicuous and unnoticed as Sara's parents worked in knee deep mud to gather remaining fruit and straighten the worst of the tangled cranberry vines. It was work filled with sorrow and bent-over backs. Some of the vines in the original beds had been groomed straight for a hundred years. But when two police cars, red lights spinning but sirens silent, sped up the same drive heading for the house, all the Koleskis dropped their buckets and slogged toward their home.

Sara had wrapped Jack in a thick quilt and parked his dripping body in the family's kitchen, close to the waves of heat radiating from their large, cast-iron wood stove. Hearing cars speeding to the house, she quickly moved to the front door to intercept whoever was approaching. From the porch she immediately recognized the nearest person driving the car. It was the man she hoped would come when she made the phone call and talked to the operator. She also saw in the distance her family hurrying to the house as well, but it would be several minutes before her dad, mom and uncles would arrive.

"Sara, is Jack here?" Sheriff Grey Fox jumped from his squad. "Is he ok? What's going on?"

Sara motioned with both her hands pushing downward, trying to tamp down the flurry of inquiries. "Jack's here, Sheriff Jo. But I don't want my family to see him. If they do, I am afraid of what they might try to do to his family."

"Right," said Grey Fox, and he turned to his fellow officer. "Deputy Drinkwine, I want you to go into the house with this girl and quickly escort her boyfriend back to my vehicle. Cover him with a blanket and do not let anyone come near to see him." The deputy sprinted into the house with Sara and returned with Jack and a blanket, quickly deposited him in the back seat of the sheriff's squad car and motioned his two fellow officers to keep everyone away.

"Now what's up, Sara? I thought Jack was somewhere in protective custody. Suddenly he turns up here with you."

"His family blew up our marsh, and after he told on them, they found out where he was somehow and brought him back to their trailer. They marched him out in the swamp to murder him, Sheriff, but my Jack got away and came to me here. Now they are after him!"

Grey Fox expression turned Lannon stone grey. He solemnly pointed to the sky. "By the powers of Earthmaker, our god, Sara, I will protect Jack and you." Then glancing back down the driveway, Grey Fox shouted, "Deputy, have Jack lie down in the back seat and put the blanket over the top of him so he is not recognized!"

The back door of the squad car shut as the rest of the Koleskis reached the edge of what remained of their dike. They pulled themselves up through the brambles of the berm and rushed to the sheriff. It was Peter Koleski, Sara's father, who arrived first. "Hello, Josiah," he said pulling off his faded Packers cap out of respect for the policeman. "What's all the fuss about? I thought I saw someone leave my house bundled in a blanket."

"You saw right, Pete. But I want you and everyone else here to forget about what you just witnessed. I can tell you what is happening involves the bombing, and that's about it. Whatever you do, please do not ask your daughter any questions about this. It is vital that what she knows remains with only her and me in order to protect her and other innocent people."

Sara's mother, Rachel Koleski, rushed up to her and gasped, "Oh, my sweet girl, are you all right?"

"Yes, Mom. I am fine. But please don't ask me any other questions. Like Sheriff Grey Fox just said, I must remain silent about some things in order to protect other people."

"And speaking of protection," the sheriff intervened, "I am leaving one of my deputies here with a slug shotgun. Peter, you and your brothers break out your deer rifles and take up defensive positions around your home until I can get more police power here. Better do it right now."

Peter Koleski's face blanched white. Fear and uncertainty nearly overcame him, but he instantly composed himself. "All right," he called out to his two brothers who just entered the room," get your .308's, boys, and pick your positions. If anyone but a cop car drives in, cover me when I approach. Shoot if they shoot! Don't miss!"

Koleski's words bounced off the back of Joshiah Grey Fox's ears. He was pointing for Drinkwine to grab the pump twelve gauge and head for the house as he threw open the door to his squad.

"Jack, stay down in the back seat," he said and grabbing the Koleski's home phone, he started dialing. "Dispatch, this is Grey Fox calling."

"Yes, Chief. Go ahead" replied the young female officer at Ho-Chunk headquarters. She was the sheriff's niece and someone he counted on to get things right by messaging.

"This is top priority, Christine. Call the State Patrol Office by the Hamot intersection of I-90 and I-94. Tell them to break out their heavy weapons and to beat feet out to the Koleski Cranberry Marsh. There is a family to protect. No sirens to be used! Got it?"

"Copy, Sheriff. Will do!"

As he spun his vehicle back out of the driveway to head north for the reservation, a small voice from the rear passenger bench spoke up.

"Sheriff, could I please tell you something?"

"Sure, Jack, sorry to be in a rush, but I've got to get you to a safe place."

"I don't mean to be disrespectful, sir," replied the boy, "but there is something more important you have to do than take me to your office."

"What on earth can that be?" snapped the sheriff. Then remembering the teenager in his rear seat was uncommonly mature, he softened his voice and said, "Sorry to crab at you, Jack. Just feeling some pressure is all. Now what do you think needs doing first?"

"We've got to stop at my house, first," Jack said. "There is you, and your two deputies are in the other car behind us. My grandpa and my uncle Adolf will come out of the woods looking for me back at our trailer. The quickest way to keep me safe is to surround them, take their weapons and arrest them right now. You have three men to their two, and you know where they'll be. Get them before they escape and start hunting me down."

Grey Fox stopped the car. He realized in the next moment what he did about Jack could mean the difference between life and death for the boy, his deputies, the von Himmels, and finally, for himself. Reaching his decision, he looked back to the squad following him, raised his right hand to make the outline of a pistol, watched to see an acknowledging nod and handed his pistol to Jack.

"In the worst case should you have to protect yourself, Jack. Use this .357," and he handed the weapon back to the boy. "It's single action, meaning you have to cock the hammer each time you want to shoot. Aim low because it kicks like one of Dewey Lassiter's Texas mules. I'll use my shotgun next to me up here."

The sheriff gave Jack a quick, hard glance to appraise the effect of what he just said. The boy simply swallowed hard, took the gun in both hands, and stared straight ahead.

"That is some kind of young man," thought Grey Fox. "If we live through this, I will ask our War Chief, Gully Hanging Moon, to initiate him into our warrior clan." Then with the knowledge the von Himmel place was less than two miles up the road, the sheriff mashed the gas pedal of his squad car tight to the floor.

Chapter 44

JOSIAH GREY FOX thought hard about calling some of the State Patrol to back him and his deputies up at the von Himmel place. Then he decided against it. Only *Ma'una*, the Earthmaker, in his infinite wisdom, knew what would be waiting at the trailer. Should he and his men get there ahead of the von Himmels, the last thing he wanted was for a late arriving patrol car to roll in and its siren alert the suspects. Grey Fox decided he needed to make an offering of tobacco to the Maker after the ambush was over. The Maker would be expecting it.

Stopping his squad down the road and out of sight of the von Himmel driveway, the sheriff spoke firmly but with encouragement to his passenger. "Don't be afraid, Jack. You are a warrior now. Just stay low, keep ready, and don't come out unless you see a policeman in uniform talking. Right?"

"Yes, sir. I will," the boy said in the steadiest voice he could muster and slid down in his seat.

"Lock and load, men," said Grey Fox to his two deputies. "We'll keep low, move to cover around the house and wait," he said with a bit of smile, "wait until you see the whites of their eyes. There are two of them. They're likely armed. If they move a gun even slightly toward you, fire first! That's a command. This family has already murdered one police officer who ordered them to stop. Their guns come up, shoot first and ask questions later."

Like their Great Lakes' Forest ancestors four hundred years before, the three Ho-Chunk tribal policemen moved as one with the silence and deadly grace of a lynx stalking a whitetail. Following gestures from their sheriff, both deputies took up hidden positions diagonally opposite each other along the margin of the swamp near the von Himmel trailer. Grey Fox himself surveyed the landscape for his most advantageous ambush spot. Down by the family shed, he saw a small, open feed door on the second floor and a ladder lying against the side of the building. He and his men would have a perfect triangle for shooting without hitting each other.

"That's it!" he decided, and in swift fashion grabbed the ladder, swung it to the window, climbed up, lifted the ladder in behind him and lay down with his shotgun barrel barely extended, pointing beyond the bottom edge of the door. His trap had been laid.

It took longer than the sheriff thought for him to hear footsteps approaching from below him behind the barn. It was just after sundown when they came. The last, mid-September crimson sun rays of the western horizon challenged the icy, blue-black night sky when the von Himmel's heavy footsteps and raspy breathing betrayed their presence near the south side of the barn. Flitting beams of a crude torch broadcast their progress alongside the barn. Just at the front edge of it, Adolf said something to his father about "the long, disgusting, shitty mess we just finished."

The sheriff waited for the men to move to the exact center of open ground in front of him before he rose to his knees and shouted down from his perch, "Police! Freeze or die!" and at the same moment his two deputies arose from the marsh grass with their weapons centered on each of the nearest von Himmels.

"Drop your weapons slowly and raise your hands!" Grey Fox ordered from behind and above the two men. To his surprise, both men followed his command. The younger man who the sheriff recognized as Adolf slung his carry bag to the ground. The older man dropped a crude torch he carried. With his hand empty and at his sides, old man von Himmel simply stood in place.

Instinct told Grey Fox something was wrong. "I said raise your damn hands!"

"Drop!" shouted Adolf to his father as he whipped around, pulling the Luger from his waist. Two shots from the automatic handgun careened off the barn door just above the sheriff's head, as both deputies from either side opened fire in a fusillade of lead. Grey Fox leveled his front sight on Adolf's extended gun hand and snapped off a twelve-gauge slug.

The von Himmel luck still held, mostly. Adolf's burning torch of marsh grass and pine branches obscured him with enough murky shadows that he was only hit once, but it was deer slug, and its impact blew the pistol and most of his right hand away. He fell to the ground squealing in pain. Herman von Himmel lay absolutely still with his arms spread.

Both deputies rushed both von Himmels, kicked the pistol away from Adolf and handcuffed them to each other using the wounded man's only good arm.

Grey Fox came down from the second floor quickly, covering the two suspects as often as he could. "When we get them to my squad, use my set of leg irons, Officers." Then the sheriff unbuckled his belt and wrapped it tight as a tourniquet around the shattered arm.

"You shot my friggin' hand off! Where in hell did you goddam Indians come from?" Rage and bright red blood spewed out of Adolf von Himmel. The wound was not exactly a square cut. There were bone fragments and ligaments dangling out, and as he writhed in pain on the ground, he had managed to rub dirt and debris into it.

"We are Ho Chungra of the Trout Nation. I am Josiah Grey Fox, sheriff of the Ho-Chunk Nation Tribal Police. You are under arrest for attempted murder of your grandson, a crime you committed on reservation land. If you try anything, we will send you both to a real hell," replied the sheriff. "Now move to the second squad car before we decide that you tried to escape and had to be shot down and scalped before you died.' The von Himmels didn't see the sly wink the sheriff shared with his two deputies before he said, "We usually eat our enemies!"

Lowering his shotgun, the sheriff turned to both fellow officers. "I might have guessed I shouldn't take you two brothers on this mission," Grey Fox said. "All that lead you released and neither of you hit the gunman! Tobias. Tomas. You must better uphold your Two Boys' family name. More target practice for both of you!"

The brothers cringed under their sheriff's scowl.

Grey Fox had Tobias move ahead of the prisoners with the orders to take the boy back to the tribal office for safekeeping. Speaking in a whisper, the sheriff said, "Under no circumstances, Tobias, should anyone else know we have Jack."

Then returning his attention to Herman von Himmel, he raised the shotgun again and said matter-of-factly, "Move to the other squad out on the road. I'll patch your wound there while Tomas covers me, unless either or both of you want to find out about the Happy Hunting Ground real soon." A minute later the screech of tires on gravel told the sheriff Jack was safe.

When the group reached the remaining squad, Grey Fox opened the trunk, removed the first aid kit and leg chains, shackled the old man, and pushed him down on his side on the back seat of the vehicle.

"You," he said speaking to Adolf, "you sit here on the edge of the seat while I try to clean and bandage your wound the best I can. At least the tourniquet is working. Tomas, cover both with my shotgun." Tomas stood back to give himself a wide pattern of fire as the sheriff removed the tourniquet and attended to Adolf's wound.

"Man alive! —you both stink of guts and old blood!" said Grey Fox as he finished. He reached over to Tomas's belt, pulled up a flashlight and started examining Herman from top to bottom. Then he had the younger von Himmel stand up. "What are you doing with blood on your rump? You were hit in the hand!" Sheriff Grey Fox swung the flashlight to study Herman von Himmel's appearance again. "Man, you stink!" A few more swings of the flashlight confirmed major blood stains and smears on both prisoners.

"I smell black blood on 'em, Sheriff," said Tomas. "It isn't theirs!" Pointing the shotgun right into Adolf face, the deputy asked, "Who you been cutting up, boy? Is that the mess you mentioned back at the barn? Sure don't look like you were doing it to yourself!"

"You're right, Deputy. When we get them back to the jail, we will have these losers stripped clean and have their clothes bagged for evidence."

Fifteen minutes later a brief stop at the Koleski home allowed for the State Patrol there to stand down.

"We've got two of the von Himmels, Commander," explained Sheriff Grey Fox. "We found congealed blood, likely somebody else's, on both crooks. They reek of it. Make sure they are stripped, and their duds bagged for crime lab study. They were coming out of the Goodyear Marsh when we caught them. The young one said something about a disgusting mess they left behind—and you've got to get him to the Hamot hospital. I shot his hand off. The wound is a dirty, ugly mess. Likely lead fragments in it because I hit him with a twelve-gauge hollow point slug."

Commander Post finished the thought— "Right, Sheriff. I know the best crime lab person in the country. I just bet the FBI will let us bring her here and go to work; there's been a bombing, after all. She's Lucille Mountain Wolf. I think she hails from the separate Winnebago Reservation in Omaha, Nebraska. Hell, she could nail these yahoos for blowing up the marsh and figure out what they were doing back in the swamp to boot!"

"And any time we need Jack's dad, Gunther, we'll just send a couple of your men to the County Line Tap up the road about five miles, Commander," Grey Fox added, "I am releasing all of them to your custody and the Hamot jail."

"Good enough, Sheriff. Glad to avoid any jurisdiction and custody fight," said Commander Post. "Great work! You and your men are the real deal!"

"Another thing," said Grey Fox. "On our way out of the driveway, I saw a dark sedan with Minnesota plates parked off the road just north of the von Himmel property. That's suspicious to me. No one parks their vehicle next to marsh and muck without a good reason. With the two Nazis we now have in custody who both emerged from the marsh as well, there could be a connection."

"You're right, Josiah! We'll take these two into town now and book them. Adolf will go to the hospital briefly to clean out his stump while I will search their possessions and start to interrogate each separately. Both von Himmels probably lawyer up instantly, but we can question them tomorrow morning when their counsel shows up."

"Tomorrow morning, I have more to tell you, Commander. It's about Jack and Sara."

"I'll look forward to your report, Josiah! Thank you and your deputies again for your excellent work!"

Post swiveled then to face two of his officers and issue orders, but Grey Fox leaned forward and added with his dry humor, "Of course, Commander, just remember when you do decide to arrest Gunther, your men should take every precaution. The most important thing is for you all to stay as low as possible. —likely they'll have to pick him up off the bar floor to do it."

The mountain wolf and his pack watched the gunfight from the edge of the reeds and tall swamp grass just beyond the von Himmel shed. The gunfire made them retreat momentarily, but they quickly realized it was not directed at them this time. And, later, when the commotion settled down and the humans all left, he and his family were able to lick up a few splashes of von Himmel blood and part of a hand.

From their point of view, revenge was best served warm.

Chapter 45

SHERIFF JOSIAH GREY Fox reported to the Hamot jail early the next morning following the agreement to avoid any immediate contact with the von Himmels' defense attorney. Right before they split up the night before, the sheriff and Commander Post decided to meet at 6 AM and sort out what had happened, what charges could be immediately brought, and what to do next.

District Attorney Tamara Blake, Commander Post and Chief of Police Stone all greeted him as he noisily stomped inside the front door of the Hamot PD. The heat and humidity of the jailhouse rushed to penetrate the sheriff's heavy woolen jacket resulting in a shroud of steam oozing up from his clothes.

Thumping his arms against the opposite shoulders of his thick, red and black striped wool coat and blowing hot breath and steam onto his hands, the sheriff entered the Hamot PD precisely on time. "Daylight in the swamps, folks!" he said and nodded good morning. "This early freeze up is weeks ahead of time," he said. Then with a wide grin, he quipped— "In fact it's so darn cold this morning, I saw a dog frozen to a Hamot fireplug!"

"Very funny, Sheriff!" retorted D.A. Blake. "I see you listen to Johny Carson too," but she gave him a bright smile and stepped behind him to help him with his coat.

"Let's get right down to work," said Post, assuming his usual take-charge demeanor. He opened an office door, signaled for the others to enter, and to take a seat around a conference room table equipped with hot coffee, note pads and ink pens.

Motioning for everyone to take a chair, the commander began by gesturing toward the sheriff and saying, "As we were wrapping up the capture of the von Himmels last night, Josiah told me he had some more news on the case, something more about Jack and Sara."

"That's right Commander," the sheriff agreed. "Earlier in the evening, I received a desperate phone call from Sara Koleski. She told me that Jack von Himmel had just come staggering up their driveway, dripping wet and in fear for his life. He had escaped a murder attempt by his own family."

"My God, that poor kid!" exclaimed Blake. "What was going on?"

"Until Hamot's new Chief of Police—" and Post nodded toward Stone, "figured out what Flaherty was doing, we believed that Jack was in protective custody somewhere."

Stone interjected then, "Right, but when I questioned Flaherty, his answers just did not add up. I called the Wisconsin Rapids PD where the chief said he had the boy. I wanted to inquire about Jack, and they told me they had no idea there was someone named Jack von Himmel in their custody. Then I called Commander Post, asap."

"Correct, Chief! Good job showing initiative and not being put off," said Post. "I raced over here from our office on the Interstate highway and cuffed Flaherty. When we questioned him, it was clear he had no idea that Jack had been taken from his elderly parents' house in the Rapids. Turns out Flaherty was just trying to run a pathetic little scam by claiming he was protecting Jack and therefore should be able to take the extra pay for himself."

"And for that, he's going down for felony witness misuse, felony police misconduct and felony attempted fraud—maybe more!" Tamara Blake's angry face looked as red as her vivid hair. "When we are done here, John, I want you to send Flaherty to the county seat's jail in Sparta. No sense in keeping him here a couple of cell doors down from the von Himmels."

"Right! I am seeing a little more of a big picture," said Grey Fox. "To continue about Sara, when she saw Jack, he told her that two men who appeared to be state patrol detectives came to Flaherty's home in Rapids, flashed some papers and badges, and lied that all charges were dropped against his family in the bombing case. They told him all was forgiven and brought the boy back to the von Himmel trailer around 9 am yesterday morning."

"So how did the boy wind up at the Koleski's marsh, Josiah?" asked Chief Stone.

"Jack told me that when the men initially dropped him off, his grandfather and uncle were the only one's home," the sheriff explained. "They took their cue from the two fake detectives and pretended everything was fine. After cooking the boy breakfast, Old Man von Himmel told Jack he needed help from both his uncle Adolf and him to dig up money he had buried deep in the Goodyear Marsh. The lawyer had to be paid, he said."

"But they obviously just planned on getting the boy way out in the boonies so they could kill him, and no one would ever find out. Correct?' As Tamara Blake asked the question, she was furiously writing notes on her yellow legal pad.

"Good," said the sheriff. "Apparently Jack's dad, Gunther, was sent to work at a nearby marsh that day. Probably, the old man just didn't want Gunther to let any fatherly emotions get in the way of murdering Jack. Then, Adolf, Herman and Jack waded a couple hours deep into the Goodyear until they came to a big marsh lake out there."

"I've heard of the place," said Stone, and he swept his right hand across the conference table, unconsciously trying to remove the remaining issues.

"Once they arrived, Jack said his grandfather gave him a long knife to defend himself with, and while Herman was distracting the boy with nonsense about how Vikings go to Valhalla if they die with a blade in their hand, Adolf was sneaking around the kid to hit him in the head with a hammer."

"That's evil and sick!" Blake stopped writing out of sheer disgust.

"Just when it looked bleak for Jack, the two fake cops jumped out of the pines behind the von Himmels and with guns drawn demanded whatever money or gold Herman had for themselves. Jack had no clue how they knew about the buried loot. He's not even sure there was any out there," Grey Fox added.

Post interrupted— "Well, it's too bad the old couple didn't know the state patrol doesn't have any three-piece-suit detectives, but what I want to know is how the boy saved himself?"

"He said all the focus was on the two von Himmel men on one side and the bogus detectives on the other. Jack, who is pretty darn brave young man I might add, slammed his knife into one of the fake cop's guts, then dove into the marsh lake. All hell erupted then," he said, "but when the shooting was done, he was already well out in the lake and up the shoreline far enough to get away."

"That boy has to be a quick thinker!" Blake said. "Since the two von Himmels are here in our lockup, I assume the two unidentified fake cops are lying dead out there in the marsh. Right, Josiah?"

"Well, not exactly lying out there as two bodies."

"What do you mean, Sheriff?" Blake responded.

"After the shootout back at the von Himmel trailer when my two deputies and I captured them, both Jack's grandfather and uncle were covered in blood. Plenty of it was somebody else's blood, and the two stunk of cutting up guts. If you've ever field dressed a deer, you would understand. I think we need to get a crime lab person out there to see if he or she can resurrect whatever dismembered little pieces of the two fake cops sitting on the bottom of the swamp lake. Maybe another murder charge against the von Himmels if we can do it, Tamara?"

"I don't get how the von Himmels figured out where Flaherty took Jack," Post asked. "How would they know Jack in the first place, much less see him at Flaherty's home in Rapids?"

"I hate to tell you all this, but there is only one way," Grey Fox said. "They have to have other Nazis watching police stations, safe houses and God knows what else across this state—maybe plenty of other states too. I think they've developed a spy system to survive. It's real possible they are watching this station even as we speak!"

"That can't be!" exploded Chief Stone. "I've lived in Hamot all my life, and I've never heard anybody say 'Heil Hitler' or do the Nazi salute. Never!"

"Then you haven't looked at the far corner of your own building, Chief." Tamara Blake sadly shook her head in disagreement. "In case you haven't noticed, there is a swastika carved into the Lannon stone on the southwest corner of your PD." She shook her head again and added, "Sorry, but Sheriff Grey Fox is dead right. They have been here for a long time, and because they are religious fanatics as well as murdering scum, they likely keep a pretty low profile and a very close watch on us."

It was Commander Frederick Post who asked the single most important question of the discussion. "Josiah, you keep saying that Jack has told you all these things. But he isn't here to tell us. Where is Jack now? Why didn't you bring him here?"

There was a long, significant, and awkward pause in the room. Blake and Stone rose to stand with Commander Post. The mood in the room and the expression on their faces hardened.

"He is somewhere safe on our reservation," explained Josiah Grey Fox in a voice that clearly would accept no argument.

"What in the friggin' hell are you talking about, Josiah?" demanded Hamot's new police chief. "It's our case! He's a white kid! He belongs under my protection!"

"Please excuse the chief's rudeness, Sheriff," Blake interposed instantly. Then turning to pat the Chief on his nearest hand as it was curling up into a fist, she did an attorney's best to soothe over the bad feelings on both sides. "I am sure he is just expressing everyone's grave concern for Jack's safety."

"John, don't ever talk to me like that again. Not ever," said Grey Fox. "Not if you want any cooperation!" This time it was native sheriff's moment to stand and deliver. "I've thought about this all night. And the situation is that we the Ho-Chunk Nation are a separate country you folks call a reservation. We have a separate treaty with your nation, and that includes basic property rights for us and our own judicial system."

In nearly that same soothing voice but tinged with some alarm, District Attorney Blake said, "But surely, Josiah, you don't mean you will keep the boy with you on the reservation?"

"That's exactly what I mean," said the sheriff.

"But you can't guarantee his safety!" Stone intervened.

"Oh really?" asked Grey Fox. "Like the safety the Hamot PD has provided lately?"

It was Post's turn now. "Sure, Sheriff. You are right. One weak cop gave into greed and put Jack in jeopardy. But I am a State Police Commander. We would take Jack into protective custody. In fact, given there was a bombing, kidnapping and now murder, it won't be long before the FBI shows up to take over the case. I called them." Then Post leaned toward the sheriff in a manner stiff enough to betray his irritation. "Just give the boy to me, Josiah. I'll protect him."

"Like Flaherty did?" retorted Grey Fox. "Sorry, Commander, but you need to ask yourself who did Sara and Jack go to when they needed protection. It sure wasn't you. And I think even the FBI will have to admit, the boy was on reservation nation land guaranteed to us by a treaty the Supreme Court of the US has verified…so he is ours!"

The facial expressions of the listeners solidified as the sheriff continued, "Think about it for a moment. District Attorney Blake just agreed with me that the Nazis are watching all of you and your buildings. How many spies do you think they may have planted in and around police and government building across Wisconsin?"

"But you don't know there are any spies, Sheriff," argued Post.

"I do know there aren't any Nazi sympathizers among our Ho-Chunk First Nation people," responded Grey Fox. "Not too many fascists living on Indian reservations these days."

"I'll just take a short coffee break down at the Rexall Drug Store across the street," said Sheriff Grey Fox. "I think a little cooling off period would do everybody some good, and when I come back, we can discuss charges for the von Himmels, search warrants for their property and how to get a good dog to lead us to the likely murder scene."

The sheriff carefully stepped around Chief Stone, and as he opened the conference door to leave, he added, "And don't forget to send Flaherty over to Sparta. He'll love his first official trip to the county seat!"

Chapter 46

"**THIS IS THE** Ho-Chunk Police Department. I am Officer Christine Grey Fox. How can I help you?"

"You answer the phone too politely," kidded Josiah Grey Fox.

"Oh, that's just me I guess, Uncle. Now why aren't you using your patrol car radio, and what do you need?"

"Pretty serious stuff, Christine," explained the sheriff, "and I don't want to take any chances being overheard by some ham radio buff, so I'm using a phone in Rexall's."

"Right, Sheriff," she agreed. "You must be calling about our boy, Jack."

"Yes, I am. There was just a meeting at the Hamot PD with the new chief of police Stone, District Attorney Blake and State Patrol Commander Post. They said they expected us to turn over Jack von Himmel to them for safekeeping."

"And, of course, you refused. He is under our protection."

"Yes, he is. And to keep it that way, I want both Two Boys' twins to take Jack out to our chief's lodge back up Cheney Road to Big Stony Lonesome."

"Yes, Sheriff. No one will ever be able to sneak up on Gully Hanging Moon out there or anywhere else."

"I agree, Christine! Right now, I'm still in Hamot. After a little timeout, I'll be going back to finish up some more plans at the jail. Tell Tobias and Tomas to take one or two of our .308 lever action rifles and a couple boxes of shells up to the chief as well."

"Yes, sir. Will do. But you and I both know that Chief Hanging Moon will use his bow and arrow and throwing lance first. Over and out!"

Chapter 47

As LUCK WOULD have it, as the Sheriff Josiah Grey Fox approached the front door of the Hamot PD to resume the planning session, von Himmel attorney N. B. Forrester was there to open it.

"Ah, Sheriff. All of you good officers of the law and of the court must be trying to get a head start on me, I see. Having your little early morning planning session and breakfast chat, are we?" Forrester was exuding his usual self-confidence and slightly detectable smirk as he spoke. "Word spread fast that you have my clients here again."

"Who are you? How do you know me? How did you know the von Himmels are here?"

"Oh, a brave, I should say a brave man, like you, Sheriff, is widely known. You are the man who blew off one of my client's right hand with a twelve-gauge slug I believe. Adolf thinks you must be quite a marksman. From what Herman von Himmel told me over the phone, however, your half-blind deputies couldn't hit a thing. By the way, you can call me Forrester. No first name. Just Forrester. You can think of me as the very opposite of the pathetic smoke-skinned forrester people of your tribe who dwell back in the scrub oaks and live off pinecones." N. B. Forrester chuckled at his own cleverness.

"Well, if they do, Forrester, they have two hands to do the gathering!" and Grey Fox saw Forrester's face darken... no one could be the clever one except himself.

"What's wrong this morning, Forrester?" continued the sheriff. "Your little Adolf having trouble wiping his ass with only a left hand now?"

"You'll be sorry for that, cop! The surgeon said Adolf has blood poisoning in his system. I'll get you for that!"

"Oh, threatening an officer of the law now, Forrester? You could go to jail. You could lose your license to practice defending bottom suckers like your Nazis sitting down the hallway. I would be so very happy to lock you in our reservation jailhouse. So many red friends waiting to welcome a racist ambulance chaser like you."

Forrester paused stalling for time. He wasn't used to someone matching him word for word, jibe for jibe.

"Glad to see you're back, Josiah. We've all calmed down a bit." It was Commander Post who stepped out from the conference room door to shake Grey Fox's hand.

"Good to be back, sir," replied the sheriff.

Forrester realigned the front of his vest to parallel the lines of his powder blue seer sucker suit and generally tried to fluff himself up. "Before all you good old boys get together to plan my clients' fate, I demand to talk to them. They have the right of counsel!"

"No problem, Attorney," said Post. He called to Stone to come out and escort Forrester for the private visit.

When the new chief of police returned, he feigned wiping his arms and shoulders off with a make-believe towel. "The manure on men like Forrester, you know!" he quipped.

Then, tapping the sheriff on the shoulder, he added— "Apologies for the dust up, Josiah. These bad guys and their lawyer make me wanna puke. I was out of line. Just make sure you folks protect that boy, ok?"

Commander Post poked his head into the conversation too. "Right. The feds won't be happy, Josiah, but it will take forever to figure out the extradition laws between first nation tribes and the U.S. government. I'll still get their crime lab specialist here, and maybe a bloodhound, but it's on you to protect Jack."

"Agreed. I will!" said Grey Fox, and the three men walked back into the conference room where Tamara Blake sat patiently awaiting their return.

Chapter 48

WHEN THE TWO Boys' brothers turned off Cheney Road's gravel and slowed their Ho-Chunk squad car enough to negotiate the narrow lumber trail and its many forks which led uphill toward Big Stony Lonesome Peak, they stopped the vehicle well before their chief's lodge was visible and exchanged anxious glances. The mountain's rising landscape of sparse, yellow grass bundles, the burnt ochre of oak leaves and the pungent scent of jack pines in early autumn weren't enough to provide welcome for the two brothers and the boy.

"Why are we stopping here, Deputies?" asked Jack. "I don't see anybody's house or anything."

Deputy Tobias Two turned from the driver's seat and smiled at the teenager. Even with the wide gap between his two front teeth, he emanated a pleasant and understanding quality. "It's not about what we can't see, Jack." The deputy swiveled his head to gesture out the front window. "It's all about what our chief has already seen approaching … and that's us!"

Forcing another smile at the boy, he and his brother Tomas slowly opened the car doors, held up the rifle they had been told to bring along and without making any sudden movements, stood silently waiting.

An arrow buried itself in the rifle's stock. It hit with such force it ripped the weapon from the deputy's grip and carried it several feet through the air before leveling off and falling into a bed of white pine branches. Fortunately, it was unloaded so it couldn't discharge.

"Holy cow!" shouted Jack. "Get your pistols! Someone is attacking us!"

"Nobody is attacking us, Jack," quietly replied Tobias Two Boys. "Just make sure you stand real still." Then gingerly looking over to his brother, the deputy grimaced and said, "I take it that's the chief's way of telling us he still doesn't like guns of any kind!"

Tomas stifled a chuckle, rearranged his reservation police baseball cap and swallowed hard. "Well, brother, it's not true that Gully Hanging Moon is our chief anymore, you know. He is just chief when he wants to be. Just chief of war things he decides are important enough for him to see get done right. He lets our mom, Teresa, be the peace chief."

"But don't you dare tell him that, brother!" cautioned Tobias. "The last thing we need is to make him angry. No sir, we don't need our tires shot full of arrows...or us shot full too!" and all three members of the arriving party looked up hill in the direction of where the arrow had been launched.

"What kind of hunters have you become?" the question sprang from a clump of buck brush below and behind the vehicle.

"*Haho*, Chief Hanging Moon!" Both the twins eased around to face downhill to welcome their chief at the same time, although he chose not to reveal himself.

"*Pinagigi*, men of the Two Boys' clan," said the chief. "Thank you for speaking your native language! There may be hope for you yet—once you learn to move more silently and use quiet weapons like mine!"

"Who are you two guys talking to?" complained Jack. "Why doesn't he come out from wherever he is hiding?"

"I will come out when I know who you are and why you have come, young boy! You must learn what your white brothers have forgotten or ignored—you must learn how to be safe," the chief replied, still screened by brush and bush.

"*Safe*!" There was that word again coming back like a bad penny—the most essential word Jack had ever confronted, had ever struggled to understand, had ever hoped to feel. Like a magnet, the boy automatically was drawn to the strong, calm voice who spoke to him of safety somewhere back in the tangle of rocks and pines.

Without waiting for the deputies to do any introduction, Jack stepped toward the voice and explained, "I am Jack von Himmel, Chief. Sheriff Grey Fox has me sent me to you because I testified against my family for blowing up the Koleski Cranberry Marsh dike. They tried to kill me, but I got away. My grandfather, my father, and my uncle Ade all are Nazis. I am here to ask you to keep me safe."

"Well spoken, Jack of the von Himmels," the chief said, and he stepped from behind a screen of buckthorns and brambles. "Your public name now will be Little Hare. Your Ho-Chunk name is *Wash-ching-geka*, for you have already been tested and survived by your wits like the wise rabbit of our culture."

Jack wasn't prepared for the human being who now revealed himself. To the boy, Gully Hanging Moon appeared to be immense. He was a red-brown man with features sculpted in moist clay. His dark brown, luminous eyes seemed to search Jack inside and out with a searing intensity. He wore a worn, tan leather shirt and vest with some sort of beadwork across the chest panels; his hair was in long, black braids interrupted in the back by a single eagle feather; he had an old pair of jeans for pants and moccasins with high-ridged seams for footwear. In his right hand he carried a long bow, his quiver of arrows hung loosely from his belt near his left hip. Lean, tall, powerful and frugal with his words, the chief projected both an intolerance for weakness and the unnecessary, as well as an overwhelming aura of integrity.

"You come with me, Little Hare. Earthmaker, our god, his name is *Ma'una*; he and I will see to it that nothing wicked comes your way here." Turning to the deputies, the chief offered a wan smile and a bit of rebuke. "You both can go now, Tobias and Tomas Two Boys. Make sure you practice with bows and arrows today, and next time you come back and bring a gun—make sure you come more quietly."

Without further small talk, Hanging Moon glanced at Jack and started walking back up the hill. Jack didn't wait for an invitation to follow.

Chapter 49

MAYBE HE HAPPENED to be sitting in a Hamot jail cell with his two clients, but N. B. Forrester, the von Himmel's attorney, was in a perfect courtroom lather as he summarized the situation Adolf and Herman had just described. "Ok, you both are telling me that you had to kill two Nazis from the Twin Cities who you had swipe Jack from protective custody in Wisconsin Rapids. After Herman here paid them off in gold at your trailer when they delivered the boy, they returned and tracked you into a great big swamp to get even more. You tricked your grandson into following you out into that hopeless mire under the guise of digging up enough loot to pay me."

"But you just told me you intended to kill the kid to prevent him from testifying," the lawyer continued. "And it just so happened that Jack was smarter than any of you and escaped. You did, how-ever, manage to eliminate both fake cops. They are dead and fish food out in the swamp. Now neither of you knows where Jack is, but we must assume he will be with law enforcement soon. Right!"'" Forrester was beside himself with loathing.

"*Ya, das* right, Lawyer Man," indifferently agreed Herman von Himmel.

"And you expect me to continue to represent you morons with major risk to my reputation after you just confessed to me of kidnapping, the felony attempted murder of Jack and felony second degree murder of the two crooks who tried to stick you up!"

"*Ya, das* right, Lawyer Man," continued the old man.

"Well count me gone!" shouted Forrester. "I'm disappeared back to Madison where the only insanity is liberal politics!" and he started putting his pen, legal pad, and law book into his Corinthian leather briefcase.

"Oh no, Shyster Man," said the old man smiling broadly. "You don't go nowhere. You stay right here and defend us. That's what you got to do."

"I don't have to do anything of the kind, you crazy old coot! I don't care how much money you've donated to our KKK. I'm not going to go to jail for any Nazi nutcases like the two of you!"

"Maybe you don't care. So what? Your boss cares, and that is all that matters. I just talk with him on the phone. I promise him a million dollars for your cause if you stay on the case and you get us off." Von

Himmel's confidence was unnerving, and Forrester instantly began to worry.

Herman von Himmel continued— "And he said you damn well better deliver or else!"

"What do you mean, 'or else'?"

"You such a smarty, you figure out what he means Lawyer Man!" Von Himmel sneered. He clearly realized he had the upper hand and was enjoying himself.

Forrester gasped audibly. If von Himmel had talked to George Sheldon, the national head of the Ku Klux Klan, and the crazy old Nazi had promised a million in gold for a not guilty verdict, 'or else' meant that Forrester would not survive a loss at trial. Sheldon was as dangerous and crazy as old man von Himmel, and the Klan had plenty of goons who would love to indulge their need for violence by traveling to Wisconsin to bump off a southerner who in their eyes turned Yankee and failed in his obligations to the Klan.

Forrester knew he had to make an instant calculation…either get these idiots off if possible, or if not, find their buried horde of Nazi gold for himself as soon as possible and disappear, even if it meant escaping from the trial at verdict time. "Go big or go dead!" Forrester said to himself. "Go big or go dead!"

"All right, Herman. I think I can get you out of this jail again on bail," explained a suddenly confident

Forrester—"but the price of your bail bond will be sky high. It's likely they will try to charge you with murder or attempted murder—but since you said you destroyed the bodies; I have a good chance at least to get you off at trial."

"*Ya, das gut!*" von Himmel said expansively. "I heard of *habeus corpus* all right. They got to have bodies, identify who they were, and prove we killed them. Our bloody clothes prove nothing. They can't find nothing out there in that bog."

"But the trouble comes with wherever Jack is and who he is talking to" replied Forrester. "And regarding Adolf, I am sorry to tell you both that when he took those two shots at that redskin sheriff, there won't be any bail for him. Threaten me all you want, Herman, but no lawyer is going to get your son here off Scot free. With some hard work and fast talking, the best I can do is get a reduced sentence for him in a plea bargain deal at trial."

"How you do that?" old man von Himmel asked.

"I'll argue that you both were taking target practice out there in the marsh. You came home late at night and suddenly someone shouted threats at you. Adolf panicked and rapped off a couple shots out of self-defense for him and you. As he has no real record, I will plead for leniency because he is a first-time offender. I'm good at that kind of argument. He'll get a few years, but even those will be reduced by good behavior…and having me bumped off won't get anyone less jail time. I remain the best attorney in this country to save your necks."

Herman von Himmel sat motionless for a full minute, then nodded his head in agreement. *"Ya,"* he finally said. "I think what you say is true enough. My son Adolf, he was just trying to protect me. Maybe a couple years in the jailhouse will do him some good…make him tougher and wiser like I want my sons to be." The old man swung to his left toward Adolf and patted his heavily bandaged stump. "He is a good son. We gotta face the facts about what he did to save his *vater*. He gotta pay the price. It was just what my *vater* Karl tried his best to do for me too."

Adolf's face was an expressionless mask as he listened to his father turn the whole desperate events of the previous night into a radio ad of total self-promotion. It made him hate his father even more. After all, wasn't it true the old man just gave up when the sheriff and his men drew down on them last night? Why didn't he try to fight back too? – or at least try to draw their fire away? His do-nothing choice cost Adolf a perfectly good right hand, and now he had to move around with an IV bag drip next to him because the wound was still infected and beginning to stink.

Adolf von Himmel knew in his heart what he had to do. He swore a silent oath to himself. If he ever got the chance, Adolf would kill his father—but not until he slowly cut off a few parts of the monster Herman was and watched his old man writhe in pain, and he'd probably start with a slow amputation of the same hand the old man used to pat Adolf's wound.

Chapter 50

As Jack reached the top of Stony Lonesome peak, he had the urge to verbalize two strong impressions the scene provided him. First, the boy wanted to say something about the magnificent view below of miles of lime-tinted moss and pine forest studded with sharp rising gunmetal gray rocky bluffs. The second thing Jack nearly blurted out was that he saw no cabin. A quick look at Chief Hanging Moon's solemn face silhouetted against the eastern horizon told him to keep silent. Silence, as the chief had just told the two deputies, was something to be greatly valued.

"You have been wise to say nothing to waste time and simply fill the world with useless sounds, Little Hare," explained the chief as if he had been reading Jack's thoughts all the way up the climb. "Silence, *Wash-ching-geka,* is the first and most basic step to always remaining safe."

"Yes sir—I mean, yes, Chief," Jack agreed.

"Think for a moment. Not only does idle talk prevent you from hearing danger approaching, but it also tells your enemies exactly where they can find you."

"Yes, Chief. I am learning." Then following Hanging Moon across the ridge, Jack moved in the same measured pace he had adopted from the chief as they came up the hill. The pace at first seemed too slow for the boy, but he soon realized he was able to move higher without any fatigue, which would have been a problem had he started rushing to the top.

As the two crossed over to the downside of the ridge on its warmer western edge, Jack saw where he would be living. Thoughts of a majestic teepee or cozy cabin vanished when the boy saw a bark and brush-mat covered lodge looking like a long, narrow tube, perfectly camouflaged to its dark pea-green forest and slate gray granite setting.

"I am learning lesson two to be safe, right, Chief?"

"Perhaps. What has Little Hare learned now?"

"After silence, I am learning to blend into whatever natural surroundings I find myself in. To be inconspicuous, especially in my choice of home," said Jack in a voice which unveiled little pleasure in his word choice. "It will also help me stay safe."

"Inconspicuous! *Haho*! Good enough," said the chief. "Enter my lodge. We will feast tonight because you are my guest, and Gully Hanging Moon rarely has visitors, much less ones to share a meal."

Jack was surprised to find the inner furnishings of the lodge actually quite comfortable. The walls held colorfully beaded decorations, feathered pipes, quivers, spears, and animal skins to provide insulation from the cold. The floor was covered in reed mats and blanket cushions for seating. Pumpkins and squash lay tight to the uneven curves of the walls.

"We eat now," announced the chief, and Jack was handed a large wooden bowl filled with dried meat, fresh wild onions, pumpkin mash, and blueberries. A simple wooden cup provided a cold beverage.

"The meat is dried venison. We drink spring water," explained Hanging Moon, always a person of few words. The food was consumed in silence, but Jack found nothing uncomfortable about it.

"*Pinagigi!*" exclaimed the boy as he finished his dinner. "Thank you so much for the delicious meal, Chief!"

Hanging Moon almost broke into a smile, but Jack could still see his host was clearly pleased and impressed that a fifteen-year-old boy under terrible circumstances still had enough presence of mind to decipher the earlier greeting the chief had given the two Two Boys' brothers when they spoke in their native tongue.

"I like you, Little Hare. Tomorrow we will continue your education," said the chief. "We will sit on the bluff top now."

"Oh, yes. I would love to take in the big picture of all the woods and hills and water!" exclaimed Jack as they strode to the peak and sat among the rock ledges.

"It is true that the view is full of beauty. And beauty is good for the mind and soul. But that can never be a warrior's first purpose, never be his first obligation, young brave."

"Well, what is...what is a warrior's first duty, Chief?"

"You will think on this and tell me tomorrow morning if you want another good meal. For now, *Wash-ching-geka*, you and I will listen to the woods, the wind. Then we sleep."

The mountain wolf had carefully observed the human comings and goings up and down Big Stony Lonesome. He was familiar enough with the two men who came to visit their leader who lived on the bluff, but he and his pack were surprised to see a boy also arrive. The alpha wolf and his mate quickly identified their new company. It was the young human who had fed them, and the timber wolf knew the boy presented no threat. The pack leader

and his she-wolf lay down in relaxed body positions, assuring their family members none of the humans were cause for alarm. Indeed, the leader of the Black River Falls pack took some pleasure in seeing the boy in the company of the man who lived among the wolves. Two human friends were better than one.

Chapter 51

"**AND WHAT DO** you have to say to me, Little Hare? There is breakfast for the right answer and nothing if you are wrong. That is the lesson life teaches us every day if we are paying attention to what matters and what doesn't," said Chief Hanging Moon.

Jack was quick with his response. "A warrior's first duty is to make sure those he protects are safe, so he must be quiet," Jack reported. "His second duty is to ensure that he himself is safe, for if he is injured or dead, he cannot protect anyone else. My guess is e sat on the top of the bluff last night to watch for approaching danger."

"Well said, Little Hare! We will see if you remember that. Now we both can enjoy more of the same meal we had last night." Hanging Moon quickly produced bowls of smoked venison strips, onions, pumpkin mash and dried berries. Then he dipped a cup into a bowl of pottery with strange lettering and handed Jack a cold cup of spring water.

"Today, your lesson will be how to catch fish," announced the chief.

"Fishing is always fun," replied Jack, and in the exuberance of youth he continued—"and I'm excellent at it too. Last year in the springtime my family took me to the Granite River. We fished right next to the dam."

The boy realized he was starting to rush his words, so he paused before continuing. "Just a mile from the dam is a very high hill." Jack twisted his body and stretched out his right arm to point to the south and east. "On the top of the bluff is a Nazi gathering place like an open-air theatre. In front of where the benches are is a tall shrine called the Irminsul. It has an eagle's head carved out of rock for its top. My grandfather Herman took me there once, but I was so young I don't really remember what happened."

The chief's face showed no reaction. Choosing his words with great care, he said to the boy, "It may be well for you that you don't remember what happened, young warrior." Bad memories of name-calling, teachers beating him for speaking his native language, and constant harassment at school, flooded Hanging Moon's mind.

Returning to what he could remember, Jack couldn't contain his excitement about the fishing trip. "Down by the spillway," he said, "I caught lots of walleyes all day long!"

"And how did the fish taste when you brought them home to eat, Little Hare?"

Jack's face sagged. "They tasted and stunk like burnt sulfur. They were so nasty we couldn't eat many of them."

"Hmmm. But you did eat enough of the fish to fill yourself with a large helping of self-pride, my excellent fisherman?"

Jack's head sunk low on his chest. "Yes, Chief. I guess that is lesson number three."

"Humility in a warrior is vital, Little Hare. If your mind is filled with thoughts of your own greatness, there is no room for thoughts of who is sneaking up on you and what you better do about it." If there was a sharp reproach in the chief's placid features, the boy didn't see it. Gully Hanging Moon's body was as long as it was narrow, but his luminous, for-giving brown eyes missed nothing.

Jack nodded in agreement. He was crestfallen for a few moments, but as he finished his food, he resolved to do better at the very next opportunity.

"My people are Ho-Chungra of the Trout Nation, Little Hare. That is what we go catch now," explained Hanging Moon. He stood, placed the empty bowls and cups in a small woven basket, and led the way out by sweeping aside the lodge blanket covering the front door. Jack was about to ask why they weren't taking fishing poles and bait—but he had already learned not to ask unnecessary questions and produce unproductive noise.

A half-hour of walking downhill in complete silence at the same measured pace brought both teacher and a rather impatient student to a wide, dark, fast-moving creek.

"This is Robinson Creek, Little Hare. Remember one thing about this water. It is black, and it smells musty in the slow back eddies out of the current. But Ho-Chunk are the People of the Smelly Water and Nation of the Trout. This water is us. We were created from it."

The Chief moved close to Jack, emphasizing his words. "When our Lord *Ma'una* created the world, he began by crying tears of loneliness which formed the waters. That is the smelly water which Earthmaker made land to hold, and he made man to be on the land and converse with him so he would not be lonely."

The chief paused momentarily, then continued— "We are the Ho-Chunk. Unlike all other tribes we do not move around and use up resources until we are forced to move again. We Ho-Chunk stay in one place. We learn how to live with the land, not to slowly use it up. We discovered this land produces whitetail deer, ruffed grouse, tobacco, beans, and squash among other things. These gifts from the Creator regenerate, they replenish if planted and harvested frugally, without selfishness or excess."

"Yes, Chief. I do not mean to be rude, but I don't understand why we don't talk more ourselves when it is safe?" Jack still found it frustrating to remain quiet for long periods of time.

"Your questions are not rude, Little Hare. You cannot learn without asking them," said Hanging Moon. "The first answer you seek is one I have already given you. We don't talk between ourselves without a good reason because our first duty is to be safe. I asked you before to remember that."

"Yes. Ok. I guess I get it," said Jack.

But Chief Hanging Moon's reply only deepened the boy's confusion. The chief nodded to the boy gravely and said, "People do not have to talk out loud to say things to each other."

Jack wanted to agree, but he really did not understand.

"Right now, young brave, you want to ask me where our fishing poles and the bait are to catch trout. You have been saying this to me all the way from my lodge."

"Why...yes. That is exactly what I have been thinking but not saying. How do you know this?" Jack answered.

"You already have the answer, young brave. Slow your thoughts. Let the silence of the forest calm your spirit. Then tell me how I heard your thoughts."

Jack was stumped at first. Then he realized he should give the chief's advice a chance. The boy found a nearby tree stump and once perched on it allowed himself to take a couple of deep breaths to clear the clutter of impulses racing in his mind. The answer came to him almost before he started to consider it.

"You knew what I was thinking because I had to have those thoughts," explained Jack, and the boy studied his teacher for some kind of response. Seeing none, however, the teenager continued. "I bet you looked at me as we walked here and read the frustration in my gestures. The situation already was understood, and I was talking out loud with my body. You didn't have to hear my voice at all to know I felt badly about bragging about my fishing skills and would be wondering how I could catch trout without the usual equipment."

"Yes, *Wash-ching-geka*. What you call our situation spoke loudly to me, and one glance at how you pounded your feet and furrowed the brow on your face told me everything without you or me making any needless sounds."

The Chief paused significantly but his expression said he had more to tell Jack. "Again, I ask you to remember the first duty of a warrior. And now I teach that you can speak to others and listen to what they say without using noise which betrays you to your enemies."

Jack simply nodded his head. He had no intention of saying anything out loud at that point…but he changed his mind. *"Pinagigi!"* he said to the chief and smiled.

For the first time Hanging Moon smiled in return. Jack felt an immense sense of relief and acceptance from it.

"Here is how we will catch our fish," said the chief as he moved toward the nearby water. As he stepped nearer to the creek bank, he looked back at Jack with a hard glance and said, "Never put your hand on creek banks to enter or leave the stream, Little Hare."

Jack suppressed an urge to ask why and instead stood still. The chief bent down, picked up a fallen tree branch almost as long as Jack, whirled around to enter the creek and pushed the stick down into the grassy edge of the bank.

"Watch carefully, young brave!" said the chief, and he swiftly brushed the end of the branch along a few feet of bank. Suddenly there was a commotion in the grass and a mottled brown and reddish head rose up from virtually nothing but plain dirt, flicking its long, black forked tongue toward the chief.

"Rattlesnake! Where did that come from?" Jack gasped . . . then grimaced as he immediately realized he had just broken a warrior's first duty.

It was if Chief Hanging Moon had again read Jack's mind. "Snakes do startle us, Little Hare. Which is why you must be more wary so you can keep silent when you find one."

Jack swallowed hard and began to edge away from the nearby creek bank.

"No, young brave. Do not step away. You cannot fish if you do not enter the water." The chief nodded back toward the snake. "You must learn he just looks like a rattlesnake but is not. Your snake brother looking up to greet you is a northern water snake. They grow to over four feet long. They are thick-bodied but have no fangs. Instead, they have a mouthful of razor-sharp spines."

Hanging Moon waited for his words to sink in, then added, "You should have known it was not a rattler, Little Hare. Provide me a good answer why and you will have a fine supper tonight."

"Because I never heard it make a rattling sound when you poked it?"

"Good, Little Hare! Your ear for detail provides you a good meal this evening." Then the chief returned his attention to the creek bank and its surprise occupant. "We Ho-Chunk name him 'waką' and to ask his forgiveness for my stick poke I will leave him a pinch of tobacco. Because these snakes are without a rattling tail, does not mean they will not strike if someone carelessly puts a hand next to their resting place on creekbanks. The big ones are aggressive!"

"Yes, Chief. I'll remember," Jack said, and he meant it.

"Now when we enter the water to fish, you must also remember that water snakes like to eat small trout just like we do. You must look for snakes not only on streambanks but also hanging by their tails from tag alder branches which hang low over the middle of the creeks. When the trout swims by, the snakes drop on top of them to catch them. A single low-hanging tree limb can have a half-dozen on it."

"So the snakes bite the fish with their spiny needles and inject the trout with poison?"

"No, Little Hare. Their teeth needles are only for grasping frogs and quick little fish. They have nothing to inject. Nonetheless, even without fangs and poison glands, the bite of a water snake is most unpleasant. You will not die from its bite—but with a few bites, a day later you will be sick enough from it that you might wish you were dead."

"Yikes!" Jack said and his comical face brought a laugh from his teacher.

"*Wash-ching-geka* has a good sense of humor!" Hanging Moon chuckled. "Now we will fish."

Jack watched the chief probe the bank again for snakes, then softly ease himself down into the creek bed. Without words, Hanging Moon gestured for Jack to move down the bank far enough to get below a sharp turn where the current cut underneath the bank. Jack quickly walked to where he could enter the creek, grabbed a stick and probed the bank, then finding nothing, he copied the chief's soft entry into the stream.

Without asking, Jack silently answered a question which sprang to his mind. "Why walk so softly?" and the answer returned —"Because the fish would feel the vibrations from heavy steps and swim away."

A nod alert from Chief Hanging Moon and Jack watched him remove a folded parcel of what appeared to be plastic strings from a vest pocket. The packet came sailing to Jack, and he caught it in the air. When the boy started unfolding the parcel, he realized what he was opening was some kind of net, but its material wasn't plastic, wasn't what his own father had called 'monofilament line' when they fished below the tall bluff at the Granite River Dam.

"It's cat gut, Little Hare," explained the chief, and Jack decided he needed no further information on its origin or manufacture. It came to Jack, as if he was beginning to listen to the situation and the chief's thoughts, that he needed no instruction on what to do next. Fastening one end of the net to the underside of the bank where it rose from the dark creek bend ahead of it, the boy stepped out deeper, spreading the net until his foot found a good-sized rock. The boy slipped the bottom end of the net under the rock, stepped back toward the middle of the lines to hold the net's top as high as possible with both hands and nodded back to his teacher.

Hanging Moon's branch smacked the creek bank and then the creek itself, sending a shower of spray toward the boy. Jack reflexively ducked, then as he started to stand up, he realized the net was throbbing in his hands. With a sharp tug on the net bottom fastened to the rock and a hard sweep to swing the net's far end to the near end of the trap hooked to the bank, Jack discovered he had netted about a half-dozen indigo, cream, and crimson-dappled brook trout. With one more swing of the net, he tossed it and its flopping contents far up from the bank edge, reached for the creek bank top to support his exit, then just as quickly pulled his hand back.

"*Haho*, Brother Water Snake! You'll not bite me today!" said the boy, and he hauled himself up the bank using his stick to clear the grass and to support his climb.

Gully Hanging Moon had to say nothing to Jack. The boy heard the chief talking without words all the way back to the lodge. The conversation was about how to cook brook trout.

Chapter 52

FORRESTER'S PREDICTION WAS all too accurate. Herman von Himmel had to come up with another hundred thousand for bail for Gunther and him. Adolf would have to stay locked up. The old Nazi provided Forrester directions to another small stash of gold out away from the shed near the northeast corner of the barbed wire fence which kept the family's animals. Two days later, the men strode out the Hamot PD front door and braced themselves against a wind chill of five degrees below zero.

"I am damn tired of cleaning out your barn, watering your critters and throwing down hay for them!" the lawyer complained. Of course, Forrester neglected to mention that the permission he received to collect bail money from the property allowed him all the time in the world to continue his yet unrewarded search for von Himmel's buried treasure himself, a wolf pack notwithstanding.

"*Ya*, Lawyer Man, my heart breaks for you," replied old man von Himmel. Then in a hoarse whisper he said, "Now tell me that you have explained just enough of all this to Gunther, so he does not get suspicious." Gunther had already separated himself in order to grab a quick smoke.

"Yes, Herman. I did that, but sooner or later he is going to find out about your actions to kidnap Jack and your attempt to kill him.'

"I will make everything right with Gunther tonight when I take him and my son Karl's ashes to Monroe where we have our Nazi shrine. We call the rock bluff an Externstein here in Wisconsin just like in Germany. Our Irminsul is the shrine on top where we give sacrifice to Odin."

"And what on earth can you guys do at that hilltop shrine? You can't burn Karl's body on a funeral pyre of dry wood because he's already a jar of ashes. You sure as hell can't put him on a Viking longship and send him off into the Granite River with fire arrows because from what I've seen driving by, you are way the heck up on top of an impossibly tall bluff. I can't even figure out how on earth an old geezer like you will get up that big rock!"

"None of your business, lawyer man. As a younger man, I climbed. As an older man, I figure another way. Just understand this—tomorrow we don't have no more issues in the family about Jack.

Now just drive me to a phone booth again, then back to my trailer."

Forrester was just about to make a snappy reply, but something stopped him. Maybe it just was the strange way that von Himmel said "no more issues in the family," but the attorney's instincts rang the alarm bell in his brain to keep his nose out of whatever fanatical business the old Nazi was planning. Maybe von Himmel planned on divine intervention? Maybe the old Nazi would put in a long-distance call to Odin himself and resurrect Karl like a phoenix rising from ashes? Who the hell knew? What could it possibly matter?

It wasn't until late that afternoon that Herman von Himmel told Gunther to warm up the family pickup truck and bring it to the trailer front door. It was just about 4:00 pm, but the blustery grey sky and unusually bad cold snap made the day feel like late November. The single exception to the bleakness were the stunning little black and bright metallic-colored birds flitting around the von Himmel barnyard. Appropriately enough, they were goldfinches.

When Herman decided the old F-150 was ready, he stepped out the front door with his hands full of plastic-wrapped sandwiches, two coffee thermoses, and an urn containing Karl's remains.

"*Ya,* you warmed the truck nice and toasty, Gunther!" exclaimed his father as the old man slid himself onto the front seat bench and laid down his packages between them.

It was the first nice thing Gunther could remember Herman said to him all year long. That realization, however, left his son with only a residue of sour memories.

"Now, Gunther, I don't think you remember how to get to the Granite River dam." his father said.

"I just remember how long the drive to get there seemed, how big and fast the river was, and how awful it was to climb up that big bluff. When we got on top, I was so afraid of what was up there, I really can't recall what I saw. It's still a blur."

"It was all right to be afraid then. We worshipped Odin there," explained von Himmel. "Odin, he is a god of blood, death, and war. The ritual was to appease him with violence and sacrifice. You are better off not remembering what I did there or who I did it to."

"Ok. I'm heading into Hamot now. What road do I take next? How far is it gonna be?"

"You go close to town, then turn left on Highway 21 and drive for about an hour. A few miles past the town of Monroe we come to the bluff on the right just as we approach the river."

Herman von Himmel cleared his throat with a customary cough, and Gunther knew that was the signal for questions and conversation to end. A cup of coffee and a sandwich was set on the dash for him, but what he wanted was to ask his father what exactly they would be doing when they arrived. He wanted to ask how on earth someone approaching age sixty would be able to make the brutal climb up the bluff. But more than twenty years of screaming threats, shaming dramas and terrifying blows spoke in very convincing terms about the risks of talking out of turn. Gunther cleared his throat too. The gesture made him feel a little more equal to his father. One day Gunther decided the time would come....

The trip to the Granite River dam didn't take as long as Gunther thought. The food and drink tasted good enough to ease the tension. The highway had little traffic and despite the early freezes no snow had begun blanketing the roads and slowing speeds to a winter crawl.

"There is the Externstein bluff and on top, our Irminsul!" the old man told Gunther, announcing the obvious to his son. The height of the bluff as the road led them near, its steep upward angles and sheer rock face made the notion of a climb a daunting idea. Maybe there was secret path wondered Gunther?

In the next instant everything came clear. The truck had to drive past the bluff, over the bridge to its far southeast side and use the parking lot down beside the Granite River. As he slowed the pickup to prepare for the entrance just past the parking lot, Gunther was absolutely astonished to see a military helicopter there with the words "Air Force National Guard" stenciled across the bottom of the pilot's windshield. Then below those words were more that proclaimed the chopper came from the nearby air base at Volk Field in Camp Douglas. Gunther braked hard, swiveled the truck into a sharp right turn and allowed its remaining speed and gravity to coast them into a parking lot space.

The truck had not even come to a full stop before the pilot switched on the power and the rotor blades started to spin. His face was covered by a dark visor, but his continuous glances and nervous head bobs made it evident he was likely doing something with the aircraft that he shouldn't be doing and wanted to get this flight over fast.

As the von Himmels opened the aircraft door to squeeze inside, the pilot kept his visor down to conceal his appearance and spoke in an affected lower tone of voice. He looked directly at Herman and said— "After your phone call, somebody told me to give you a lift up the bluff. You'll have to make your own way down," and before old von Himmel could open his mouth to reply, the pilot jammed the accelerator forward so quickly the entire aircraft shook as it lifted from the parking lot. In a dizzying rush of speed, ear-splitting noise and altitude, the helicopter shot straight up in vertical ascent.

The pounding vibration and sickening acute angle of rise made Gunther force back a mouthful of bile and phlegm. Then, before he had adjusted to the ride, they were on top of the bluff, and the man with the dark visor was pointing to get out. Herman von Himmel scrambled to grab the urn, leave the plane, and walk low far enough away to be safe from the whirling blades. Gunther was right behind and just as he put his first foot on the ground, the copter jerked up and away from the two men, speeding off to the west head for Volk Field.

"My old man is one mean S.O.B.," thought Gunther, "but his Nazi contacts are amazing! Who would think old Herman could dial up a helicopter ride to the top of this river bluff to bury his son?"

Gunther von Himmel shook his head in small wonderment at that thought, but as he looked up and around him, the hilltop scene sucked all the breath from his body. While the flight to the hilltop had been crazy but short, what Gunther took in now as he looked about was nearly indescribable. At first it wasn't about anything he saw—it was about what he felt. He felt the bitter north wind racing across the bluff top sawing him in half with teeth of pure ice.

The vista jumped out at him next. Gunther faced northeast and from that vantage point he was looking at the massive Granite River reservoir held back by an earthen dike that seemed to stretch forever eastward. Spewing out of the spillway, the turgid, swirling currents of the wide river tore southward the evil spirits on a Halloween night ride. He was a small child on his first visit here. Now nothing could have prepared him for this portrait of raw power.

Off to his left, the western horizon still glimmered with blaze orange and hot pink embers of a setting north country sun. Front and center, Granite River dam loomed darkly up from misty tangles of tailrace water, a medieval stone bastion of power, ablaze with miles long strings of spotlights conjuring an incongruous landscape of forest tangle and the vast poured-out motion of a raceway producing a roar clearly audible all the way up the bluff.

A thunderous whuff and sudden swirl of combusting air ripped Gunther's attention away from the north and its dam, demanding instead he turn and face a conflagration of fire and smoke behind him to the south.

There, towering with black magic majesty, rose a gigantic swastika, its limbs so large it seemed impossible to have been carried to this place. Inside the two crooked pieces of the Nazi cross, spearing the night sky like a Teutonic lance, rose a rugged, twisted wooden telephone pole with spiked steps. And the crowning centerpiece atop the Irminsul spire rested the fierce head of a monstrous stone eagle, a delicately balanced candelabra of pure menace, its deadly eyes reflecting the instant flames from the funeral pyre the old Nazi set for his lost son.

Had Forrester been there he would have chosen the word 'phantasmagoria' as an apt descriptor. But he wasn't there, and Gunther had no eloquent words. In fact, he was petrified, and his situation was only intensified by the sight of his father, naked before the swastika, one eye removed, a dagger in his belt, insanely dancing about as he swung his necklace in one hand while holding Karl's urn in the other. Herman was wildly chanting something like a German prayer, but his ritual had transformed him into a Satan of the bizarre.

At the orgasmic peak of the chanting and dance, the old man, now lathered in sweat and smoke, firmly gestured for Gunther to meet him in the center of the spectacle. When his father started moaning the phrase 'Odin be praised,' Gunther realized there was no choice but to obey. No sooner than he stepped into the bonfire's circle, however, than his father threw himself upon his son, cracking the urn and strewing his brother's ashes over both, and kissing his son forcefully on the mouth while simulating intercourse with Gunther's groin.

It was, in a single word that burst into Gunther's mind . . . insane.

Then the orgy of death and sacrifice ended as abruptly as it had begun. While Gunther staggered away to try to reassemble his sanity, Herman von Himmel tossed the remaining pieces of Karl's urn into the funeral pyre, sliced a tiny cut into his forearm with the dagger, spilled a few drops of blood on the eagle's head pole and silently walked away to put his clothes back on. After a few moments, fighting back waves of disgust, Gunther followed his father to a small opening in the rock wall surrounding the altar area, and together, a torch in Herman's hand, they began the long descending path back to the parking lot.

Chapter 53

WHEN HERMAN SUDDENLY decided to stop as they walked down the chiseled rock steps cut into the bluff, Gunther nearly jumped out of his skin. His mind was still in tumult from the events on top at the altar. He subconsciously leaned away from his father when the old man turned to address him.

"Now, my son, I got something I got to tell you about. It's about Jack."

From somewhere deep inside Gunther anger and fear wrestled with each other in a life-or-death match. "What about my boy, Jack? What has happened to him?"

"He is alive, Gunther," said von Himmel. "But he told the cops on us, and that includes you! The chief of police hid him away until our trial comes due." The old man paused for a moment, then added, "I knew we got to get him away from those police boys and convince him to change his testimony."

"Then I found out where Jack was being kept," said his father. "I had two other Nazis steal him away and bring him to our trailer. After I paid those two men off with some of my gold, he and Gunther and me went way back in the Goodyear to dig up some more of my loot in order to pay the lawyer man I got to defend us."

"Ok. I am following what you are saying, but it was a big mistake to show those two bad guys from the Twin Cities that you had real gold," said Gunther.

"*Ja*! That's true. It was a bad mistake all right," von Himmel confessed. "So when we got out to the marsh lake where my money was hid, those two Nazis popped out of the woods and demanded more. I stabbed one of them with this knife here," and von Himmel pointed to the knife in his belt. "Adolf hit the other over the head with a hammer. Jack dived into the lake to get away. The boy doesn't know how it all turned out. He just decided to run for his life."

"What happened after that?" Gunther asked.

"After they tried to shoot us and the struggle was over, me and Gunther eventually killed them," explained the old man. "I sent Adolf to save Jack, but he couldn't find him. Later, Adolf came back empty-handed so he helped me cut up the bodies, break the bones and throw the mess into the swamp lake where the cops can't find anything."

"And when you finished disposing of those two guys?"

"Adolf and me, we head back to the trailer. But the Indian cops were already there waiting in ambush. I fought it out with them, but their sheriff aimed a shotgun at Adolf and blew off his right hand. Then they took us into the Hamot jail. Forrester got me off on some more bail, but Adolf has to sit because he took two shots at those Indians."

"My god! Tell me if you know where Jack is," demanded Gunther.

"I am hoping you can tell me, my son."

"What in hell do you mean—'I can help you locate Jack.'"

Von Himmel wet his lips before continuing. "I think the Indian cops must still have him. If they do, then he would be held by their best leader and fighter, I think, and kept way out in the reservation woods where nobody can find him."

"Stop right there, *Vater!*"

"What you mean—you telling me to stop!" von Himmel was about to blow up one more time, but Gunther's expression stopped him.

"I absolutely know the area where they must be hiding Jack."

"*Got in Himmel!* How you know that?" Herman von Himmel was mystified.

"It's easy for someone like me who worked for many years beside plenty of Ho-Chunk who help harvest cranberries in the fall. They often talk about life on their Black River Falls reservation, and many of them like to brag about their war chief. His name is Gully Hanging Moon—"

"What the hell kind of name is that?" interrupted von Himmel.

"Hell, I don't know," Gunther said. "But the man, according to the people from his tribe I talked to, is one big, tough son-of-a-gun who lives out somewhere on Cheney Road, up on Big Stony Lonesome Peak by himself, and nobody dares mess with him. The best part is he never has a gun!"

Old man von Himmel was in pure ecstasy with this news. He grasped Gunther in a man embrace, slapping him on the back and laughing hysterically. "Odin be praised! This is the best of news we could get, Gunther! You and me, we go find Jack and rescue him from that Injun man. Right? Then we convince him to change his testimony, and we are free!"

It was all too much for Gunther. He had to lean into a small crevice to sit down for a minute. Digging into his coat pockets, he found a pack of Marlboros, shook out a cigarette, lit it, inhaled deeply, and in the most serious tone he could muster he said, "You're right, Dad. We do have to get Jack away from their war chief. It helps that he has no guns."

"So what is the problem?"

"The problem is just climbing that hill could kill both of us," and Gunther took another long drag on his cigarette and coughed. "Maybe me, but you can't hike up the Stony Lonesome, much less sneak up on somebody as skilled as I hear that chief is."

"Then what are you saying we should do?"

"Send in hired guns with me, that's what!" explained Gunther. He had to choke off a smoker's cough before continuing, "Your Nazi contacts won't likely be sending us any more help, but this time, get your lawyer buddy to send us three hitmen from the KKK. We can sneak up that hill from each of the four directions. It won't matter if we use cannons to kill the chief 'cause nobody will hear the shots way out there anyway. And who would KKK people like to kill besides niggers, huh? I bet they would see this as a good chance for a little sporting fun and live target practice on redskins!"

Herman von Himmel scratched his chin, his face revealing instant calculations he was making. "This I agree with," he said. "It will cost me about a hundred grand for three of their killers, but that still leaves me with a little more savings from my *vater* that I will show you about when all this is over. Remember my gold is the support for our family!"

"Right, *Vater*!" and Gunther's face blossomed into a wide grin. Inside, however, he understood the day that his father showed him where the gold was, would be the old man's last day in this world. The thought made Gunther smile even more broadly.

"Let us get down this bluff now, Gunther. We go home and tomorrow you drive me in to see Forrester. If I offer him enough money, he will do anything to get it."

"Sounds like a typical lawyer!" Gunther said, and both men joined in a good laugh.

Chapter 54

JACK DECIDED THAT smoked brook trout cooked with the skin on, split open on a stick over a bed of fruit wood coals and a bowl of wild rice with cranberry slivers and blueberries was the most sensational meal he had ever tasted.

"Whoa! —do not eat so fast that you choke yourself, Little Hare," cautioned Gully Hanging Moon. The two of them were seated around the last remains of a campfire. Jack hadn't heard the old joke about Indians make small fire, sit close—white men make big fire, sit far away, until the chief began preparing their first hot meal together. When Chief Hanging Moon told the old joke that evening, Jack laughed out loud. When he thought back to the few bonfires his family ever had out in the marsh, the size of their bonfires was enormous and wasteful.

Now, with the temperature in free fall so early in October, there was great comfort and warmth sitting close and looking into the flaming shards of the fire, even if the campfire was a small one.

"We must do some thinking and deciding now, *Wash-ching-geka*!" and when Jack heard his teacher use the boy's native name, he instantly came to taut attention. Jack tamped down hard on his natural tendency to say something like "Yes, Chief," in return. He realized his straightened posture and focused eyes already used the body language he was learning to speak with. Jack just sat, listening, and waiting.

"I have tried to teach you some basic duties and skills of a warrior. Tonight, we take another step." Jack leaned forward slightly and simply nodded.

"First question to you, young brave. What is the first duty of a warrior?"

"To be silent in order to protect his loved ones and to protect himself."

"Yes. Good. But how do you best do your duty to communicate and protect?"

Jack was still doing well in the test, he thought. He answered immediately— "Silence allows me to listen. I can hear what others are saying and doing if I am quiet. Their bodies will talk to me. My body can talk to whatever person I want when they see me."

"That is so, Little Hare," said Hanging Moon. "Now here is a tougher question, but one you should have the answer for—how do you listen and talk when you cannot see or hear your enemies or friends?"

Jack almost stood in his eagerness to answer—"By knowing and thinking about what we both now call ...the situation. If I think hard about what you refer to as 'what has to happen' in a situation, if I listen to what I can anticipate must happen, I can know and do what has to be done."

"*Haho, Wash-ching-geka!* You have earned a fine breakfast tomorrow morning!

Jack breathed in a lungful of cold, night air. It was wonderful to pass what he realized were tests each day that had immediate and negative consequences if he failed—but wonderful positive rewards when he succeeded. Yes, he decided, there was nothing so sweet as passing the test.

"Now for your supper tomorrow, I have another question for you—and one if you use what you just told should have an obvious answer," explained Hanging Moon.

Jack gulped. He had not expected two tests all at once, but as he considered it, he realized that the tests naturally had to become more and more challenging. He looked at the chief and nodded he was ready.

"My question to you, Little Hare, is this: What has to happen next?"

Jack felt his hear sink, and it had been such a wonderful day until this moment. Nobody could read the future, right? He would have to go hungry tomorrow at suppertime. The boy truly hated the idea of admitting failure. He despised the idea of disappointing the first adult male he had grown to respect and admire. Then as Jack looked down into the campfire, it came to him. He could use the lessons he had just enumerated to say what the chief required.

"What has to happen next? Well, the situation is that I am here hiding with you from a family that has tried to kill me, and you are teaching me how to survive," summarized the boy.

"Yes. That is true," said the chief. "But I am not asking what the present situation is. We both know what that is. I am asking you to tell me what you should know must happen in the future."

"They must find me and kill me. I must learn from you how to fight and defeat them."

"I see another dinner of brook trout and wild rice in your future, young brave!" grinned the chief. After a few seconds of considering his future, Jack decided he could smile a little too.

"Without you asking me, I want to go ahead and think some more about what has to happen, if that is all right to you, Chief," said the boy.

"This is good. A young warrior just like a growing young bird must begin to leave the nest and survive on his own," affirmed Hanging Moon.

"I must learn to use a weapon. I expect that you will help me choose and practice with it," said Jack.

"That is so, Little Hare. My weapon is a bow and arrow. It shoots as far as I can see in these dense pine forests, it does not malfunction in the cold or wet, and most of all…"

"It is silent!" Jack exclaimed. And in the same breath, the boy said, "but a bow and arrow is not a good fit for me."

The chief remained silent and expressionless at this announcement, waiting on the boy.

Jack continued— "It seems to me that I must pick a weapon I can learn to use quickly. A bow and arrow will take too much time considering men could come for me tonight. I need something that is easy to learn to use, and I obviously need it to be absolutely silent!"

"What will be your weapon, Little Hare?"

"A lance that I can jab with or if I have to, throw!" and both man and boy passed a knowing look between them. This next lesson would be one of life or death.

Chapter 55

"**HELLO, FORRESTER!** —**AND** don't bother turning on the room lights, my friend."

N. B. Forrester didn't need to turn on the lights to know that George Sheldon was sitting in the dark at the back of his motel room. Of course, as Forrester parked his car outside just outside, he had checked to see the lot was empty. But finding the KKK's president was not an entire surprise.

"How do, George!" replied the Midwest Director of the KKK, affecting a palsy, southern good old boy affectation in response. "Must be terribly hot down in Georgia to bring the head of the clan all the way up to the frozen tundra of Hamot, Wisconsin."

"Is that a question or just an observation?" The voice in the dark corner brought a tiny red dot to his mouth and blew a long puff of cigarette smoke in Forrester's direction.

"Maybe both, Mr. President. How long have you been sitting here in the dark waiting? If you had told me you were up for a visit, I would have selected a little supper club with some good red meat and strong beer."

"Oh, I wouldn't want any meeting like that for what business needs to be transacted tonight,' replied the president, and turning toward the door to the bathroom and the feeble light its partially opened door provided, he said in a louder voice— "Step in here, boys. I want you to meet the worst attorney the Klan has ever hired."

The door swung fully open, and two men silently walked out. Forrester didn't recognize the first one, even in the improved light. He was rather short, had skiss, razor cut bleached hair, wore a pin stripe dark suit, and restlessly wormed a toothpick back and forth across his tight, expressionless lips. As the new man moved to stand on the far side of Sheldon, the President slapped the man's rear end and said, "This is, Danny, the second-best problem solver in our organization, Mr. Lawyer Man!" and the intentional reference to von Himmel nearly paralyzed Forrester. He began to count how many minutes he had to live.

The second man emerging was a near giant and someone the lawyer recognized instantly. Forrester tried to force a bit of smile as he said, "Hi, Fritz! Long time, no see!" But the huge man only raised one massive arm, his left, to stroke his completely bald but tastefully tattooed head. Then he stood by

Sheldon, rivetted in place except for a quick twisting of his neck from side to side. The lawyer could hear muscles and ligaments snapping in place.

"You already are friends with Fritz, here," and KKK leader slapped the giant's backside too. "I don't have to tell you that he is our number one problem solver, do I?"

"Nope, I know all I need to about how Fritz solves problems," replied Forrester and desperately trying to use surprise to his advantage, the defense lawyer added— "and all of you couldn't have come to help at a better time!"

"Whaddya you mean—help?" Sheldon angrily responded.

"Well, of course I mean help," replied Forrester who knew he had to seize the offensive while the opportunity was there. "I know Herman von Himmel has offered a million bucks to our organization providing we get him and his son Gunther off entirely and Adolf only does a couple years…there is nothing that I want more dearly than to make sure we get that money."

"Glad to hear it, Forrester, but Herman blames you for all his problems and is telling me that he's not so sure you are up to the job. The boys and me just made a fast run up to this Siberian nightmare of a town to find out for ourselves what you are doing, or maybe not doing."

"And has Herman told you what he has been doing without telling me?" Forrester was on the attack now and he felt good about it.

"Doing what without telling? You're his lawyer! You're our lawyer in this!"

"Oh, you mean he didn't tell you how on his own he had two Nazi hitmen from St. Paul kidnap his grandson out of protective custody? He didn't tell you that Adolf and he tried to take the boy out into the marshes to kill him but were surprised when the hitters showed up for more loot and had to die? And I'm wondering if old Herman happened to mention that his son Adolf shot it out with Ho-Chunk deputies back at their trailer and lost his right hand in the process of letting Jack get away? Or that Adolf is back in intensive care full of gangrene!"

His fast summary hit its mark. Sheldon shuffled nervously in his seat and, a nervous tick jittered across his right cheek and eye making it look like he was constantly blinking at Forrester.

"Uh—no," admitted the Klan leader. "He didn't tell me anything about that. And if all that you are saying is true, then it changes things."

"You damn right it changes things," Forrester said. "Herman von Himmel is doing to us what he constantly does to his own family—he tells them just enough of the truth to hide his lies and manipulations. Can't you see he is dangling a million bucks

in front of us to keep us from taking the lead ourselves? His game is to play everyone off each other—
divide and conquer. He'll sacrifice his entire family
and all of us to keep himself free and blameless."

"But a million in gold, Forrester. Think what that
kind of money would do for our cause!"

"A million from him I believe is pennies on his
dollars. He's got to have many times that amount
hidden out around his trailer and maybe other
places too," Forrester explained. "That is why,
George, it was brilliant on your part to see what he
was up to and come up here, like I said before, to
help me. Together the four of us can take control,
clean up this mess, and blackmail or torture that
crazy old Nazi into revealing where all his treasure
horde is hidden!"

George Sheldon laughed heartily and long.
"Damn, Forrester. I really didn't want to come up
here to Yankeesville and kill you! You've always
been so frickin' smart with all our previous cases."

The leader of the KKK stood up, walked across
the room, turned on all the light switches by the
inside front door and slapped the lawyer hard on his
near shoulder. The admission, while not a major revelation, still left Forrester shaky, his legs shivering
out of a combination of relief and tension. "Glad to
hear you say that, George!" and Mr. KKK laughed
even harder at Forrester's admission.

The president looked back to his associates and said, "Ok, boys. I've decided to let Mr. Lawyer here bring us way more than a measly one million. Our southern lawyer in the north just said we must take control. And that is dead right, providing that control brings us the von Himmel fortune."

Opening the door but holding out his left palm to indicate to his two assistants they should stay, Sheldon offered a couple of concluding remarks. "My two helpers over there," and he pointed to Danny and Fritz, "are now your helpers. Old Herman wanted three, but there's more fortune divided two ways, fifty thousand a piece. They will do anything you ask, no hesitation. Right, men?" and the two clansmen just barely moved their heads in assent.

"Tell me exactly what you plan to do with your new assistants, Lawyer Man."

Forrester had been preparing for this. The question was inevitable. "I want them to start hanging out in some broken-down old taverns near the Black River Falls' reservation and try to learn more about the leadership of the tribe from whites and natives alike. I want them to take Gunther von Himmel out drinking without letting Herman know about it. Once the boys here get Gunther drunk enough, it shouldn't be too hard to get him to tell everything he knows and plans. And as soon as we can get a good line on Jack's hiding place, we offer the von

Himmels some assistance in getting their boy back. In fact, Gunther can help!"

"You're making sense, Forrester," Sheldon said, "keep going...."

"The more I think about it," explained the lawyer, "I'd bet that old Herman is already trying to hire his own killers through the Nazis he knows. But his last two hires didn't work out too well, so when I offer him our two boys that could work very nicely in our favor."

It was much too fast for Sheldon. "How so?" he asked.

"I know your two men here are experts in death," Forrester said gesturing to Danny and Fritz. "When they track down and offer the ultimate test to Jack von Himmel and whoever is hiding him, there can be only one test result—one hundred percent murder!"

"Me like um your plan, Forrester!" chuckled Sheldon. "Just make sure you find us all the gold or coins or paper money out there." The KKK president turned to leave but thinking of something looked back over his shoulder and said, "You boys know what I expect. I expect results. Have some fun gunnin' for redskins and a high school kid!" And with that, he stepped out into the blackness of a late-night, small-town parking lot and literally vanished like a demon spirit in a cheap horror movie.

Chapter 56

"SHERIFF JOSIAH GREY Fox, let me introduce crime scene investigator and Director of the Federal Bureau of Investigation's crime lab—Lucille Mountain Wolf!" said Commander Post. He adroitly stepped from behind his office desk at the interstate headquarters building just outside of Hamot and brought his two outstretched arms together to bring the two individuals a little closer together.

"I am pleased to meet you, Ms . . . Mountain Wolf?" asked the sheriff.

"Just call me Director in front of the public and Lucy in private, Sheriff," and she extended her hand and provided a surprisingly strong, sure grip when they shook hands. "And I'm confident a tribal sheriff like you dismissed all that nonsense from the Commander about my titles" Looking at Post in mock-anger, the director said, "Shame on you, Fred!"

Grey Fox paused to assess what he saw in the Mountain Wolf. She was a bit taller than most First

Frederick Poss

Nation women, wore no makeup despite being a national administrator and scientist. Her strength of body and character spoke volumes. She wore her black hair straight and unadorned, which he liked. Her gaze and manner were direct, confident and she wore no wedding ring. The sheriff decided she was likely the perfect woman for him and just as likely completely above and beyond his life situation. A career woman, he decided...no chance!

"I grew up with the separate Winnebago tribe in Omaha when my father moved me there," Lucy continued as the three of them walked to a conference table across the room."

"But your grandmother was the original Mountain Wolf Woman of our Black River Falls tribe," finished Grey Fox with a knowing smile. Hey, he thought. No harm in trying!

"Why, yes, she was, Sheriff!" and the director's smile, Grey Fox realized, was the most beautiful aspect of her entire appearance. It was engaging, almost magnetic, and he felt that despite their status differences she truly appreciated he knew of her background.

"I love her and miss her still," Lucy said. "Before she passed in 1960, she was known as a strong leader even though she never was elected a chief!"

Sensing a little edge, maybe an agenda in the director's voice, Grey Fox nodded and replied,

"Perhaps she chose never to run for office? But, if she did, having met you, I think she would have made a great chief, whether in peace or in war!"

His remark seemed to be exactly the right thing to say now. When the director smiled broadly in return, it was not the public, political smile national figures use like throw-away tissues. Mountain Wolf's granddaughter truly appreciated Grey Fox for his comments as well as his understanding of a sensitive topic to her. The sheriff wondered if she was expecting a more dismissive remark about females as leaders from him. If she was, he was glad to disappoint. The long history of his tribe, he knew, proved they had often selected females in charge, even though the white society of America still hadn't elected its first woman president.

"All right, let's get right down to business, shall we?' asked Commander Post. Grey Fox had to stifle a grin. "Post says 'Let's get down to business" . . . what a surprise!"

"Yes, Commander. I completely agree," said Director Mountain Wolf. "And as I anticipated some of what must be done given the facts of the case, I have made a short list of steps I want to offer. Of course, I realize there is overlapping jurisdiction potential here. But I am here to get to the facts of murder, not play politics."

"Wonderful!" said the sheriff. "What are you thinking?'

"Yes," added Post. "The sheriff and I have agreed to an understanding about protecting Jack by keeping him safe on the reservation currently. He in turn has released Flaherty and the von Himmels into our custody and justice system."

"Works for me!" Lucille said. "Here is what I'd like to undertake. First, I need a room to sleep, some warm work clothes and hand tools to dig. Second, I need a couple helpers to bag the evidence I collect out in the marsh, providing we find a crime scene out there."

"What I need to find is tissue, fingers, or something that I can match to the fingerprints we already have on file from the men we suspect were murdered and dismembered on the marsh lake. If their bodies lie in little pieces on the bottom of a lake, a jury will likely conclude they were killed. The fact that Herman and Adolf von Himmel clothes carried the same tissue and blood evidence will make the connection that they did the killing. Third, I need a rubber suit if I am to be neck deep in a frozen marsh lake. Fourth, I need some propane heaters to keep people and any evidence from freezing solid . . . freezing could destroy the chemistry of chemical compounds I discover . . . we want to take every precaution. And fifth—

"You need plenty of hot coffee!" laughed Grey Fox, "just like the rest of us out there in the Goodyear Swamp!"

"But I think you forgot something you need to add to your list," said Commander Post. "Don't you need to bring in a bloodhound from somewhere to find the trail the von Himmels used when they took Jack out to kill him? And the dog we get should search beyond the burned area that Jack has described where the gunfight took place too, right?"

"I said I had anticipated some of what I need to investigate what happened out there, Commander," the director explained and reaching down into a large bag she pulled out a dog collar and extension leash. "You see, the wolf inside me already found a dog to live in my pack! I brought my own blood-hound—although when you meet *Cμkdjąk*, my pet, I think you will be looking at someone who is more than dog! Call him Wolf. I do."

Post sucked in enough flabbergasted air to last him into the next year.

"Of course!" exclaimed the sheriff. "We shouldn't expect anything less from a granddaughter of Mountain Wolf Woman!" Grey Fox beamed at Commander Post. "She's the real deal, sir," and he playfully added, "with a pet who has the Ho-Chunk name 'Wolf.' Maybe both get their noses to the ground and hunt together!"

Somehow Director Mountain Wolf didn't find the comment all that humorous. "You're wrong, Sheriff!" she said sternly. "But if Wolf needs any help, I'll just shape-shift myself into his mate, and we'll hunt down whatever or whoever we need."

Sheriff Grey Fox instantly regretted his words. "Please excuse my ignorant comments, Director. It's my nature to try to be a little humorous, and obviously, I wasn't. I apologize! I was wrong, and I am sorry." Then before the director responded, Grey Fox stepped closer to Post, whose face told everyone in the room he was lost in the threads of the conversation.

"Commander, I owe you an apology too," the sheriff said. "You probably don't know that a basic tenet of some First Nation religions is that some humans are not what they appear to be. A man or mountain wolf may look like a human being but in truth, he or she or it may be a shapeshifting, animal spirit."

"Uh—like a wendigo? Or a windigo?" offered Post.

"Something like that, Commander," explained Lucille Mountain Wolf. "Our Navaho brothers call them witches, other tribes call them shape shifters, but Ho-Chunk people do not accept belief in shape-shifting. Various Europeans and white Americans have named them wendigos, vampires, and every-thing else. There are big arguments about how all these beings are separate and different from each other. Even little kids call them boogey men, right? —and by the way Sheriff, apology accepted."

"Ok, I think I am beginning to get what you mean, Director," Post said.

"Every culture has some kind of name for people who are so evil they act like animals or for forces no one can explain," Grey Fox explained. "You and I meet some of these killers or their work at the worst of crime scenes. When captured, serial killers only look like they are human, but they have no con-science—only the animal need to kill and destroy. Call them whatever you want.

"But there is always a natural balance of things," the sheriff said. "We have names for heroes and beings that fight back against evil, too. Little kids have their Superman. Grownups have S.W.A.T. and SEAL Team members. Who knows? Given the evil the von Himmels are generating, maybe Earthmaker, our god, will send us someone who looks human but is an avenging animal spirt instead…just like Madam Director said."

"Or vice versa, Sheriff," the director replied, and a curiously serious expression passed across her face, like a small storm cloud on an otherwise sunny day. "Maybe Earthmaker or perhaps God the Father or Zeus himself sends us a straight up avenging animal spirit—period? No human or animal form to complicate matters. You know, there's nothing quite like the ghost of a black bear or a timber wolf to settle a score. Right?" A wry smile creased the director's lips.

"I think people make religion way too complicated," Mountain Wolf added. "The world is full of religions that have different names for evil beings. There is Satan, the devil, banshees, skinwalkers and so on. In the same way, there are different names for good spirits. Sheriff Grey Fox and I honor Earthmaker, Christians and Jews pray to Jehovah, Buddhists have their Buddha, and so on. Various names, but still just one God." Another wry smile appeared. "Maybe our beliefs are much more similar than different? . . . and by the way, my name is still Lucy, Sheriff," When he nodded in agreement, she coyly asked, "and can you help a girl move her luggage into the barracks down the hallway?"

"Sure thing. Just don't growl too much or haunt me, Lucy!" replied the sheriff, and all three of them had a good laugh.

Chapter 57

N. B. FORRESTER was feeling especially successful. Not only had he used his quick thinking and attack style of argument to save himself from George Sheldon and associates, but he also believed he had demonstrated his intellectual brilliance in other ways. After all, Danny and Fritz were temporarily defanged, sacked out in the motel room next to his. The poor babies were all worn out from the non-stop drive from Georgia to Wisfrozen, the lawyer decided.

And, just like perfection itself, his Mercedes Benz 280, four-door sedan—a vehicle he liked to call a sports car even with its luxury appointments—had started up the first time he turned the key, despite the crazy cold 10° temp at 5:00 AM when he awakened. Of course, getting up this early was not usually on Forrester's agenda, but he did not see much hope for getting the von Himmels off as lightly as expected. No, not likely…so that naturally provided

"And what are you doing out here, Attorney Forrester?" At his window, coming from behind the trailer, was Commander Post, and he wore a huge grin that almost matched the size of his winter parka.

"Right, Commander. I might ask you the same question," deflected Forrester.

"Oh, we're here to find evidence of the kidnapping and attempted murder of Jack von Himmel, as well as the murder of two Nazi hitmen that Herman von Himmel hired and later

disposed of." Then Post gave Forrester a broad smile, dazzling enough to match any that the attorney could paint across his surprised face.

"And you'll be happy to read all about it in these search warrants!" said the commander as he reached inside his coat, removed the legal documents, and waited until the attorney lowered his car window to examine them.

Forrester was still looking through the warrants when Commander Post added, "Of course, if you remain entirely out of the way, you can observe from a distance. But make the mistake of getting in the way, and I'll have you thrown out of here faster than you can say 'Jack Scratch!'

"I don't need some overly promoted token black to make any condescending warnings to me, Commander. I know the law, and the law allows me to observe—even if it is at a distance," Forrester retorted. And the defense attorney was just about to slip on a pair of thick gloves he purchased at the Cash and Carry, when his peripheral vision picked out two unusual objects.

Advancing out of the von Himmel trailer was the largest, collared grey wolf the lawyer could possibly imagine, and holding its leash was an incredibly good-looking woman despite the fact she was nearly engulfed by a fur-lined, snow-white parka that had F.B.I. stenciled across the left shoulder in bold, blue letters.

The animal and the woman were all business. They came out of the trailer almost as if they were in hot pursuit of escaping suspects. Ignoring what Post had just said, Forrester sprung out of his car door and sprinted toward the two hunters. His door slamming shut temporarily halted the search.

"Whoah there!" he called out. "Wait up for a minute!" Forrester pleaded as he rapidly approached the woman and her wolf. The problem was the attorney, thoughtlessly filled with ego and overconfidence, came on a bit too fast and a bit too close. The wolf on the leash, without a hint of noise, whirled back from the trail and lunged at him. Forrester needed all his athleticism to leap back just in time to avoid its snapping jaws.

"Damn that thing!" Forrester screeched in a voice a bit too high to convey his usual masculinity.

"Be nice to pets, and they will be nice to you... don't be nice and—" The huntress holding the leash provided a sweet smile but made no attempt to pull her dog back from its attempt to remove Forrester's left foot.

"You can't threaten me with that wolf!" snarled Forrester.

"I'm not doing the threatening. You are!" she stated in a reasonable, steady tone of voice. "Whoever you are, this is a police investigation site. Not only shouldn't you be this close to me—for your own safety, you shouldn't be close to my dog. If you take just a minute to look around, you'll see that not even police officers who do have permission to be near me have any intention of getting close." Then the woman said something to her pet that Forrester couldn't quite make out, and it returned to her side while never taking its eyes off the attorney.

"I am Lucille Mountain Wolf, Director of the F.B.I.'s crime lab in Washington D.C. And you just met my tracking dog, Wolf! He's g part grey wolf and part me! He's smarter than most crooks and tolerates no one around us that he doesn't know." She reached down, roughly stroked her dog, and looked back up at him. "Who the heck are you?'

Unconsciously, Forrester stepped back from the director and her dog, then gained his focus and replied, "I'm N. B. Forrester, the von Himmel's defense attorney." Then stepping forward to his original position, the lawyer sneered, "and I know all about you, Lucille!"

"So—you're Forrester, the Midwest lawyer for one of my favorite targets to investigate—the KKK! And if you call me by my first name one more time, I'm going to accidentally lose my grip on Wolf!" And if the dog did not understand her words, certainly he understood her tone and strained forward against the leash to get at the lawyer.

"You can't—" and then the lawyer took a close look at her pet and decided the better part of valor was discretion. "So how come your, ah, animal doesn't bark, doesn't make any noise?"

"Because he was supposed to be roadkill, Forrester. I found him on a logging road, hit by a lumber truck I guess, nearly dead and vocal cords smashed," said the director. "Wolves have absolute love for their mate. In caring for him and saving his life, I became his packmate—and he became mine. You likely can't understand the concept of living things sharing their innermost spirit in a lifelong bond—but make no mistake, Wolf and I have that."

Then pulling in Wolf by an extra arm length, Director Mountain Wolf stepped forward toward Forrester and said, "Now get off my crime scene!"

Forrester stood transfixed, a tumult of emotions swirling inside him. He had never met a female that rivaled him in confidence, intelligence, and good looks. Lucille Mountain Wolf was the most perfect woman Forrester had ever met. He was overcome with her magnetic strength and beauty. His heart and brain shouted, "This is the woman of your dreams; the mate your heart and your mind have always craved!" Lucille wasn't a sweet little pluckable peach like Sue Ellen, his secretary. Lust, in its purest form, had been a desire unknown to Forrester, unknown until this very moment.

"Yeah, sure. I will step back to my lawful place, Director," the lawyer said in his most congenial manner. "Just keep a good grip on our mutual friend Wolfie there," and with that, the von Himmel attorney slowly backed away without losing sight of the dog. Forrester immediately strode back to his vehicle, turned on the engine to let it warm him and tried to understand what had just happened.

Across the yard, he saw the wolf and investigator already entering the marsh grass near the shed. Upon seeing the animal go to work, Forrester's first thought was how deadly a silent wolf attack would be to an intruder. No warning growl, no warning anything! Just the sudden snap of a foot leaving an ankle bone. Or the whoosh of a throat instantly torn out.

But these thoughts were deeply enticing to the lawyer. He craved raw, bloody violence—it was his turn on! The sheer savagery of teeth ripping flesh and breaking bone excited him, mentally, emotionally, and even sexually. Lucille Mountain Wolf was every bit as wild as her wolf dog. The thought of rough sex with a native woman from a race he considered savages excited Forrester enough to kiss his lips in pleasure.

Yes, she was every kind every kind of forbidden fruit the lawyer could imagine—a redskin who the KKK boys would love to rape, humiliate, and maybe even kill; a bold, brash female in a position of power that his Klan brothers would hate even if she were white. And worst of all—she was a leader in an organization sworn to defeat the purpose of his hate group. The more Forrester considered her, the more desperate he became to have her in every way he could...if only once!

Chapter 58

"COME, LITTLE HARE," said Gully Hanging Moon as Jack and he cleaned their breakfast bowls. "This morning you will begin to learn how to use a spear."

"That is good!" Jack replied, trying to be brief with his words. Yet, in the boy's mind he couldn't help but think the lesson would only last a few minutes. Pick up lance. Reach back. Throw! —or at least stab with it! What else could there be?

"*Wash-ching-geka* thinks there isn't much to learn about fighting with a lance?" The way the war chief of the Ho-Chunk tribe asked the question, it sounded very much like a conclusion.

"Sorry. I keep forgetting that my body is talking to you all the time," Jack affirmed. "And, yes, that is exactly what I was thinking."

"I say yet again. Little Hare must never forget the first duty of a warrior if you expect to survive what we know inevitably must come up the hill for us."

"You are right, Chief. I must learn, and I must learn now!"

"Let us go outside my hut. We will pick a limb for a shaft, decide if you want a spearhead or not, and finally learn to jab, parry and throw it."

"*Pinagigi!*" Jack said, and with the typical energy of a fifteen-year-old on an adventure, he asked, "So what kind of tree limb do I need? A six-footer? Less? More?"

"First things first, Little Hare. Before you select a tree limb length, you must first decide what kind of tree you will use."

"So the type of wood actually matters, Chief?"

"Yes. If you want to always keep the weapon in your hands, then you need a strong wood like oak to jab and parry," explained Hanging Moon.

"And if I decide to take the one-time chance to throw my lance and maybe lose it, I will need a lighter wood…maybe willow or ash?"

"Yes, Little Hare. That is good thinking. But you must decide now."

"Then I decide to have two spears, Chief. One of oak and one of willow. If I keep the weapon in my hands, I drop the willow and use the oak one. If I throw the willow, I keep the oak one for backup."

"Excellent, young brave. But having two lances, one in each hand, has some problems too."

"How can that be? Aren't two weapons better than one?"

"Perhaps," nodded Hanging Moon. "But it is harder to be quiet with two spears banging against brush and trees. It is harder to run fast with two spears. If you jab, you need to use both hands, so you must drop your throwing lance. What you gain in quantity, you lose in quality. This is why your final decision may determine whether you live or die in battle."

"I would have never thought of that, Chief!" the boy answered. "But somehow the idea of two spears—one to throw and one to jab—feels right in my heart and mind."

"Then two it is! First look about this hillside. You will find a good oak limb up here. As you are a tall young warrior, your jabbing spear should be a foot longer than you are," explained Hanging Moon.

"I'm tall for fifteen...almost six feet, so I'll find an oak limb seven feet or a little longer," Jack announced.

"That is good, Little Hare, but make sure the limb is straight and has no knots in it.'

"Why make sure there are no knots?" asked Jack.

"Because the knots are weak points where the spear can break under stress!"

The advice rang true in the boy's mind, so he immediately began casting about the hillside for the limb he needed. The search took more time than Jack anticipated, but twenty minutes later he found a straight piece of oak wood, without knots and with a taper that fit his hands.

"What's next, Chief? Should we look for a willow or ash limb next?"

"Perhaps, Little Hare. We could also finish what you found before we look for something else."

"Ok!" Jack agreed enthusiastically. "How do we make a jabbing spear?'

"First, you must find the exactly right weapon that is hiding in the limb you picked," explained his tutor. "Hold the limb in your hands, use both. Find the exact balance point in the limb that also matches a comfortable grip size for you to hold. The gripping spot should be a little bigger than your hands, so it provides strength and power for close-in fighting!"

Jack struggled with this decision. He moved both his hands up and down the length of the limb before settling on a gripping spot slightly higher than the middle.

"This is the spot, Chief Hanging Moon. It feels just right to both my hands."

"Then young brave, you are ready to cut off the ends of the limb to the exact length and thickness you want but leave a little extra near the narrow point in case you want a sharp point."

"I don't want a spear for hand fighting that has metal or sharp rock at the narrow end. I think my enemy could use the backend of the blade to get leverage and force the weapon out of my hands!" explained the boy. "I'll just go with sharpening the wood into a point."

"That is a good reason, Little Hare. But if you do that, remember it means you must use all your force to drive the wood point as deeply as you can into your opponent. It is a hard job physically. It is even a harder thing to do in your mind and heart."

"Yes, Chief. But I am certain that is what is best for me."

"*Haho, Wash-ching-geka!* A warrior must know his own mind!"

"What are all the rest of the steps for my jabbing spear, Chief?" The boy's excitement was irrepressible.

"We must cut it to the exactly right length. Then you must shave off all its bark to make it smooth but still balanced. Next, you must make a point and harden it in fire to keep it strong. Finally, the spear should be stained with a dark oil to make it hard to see."

"Yes, Chief. But before I start finishing this weapon, I want to get the throwing lance limb so I can work on both weapons one step at a time. My *Opa*, uh—my grandfather talked to me about the the

Spear of Destiny, a weapon belonging to Odin, the god of Viking warriors."

"Yes, Little Hare. What of it?"

"Well, I will go Odin one better," the boy announced. "I'm going to make myself two of them…and then I'll have both Spears of Destiny, one for Odin and one for me. That's what!"

"Very good, Little Hare. Follow me to the trout stream where there are many good willow limbs— and a few snakes. We again will pick a straight limb without knots, balance its length, find a gripping spot, cut its ends but leave an extra length for the spear tip, shave it, split the narrow end, insert a spear point, bind it to the wood, then fire harden the entire weapon."

"And after that, Chief, you must teach me how to use my spears of destiny to jab, parry and throw," said Jack.

"Yes, I do, Little Hare . . . but you did not need say that out loud."

Chapter 59

"**IT ONLY MAKES** sense for your family and my Klan brothers here to join up," Forrester argued to Herman and Gunther von Himmel. At the lawyer's suggestion they all met up at the Townline Tap, a local watering hole—emphasis on hole—for a few brews and a meeting of the minds.

"Damn, that's good beer!" exclaimed Fritz. "Who in the hell makes this stuff? I've never tasted anything as good before down South!"

Forrester frowned. He knew if the conversation strayed off target into beer quality, he could never get the two sides to agree to join forces and hunt down Jack von Himmel.

"It's called Leinies," explained Gunther as he threw down a half-bottle in a single swig. "Look at the label. It says Leinenkugels. Best dang beer east of the Mississip, and you southern boys should like it 'cause it's strong. It's got extra juice above your run-of-the-mill light beers."

"Lemme try some of that there Wisconsin brew—" said Danny, as he elbowed his way through some local toughs to get his place at the crowded bar. He took a minute to dust off what he perceived as some kind of particles of dust from his suit jacket after encountering the suspenders and farm overalls of the man next to Forrester. Once he accomplished the cleaning routine, he had to slowly and with great deliberation remove the ever-present toothpick from his mouth.

"Damn—that is good beer!" Danny exclaimed. "Strong stuff, too!"

"*Ja*, your buddy already said that!" snapped Herman von Himmel, as his immense right hand engulfed a second bottle.

"Ok, everybody's got a beer now. Let's take this meeting over there to a nice, dark corner table and find some privacy," suggested Forrester. Once he heard the jeering quality in Herman's voice, the lawyer immediately knew he had to get the topic of hunting down the kid re-established. He put his arms around Herman and Fritz, nodded to Gunther and Danny and gently pushed them toward the far corner table just beyond the pool table.

He felt much better once everyone finally sat down.

"I have a mutual solution to a mutual problem," Forrester suggested.

"But you don't got no bottle of beer, yet!" growled Gunther. "Take one of mine. I still got two more," and with the gifted beer came a profuse cloud of cigar smoke.

Forrester suppressed his urge to take the bottle and smash Gunther across the top of his head. Instead, he responded to a man who clearly liked beer as much as a bar fight by offering him a wide smile, a wink of the eye to say 'you're right' and a friendly pat on the back.

"Thanks, my friend. Now I'm all set!" Forrester said as he took the beer bottle offered and intentionally slowed his pace down to accommodate the situation. "I propose a toast, gentleman!" he said next.

"To what, Lawyer Man?" Herman asked sharply.

"Crime, Herman. Here's to Crime! Bottles up!" and Forrester forced down a serious gulp of Wisconsin's finest. As he did so, he took the time to glance at his drinking audience. His toast had been the perfect tonic to set the tone of 'Hail Fellows, Well met!" Now the group was united in spirit and spirits.

As he was first to drink, he was also first to finish. Forrester seized the opportunity. "The way I see it is just as Herman sees it," the lawyer said giving a flattering nod to the old Nazi. "If the von Himmel family is going to stay out of twenty-five years or more of prison, they have to find where Jack is being kept, get him away from there and convince him to change his testimony about the bombing."

Gunther belched, then leaned forward over the table, pointed his beer at the lawyer, swung it to include the rest of the group and said, "Gently! We gotta gently convince Jack. After all, he's just a dumb kid. Just a freshman in high school. A *dummkopf* just like my dad has said before."

Then Gunther belched again. "He's my son, ya' know. I don't want no harm coming to him from you two guys Mister Lawyer here brought up."

It was Fritz who reached over and patted Gunther's forearm in a reassuring gesture. "Well, of course. Danny and me work for the same purpose you Nazi boys do! Forrester here just asked us to come up to Hamot and maybe help find your boy and straighten him out—gently!"

Fritz's move was as unanticipated as it was clever, thought Forrester. Much better that the stranger said it than some comment loaded with self-interest coming from a lawyer the von Himmels distrusted. There was a good reason why Sheldon had selected Fritz as his number one problem-solver, Forrester decided, and his confidence that Fritz would dupe Gunther into trusting him took a major leap forward.

"Me and Danny both know the problem you von Himmel boys have. Mr. Forrester here, already filled us in about how your kid was intimidated into spilling his guts about your bombing. All we have to do is steal him away from those goddam injuns who have him and talk some sense into him so he don't betray his father and grandfather into long prison sentences."

Forrester could see how persuasive everything Fritz said was to the von Himmels. They didn't know him or Danny until this moment, but my goodness was he make a convincing pitch. Of course, the lawyer had taken the time to educate both hit men that they at least had to kill Jack—maybe even Gunther—to assure there would be a not guilty verdict for Herman and a short sentence for Adolf. Then again, a guilty verdict or death for Herman wasn't a bad outcome either. Heads I win, tails you lose . . ." thought Forrester.

"*Ya, das gut!*" exclaimed Herman, and the old man swiveled in his chair to face Forrester. "By God, Mister Lawyer Man, you finally done a good thing for us! I like both these guys! I think Gunther and I join up with the three of you."

"Excellent, Herman! We'll make a team of Gunther and my two guys" Forrester agreed.

"And our next step is to take a look at the area Jack is in hiding," explained Fritz.

"Yup. That's right, partner," said Danny, as he replaced the toothpick into the exact left lower corner of his mouth. "We don't want to just go clomping up into a huge forest and hill or swamp area. That could give us away. We need to make a few trips there, each time getting a little closer until we know as much as we can about what we are getting into."

"And I can help with that!" affirmed Gunther. He sat back, reached into a shirt pocket and pulled out a pack of Marlboro's. "Give me that paper placemat on the next table, Fritz. Forrester, a lawyer like you has to have a pen, right? I'm gonna draw out a rough map of the road through the reservation and give you an idea of how big the set of Stony Lonesome ridges and hill is."

Fritz smiled a bit and shook his head in agreement. "Danny is absolutely right," he said. "And I brought several M-16 A1's and GEN-1 night vision goggles to assist our hunt! Viet Nam surplus I confiscated for the Klan!"

"*Gut!* Then you men can get started. You go there tomorrow morning so you can begin getting the lay of the land," announced Herman. "You go early in the morning. Three times is da charm!"

Chapter 60

"**WELL, IF IT'S** any help as you are walking out to the spot on the ice that Wolf indicated," State Patrol Commander Post was saying to FBI Director Mountain Wolf, "the word from the hospital is they'll have to start large-scale amputations to save Adolf von Himmel."

"Nice, Commander! But I'm afraid after I punch a twenty-foot diameter hole in this frozen swamp lake, even my dry / wetsuit isn't going to prevent some of my limbs from freezing and later amputation, too!" Lucille Mountain Wolf had just finishing putting her flags around the circumference of the area that her wolf dog furiously scratched up following the scent trail he gleaned from Jack's clothing in the trailer. "And the worst part of it is, we still don't have any clue as to how deep the bottom is here. It looks to me like I need to skip using an air tank and flippers in crime scene circle. They will kick up so much mud, I'll never find any evidence."

"Right, Lucy!" chimed in Sheriff Grey Fox. He clapped his arms against his heavy coat and called out to her, "but our search of the license plates on the abandoned car near the von Himmels could lead you to find at least one or even two Nazi bodies out there. One might be Grier, and the other could be his partner in crime, Harold Reeves, alias Reig."

"I like your positive thinking, Sheriff," said the FBI Director as she revved a small chain saw into action, "but unless I miss my guess, there won't be anything as big as a body or two underneath me. If we're real lucky, maybe an identifying chunk or three." Then she put the saw to the ice and began cutting down and through.

Patiently, she slowly and carefully walked her chain saw back and forth along the entire perimeter of flags encircling her investigation area. Clearly, her plan was to make long parallel cuts within the circle running east and west, followed by similar cuts running north and south. Once the ice was in small enough chunks, she could latch onto them with a hooked pole and drag out just enough for her to enter the water.

"Time for me to dump my warm and wonderful, white parka," she said taking it off as she finished the last cut. "Don't think the Bureau would appreciate me drowning all its down in marsh water and bog slime. Besides, I'm tired of looking like White Fang or Nanook of the North!"

Grey Fox and Post cracked up at her jest, then just as quickly went silent as they watched as the best forensic scientist in the country lift out several heavy pieces of ice, sit down on the edge of her opening and gradually lower herself into the icy lake, feeling for the bottom with her feet as she descended.

Inhaling deep breaths several times to maximize her oxygen load, she went under. Both men jumped to their feet and sprinted toward the hole. Three agonizing minutes passed.

"I'm back!" the director shouted as she bobbed up to the top. "My darn foot slipped when I hit bottom. It's about nine feet deep here. Now I'm going to have to ask one of you gents to hand me a towel, so my face doesn't freeze."

"My god, Lucy! You scared us half to death when you went down!" The sheriff's face had turned as white as the director's parka. And now, the hair around her skull cap and both eyebrows were snow white with frost too.

"If I didn't know you were an FBI agent, I'd swear you were one of those shape shifter things coming out of the depths to swallow us whole!" said Commander Post. "You look darn right terrifying!"

"Love you too, Commander! Now get me a towel for my face please. It's hard to hold onto the ice edge, and I need to keep my feet off the bottom as much as possible."

"Here's your towel, Lucy," said the sheriff. "I'll cut a sapling with a notch in it to push your test tubes and such out there."

"Good. Thanks, Josiah!" and after drying her face, the lab director looked directly into the sheriff's eyes and smiled the kind of smile a woman uses intentionally when she pronounces a man's first name slowly.

Grey Fox's knees buckled. Then he watched in sheer fascination as Lucille Mountain Wolf grabbed a fistful of evidence bottles, inhaled deeply three times, and ducked under again.

Both Post and the sheriff had to give up holding their breath before Mountain Wolf reappeared. From what they could see from shore, her bottles were full of dark mud and other dark pieces. The caps had been sealed under water. And without allowing her face to start freezing, the director took more jars, three more deep breaths and sank below the surface again.

When she came up the next time and placed the sealed jars on the rim of the ice circle for collection, Post and Grey Fox had several propane heaters going. The unspoken routine for the rest of the day was simply for them to slide out empty evidence containers, retrieve the full ones, place them near the heaters to avoid freezing and offer encouragement to a female stronger than both of them together. On the rare occasion the ice one her eyebrows, eyelids, nose and mouth grew impossibly thick, the director crawled up far enough out of the water to put her face close to one of the gas heaters, then wiped it with a towel before resuming her search.

The pale yellow, late autumn afternoon light began to spread like jaundice into the nether world of dusk and night. Lucille Mountain Wolf, her face a mask of ice and mud, bobbed to the surface in exhaustion and pain. "That's it for today, guys," she tried to say with frozen lips, but it sounded more like "Thast for taday, eyes."

"Sweet Jesus, Lucy – I don't know how you lasted this long," said Post. And before he could say anything else, the director reached under the water, fumbled with her suit, brought up a spool of tape and started to mark off the area she had finished investigating.

"Lucy," the sheriff said with real anguish in his voice. "That only sets off one-third of your circle! You can't possibly keep going another two days, can you?"

"Oh, she sure as hell can!" All three investigators spun around to see Forrester standing behind them, sarcasm and smirk already in place. "You're tougher than all four of us, aren't you, Lucille!" he said.

"And I said if I ever heard you use my first name again, I'd sic my little grey pet on you!" the director said in something as close to a snarl as she could manage given her face was just beginning to unthaw.

"Oh, just came out to pay you all a friendly visit. Thought you might want to know the sheriff here used a hollow point slug in his shotgun, so when it hit Adolf, the lead fragments splattered every which way. And worse, the local quack doctor in Hamot couldn't find and remove all the tiny metal particles in Adolf's wrist. Poor man just lost his right arm up to his arm pit, but there are so many black lines running across and down his entire body, there's no telling what all they'll have to chop off before they're done!"

"Boohoo!" replied Grey Fox. "Then again, I have already explained to you how that pathetic Nazi can wipe his ass with his left hand, once he gets enough practice."

"Very, very funny, Sheriff," Forrester responded. "But that requires they stop the infection real fast. Otherwise, just remember the more body parts he loses, the more millions I'm going to sue the Hamot PD, the Black River Ho-Chunk Tribe, and you, pal! Plus, I get at least a twenty-five percent cut of the lawsuit pie!"

"Cry me a river, Forrester…that is, if that doctor you mentioned doesn't remove everything above Adolf's neck! Or have you already forgotten that he opened fire first?"

"Commander Post," Lucille mumbled as she pulled herself up out of the lake, "get on the horn and have someone get Wolf from my van and bring him out here, please."

"Now no need to get touchy, Director," smiled Forrester as he backed away from the group. "No need to show me to the door. Your rope trail will get me back to my vehicle. It's a Mercedes, just like the ones all you public servants can afford too, right?" And as he turned to walk away, the lawyer called back – "Enjoy your pool party for another two days! It should be a real cool event!"

Chapter 61

THREE DAYS LATER, Forrester was getting more than a little nervous. The ease of finding Jack and his protector somewhere up on the Big Stony Lonesome that Gunther had boasted about was turning out to be a desperate endeavor. Aside from the absolute certainty that the boy had to be found and killed before there were any court proceeding, each night after searching, Gunther, Herman, Fritz and Danny were at the bars right up to 2 am closing time, guzzling Leinies and throwing down shots of Jack Daniels. That meant the great and terrible search party wasn't climbing out of their beds and hangovers until almost noon every day.

The decision to move Herman and Gunther into the motel room next door to Forrester had seemed to the defense attorney like a good decision at first. No wasted time to get the morning searches underway. But the law of unintended consequences popped up out of nowhere and provided an easy means for the threesome to hook up each night and get dead drunk.

Forrester's gut ached from the stress of it all as he sat at the little worktable his rented room provided.

"Hey, buddy," said Gunther as he slapped the attorney on the back and blew a nasty grey cigarette cloud into his face. "Tonight, after we're done lookin' for my kid, you gotta come with us. I'm gonna introduce your boys to snowshoes!"

"They don't need snowshoes, Gunther," Forrester replied with obvious irritation. "First of all, while you and Herman ride in the front seat of your broken-down pickup truck, my two guys have to ride in the bed. But it is a vehicle! They don't have to walk anywhere. In case you haven't noticed yet, despite all the below freezing end of September weather we're enjoying, there isn't any frickin' snow either! No snow—no need for snowshoes!"

"Up yours, Lawyer Man," Herman von Himmel replied as he stepped out of Forrester's bathroom. "My son, he is not talking about the snowshoes we wear on our feet. He is talking about the jiggers of Wisconsin brandy topped with German schnapps that old lumberjacks and cranberry men like us swallow in a single slurp! That's what we mean when we say we're introducing snowshoes—their big shots of booze!" and there was an explosion of laughter from the others in the room.

"Double bubbles, tonight, boys!" Danny shouted. "First the brandy, then top it off with the frickin' schnapps!" He swiveled on his seat at the end of his bed to look at Herman. "You Germans are as crazy as pet raccoons as far as I can see—but my gracious, I ain't never had a shot of that there schnapps stuff you brag on! Gotta have me some of that!"

"It'll put lead in your pencil," offered Gunther. "Then all you'll need is someone to write to!" and another cascade of belly laughter filled the motel room.

Amid all the liquor talk, the phone rang. Herman von Himmel instantly answered it. "*Ja*?" he said. "You are sayin' what about my son Adolf?" The man's father listened with deep anger lines criss-crossing his face until the call ended.

"What's goin' on, *Vater?* Is Adolf getting' worse or what?"

"That damn Indian sheriff who shot him with that shotgun slug poisoned my son all right," explained the old man. "That call was that damn Jew doctor's nurse. She said Adolf has got to go back into surgery right away or he's gonna die."

It was Forrester's turn to complete the interrogation. "Ok, Herman. What do they need to amputate now?"

"Well, they already hacked off most of his right arm, don't cha know! Now they call me since he is not conscious and ask to cut off half of his right leg! The nurse said it's either that or the gangrene goes to his heart and kills him. I had to say go ahead."

"Frickin' A!" bellered Gunther. "That doctor keeps this up and there won't be anything left of my brother."

"That's a Jew for you, my son!" concluded old man von Himmel. "They take and take until there's no more left. But don't you worry none. Maybe the snowshoe shots have to wait a little bit until you three men find Jack. But once we get him back and set him straight about our family, don't you worry about nothing."

"What do you mean, *Vater?*"

"I mean once things settle down, you and me will make a house call ourselves. We sneak into that surgeon's home and do some amputating on our own . . . and we be really slow about it too!"

Danny and Fritz chuckled and nodded affirmation. Forrester was beside himself. "I didn't hear one damn word you just said. As your attorney, I can't be party to anything illegal, and you all know that! —so just do your vengeance planning when I'm not in the room."

"Ya sure, you betcha Lawyer Man!" Herman replied. "And, of course, it wasn't you who put the four of us together to kidnap Jack away from the cops either, right?"

Frederick Poss

Before Forrester could answer, old man von Himmel was up and pushing Fritz and Danny off the bed and toward the door. "Come, Gunther. You got to help these men find Jack or I have to kiss the rest of my life goodbye. Just too old, I am. Twenty-five years in prison is the same as the death sentence for me . . . so all of you just get out the door!

Chapter 62

As SOON AS Gully Hanging Moon put down his bowl in the middle of a silent breakfast, Jack knew something was very wrong. His face was a study of human crisis. The chief stood abruptly, turned his left ear to the window and cupped his left hand to his head to listen. Jack did the same and tried to focus with all of his being. At first all he could hear were the usual sounds of the north wind among the scrub oaks and jack pines with an occasional leaf in the tall grass skittering by the lodge. The he decided on another tactic—he tried to ignore everything familiar he heard and pick out only that which did not belong. When a branch off in the distance made an unnatural cracking noise, the boy knew someone was coming up the hill directly below them!

Hanging Moon's head leaned into the open window slot, then pulled back. He gestured to Jack to pick up just one weapon—the oak spear for hand fighting. As the boy did this, the chief delicately removed his bow and quiver from a deer's horn hook on the wall, and both warriors left the hut to begin a hunt, neither knowing what they would encounter. Jack saw his mentor walking cautiously, stepping only on the balls of his feet, moving forward and slightly on a diagonal down the hill. The boy realized a second advantage of being at the top of the peak was that the wind carried sound uphill while pulling it away from those who caused it below.

Another branch cracked but this time just a bit closer. Jack almost coughed from the quick rush of cold autumn air that hit his lungs. Never in his young life did he have to instantly tighten every muscle, conserve every breath and step so silently. It hit him hard that he and the chief had never practiced an actual stalk. Hanging Moon's observation about how difficult it would be to actually shove a wooden spear into somebody flashed across the boy's consciousness. How hard would it really be? Could he actually do it? What if he hesitated?

The chief turned to Jack. The boy had never seen any human being look so riveted with deadly intent. Jack realized his life depended on learning this lesson in real time. With slow but intentional motion, the chief pointed for the boy to take up an ambush position behind a pair of granite boulders and ready his weapon. Jack followed the instructions, but his body was screaming from the tension and muscle ache he had to endure.

The fighting spear which until this moment had seemed more like a novelty than a combat weapon, grew heavy and awkward in his hands. The pine pitch the chief used to stain and preserve the wood, felt sticky and clumsy now. The boy realized he had given into a moment's laziness and ignored Hanging Moon's advice to wrap the handhold with leather.

Then Jack heard two definite footsteps, maybe forty feet down and to his left. Like a heavy fog on a rain-sodden day, the boy saw the chief drift down and to the left as well, countering the direction of the person or persons who advanced. His mentor soundlessly notched an arrow and drew back his bow, sighting along his left forefinger to center the target.

Hanging Moon was at full draw when a voice called out— "Jack? Jack, where are you? It's me, Sara! Are you up on the hill somewhere?"

But the chief didn't instantly relax his drawn bow. He studied the area behind the girl and on both sides of her as he continued her climb. Jack realized there could be a trap and Sara could be the bait!

"Jack, it's me! You and the chief have to be up here. The deputies told me to come this way." Sara's voice sounded as tense and desperate as Jack had been just seconds before. Then the boy saw the chief lower his bow, relax his draw, and step out from behind a screen of tall grass to reveal himself.

"You are Sara of the Koleski clan. I am War Chief of the Trout Nation Ho-Chunk. I am named Gully Hanging Moon," he said in a formal monotone. Then he grinned at the girl and conversationally added, "But you can call me Chief."

"How do you do, Chief," said Sara. "Is my Jack up here somewhere too?"

"Yes, I am!" announced her boyfriend as he rushed out from his rock pile and wrapped Sara in a squeeze so hard it almost took her breath away. She hugged back just as fiercely, then kissed Jack full on the mouth with all her strength. "Oh, Jack, I've been so afraid for you I just had to come!"

"Oh, Sara! I've missed you so much at times I couldn't think straight," Jack answered, and he kissed her back.

"Enough!" It was the chief speaking and his tone announced there could be no disagreement with his order. "We talk too much here, and we are out in the open," he said. "Follow me. Do not—!" then impossibly fast Hanging Moon whirled around, knocked an arrow and at full draw aimed down his left forefinger.

"Wait, Chief," shouted Sara. "It's just my dad, Pete!"

Her words carried a wave of relief over Jack, and he relaxed his guard momentarily until he saw that his teacher had not relaxed anything. The boy could see the chief's finger moving in tiny gradients to his right, following an invisible target.

"I'm coming up the hill with my hands in the air, Chief!" called Sara's father, and with that he strode into sight between two gnarled jack pines.

"Nobody followed me, Chief," explained Peter Koleski as he drew close and reached out to his daughter Sara. "It's safe."

"Safe!" There was that word once more. Jack shivered when he heard it.

"Safe? And how do you know this?" Hanging Moon only slightly relaxed his drawn bow.

"Gosh. I guess I really don't know entirely, Chief," Sara's father said and grimaced as he looked back down the hill. Turning back to continue the conversation, he extended his hand toward Hanging Moon. "I'm Pete Koleski, Chief. Sorry, I just assumed with it being so darn wild out here that—"

"The worst thing you could do to Jack was for both of you to come here," Hanging Moon said matter-of-factly. There was no affect in his expression. He was berating no one, just emphasizing what should have been painfully obvious.

"Why, Chief?" asked Sara. "Everyone in my family says Jack is perfectly safe with you up here on the Lonesome's peak. And it's such a huge place, no strangers could ever discover your hiding place.

"It's not too hard, even for a stranger, to ignore a car parked directly below my lodge, Sara Koleski."

"Oh, wow! It's all my fault, Chief," admitted her father, Pete. "My head told me not to give into my daughter and bring her out here, but she was crying herself to sleep every night with worry. I kept nagging at the Two Boys' twins to tell me where we could look."

"That's two mistakes they have to answer for," said the chief.

"Ah, please don't blame them. The blame is all mine," Kole ski said. "But I've got a couple of Winchester lever-action .308's locked up down in my truck, and I brought enough food to feed a small army. Sara and I won't be any bother, and I can help you protect our—."

The crash of shattering glass from the bottom of the hill ended any more speech. Hanging Moon impassively stared at the two visitors, then forcefully pointed up the hill.

"No talk!" he said in a fierce whisper and swiftly led the way up to his lodge.

Chapter 63

"**Just your favorite** defense counsel on the telly, Director!" Forrester said when Lucille Mountain Wolf answered. "And it took you three rings to pick up, Miss FBI. Could it be that you're still suffering the ill effects of the ice bath you enjoyed for the previous three days?"

"I'm always slow to answer the phone when I can smell it's a call from you, Mr. KKK," she replied. "What has dragged you out of your hole far enough today to call me up?"

"Surely you jest, Lucille! By now you must have our little question-and-answer dance steps down to a fairtheewell," said the von Himmels' attorney. "And best of all, not only is today an auspicious event because I am giving you the pleasure of a telephone chat—but unless you don't know—today is September 26!

"I don't have any kind of routine with you! And you keep forgetting about how my pet wolf will turn you into puppy snacks if you insist on calling me by my first name. And, yes, I know that today is semi-special! The actual lunar eclipse is not until a little after one tomorrow morning, so along with everything else you mistakenly believe—you have the wrong morning for the eclipse!"

When there was no snappy reply, the director added – "and I do know the von Himmel's lovely little nickname for you, Lawyer Man."

"Well then, to quote a State Patrol Commander named Post, 'let's get down to business,' Forrester said. "Of course, I am willing to cut you some slack, given your unfortunate racial background, Director. I don't think even God herself could have scavenged any useful evidence out of that ridiculously frozen slushie the locals call the Goodyear Marsh Lake."

"But a prediction like you're making means you must be one of the all-knowing Trinity yourself," said the woman. "Let's see now, even though it's a religion I have never subscribed to, my guess is that you think you're the omniscient God the Son…" and for a little extra jab, the FBI Director added, "and since big vocabulary words are hard for you, omniscient means all-knowing!"

Forrester chuckled. He loved the give and take with an intelligent adversary, just as long as he was always winning. "Well, that's right, Madame Director. I am God the Son. A Mr. George Sheldon,

President of the KKK, is God the Father. Presidents are always like that, you know."

Madame Director simply chuckled back, which irritated Forrester, of course. It was intolerable for him to be dismissed with a laugh to second place in the war of words.

"Come on, Miss Never Defeated in court forensic FBI scientist—tell me what gives with your lab testing of the evidence? Inquiring minds want to know."

"Well, Attorney Forrester, the first important point is that I have only preliminary results. I sent the evidence jars to the crime lab in Madison—your stomping ground I believe. It will be six weeks before I make my official results public to reveal my immediate findings."

"You have findings? From this morning? You're kidding me, right?" Forrester's emotional level went from playful to Def Con Three in a nano-second. "How in the hell can you talk into that state patrol phone and tell me you already have some kind of half-baked theory? That's just plain impossible!"

"Not when I find certain types of evidence items at likely crime scenes, Lawyer Man! And I have way more than a tentative theory. Little items like finger-nails and thumbs, for instance, can show up at even the most difficult crime scenes. Stuff with finger-prints can pop up out of the mud even if the lake top is frozen. I can tell you for dead certain that I have one hundred percent proof!"

"Cut it out, bitch! When I called those quacks at Hamot Hospital this morning, they said that Adolf had to have his entire right leg and part of his left amputated at three in the morning because of the infection racing through his veins. And his left hand has started swelling. Don't play any coy little games with me. What you got?"

"Oh, temper, temper, Counselor!" chided the director. "I didn't think someone who hasn't been defeated in court—up to now—would get so touchy."

"Dammit! If you have conclusive evidence that there is debris from the bodies of two Nazis from St. Paul, then I must convince what's left of Adolf and all of that which is Herman to cop a plea. Even before the bombing charges come from the feds, I have to talk that sharp-tongued banshee Blake into accepting guilty to second degree murder charges. Maybe with my offer, the bombing charges can go away? Who knows? But I am certain I can't take a chance of my two guys being found guilty of first-degree murder. Neither Adolf if he lives or Herman can do a life sentence, parole eligible in twenty-five years. The first one is too handicapped and the second is too damn old!"

"To quote an intrepid lawman, Forrester… 'Boo hoo!'" said the director.

"I asked you a frickin' question, Mountain Wolf. What's the level of certainty you have for your evidence?"

A long and very pregnant pause ensued, while Forrester fretted. He knew the Klan would likely kill him now unless he could sweet talk old von Himmel into forking over at least several million. Finding the treasure trove himself was not working out too well, but there was always a chance. Why wasn't this red skinned woman telling him what he already was sure of—she could prove nothing.

"Well, I am still waiting for you. You have nothing, I know it, Lucille!"

"As I already just told you, Forrester, my evidence is one hundred percent certain!" She waited for a few seconds and added, "I am one hundred percent confident in what my evidence proves about your clients murdering two men!"

"But, but...how can that be?" shouted Forrester. "Even a layman like me knows that bogs are incredibly acidic. They dissolve everything, and they do it fast!"

"Maybe fast in warm water with high bacteria counts, Mr. Lawyer. But you forget basic chemistry. The lake just froze. Not many of those hungry little summer-time bugs and bacteria are chowing down right now, sorry to say. They are all snug in their beds fast asleep."

"But the bodies were in tiny little pieces and chunks, for God's sake!"

"And just how do you know that!" Suddenly the FBI lab director was sounding like a lead prosecutor.

"Forget it already! Just my manner of speaking," Forrester raced to explain.

"I won't forget it, Forrester…and neither will the tape recorder the State Patrol Headquarters has running on phone calls here either. Another certainty is it won't be long before it will be time for them to say, 'See *you* in court!'"

"All right already. You can win this round! I will call the local judge—his name is Windshill and Tamara Blake, the local district attorney. I'll tell them my client or clients will admit guilt in exchange for a sentence on second degree murder. They will testify that those two goons from the Twin Cities followed Adolf and Herman out into the bogs looking to get money the old coot supposedly hid out there. Hey, my guys had to defend themselves!"

"Sure, Lawyer Man," responded the director. "And innocent victims always take the time to cut their enemies up in little pieces, right?"

Forrester paused to clear his throat and his mind as well. "If there was even one percent chance of uncertainty about your evidence, I'd take you on in a trial and smash you on cross examination. Just drop the attorney misconduct stuff . . . as a little favor."

"Uh huh. Right, Forrester. No promises until I hear your Nazis admit some guilt. Like I said before, in court tomorrow, I will put my right hand on the good book and testify that my evidence is one hundred percent certain. If you want to plead out thinking someone can avoid a longer sentence, go ahead. I'm just a scientist explaining the facts."

When no smart reply was forthcoming, Lucille Mountain Wolf concluded the conversation with some advice. "Now, Mr. Lawyer Man, I suggest you take two aspirin, put a freezing cold compress on your feverish brow like I've had to do the past three days, and figure out how in hell you're going to tell the von Himmels and your Klan buddies that you screwed the pooch! Now you all have a real nice day!" Lucille said and hung up the phone.

"Bitch!" she added and had a good laugh.

Chapter 64

HERMAN VON HIMMEL opened the motel room door so quickly Forrester was still in motion of making his second rap on the knocker.

"*Ja?* What good news you bring me now, Lawyer Man?"

"Just let me in the door for god's sake, Herman. A completely naked old man standing in an open doorway at one in the afternoon of a bitter cold late September day can get you yet one more charge—indecent exposure. And, frankly, I don't defend sex offenders." With that reply, Forrester just pushed his way past the old Nazi and once inside, slammed the door shut.

"Herman, I have to tell you that we've had a setback in your case," Forrester explained glumly. "The FBI sent out their best scientist out here to dig up evidence where Adolf and you disposed of the two bodies out in the swamp. Her wolf dog led her directly out to the spot you described the killings took place. Worse, the dog ran out on the ice and scratched out a little circle. The Mountain Wolf spent the last three days diving down and filling evidence containers with muck from the lake. She just told me she has one hundred percent evidence of what she found down on the bottom of that marsh lake!"

"Baaah! I don't believe nothing like that coming from some storm trooper army woman! Did you ask her exactly what type of evidence she found, Mr. Shyster?"

Forrester could see the beginnings of a temper eruption building in the old man. He had anticipated as much and therefore had decided to let his Mercedes running out in the parking lot.

"She said she had chunks of human evidence, Herman. You think back real hard to how Adolf and you handled cutting up the two guys who tried to hold you up out there. Did either of you throw something like a finger or a thumb in marsh lake?"

"Ya, sure, you betcha!" Herman admitted, "but we didn't leave no face for the cops to recognize. We took care to destroy any way to link the little hunks to a certain person. Adolf and me, we just chunked them two into venison sausage-size pieces. Fingers and thumbs can't tell who their owners were, *dummkopf!*"

"You're the dummy! With fingers and thumbs, she'll have fingerprints!"

"Ya, so vhat?"

"So those two were long-time crooks who must have been finger-printed, that's what! Mountain Wolf rose to the Directorship of the FBI Crime Lab because she has a one hundred percent conviction record, Herman. She's never made a mistake. Never been overturned in cross examination during a trial or by some expert witness the defense hired to show she was wrong. She just told me her evidence is one hundred percent conclusive! —and every jury in the world is going to believe her."

"That can't be, Lawyer Man. I don't believe no person is totally perfect except for the one Hitler said could be created!"

"Oh my God, spare me your Nazi religious hocuspocus. I don't have the time or interest!"

"Mein Aas! You know nothing for certain about the evidence. And you know less than nothing about what our great leader of the Third Reich predicted for the world. He wrote that someone with the Spear of Destiny, *'Der Speer des Shicksals'* could use its power to impregnate a woman at an Irminsul on a moon eclipse and produce the perfect Man-God, son of Odin himself!"

"Give me a freaking break! I'm trying to talk immediate prison consequences to you, and all you can do is quote your insane German dictator from World War Two."

"Nothing insane about the power of the *Speer*, Lawyer Man. And I do know history. My *vater* Heinrich taught me it was the weapon of Alaric who sacked Rome. Charlemagne the Great carried it into forty-seven battles, all of them victories, until he accidentally dropped it."

"Ok. If telling me all this bunk is going to get us to talk about reality, explain to me what happened when Charlemagne dropped the Spear of Destiny."

"Do not talk lightly of its power! Charlemagne let it touch the ground and died for his carelessness. The spear came from Odin, himself! A Roman soldier used it to kill the Christian Man-God, Jesus the Christ. If you don't believe this, look up for yourself what happened to Barbarossa when he dropped the spear into a little stream. He too was dead within minutes."

"Those men may be real people in history, but I only know U.S. history and the law. If what you are talking about really happened, then how did Adolf Hitler get hold of it?"

"He took it from a museum in Austria when he liberated the country from the kikes and the gypsies who had corrupted it. He said the spear held a hostile and evil spirit which would give its owner power over the entire world when he used its energy on the night of a moon eclipse to impregnate a young virgin and give birth to the Man-God."

Forrester struggled not to laugh. "Oh, Herman! That's a great story. Let me know whenever the next owner decides to use the spear, please. I'd just like to see a virgin impregnated with a spear! I guess that event is going to rival the Catholics and their silly myth of Mary's virgin birth! Ha! Ha!"

"For your information, Lawyer Man, no one needs the whole spear. They just need a little piece of it to connect with any metal spear, if they are joined together with a golden scabbard when they are at an Irminsul, a special mountain shrine!" Something about the way von Himmel said this struck Forrester as strange and uncomfortable. The feeling temporarily silenced his interrogation of the old man. For a moment he felt like he was listening to a voodoo priest, not a client.

Von Himmel sensed this unease. His facial features and body posture seemed to rise and expand. "And who knows, Shyster Man? The tip of the spear got broken off. Nobody don't seem to know where it is either. Maybe I find it on the night of a lunar eclipse? Maybe I become immortal with Odin when I make him his God-man?"

"And maybe you're full of crap! Enough of your science fiction and Teutonic nonsense, Herman. I came here to discuss a short-term prison deal like you said you could live with when I talked with Adolf and you earlier."

"*Das* right. The deal was that Adolf pleads guilty to a sentence of a few years, and he says I had nothing to do with nothing."

"Uh huh. But the problem is that the cops found the men's car parked just back from your driveway, remember? Some of the blood stains on Adolf and you weren't from either of you. It won't take long for the state crime lab in Wisconsin or Minnesota to find out if one or both of those dead guys ever were in the service or ever donated blood. And FBI Director Mountain Wolf already says she has totally certain evidence, like a finger or thumb to be printed and matched."

"So where you going with all this, Lawyer Man? What you say is to be done?"

"Well, we had a good deal until this FBI scientist came along. Remember that story we agreed to was because the two of you were just using your weapons for some target practice back in the swamps. I planned on arguing the theory the Indian cops ambushed you both and out of surprise, Adolf set off a couple of rounds."

"You say now we need a new deal?"

"That's up to you and Adolf, Herman. If we go to trial, you both are going to be found guilty of first-degree murder unless I can successfully argue self-defense. I have a chance with that argument, but the prosecution is going to throw in the suspicious disappearance of your grandson from the safe house in Wisconsin Rapids right after he blew the whistle on you.

Forrester felt he was beginning to sound convincing. He continued with fresh energy. "They will also point to the fact that your son Karl must have had something serious to cover up because he shot it out with the state patrol, killed a Hamot police chief, and died in a hailstorm of lead himself. Bombing, kidnapping, the murder of a cop? Sorry, old man, but you and what's left of your amputated Adolf will get life in prison with no chance for parole if you face a jury. That's a certain fact!"

"But I am paying you lots of money to get us out of that stuff, Mister. What you got for a new plan for us?'

"I think we must do a couple of critical things, Herman. First, we need to have Adolf plead guilty to everything, including the masterminding of stealing Jack. He must take the whole rap if you can get him to do it. But if he does—and this needs to happen before tomorrow morning, you remain free up and to the point where Jack comes forward and testifies against both Adolf and you."

"And just how am I gonna get Adolf to sentence himself to twenty some years in the lockup, huh?"

"Shouldn't be too hard actually. But we have to visit him today and get that confession witnessed by two people. With the way his infection is spreading, he might die before tomorrow when we go to court and plead out."

"But I just come from the hospital. My son is barely conscious, but he ain't gonna die. Why would he take all the blame when there is such a long sentence for him? Tell me that!"

"It will be simple, Herman. You're his father. When we go to his bed, a nurse we can bribe and me will both witness he whispered to you that he did it all and wants to confess because he is so sorry for what he's done. And even better, in front of the judge tomorrow, I'll ask for mercy for him. He could be a quadriplegic for crying out loud, incapable of moving around much less hurting anybody. With a little luck and lots of crocodile tears from you about what's happened to your family, he could still get just the two or three years we had in last plan."

"Lawyer Man, I don't think I ever liked you. But I got to admit, you're a very smart man. Adolf gets just a couple years. I go free. And the state has to pay Adolf's bills as he recovers in their jail." Then a faint smile crossed Herman's lips, sly and full of menace.

"Of course, should Adolf actually get better at some time down the line and decide he wants to change his confession to include me, that won't be much of a problem," the old man said.

"I don't follow you. Of course, a change in his confession to include you will be a huge problem," explained Forrester.

"No. Not no way. Lots of our Nazis and Aryan Nation brothers in the big prisons. I could pay them to make a short visit to Adolf when no one is looking. That would keep me free for
  good!"

"I didn't hear you say that, Herman. Now get dressed. We have to get over to the hospital asap. I'll have us stop at the Farmers and Workers Bank downtown and withdraw twenty grand from the escrow account to pay off the nurse. I'll get the court time for offering up Adolf's confession tomorrow, and phone it to you, so after our hospital visit, don't leave the motel room until you hear from me. It is essential that you appear in court with me to show that you have not violated the terms of your bail. You'll lose your bail money if you don't show. Got it?"

"Don't worry about me none, Lawyer Man. And I sent out Gunther and your two hunters from the Klan just before you knocked on my door. Maybe they get lucky and we don't got to concern ourselves no more about what Jack might say! Three times da charm, you know!"

Forrester swallowed hard. How in hell did he ever get himself into this?

Chapter 65

JACK KNEW HE had to finish his gathering before late afternoon turned to dark. At first, Hanging Moon raised his hand to silently ask Jack where he was going when the group climbed back up to the chief's cabin. But the boy just raised the carry sack he took off the wall and pointed east away from the southern trail where the cars had to be parked. Then Jack brought his finger to his lips in a gesture to Sara to remain silent. As Hanging Moon pulled out a basket of food and a jug of spring water, the boy gave a purposeful look to the chief and was out the door.

It only took an hour's travel to collect what he needed and make the tie string tight at the top of his bag before Jack headed back up the hill. "Still time to prepare," he told himself as he studied the western sky. It might be late afternoon by the time he returned to the lodge, but now his materials and strategy were both in place.

Sara was sitting just outside the lodge door, her hands clasped like iron rings around her knees. Her head was down, and she simply rocked back and forth. Of course, Hanging Moon had heard Jack approaching, so he came outside too.

The chief said nothing at first, only taking a long minute to study Jack's wet jeans and heavy sack. His fkisser of a smile said to Jack his friend now understood the boy's preparations. Then Peter Koleski emerged from the lodge to join the meeting.

In a hoarse whisper with Sara beside him, Hanging Moon said, "Little Hare, you will give Peter your oak spear because he needs a weapon and has no practice throwing a lance. At least you have some. I will place Peter in the center between us and higher up. I have told him he will hear our enemies' approach because they will be too confident. When they pass where you and I are hiding on their two sides, I will hoot like an owl, and he is to make a little noise with his feet. They will move quickly toward him. That is our chance to attack from underneath. After we make our move, he can fight with your oak spear. He has one of my hunting knives to use after that."

Sara started to speak, but she saw the frown on Jack's face and decided to remain silent. Hanging Moon whispered to her instead. "You must stay behind me and follow quietly wherever I go.

Whatever happens, you must remain silent. This you must do!"

Jack picked up his throwing lance from the side of the lodge, hefted it, entered through the front door and emerged with a length of leather wrapping. Carefully balancing the spear in his right hand, the boy began making a tightly bound handhold. Mentally, he kicked himself for his limited throwing practice, but there was no longer time for that.

"Too many of us to run away. The noise will be our death," said the chief. "But our enemies will wait for dark before they come up here. There are three men. When you were gone, Jack, I worked my way down far enough to see them. They were practicing putting on night vision goggles. They have automatic rifles that soldiers use too."

Jack just nodded and gritted his teeth.

"Before I give you any instructions, Little Hare, you must take this small pouch. Keep this around your neck, never to leave." In one simple but elegant gesture, the chief put string over the boy's head and centered the small pouch it suspended at the top of his breastbone.

Jack only nodded. He knew Hanging Moon would tell him what he needed to know.

"As war chief of the Trout Nation Ho-Chunk Nation, I have named you 'Wash-ching-geka'. While we Ho-Chunk do not have various clans in our tribe,

at this moment, you are now a man and warrior."
The chief reached into his vest pocket, removed a
small handful of tobacco, and sprinkled it in all four
compass directions.

Jack knew his chief was speaking to Earthmaker
as well as addressing Jack himself. "Warrior, you
now have your war bundle to bring you ferocity
and good luck. It contains soil mixed with water
because it is what we are. It contains wood shavings
of oak and willow from your spears of choice. Last,
it contains the shed skin of a northern water snake
for its selection of you and its protection as a spirit
brother which was announced to us when the first
one greeted you at the creek." And with that message, the chief sprinkled bits of tobacco over Jack,
took his head into both hands and said, "Remember
the first duty of a warrior!"

Sara could no longer contain the flood of emotions that washed through her mind and heart. "Oh,
Jack!" she whispered, "if I am to die tonight, I want
it to be here with you! I am yours—yours now and
always!" She threw herself into his arms, shuddering in silence.

Jack held her close, stroked her hair and let the
sobs slowly disappear. When she looked up, he
kissed her lips and smiled. "I know my fate will
not end tonight, Sara, and neither does yours."

"How do you know, Jack?"

"I know because all the gods, Christian, Viking and even First Nation have protected my life for me to be here in this moment. It was meant for me to be here with you, Sara, protecting you as I have from the first time we met."

"Oh, Jack, you are what is good and right," Sara whispered. "You are not the darkness that surrounds us. You are not the evil coming up the hill." With lingering tenderness, she kissed him fully on the lips. "You are the light that gives me hope. I love you."

Jack set down his spear and held Sara's head in both his hands. "I've always believed there is nothing more important than being safe. But tonight I know that I can feel love for you, Sara. I fight with my chief for the family one day I want us to have."

"*Haho, Wash-ching-geka!* You are a man who will make his mark!" Hanging Moon whispered. "Now you go back to your rocks from earlier today and take your throwing lance when you've finished the wrapping."

Jack nodded.

"You will hear our three enemies coming. They do not know the first duty of a warrior. Let them pass uphill. I will be on the far side with Sara. I will let them pass by too…but only for a few seconds if I can. Then I will signal Peter."

"Yes, Chief," Jack whispered in return.

"I willl put an arrow through the nearest one. You will know it by the spray of gunfire when he is hit, but they will not see me with their goggles because they will not know where to look at first."

"Yes, Chief."

"When you hear gunfire, get ready to fight. The leader will be first to head downhill past where we hide. But there is sure to be a follower. The follower will come down the hill too, but he will hang back moving slower. His focus will be on what is happening below him, not on you coming from his back above him."

"Yes."

"You must kill that follower. Leave their leader to me. If I am still alive, I will try to surprise him with an arrow or cut his throat. When you've hit your target, pull out the lance and let your enemy bleed out. Then you and Peter rush downhill making noise to distract their leader."

Jack nodded in silence.

"Their leader will turn back toward the noise. He will need a few seconds to locate you and aim his weapon. Those will be the last seconds of his life or mine."

Chapter 66

JUST BEFORE SUNSET, Chief Hanging Moon rose from his seat next to the lodge door, gestured toward the spears and without a word, took his bow and quiver of arrows as he led Peter, Jack and Sara quietly into war. As they stood to follow, the chief turned back, removed tobacco from his vest pocket and sprinkled them with it. During their final wait, Jack had found more leather and wrapped Peter Koleski's spear handle too after the man found the balance he needed.

Carefully, walking on their toes as the chief had indicated, their small war party moved purposefully down from the peak of Big Stony Lonesome. The temps had been uncomfortably cold, near freezing in fact, with occasional snow flurries throughout the last part of the day. But now, as they walked in silence to the fight, Jack felt warmer and stronger than he had ever been. He knew he could allow nothing to stop him.

They eased their way down for about ten minutes before Hanging Moon paused, looked at Peter Koleski, pointed to a thick clump of buck brush with a rock in front of it, and nodded for him to take his position. Koleski understood he was to be the bait for the ambush, and he welcomed it. If only Sara could live through this fight, he prayed, he would die as a man at peace with himself but filled with the grim determination to take at least one enemy with him. He began reciting his favorite psalm in his mind—"The Lord is my shepherd . . . ."

Another twenty yards by Jack's estimate, the chief paused again. Jack nodded to him. "Yes," the boy's body told the chief. "Off to my right is my hiding place." The chief nodded in return, then gave Jack a look of respect and deep concern. He raised his bow, pointing the tip at the boy warrior. Jack, in turn, raised his lance and pointed it at his chief. In the next instant the moment was gone and so was Hanging Moon and Sara.

Night fell hard and fast as it always did in the place people in gentler climates referred to as "up north." One moment the western edge of the world was a kaleidoscope of autumn oranges, scarlets, and smoky grey. A nano-second later, all was coal tar black.

Just as Hanging Moon had predicted, Jack heard twigs snapping unnaturally well below his rock pile.

The chief had said the men were not warriors, did not understand the absolute need for silence and would carelessly rely on their advantage in fire-power to achieve their goals.

Up to the very last second before any shape came into sight, Jack's mind suffered lapses of confidence. But when he saw the tiny aquamarine spots of light, swinging about head high, the only thing he thought of, the only emotion he felt was complete and unlimited anger. His life had been one of torment and abuse. Time for a change!

The shrill screech of an owl from below, kept Jack and Peter Koleski well-informed. The boy crouched as low as he could when the steps and sounds drew even with his ambush rock. From above, Jack heard Peter Koleski's rustle of weeds and a few footsteps on the ground. He willed all of his power into his hands.

Then the hunting trio of men stopped dead. Jack could see the nearest one slowly turning his face back and forth, his eyes under the metal and glass of green light night vision. "They're trying to locate exactly where Peter is..." the boy realized. Then Jack watched as his man turned to his right, away from him and looked to the man in the center of the group. "You're a follower, just like my chief predicted!" thought Jack. "Now just take a few more steps up. . .."

Another pounding and rustlings from up the hill were all that was needed. The man in the middle of the killers signaled for the other two men to move up and slightly out to their sides. Jack watched as he stood there waiting for his partners to get to the edge of their prey. They would flush whoever was in front of them and spray him with bullets.

"Uggghhh—" a heavy thud and the sound of a man's desperate gargling and thrashing on the other side of the hill rushed to Jack's ears as fast as Hanging Moon's arrow snatched away the life of the man called Danny. Jack didn't know it, but even being hit squarely in the middle of the neck doesn't always instantly kill. There was more gargling and thrashing about. Jack raised himself ever so slightly anticipating the downhill rush of the follower nearby.

The hill erupted with automatic rifle fire. And just as the chief had predicted, the rifle fire was wild and badly off target. Then the boy heard the chief's body say, "After they pass back down, move from above them down the outside edge of the sidehill while they are aiming down the middle of it!"

The gunman with his back to Jack rattled off a long spray of rounds from his M-16 A1, then surprisingly, lowered his weapon and started to remove his night vision helmet. "The bright lights from the muzzle of the gun must have blinded him!"

Jack realized. The boy gathered himself, raised to a crouch, and centered his lanced for the middle of the man's back.

A guttural noise escaped from the boy's mouth as he leapt, an unconscious release of fury and tension. Jack jabbed his spear forward with all his power, but the man heard noise and turned just enough for the spear point to scratch the top of his shoulder and skitter off target.

Screaming in desperation, Jack thrust the lance to inflict any damage he could. Then his enemy shouted– "Jack! Stop! It's me, your dad!

Chapter 67

JACK FROZE. HE shook his head in disbelief. "What—huh?" he managed to say. "But—you're here to kill us, *Vater*! Why?" and the boy again raised his spear.

Gunther von Himmel dropped his rifle and swung his left hand up to the opposite shoulder to press down on the gash from the boy's lance. "No! No, Jack!" he pleaded. "We just came to get you away from the cops and talk some sense to you. Get you to take back your story that sends us all to prison!"

"Liar! You brought night goggles and automatic rifles to talk to me! You spray gunfire all around into the night, maybe hitting me? Then you say you come in peace!"

"No, Jack. No!" But from above and slightly behind Gunther, Peter Koleski appeared, racing down to run him through. Jack stepped in front of his father, instantly putting up his hands in a stop gesture. Before he could say anything, a cascade of gunfire showered Sara's father with rivulets of lead, dropping him at Gunther's feet.

Gunther, standing just below his son, turned forty-five degrees to face straight across to his right. "No, Fritz! Don't shoot!" He raised his hands, palms outward toward his partner. "I've got Jack here with me. We can go—!"

A huge man with a helmet streaming a deadly, thin, chartreuse beam of light came charging toward Gunther and Jack. As his waist cleared the line of the hill, he looked squarely at the adult target and let loose with a fire storm of lead.

"Fritz—no—!" Gunther gurgled and fell to the ground. Jack had already dived back into his rocky hole.

The boy scrambled desperately to wedge himself, his lance and bag as deeply into the hollowed space as the rocks allowed. In no more than three beats on a drum, however, there was the thump of heavy boots and the wheezing breath of a man in a hurry only a few feet from his hidey-hole.

"Now I gotcha!" he heard the man his father called Fritz say, and the pair of feet a couple steps from the boy turned outwards to allow its owner to crouch down and finish Jack. The boy heard a grunt as the big man bent down. Jack saw the butt of the gun lowered to the ground first, then both knees appeared, then an elbow. The boy tensed himself for his ultimate test.

A chin came down into view, then a pair of eyes and a gun muzzle swung toward Jack. "Bang, bang," the big man said, "you're—!"

But Jack ripped open his bag and threw its contents into the confident face of his attacker. A snarl of thick-bodied water snakes wrapped itself to the man's face and neck, a writhing bundle of biting fury. Screaming in agony, the man stumbled back and tripped as he did so.

That was Jack's chance! He threw himself out of the hole, over the thrashing man, and raced up the hill toward Peter Koleski.

But the big man was too tough and too quick. In the next instant he ripped off the snakes, reached down, grabbed up his rifle and swiveled to level a burst of fire at the boy struggling up the hill in front of him.

Thhh-wukkk! An arrow buried itself into Fritz's right side. Wordlessly, he fell back from the impact. Then using his left hand, he reached across his chest and snapped off the arrow shaft. Thhh-wukkk! Another arrow hit him front center and again the force of it drove the Klan killer backward. He snapped off the shaft of the second arrow too.

"Damn! Don't you know that a Kevlar vest stops arrows! Now see if you can stop this!" and the killer touched off a long sweep of automatic fire from his M-16.

"Uhhha—!" a voice in pain cried out from the other side of the slope. At the same time, Sara's screams as she ran down the hill overpowered all other noise. Jack instantly knew her fear must have made her leave the safety of her uphill hiding spot. Like an electric charge, her wailing propelled Fritz up from his knees and into a headlong charge down the hill after her.

The boy's first instinct was to rush after the gunman. But the training from Hanging Moon made him stop and survey all that was before him. Jack made his decision. Immediately, he scrambled back to his father.

"J-J-Jack! I uh so sorry..." Alex managed to say. "It was Herman—!" and the man exhaled his last breath. The drama and insanity of it all broke through the young man's defenses. Jack dropped his head on his father's chest and sobbed.

"Little Hare? Little Hare? Are you still alive?"

Jack heard a scraping sound like someone dragging a body across the ground.

"It's me, Little Hare. I'm over by the rock pile!"

The murky outline of a head and shoulders rose out of the gloom. "Little Hare, if you are able, come help me!"

Jack was out of his cover and in seconds next to his chief. "Where are you hit?"

"In both legs," said the chief. "Here and here…" as the man took Jack's right hand and brought it to the wounds. One had torn through the fleshy part of his right thigh, the other smashed into the chief's left kneecap. The boy warrior felt for a sense of how much blood was spilling out. The thigh wound was wet but not spurting, but the kneecap was pulsing blood in heavy amounts. Without a word spoken, Jack stood, released his belt, and cinched it as tightly as he could above the dangerous bullet hole.

"I have to check on Peter," Jack whispered, but before he could rise the muffled wailing of a young female echoed up from below the two men. Then a vehicle's door slammed shut and an engine roared to life. Faint headlights from the logging trail below confirmed that Fritz had just made an escape—with Sara or without her.

"Sara? Sara!" the young man screamed into the ink of night, but the only response was the same word reverberating across the hills. Jack knew then for certain that Fritz must have taken her, and now as a man and a warrior of the Ho-Chunk Tribe, he would have to get her back.

"Mr. Koleski? This is Jack! Can you hear me? Peter, are you ok?" Jack repeated these words as he searched back and forth above from his rocky ambush spot. His left hand found Sara's father. No sound, no movement issued from his body. He was as dead as Gunther and gunned down by the same killer.

Jack wept. How many good people had to die to satisfy the hatred and greed of his family and their hired guns? The boy touched the man's face, wiped away the dirt and blood he sensed was there, and with the greatest of care, closed Peter Koleski's eyes. "May God bless you and keep you. May his perpetual light shine down upon you. . .." Jack had been to church only for his grandmother's funeral a year ago. He couldn't remember any more of the prayer, but his heart told him what he said was right enough.

In the next moment, he was back at Hanging Moon's side. "Peter is now with both your god and mine, my chief! So is my father!" the young warrior said. He sucked in a full breath, expelled all of it to release the death around him and said, "If you can take it, I think it's best for me to drag you back to your lodge and clean and bandage your wounds there."

"*Haho, Wash-ching-geka!* You are the chief now. Do what must be done."

And Jack did exactly that. It took him almost to dawn before he had pulled the war chief up the slope of Big Stony Lonesome and into his lodge. Hanging

Moon was a man of considerable size, and the warrior boy and to stop for rest many times. Jack used the break times to release the tourniquet for short intervals before tightening it back in place.

The chief was still conscious but very pale when Little Hare hauled him into his blanket bed. Jack positioned the chief to dress his wounds, then he reached down, grasped an empty, hollowed-out gourd, and lifted a long drink of spring water to Hanging Moon. The chief took it all in long, thirsty gulps. Then Jack took several long drinks himself.

"Take more water, Little Hare," explained the chief, "and wash out both sides of the wounds as best as you can. Pour the water deep into the holes to clean out everything you find!" When the young warrior finished, the chief had him repeat the process again, and then again.

"We must make the wounds as clean as we can to avoid infection!" explained the chief. "Now the washing out is done, go to the fire ring just outside my door, stir the smoldering log in its circle, throw on some dead grass and twigs. Then blow on them until they catch fire."

"Yes, Chief!" and Jack was out the door. Minutes later he returned.

Hanging Moon reached alongside his waist and removed a hunting knife. "Go now and heat it in the fire. Wait until it glows red. Wrap its handle with some cloth to avoid its heat on your hand. Then use the flat of the blade to seal the wound on my knee first . . . on top, then underneath."

Jack's eyes appeared to bulge out of their sockets.

"Do not shirk from this, Little Hare. It is that which must be done. As we have said, this is something that must happen. When you are finished with my knee, reheat the knife and close the other wound front and back on my thigh."

Jack scrutinized Hanging Moon's face as hard as the chief studied his. Without another word, the warrior boy left the lodge with the knife, returned a moment later holding it with a cloth around the handle, and pushed the flat of the blade hard against a hole in the chief's kneecap about the size of a twenty-five-cent piece. The smoke and stink of the cauterizing nearly overcame the fifteen-year-old, but when he looked down into his chief's face, he took courage.

Hanging Moon did not move, did not speak, or make a sound. He simply looked back at his young warrior and nodded approval when the first wound was burned shut.

"One more, Little Hare!" and his gasp told him Hanging Moon was in terrible pain.

Jack nodded, strode out the door, returned in a minute, and pressed the red-hot blade against the chief's thigh until the flesh stopped sizzling and the wound was closed.

"Water!" asked the chief, but the warrior boy was already dipping it for him, then for himself.

"Now before I sleep and begin to heal, we must talk of what else has to happen, Little Hare!"

"I must get Sara away from the man who took her. She is most important now that your wounds have been cleaned and sealed."

"Yes, Little Hare. And what else?"

"My father and Peter Koleski died in battle. Before I leave, I will close their eyes and cover them with blankets from your lodge. The enemy who lies dead can feed the animals and birds, but I will take his weapons with me."

"Yes, Little Hare. What else?"

"I heard only one vehicle start up. It had to be our enemy for he had to park behind Pete's truck. When I go to cover Sara's father with a blanket, I will find his keys. First, I will drive to Black River, find Sheriff Grey Fox, and have his helpers come back here to take you to a hospital."

"Yes, Little Hare. And then?"

"Then I will go for Sara."

"But how can you find her, Little Hare?"

"My heart has already told me where she is. I will go to reclaim her as soon as I can!"

"Perhaps, young brave. But do you know that the coming night is the darkest of nights?"

"No, Chief. What do you mean— 'the darkest of nights?"

It is what your world calls a lunar eclipse. It is a rare event. The moon passes directly behind the earth an hour past midnight. For several hours, the earth will be totally black. You will see nothing."

"No, my chief. Along with the killer's rifle, I will take his night vision goggles!" and the boy smiled a deadly smile. "Two can play that game! And now since you spoke of the eclipse tomorrow night, I am dead certain where Sara can be found."

"Haho, Wash-ching-geka!" and with that exclamation, Gully Hanging Moon fell into a deep sleep. Surprisingly enough, for more than five hours so did Jack.

Once the gunfire had ended and a safe space of time had elapsed, the mountain wolf led his pack out of the den and down to the killing ground. Time to eat.

Chapter 68

JACK AWOKE IN a startled shiver. It was early morning, but the night's hoar frost had painted his blanket with intricate lines of ghostly whorls. Quickly looking across the lodge, he saw his chief, fast asleep, breathing deeply and evenly. That was all good the boy decided.

Jack stood slowly, stretching out cramped muscles. They hurt like firebrands welded to his frame. Looking about the lodge, he saw a large boning knife in its sheaf, hanging from a deer horn. He took it and slid his belt back on, taking the time to thread it through the sheaf before buckling the belt closed. He took another moment to stretch and inhale deeply. As he did, the Viking necklace around his neck thumped against his war bundle. "Odin and Earthmaker protect me!" he whispered, and grabbing two blankets from a corner, Jack headed out the door and down to the bodies of the dead to do what he must.

After covering Peter Koleski, Jack did the same for his father. Gunther's M-16 lay next to him, and after some fiddling with the magazine, managed to slide it out. He found the rifle had just two rounds left—one in the chamber and one in the clip—but he took it and the night goggles before moving over to Danny's body.

When he reached the dead Klansman, the first thing Jack did was spit in his face. Then he reached down and removed the magazine from the automatic rifle. "Just my luck!" the young warrior said out loud when he found both the magazine and the chamber empty and no rounds in the man's pockets. When he removed the night goggles from the man's head and went to try them on, he discovered the batteries were dead. "But my dad might have turned his batteries off when he removed his goggles!" he remembered.

After a quick check, he happily found there was still power in his father's helmet. Jack touched his war bundle and the animals on a chain under his neck! "The gods be praised, whoever they are!" he said, then quickly rising, he cautiously picked his way down the slope.

As he had suspected, Fritz had not lingered or returned. After an intensive scanning of the area around Peter Koleski's truck, Jack approached, brushed some broken glass off what used to be the driver's side window ledge and nodded in satisfaction. The keys were hanging in the ignition! The killers had removed the deer rifles but thoughtlessly had forgotten to take the truck keys. They also forgot to take any of the food Sara's father had brought along.

Jack worked the door handle, used his long sleeve shirt to wipe off the broken glass scattered across the bench seat of the pickup, jumped in, started the engine and started slamming down a peanut butter and jelly sandwich as he threw the transmission into reverse. He tromped down on the gas pedal, spun the Ford F-150 in a tight 90-degree half-circle and sped down the lumber trail generously named Cheney Road. Jack hoped he could find the right track toward Black River Falls and the Ho-Chunk Police Department.

But he didn't. Despite hurling the pickup the length of one trail after another, it wasn't until late afternoon that Jack discovered his way out of the big woods. Just as he frantically skidded the heavy-duty truck into one more tight turn to explore the last possible trail, he had to hit the brakes. There, coming from the opposite direction, was a police squad car.

It hit its brakes too, and after the road dust settled, Jack saw two familiar faces looking back at him.

"Tomas and Tobias! Am I ever glad to find you out here!" Jack sprang from the truck and raced to the hood of their Mercury sedan, resting his hands on a large, painted emblem declaring it to be the property of the Ho-Chunk Nation.

"Easy, Jack!" said Tomas, as he was first to emerge from the passenger seat. "As I see you are driving somebody's truck, there must be bad trouble!" Tobias Two Boys was instantly beside the boy too but knew to hold his tongue.

"My girlfriend and her dad came out to me, after you told them where we were!" the the boy said, looking grimly into the faces of the two deputies.

"Damn it, Tomas! I told you it was a mistake for you to blab on where we hid Jack! Now Chief Hanging Moon is gonna punish us both hard!" argued Tobias, pounding on the vehicle's hood.

Before Tomas could defend himself, Jack raised his hands and made hand gestures to settle the argument down. He explained. "It's too late to assign blame. Three men found Mr. Koleski's parked truck, the one I'm driving now. He didn't have it locked, but our attackers didn't bother to try the door. They just busted out the front window to get his rifles, and when they did, we heard them up on our hill.

Where they threw the rifles is anyone's guess, and I don't have the time to hunt all over to find them."

"It was a bad mistake, Jack! —my bad mistake," said Tomas. "What happened after the three of them found where you were?"

"They waited for night, then came up the hill with automatic rifles and night goggles on their helmets."

"Oh, no! You had a shootout?" asked Tobias.

"Yes, we did. They killed Mr. Koleski. Then I discovered one of the attackers was my own dad! — but he put his gun down when he saw me. He was saying they just came to take me away from you guys and talk me into changing my testimony."

on"But that really doesn't make any sense," explained Tobias. "You said they arrived with automatic rifles and were wearing night vision goggles. Not exactly a peace delegation."

"Right. I know. My dad was never very smart. Right after I told him the same thing you just said, a big bald guy across from him ran up and shot my father to death. He tried to get me too, but I threw a bag of snakes into his face!"

"But you said there were three men—" said Tomas.

"Right. Our chief arrowed the third man over on the far side of the hill. But the big man in the middle ripped off a long burst of bullets, and they hit the chief in both legs. He's up in his lodge now.

I cleaned and sealed the wounds. You need to call for an ambulance and then get up there!"

"Yes, we will," Tomas said. "But you said Sara was up there too. Where is she now?"

"The big man heard her screaming, so he ran down the hill, grabbed her, and drove away."

"Oh my god, what have I done!" Tomas fell against the side of their Merc and wept silently.

"You caused Peter Koleski to lose his life protecting his daughter, Tomas," said to his brother. "But before our chief does the same thing, get on the radio and call in some help!" Tomas, fought to gain control of his emotions, partially succeeded, and swung himself into the sedan's front seat to broadcast the situation.

Tobias took the measure of the young man who stood before him, dirty, bloodstained, and fierce. "I guess it would be useless for me to try to stop what I am sure you're going to do, Jack," he said.

"Yes, Tobias Two Boys. It would be useless."

The Ho Chuck deputy nodded in agreement. "How about giving me a clue as to where we can find them and you?"

Jack just shook his head. Then, pausing briefly, he changed his mind and said— "The Irminsul shrine on top of the Ermanstine."

The deputy released a thousand-pound sigh. There was no need for wasting time in asking about what sounded like German hangouts. He simply turned to his right and pointed down the trail he and his brother had used. "That way to Highway 12. It takes you back to Hamot if you go left at the fork. Right takes you to Black River." He glanced at his watch. "It's now 4:30. Be dark in an hour or so, and tonight's the eclipse."

Jack just nodded once and held up the night vision goggles.

"I see you have the chief's knife, and you took one the bad guy's rifles from up there?"

Jack nodded.

"Little Hare, take my .357," Tomas said and handed over his pistol. "It's a heavy weapon that will stay down when you fire more than once. Not that I can ever hit anything with it. Hope you are a better shot, my brother. And don't bother to say anything stupid like 'Hands up' to whoever you catch."

Tobias Two Boys stepped back and turned to the driver's side door. Over his shoulder, he said— "Just kill 'em, Jack. Kill 'em all . . before they kill Sara and you!"

Chapter 69

THE COUNTY COURTHOUSE in Sparta was stuffed with people like dressing in a Thanksgiving turkey. Senior citizens, country folk and the usual bar-crowd element all had packed themselves into every nook and cranny of the courtroom itself as well as the hallway and even the stairsteps outside the building's pair of copper-plated front doors.

The courtroom itself was not exactly spacious. Along with a few rows of wooden benches for the public, officers always added a couple dozen folding chairs to use up the space between the last bench and the white-washed, plaster walls. The ancient windows were high up, narrow and small, giving a church-like, somber quality to the scene. And with the press of so many people, some of them fresh from chopping corn and spreading manure, a viscous cloud of pungent air hung suspended head high. Some of the more elegantly dressed women who had gained entrance and a seat, sniffed at the atmosphere through dainty handkerchiefs. But make no mistake, this was high drama for the Monroe County Court.

Forrester and Herman entered a minute to the hour. To say their morning was a tumultuous one would be utter and complete understatement. And yesterday had gone so very well, Forrester reflected bitterly as he took his seat beside his client. He and Herman had gone to the hospital first that morning. Forrester had fretted about whether he could fast-talk a nurse into being a false witness, but 'Odin be praised,' that wasn't necessary.

As the old Nazi and he entered the general hospital area, they encountered two very elderly patients. Both men were hand rolling their wheel-chairs, I.V. bags attached, like they were teammates in Roller Derby. At the sight of Forrester and von Himmel, the two men giggled, elbowed each other conspiratorially and punched an automatic door button that sat below a sign that said Critical Care.

No one happened to be at the hospital's small front desk when Forrester and von Himmel walked in the front door. A kindly, arthritic old woman with the word Anabel on her name tag that said Gift Shop just below it had seen both men standing at the unoccupied front desk.

"You can just go in and see whoever you need to," she explained as she, her walker, and her friendly smile had approached.

"We're needing to go to where the severely injured are cared for, Ma'am," said Forrester in the most polite, southern drawl he could manage. The cheery old woman's face brightened. "Just turn left through that big door," she said, "and listen for a room with lots of mechanical noise."

She was right. Along with the unsolicited assistance of the two old geezers with IV bags on wheels, Forrester was amazed at how easily they found Adolf. And the two old men, likely escapees from the Alzheimer's ward were there too, fighting to squeeze through the room entrance at the same time. Forrester's mind immediately sought to take some advantage of the situation. These two old birds would make perfect witnesses, he realized. With a little cajoling now and perhaps some brow-beating later, a tough attorney like him could wring anything he wanted out of this odd couple, now or even later. Forrester grinned and thought to himself – "Just what the doctor ordered!"

Herman, in no surprise to Forrester, simply hung back in the corridor. "You go look in the mirror awhile, Herman!" he thought to himself. "Show some love and compassion to the only person you've ever cared about, please—yourself!"

But the attorney knew better than to say any-thing to the old man. Instead, he warmed up to his two potential witnesses. "All the electric-powered motors and beeping machines in this critical care suite generate a lot of noise, right, boys?" he said more loudly and congenially than normal, guessing his witnesses were hard of hearing.

"Eh?" said the shorter of the two who sat down closest to Adolf's bed.

"He can't hear worth a damn!" giggled the taller of the two. "Now, what did you say again?"

"You guys are playing a little hooky from the senior care wing, right?" smiled Forrester, and he slapped both men lightly on their shoulders to show he was enjoying their fun too.

"Eh?" said Mister Short.

"Oh, don't mind Bill! He doesn't know a damn thing, unless I tell him what's going on," said Mister Tall.

"Well, how about you tell Mr. Bill he can join you and me as we play a little game of Operation?" asked Forrester. "You know the game. You guys get to be the doctors and write the fellow in the bed a prescription! Ok?"

"Eh?" said Herb. "What are we doing, Stan?"

"We'd like that!" said Stan, and he leaned over to speak close to Herb. "You get to be a doctor! We're writing up a prescription," and both men giggled some more.

"Yes sir," said Forrester and he removed an envelope from his briefcase, unfolded the confession he had prepared, and using the top of the case, had each man sign their names. After inspecting the signatures, Forrester couldn't have been more pleased. The hands shook with only minor tremors and the names were quite legible. William Stage and Stanley Vance. Nice!

"Ok, men," Forrester announced. "We've had our fun now. You filled out a very helpful prescription for this young man. Time to head on back to the ranch!" and he began maneuvering Stanley out the door and signaled to Herman to move the other man.

Bill said, "Eh?"

Once they had pushed the two witnesses through double doors that said Senior Care Center, Herman and he quickly returned to Adolf's bedside. Herman's son must have been partially awakened by all the talk in his otherwise empty room. His eyes opened, and despite his heavy sedation, the young man recognized Forrester and his father. Then he smiled. It wasn't much, but afterward Forrester thought it likely their appearance may have given Adolf the hope that desperate people always crave.

"Hi, Adolf!" the defense attorney said, lifting the shiny, orange oxygen tent canopy over the patient.

"It's me, Forrester. And your dad is right beside me here. We came because we thought you might be waking up a little. Looks like we are right on time!" and the lawyer lavished one of his amazing and phony happy faces on the double amputee. A quick study of Adolf told Forrester, the man was so doped up, he clearly had no idea of all the limbs he had lost.

Herman reluctantly moved to the far side of the hospital bed. He lifted the oxygen tent flap too and briefly made eye contact with his son. He patted Adolf on his son's near temple, carefully avoiding contact with all the gauze and tape that covered the area where his right arm used to swing from the shoulder. Adolf blinked and smiled again. Forrester sensed somewhere deep inside the amputations and bandages; an overwhelming amount of fear was spreading inside the young man as he lay cheek by jowl next to a truckload of gangrene.

"Adolf, since you're awake, and we're here right now," Forrester said slowly, "I have a paper you need to sign. It gives your father and me the legal authority to oversee your care and to pay the hospital for it instead of you footing the bill. Ok?"

Of course, what the lawyer had just explained was a complete lie. But it was a sure bet that Adolf would sign virtually anything a reassuring face put in front of him.

"We'll have you use your good hand, the left one on my side, please." Forrester heavily emphasized the 'please" part of his explanation. Adolf appeared to nod in agreement and brightened a bit from another reassuring smile from the attorney. Lifting his briefcase to use as a base, Forrester whipped out a pen, lifted Adolf's swollen left hand to accept it, and guided him in signing a confession that would lead to his death in prison, if not in a few more days in his hospital bed.

Of course, Forrester had little faith that the two witnesses would bear up under much serious legal scrutiny, but he also knew that such a verification process would take time, lots of it. And Forrester planned to use all that he had to find the von Himmel hoard just as quickly as he could. No good options were available anymore. Maybe Jack was already dead? Maybe not? Herman could wind up back in jail within a few hours. One of Sheldon's men could be hunting for Forrester at this very moment. If the lawyer could placate old man von Himmel or get rid of him, he just might have enough time to disappear. Millions in von Himmel gold would make that happen!

As soon as the paper was signed, Forrester gave Adolf one more gleaming smile, pulled the oxygen tent back down and walked out of the room with Herman. A brief stop at the now-attended front desk provided the perfect opportunity to call District Attorney Blake and to announce Adolf's confession in exchange for a sentence Herman said he could accept.

Once they exited the building, Herman swerved to his left and walked with determination around the corner of the building. Forrester found this surprising and a wee bit discomfiting. He followed Herman and found him standing on the southeast corner of Lake Hamot, a few yards from the hospital. There was a brutal northwest wind whipping up white caps and carrying tiny, icy splinters with it that slapped Forrester's face and ungloved hands with sassy, insouciant pings.

Both men simultaneously exhaled and inhaled deeply. Forrester, not that he really felt it, tried to say something to von Himmel with a little sympathy in it. "Sorry, Herman. You've lost Karl to the state cops, and now your boy Adolf isn't looking too well."

"*Mein Arsch!*" the old man sneered. "You don't know nothing, Lawyer Man!"

"Well, I know no father wants to see his sons suffer and die," replied Forrester, trying to remain reasonable.

"Fritz," the old man said, "came back to my motel room late, late in the night. He had some very bad news."

"Now what's going on, Herman?'

"Gunther, Danny and him yesterday found where the Indian cops were hiding Jack, that's what!" but the rage in the old Nazis voice warned Forrester to say little.

"Uh huh," the attorney agreed.

"They got in another shootout up there in the hills." Von Himmel paused but Forrester stayed silent.

"That goddam chief and my grandson weren't the only people up there. When it turned dark, our men went up the hill and were ambushed."

Forrester clenched his teeth. The news was going to be very bad indeed. He said nothing.

"So when Fritz came back, he told me that the chief killed Danny using a bow and arrow. Then the chief killed my son Gunther."

"Oh my God!" Forrester said.

"Fritz opened up with his M-16 and killed some guy running at him with a spear. He thinks it was Sara's father because he found her up there too. Then he shot at the chief. He thinks maybe he killed him or at least hurt him a lot."

"And where is Sara now? And what about Jack?"

"Fritz did real good work. He brought the girl back to the motel in the trunk of his car. I tore up some bedsheets, tied her up to the bed in my room and put out the Do Not Disturb sign."

"And Jack?"

"Fritz was about to kill him when that little *kotzbroken* lump of puke threw a bag of snakes in his face and got away."

For a split second, Forrester wanted to grin. Jack had more guts and savvy than all the von Himmels adults put together. But the realization that Jack had to die for Forrester to keep Herman out of prison, quickly dashed any fragment of regard he had for a teenager who kept finding a way to survive.

"So how soon do the cops come for you, Herman? You think they are already on their way—or maybe waiting for us at the courthouse?"

"Nope. Not for a long while yet," Herman said. "After Fritz dropped off the girl we can use as a hostage if we have to, he got more ammunition and took off straight back to the hill once he rested some and the sun come up. He still gonna kill Jack all right."

"But what if your grandson isn't up on the hill anymore?"

"He can't go nowhere, Lawyer Man!" von Himmel retorted. "He's way back in the Stony Lonesome woods, up a hill with no paddle you might say, and he might have someone wounded to fix up. For certain, he is by himself. And before anyone comes to check on him, Fritz will solve all our problems."

"And what about your court appearance? We're due in court at Sparta in just over an hour! It's a twenty-minute drive to get there."

"I go with you. Bring out the confession. I go free. Jack dies. On the way back from Sparta, I buy a car with the twenty thousand that we didn't need for no bribe. All is still *gut!*"

"And you make a down payment to me, Herman," said Forrester. "That's when all is still good!"

Chapter 70

THE **PB** AND J sandwich had tasted good going down, so Jack fumbled around the pickup's front seat and dug out another from a packsack that Peter Koleski had brought along. But there was a problem with the sandwiches. They left his mouth dry as a withered cranberry vine in winter. He decided to pull off Highway 12 and take County Truck O east into a little off-the-track lakeside spot called Waseda Park. Sara's father had said he had a store of supplies in the truck, and the young man decided he could take a little short cut through the village of Barrens, refresh himself at the park but remain alone, then continue to the Granite River.

Jack's decision to gobble down some food was a fateful one for more than himself. Fritz knew he had to hurry back to Big Stony Lonesome once he

411

deposited Sara at the motel room. He had to explain what was going on to Herman, put an ice pack on his swollen face to cool off the snake bites and catch a a quick nap. A couple lines of cocaine didn't hurt either. But after an entire morning and the better part of the afternoon driving around rural Wisconsin, he came to understand, he was lost.

Worse, although he had managed to get back to the Black River Falls area on Highway 12, it was mostly populated with First Nation families. Not exactly the type people who would appreciate his SS and skull with cross bones tattoos across his bald head. And instead of feeling better, the drugs had worn off, and his face had swollen even more. In fact, his entire body had started to ache and cramp.

To add injury to insult, his fruitless search set him back in another way. As he drove north on Highway 12, he passed by the turnoff where a couple miles down the road Jack von Himmel was drinking a coke.

Then his luck changed. A yellow and white Ford Bronco with the words Forest Ranger passed him, heading east. Fritz decided he nothing to lose except his life in a federal prison, so he followed. In a few miles, the brake lights from the Bronco lit up and the left turn signal went off. As the vehicle slowed to turn off the highway and bounce down to a familiar-looking two-tire track trail up an ascending mound. Its sign announced itself to be Indian Mission Trail. Fritz was elated. Any trail back into deep woods had to be better than using a state highway.

Ten minutes more of following and the Bronco paused at a fork in the road and turned left. The sign said Cheney Road. Fritz stopped his vehicle, stepped outside to stand on its hood, and there above the trees he saw the ridgeline of Big Stony Lonesome. Before he put his car in gear, he removed the magazine from his M-16, filled the thirty-shot clip, tapped it back in place and, turning right, tore up the lumber trail.

The approaching violence would have made most men edgy or even frightened. But in Fritz's case, the oncoming gun play soothed him like a line or two of cocaine he snorted on occasion. His body relaxed. His face stopped swelling from the snake bites. His vision hadn't cleared, but taking a life, spilling blood, was the best medicine anyone could ever prescribe. He never felt more alive!

That's when Fritz saw the Mercury squad car parked where the day before he saw a Ford 150 pickup. He eased off the gas pedal and let his car's momentum roll itself up to the police vehicle. Its near-side door announced it belonged to the Ho-Chunk Sheriff's office. And the thought of an extra killing or two only caused Fritz to kiss his lips in eager anticipation.

Once his car stopped, Fritz soundlessly opened the driver's side door, and with two hands, grabbed his Kevlar body vest and the M-16 A1. "Just like the boss said: I can dust off a few redskins along with that white trash grandson Herman wanted to remove," he said to himself.

Ten minutes later, Fritz could see the sketchy outline of the top of the ridge where he had shot it out the night before. Maybe one or two deputies and a wounded or dead chief up there, likely in some wood hovel, Fritz decided. No one was going to stop him from chasing down Jack von Himmel. The thrill of the hunt rose in his throat and drove him forward.

"Shit!" he said out loud. In his haste and excitement, the Klan killer stepped on a small branch and the snap as it broke rode upland with the rising southern breeze. Fritz stopped, but only for a few seconds. "Hell, there's so much goofy wind whipping around this high country, nobody heard that little crunch," he thought to himself.

Fritz was right about the sound of the branch snapping. He was wrong about the sound of what he had said out loud when he broke it.

All three Ho-Chunk men in the lodge atop the ridge went on instant alert. Wind may stifle twigs snapping across miles of forest, but it also carries unnatural sounds like the human voice much farther up a hill than the speaker realizes.

"No one says 'shit' on their way up here," whispered Hanging Moon, "and comes as a friend."

Tomas and Tobias Two Boys agreed but had no reason to say so out aloud. Tomas accepted his brother's pistol and checked the chambers to make sure the .357 was fully loaded. Next, Tobias lifted his twelve-gauge pump to his chest, chambered a hollow point slug and handloaded four more rounds. "You have a better chance of hitting something with this shotgun," he said to Tomas, and the two brothers exchanged weapons. Then each man crept downhill in opposite directions.

Gully Hanging Moon forced himself to rest on his one good knee. He pushed back a blanket decorating the south wall near the lodge's entrance and removed a spare bow and quiver of arrows. Fighting waves of nausea and pain, the chief dragged himself out the door and willed himself farther up the bluff to a boulder that gave him a good view below and a rock to hide behind.

Once in place, he notched an arrow and looked down to examine the new bandages the deputies had applied to his damaged knee cap. A slowly expanding crimson circle issued from the wound. Hanging Moon assessed his situation, decided he had maybe fifteen minutes of consciousness left before the loss of blood made him pass out. He raised himself up enough to get a full draw on his bow when the time arrived. What would happen next would not need ten minutes, and he tested the bow string to assure himself he still had strength to draw it back.

The nearer Fritz approached the ridge top, the more cautious he became. When he passed the blanket-covered body of the man who ran with the spear, his caution waned. Danger was a drug of choice for him. Another minute of edging up the ridge, its curve above began to slide down the other side. Fritz grinned. He could see a rooftop, its mottled bark-brown cover poking out from among its surrounding jack pines.

Just as stepped forward to get a better look, a shotgun slug exploded the branch of a scrub oak inches from his left ear. Then another. As he dove for the cover of a rockpile, two quick pistol shots from the other side of the ridge clanged off the rocks, just above his back.

Fritz laughed. "You should have got me then," he snarled at his enemies. "You missed your only chance. Now I'm gonna kill both of you!" The Klansman fired off a burst to his right, a burst to his left, and surprisingly threw himself forward, up the hill toward the danger.

Both Two Boys' brothers silently cursed their bad marksmanship and were instantly confused by the killer's move to go uphill and not retreat down.

Tomas realized their weapons, his shotgun and Tobias's pistol, were poor matches against an automatic rifle. He had been to blame for one man's death already. This, he knew, could not happen again and in that instant charged upward, slightly to his left, using the screen of pine trees and rocks to provide some cover. Someone had to stop the gunman from claiming the high ground in this fight! He threw himself up the hill, his body inhaling its own adrenaline rush from the gunfight.

A long burst of gunfire tore up the brush and rocks around Tomas Two Boys. But his charge had drawn fire away from his brother and protected his badly wounded chief. When he heard his brother touch off two rounds, Tomas dove for the next rock pile a few feet further uphill.

He nearly reached it. The Klansman anticipated the rounds from his right were meant to be covering fire for the cop on his left to make another move. Fritz just looked for the next pile of boulders above the moving deputy, and when he saw a flash of motion, he let off a hailstorm of lead. Only one round hit Tomas. It took him on the right side of his leg, mid-calf. He screamed once and lay perfectly still, his wounded leg exposed like a dead man's appendage, but his motionless body drew no more fire.

Tobias heard his brother scream, and with the singular knowledge only twins possess, knew in that split second, Tomas was not dead but at deadly risk. He slid two rounds into his revolver, shouted his brother's name and raced forward, firing non-stop as he came.

Tobias's wild charge was just what Fritz needed. The running man had no real ability to aim a steady shot, and he was crazy with fear and anger. This would be easy, Fritz knew. He just raised himself up enough to see over the small boulder that concealed him. Sighting through his 4X power scope, he centered the crosshairs on the deputy. But his swollen eyelids made him blink—

The arrow took the Klansman in the center of his forehead. He simply toppled over, a bloody ragdoll on a stone carpet. When Tomas reached the dead man, he emptied his last three rounds into the Nazi's tattooed face, then collapsed from his bullet wound. A few seconds later Tobias arrived and quickly strapped his belt directly over the bullet hole and helped Tomas back up the hill to their chief. It would take the better part of the night to care for Gully Hanging Moon, then for Tomas. It made no sense to tromp around anymore at night when killers with night goggles could still arrive on the scene, and there were two badly wounded men to assist.

After Tobias lifted Hanging Moon on a blanket litter and pulled him down to the lodge, he turned his attention to his injured twin. "Well, Tomas," he said. "You had a score to even...and you did it. But putting three shots into a dead man at close range isn't really target practice!"

Chapter 71

JACK WAS SURE that the Two Boys' twins would call for helpers and lead them to Chief Hanging Moon. And once he came to the fork Tobias had told him about, Jack turned left. His anxiety had been running at fever pitch. It had taken more than a half-hour to drive out to the main road. Fortunately, once he reached it, he calmed down a bit. Driving the truck was no problem for any fifteen-year-old farm kid in Wisconsin. Jack had been tooling around the driveway, backing up the truck to offload grain sacks for the animals since he was ten.

But another problem did present itself. Where was the Granite River flowage and how long would it take to get there? Jack knew he was close to Warrens, and he was friendly with Rosie Beecham, the easy-going, very obese owner, and ever-present counter lady of the only gas station in the village. Once he finished his sandwich and coke, he backed the Ford pickup out of the parking lot at Waseda

Park, turned east and drove back the three miles needed to see Rosie.

"Goin' to do some fishin' yet tonight, Jack?" she asked when he inquired for directions to Granite River dam. "Pretty darn dark and cold for that stuff this evening what with the eclipse and everything!"

"Well, the dam is real lit up, and I plan on fishing real close to the spillway where the walleyes like to feed," he said, reminding himself that Rosie was nobody's fool.

"Uh huh..." replied Rosie, very much unconvinced, and she swiveled in her seat enough to look out at the gas pump area. "If that's what you're up to, how come I don't see fishin' poles stickin' out the bed of your pickup? And by the way, why are you driving Pete Koleski's truck anyway?"

Jack thought fast. "Ok, Rosie. You got me! It's Pete's truck, and I'll be driving my girl Sara over there because it's a pretty dramatic scene. I've always wanted to show it to her."

"Uh huh..." Rosie replied. Then she leaned over and gave the young man a sly grin. "Anything else you gonna show your girlfriend, Jack? Round and hard but shorter than a fishing pole?" and she gave him an exaggerated wink. "It's all over town that you two are getting serious, you know!"

Jack blushed. Nothing could be hidden from those who lived in a little village anywhere in the country he realized. He needed to say something closer to the truth. "Well…maybe you might have something there," he confessed. "But please, just tell me how to get there, ok?"

And she did. The idea of buying a pack of rifle rounds briefly crossed his mind, but Jack dismissed it. Rosie would become instantly suspicious. He would head on back using County O and Highway 12 to Hamot, turn left on Highway 21, drive to the dam and start climbing the Externstein hill. He had to get there before the eclipse if he understood what his grandfather was up to. The thought ate at his mind like battery acid in bread.

Chapter 72

"**ALL RISE! DEPARTMENT** One of the Monroe County Circuit Court is now in session. Judge Terrence Windshill presiding."

Windshill nodded to his bailiff, stepped up to his platform desk and said, "Good morning, Ladies and Gentlemen. Calling the case of the People versus Herman and Adolf von Himmel. Are the people ready?"

District Attorney Blake responded, "Ready for the People, Your Honor.'

"Ready for the defense, Your Honor," said Forrester, and he opened his briefcase to remove some papers.

"If the court, please, Your Honor," began Blake, "last minute developments in this case have led to one party's confession admitting guilt to the charges and a resulting plea agreement. The defendant Adolf von Himmel has signed a confession in the presence of two witnesses in which he admits sole responsibility for the bombing of the cranberry marsh and total guilt for the charge of manslaughter in the first degree in the deaths of the two men from the Twin Cities who kidnapped Jack von Himmel from a home in Wisconsin Rapids."

"And why isn't Adolf here to admit this himself?'

"Your Honor, he is in critical condition in the Hamot Hospital Critical Care unit fighting for his life against gangrene. He has lived through two surgical amputations and is heavily medicated. However, the defense has a signed and witnessed confession that was completed when Adolf was lucid."

"Is that right, Mr. Forrester?" asked Windshill.

"Yes, Your Honor. I have it right here, and if the bailiff will take it up to you for your perusal, we can move ahead with releasing his father Herman, here by my side."

The bailiff took the confession to Windshill, who spent several minutes studying it. "The confession on its face looks genuine, Mr. Forrester. Are the People satisfied, Ms. Blake?"

"We are, Your Honor, but since this confession appeared just before trial, I want to reserve the right to open this case again if there is any false testimony or if hidden facts are later revealed. The People also stipulate that there remain other possible charges regarding the disappearance of Jack von Himmel and questions as to his present whereabouts."

"What about that, Mr. Forrester?" asked the judge. "What's prompted one of your clients to take the entire blame?"

Forrester looked across the aisle and gave Director Mountain Wolf a stare of pure hatred. "Well, to be frank, Your Honor, there are several compelling reasons why Adolf signed the confession."

"Name them, please!"

"Your Honor should know that the most compelling reason why Adolf is admitting his crimes is he has an overwhelming sense of grief for what he has done to his family, especially his father Herman, who is blameless in all this. The second reason is that Adolf is desperately ill, and he told me he can't rest without a clear conscience, sir."

"Clear conscience? The bar fights on his record don't seem very convincing he has any strong sense of right and wrong, Counselor. But is there anything else?"

Forrester sensed the judge was likely unconvinced yet. He did not have to automatically accept the plea bargain worked out with Blake.

"Yes, Your Honor, there are two other compelling reasons for Adolf to plead out to these charges. Because he has suffered the entire amputation of his right arm, and part of his leg, District Attorney Blake has agreed to a lenient sentence because the defendant literally won't be a threat to anyone anymore."

"I'll be the judge of that, Mr. Forrester," snapped Windshill. "What's your last point—and you better hope it's a good one."

"If your Honor please, the notoriety of the bombing, shooting and kidnapping in this case drew the attention of the FBI and its Crime Lab Director, Lucille Mountain Wolf, who is seated to the right of the prosecutor."

"Yes, I know that, Counselor. Go on."

"Yesterday, Madame Director informed me that in her investigation into the possible deaths of the two fraudulent state patrol officers, the evidence she collected at the bottom of the Goodyear Marsh Lake was absolutely one hundred percent certain. And given that her record is perfect, that she's never been overturned in court, and the absolute certainty of her evidence from the bottom of the lake, my client decided it was best to admit his crimes. He wishes to throw himself on the mercy of the court, plead for a reduced sentence due to the dangerous spread of his gangrene and submit himself to the state for his remaining medical care."

"So the real reason is more about absolute proof and free hospital care, isn't it, Mr. Forrester?" said Judge Windshill as he smiled. "But you don't have to answer that."

The judge turned one last time to the prosecution. "And, Ms. Blake, the district attorney's office is agreeable?"

"Yes, we are, Your Honor. We have agreed to the lighter sentence for Adolf that is contained in the documents we just provided you. Given the fact he has admitted his guilt and has had two amputations to date, we are recommending a sentence of five to seven years for Adolf, with parole available in three years counting time already served."

"And the defense finds this agreement acceptable, Your Honor," said Forrester as he looked over at Herman von Himmel. The old man's nod and cough was good enough.

Windshill's voice rivaled an ice storm from the Artic. "Therefore, the prosecution and the defense find it acceptable to provide a light sentence for a man who has admitted to a heinous bombing which destroyed an entire cranberry operation at the cost of millions of dollars to restore one day? The prosecution and defense somehow find it acceptable to make no mention of possible restitution for the millions of dollars and decades of growth time for the crop and vines lost? The prosecution and defense find it acceptable to put a man in prison for three years despite his admission to the murder of two human beings?

Forrester swallowed hard. This wasn't how things were supposed to go!

Judge Windshill lifted himself out of his chair, rested both elbows on his desktop, and almost shouted— "Well, this court does not find any of this acceptable! None of it! The defendant is hereby sentenced to a term in the State Prison of a period of no less than twenty-five years to life, without the possibility of parole! And what's more, I'll look forward to whatever new information comes out of the continuing investigation into the disappearance of one Jack von Himmel!"

"But you can't do that, Judge! We had an agreement with the prosecutor!" shouted Forrester.

"So what? You had no such agreement with me, Mr. Forrester. Remember, even you admitted the FBI Director's evidence is one hundred percent certain. Her evidence is absolutely damming for your client, and what's more, you are out of order, sir! One more outburst and you'll be held in contempt of court! This trial is over. Court is adjourned!" The judge slammed down his gavel, stood up, and strode out of the courtroom.

Forrester was a cauldron of rage. He twisted to his right to face the prosecution team. The sight of District Attorney Blake doing her best to suppress a wide grin only infuriated him more.

A heavy hand grabbed Forrester left shoulder from behind and pulled him backwards. "Adolf won't never accept any of what you done, Lawyer Man!"

"You already told me you had another solution for Adolf, you old shit!" Forrester snarled back at Herman von Himmel, his fierce whisper almost audible in court.

Then before he got into any more exchanges with the old man, Forrester strode across the aisle and exploded at his real opponent, FBI Director Mountain Wolf.

"It's all your doing!" he shouted, and the noise of his outburst drew the attention of Commander Post and the bailiff.

But Forrester would not stop. "You and your damnable tests! One hundred percent certainty you said!"

"Yes, I did, Counselor. And, for that matter, I still do say that!" replied the director evenly.

"You and your one hundred percent evidence! If there had been even a glimmer of doubt, just ninety-nine percent certainty, in cross examination I would have made you look like an unreliable, incompetent, rookie lab tech. That's what I could have done!"

"But my evidence was perfect, Counselor," replied Lucille Mountain Wolf. As she spoke, both

Commander Post and the bailiff grabbed hold of Forrester, ready to forcefully restrain him if needed.

"Yeah, right. Perfect! That's what you forced me to tell Herman here. I had to tell him that the proof you dug out of the lake was one hundred percent!"

"Yes, Mr. Forrester. My evidence was one hundred percent and still is . . . one hundred percent . . . MUD!"

. . . Forrester stood transfixed. "You say what?"

"I am saying my evidence from the lake bottom is one hundred percent mud. M-U-D! You know, the soft, brown mucky stuff that lines every lake in the universe! After all, you never asked me about what I had one hundred percent of in the collection samples!"

"But my client was just sentenced to life in prison for nothing! You can't do that!"

"I just did Mr. Lawyer Man, but it was your mistake.... Not mine!" and the director looked over Forrester's shoulder to make direct eye contact with Herman. She smiled at him and added, "You do understand, Mr. von Himmel? You are likely going to die in state prison because your ace defense attorney never thought to ask exactly what I had in the evidence jars." Then she winked at both men, turned her back on them, and began to walk away under the protective escort of Commander Post of the State Patrol.

"You timber nigger!" Forrester shouted. "I'll see you and your freaking wolf dog deader than a lynched black man!"

The FBI Director stopped, turned back, and with a baleful stare at the KKK lawyer offered a stone-cold reply: "You already had my final warning last time we argued, Forrester. Time's up. Better watch your ass!" She made a chomping gesture with both hands at the man and then left.

Chapter 73

ALL THE WAY back to Hamot, Herman von Himmel said nothing to Forrester. Forrester, in turn, tried several times to explain how the long sentence for Adolf really wasn't a problem. At the worst, he or Fritz could just swing by Adolf's hospital bed in the next day or two and put him permanently to sleep with a pillow.

But Herman would have none of what Forrester was selling. When the lawyer finally reached Hamot, he stopped to allow the old man to enter the Farmers' and Workers' Bank and extract the twenty-thousand-dollar withdrawal. Old man von Himmel returned to the Mercedes and made only one comment . . . "You just killed both of us, you fool! If I don't take some steps, they find Jack and then they come for me."

They drove several blocks before Herman spoke again. "Drop me off at the Vanfleet Ford Dealership outside town, Shyster Lawyer!" Herman would not even bring himself to look at Forrester when he said it and remained silent until they arrived.

"But I still got you off, Herman! No need to call the KKK about what just happened, right?" As von Himmel opened the car door, Forrester knew he was pleading for his life.

"I don't need to call them about you, Lawyer Man!" Herman von Himmel's eyes blazed with revenge, as he stepped out of the Benz. "Such a smart man you are, huh? You don't figure out that right away I am sure you promised them my gold? You called me stupid back there in Sparta. Well, nobody knows where the fortune is but me! It has been the support of my family always. Now when he asks, you tell your Klan boss you not only screwed up the trial, but you also lost him and the KKK millions in gold too."

"We can still get out of all this, Herman," begged Forrester. "Just trust me! I don't know what you're planning to do with the girl now, but we can blame Fritz for her kidnapping and the shootout up on Big Stony. He'll have to take the wrap for killing Jack because the both of us were in court! You can still have a good life, Herman!"

"No, Lawyer Man," said Herman in a curiously calm tone of voice. "I don't need no mortal life no more."

"What in the hell are you saying? There isn't anything else but life and death, Herman! Just let me take control and get us out of this disaster!" Forrester was beyond desperate. What on earth was this old Nazi talking about?

"You wrong, Lawyer Man. There is something better than life and death."

"Better than life? Death is not an improvement on life, Herman."

"Immortality is! Immortality with Odin in Valhalla is better than life, better than death. And tonight, with the eclipse, I have all that I need to become immortal when I make a perfect God-Man child for Odin who will replace my dead sons!"

For the first time he could ever remember, Forrester, the perfect defense attorney, had a bar exam he couldn't pass. An eclipse? Joining Odin? Herman's plans left the lawyer dumbfounded. When the old Nazi shut the car door, Forrester knew there was only one option on the table left for him: find the von Himmel horde before somebody else did! After all, didn't Herman say it had always been the support of his family? What kind of support could he be talking about? Forrester decided there was only one way to find out—start looking!

Chapter 74

IF FRITZ WAS successful, he should have been waiting at the motel room or just about to arrive, Herman reasoned. All the bad luck and wrong turns of his family life weighed like a boatload of iron ore on him. After purchasing a beefy, white Cadillac with a big trunk at the Ford dealership, he drove back to the motel room with the faint hope he would find Fritz there. If the killer had been successful in his second trip out to the hills, he should arrive back no later than mid-afternoon, Herman decided. If Fritz was a no-show by then, Herman would use Plan B, the one he referenced in his last conversation with Forrester.

At 4:00 pm, Herman von Himmel decided Fritz had failed and likely was a dead man. He phoned a Volk Field Airforce Base number, made his request for another helicopter ride, agreed to an even larger payment for services rendered, opened the large truck of his Caddy and when he was certain no one was watching, using the immense strength of his single arm, dumped in a terrified Sara Koleski. His plan was to force their way to the top of the Externstein, and once the eclipse began, he would have nearly four hours to use the girl to replace his dead children and claim his immortality.

It took just less than an hour for Herman to reach the parking lot across the river from the Externstein hill. He smiled ruefully when a helicopter swooped down out of the early evening sky to land on the east shoreline's parking lot.

"How many damn people do you intend to bury up there on that bluff, Mister?" The pilot had climbed out of the chopper when Herman signaled he needed help with something in his trunk. "I can't say the name of the officer who sent me here from Volk Field, but he told me to tell you this is the last time he's going to accommodate your requests. Ok?"

"*Ja*, sure—it's gonna be plenty ok," said von Himmel. "I will not need no help again from him or nobody else."

Herman couldn't read the pilot's facial reactions given his helmet had on a dark sunshield over his face, but for his plan to work it didn't matter what the pilot felt.

"Now I open this trunk, and you help me carry the package over to that whirlybird. Once we are on top of the Externstein, I will set you free!" explained the old Nazi.

Somehow, as the pilot heard the old man's directions and explanation, it just didn't sound right. But he decided the guy was just a weirdo who had a thing about burying family members on a hilltop.

Herman unlocked the trunk and stepped back, gesturing for the pilot to lift the top. Being anxious to get this strange mission over with as quickly as possible, the pilot put his hands on the trunk, lifted the lid and . . ..

"Now, don't you get no stupid ideas, Mister Pilot!" Herman had wrapped his enormous arm around the man's neck as he bent forward to investigate the trunk. Herman pulled his boning knife from his waistband and shoved it tightly against the pilot's neck.

"What the hell!" the pilot barked as he lifted his head slightly up and away from what he saw. "You've got a high school girl all tied up in here!"

"Ya, you see pretty good!"

The chopper pilot was both disgusted and fascinated by the girl tied in strips of bedsheets. She wiggled frantically when the lid opened. Her eyes widened in pure terror. She was trying to scream, but the linen tie through her mouth muffled both the words and the sounds. It was at that moment his military training kicked in.

With a violent spin, the pilot tried to shrug off Herman's grip and break free from a man who appeared to be a budding serial killer. He tried. But von Himmel was too strong and had anticipated the attempt.

"Not so fast, whirlybird boy!" and using his irresistible strength, Herman re-established his grip and control. Then he pushed the knife into the struggling man's neck just enough to draw blood and pain.

"Now then! I gonna keep this knife right where it is while you pick up the girl and carry her over to the machine," Herman said. "You gonna strap her in the back seat. Then I'm gonna walk us both to my seat, and after I am buckled in, you gonna crawl over the top of me into your seat. Then we fly up to the hilltop like before. Then I am gonna release you."

The knife blade was jiggling about a half-inch inside the pilot's neck. He had to move like he was drowning in molasses just to keep the pain at a tolerable level. There was no choice but to comply.

Von Himmel switched the knife to pressure the middle of his helper's spine, while the pilot lifted Sara out of the trunk, carried her to the aircraft, lifted her to the back seat and buckled her in. The soldier intentionally made eye contact with the teenager and gave her a tiny nod of his head he meant to help her.

Then in the most incredibly awkward way, Herman backed into his seat and forced the pilot to crawl over him to get to the controls. An instant later and the aircraft was clawing its way upward into the dark gloom of the Externstein and its shrine.

"So I see you got a name tag!" von Himmel announced as the helicopter came to rest just beyond range of the Irminsul shrine atop the hill. "You are called Manningham!"

Frank Manningham just nodded. He didn't want to give the crazy old man who had a knife any reason to use it. Two minutes later they were on top of the granite peak above the Granite River dam. The pilot tensed as the wing rotations of the helicopter started to subside as it hovered inches above the ground. It gave riders the feeling and expectation that the ride was over. And Manningham planned for the second that the nutcase next to him unbuckled his shoulder strap-seat belt. At that precise time, jamming the controls back and to the right, the pilot believed he had a great chance to spill out the dangerous man and make good an escape for him and the terrified girl.

"Ucccccccckkk!—" was Frank Manningham's last word. Herman von Himmel stabbed the pilot directly through his neck into the carotid artery, then swept the knife forward and out, effectively cutting the man's throat. Blood spurted and sprayed a treacherous arc across the pilot's side of the inside canopy. As Manningham slumped forward grasping at his throat and the helicopter settled down, von Himmel drove the blade into the man again and again.

"*Ja*, another problem—another dead man solution!" sneered von Himmel. Then after wiping some blood spatter off his face, Herman folded up his knife, flipped the aircraft engine switch to off, climbed out of the front seat, reached back into the rear, and dragged Sara Koleski out of the chopper.

Chapter 75

"**By Gott, you're** a full-grown woman!" he said to her as he bounced Sara Koleski in his arms. "My Jack wasn't so much a *dummkopf* as I thought." He bounced her again to assess her size and weight. "*Ja*, you would make my grandson a plenty good baby-maker. Good wide hips! Plenty good breasts!" Then his face shriveled into a badge of cruelty, and he said, "But tonight when the moon is covering the black sun, you will service another von Himmel to make a God-man in your belly!"

Sara wailed and twisted against her bindings. Herman only laughed and tied her to the shrine's pole. The next thing the old Nazi did was to disappear into the patch of woods behind the shrine on the hilltop. In a few minutes he reappeared, dragging several logs which at some earlier point had been soaked with creosote. Two more trips followed after which the man arranged the logs into a square stack about twenty feet from her. He walked behind

441

Sara, bent down, shoved on what appeared to be the base of the eagle's head pole he had tied the girl to, opened a large box-like compartment and removed several items.

The first two items the old man pulled out were a plastic bag full of old newspapers and a box of matches. He returned to his log square, crumbled the newspapers, stuck them inside the logs, dragged the dead body of the pilot to his funeral pyre and lifted him on top.

"Odin be praised," he began to chant repeatedly. "This night will ensure my acceptance into your Asgaard Palace. The sacrifices I make here will inspire you to give me the gift of immortality! It is the night of the black sun and the full eclipsis of the moon. As I impregnate this young slave, you will grow the God-man inside of her! It will be the beginning of what our divine ruler Adolf Hitler predicted—the perfect man will rule the world; he will bring forth all perfect humans for his world, and together they will enslave all the inferior races!

Von Himmel strode over to check Sara's bindings. After a satisfactory tug, he put his face tight to hers. "Know this, *Fraulein*. If you dare try to abort the Man-god child I put in your womb tonight, you will bleed to death on the spot! Odin will have his sacrifice one way or another!

"And once you give birth, Odin will send me as an avenging spirit to protect the child with his Spear of Destiny. You are a Jewess but know that your child will be a Nazi god because I will be his father!"

And shouting "Odin be praised," von Himmel lit the entire box of matches, tossed them into the fire square and watched as their flames rocketed upward to incinerate the pilot's body.

Herman von Himmel was now in a manic fury. He went back to the base of the Irminsul center pole, looked up into the fantastic eyes of the Nazi eagle head resting on top, then knelt back down to remove a very curious, leather-wrapped packet.

"Ha!" he shouted in ecstasy. *"Der Speer des Shicksals!"* and he unwrapped the leather sheets holding the contents and removed a gleaming, golden triangle. It was a hollow scabbard about ten inches long. The wide-open end was about five inches, the narrow end was open only a half-inch. He reached into his right, front pants' pocket and drew out a shiny, metallic triangle.

"Ja, das tip!" he uttered, and in one swift motion he fitted the spear tip to the front slots of the blade, sliding the long golden sheath over the spear point and up the shaft, until it perfectly snugged up against the widest section of spear and exactly covered the business end of the weapon. "Now!" von Himmel cried out. *"Ja!* I have now a full spear, a

moon eclipse, and a virgin slave . . . all together at the Irminsul!"

Sara was wild with fear and pain. Her muffled cries drew the old man's attention again. Herman walked to her and pushed himself tight to her face and body. She did her best to turn away from him, but her wrappings allowed virtually no move-ment. Herman put his abdomen tightly against hers and sneered.

"Ah my little *Fraulein*, I think you secretly like the idea of my spear, don't you?" The girl tried to shake her head violently in a useless effort to show her revulsion for the old man and what he intended to do. "I tried to pierce my son here with the spear in my pants, but it was no good! Odin be praised! —he demands all his rituals to be real! And now I have you, and I, and my babymaker will not be denied!"

Sara worked her lips and tongue enough to push the wrappings away from her mouth. "Noooo!" she screamed and spit into the old man's face. He stepped away from her only slightly, just giving him enough room to lower his gold-tipped spear to her abdomen, turn the blade flat and stroke her crotch. Wiping the spittle away from his eyes with his free left hand, he shouted—"Yes, tonight you will be the bride of Herman von Himmel. And the baby I make inside your womb must remain until it is born, or you will die smothered in your own blood if you try to remove the God-man I give you." He removed his shirt and unbuttoned his pants.

A bullet ricocheted off the golden scabbard of the spear's sheath, then another.

"Never! Never will you do this! Sara is mine!" Jack von Himmel raged as he leapt from a large rock he had just ascended. He was wild with the fury his grandfather had visited upon him.

"Now get away from Sara!" shouted Jack. He threw away the empty rifle as he cleared the rim of the hill and climbed down the rocky ledge encircling the Irminsul to fight his grandfather.

Drawing the .357 pistol from his belt, the boy approached Herman von Himmel. Jack stopped just out of what he thought was effective spear-throwing range and leveled the pistol at his Nazi grandfather.

"Step away from her, drop your spear, and I will let you live, *Opa*!"

Von Himmel grinned first, then laughed out loud. "What you think you are, little *dummkopf*! A man? Are you man enough to pull that trigger and kill the one who brought your father and you into this world with this spear of my flesh?" and the old man gestured obscenely to his groin.

"Yes!" Jack said calmly. "I'm changed! I am a man now, not a groveling kid afraid of your anger. You've done your best to kill me. I followed you out to the Goodyear Marsh where Uncle Adolf was supposed to bash my head in with a hammer. You had men come for me on Stony Lonesome, and one of them killed my father. And now you think you can make a baby inside my Sara."

Jack cocked the hammer of the heavy pistol and centered the front sight on Herman's belly, below the golden thunderbolt of Odin. "Better think again," the boy declared.

Herman made a deadly rush at Jack, the old man's long-handled spear and its mythical tip thrust toward the boy's chest.

Jack pulled the trigger. He heard nothing but an empty ckiss. He cocked the hammer again, pulled the trigger, heard only a sickening ckiss and threw himself in a dive to his right to avoid being impaled.

"Tomas! You never loaded your weapon!" Jack shouted as he rolled into brush and rock along the perimeter of the hilltop. And in the next instant, he was up exchanging the empty pistol for the boning knife he took from Hanging Moon's lodge.

Three more lunges, three more parries, each time with Jack leaping away.

"*Ja!*" screamed von Himmel in an insane fit of laughter. "What you do when I stick something else into your girlfriend? What you do then?" and the old man spun around and raced back to the pole where Sara remained tied.

Her cries ripped at Jack's heart. Out of the desperation born of circumstance he thought of the only thing he could do—he threw the knife at the center of his grandfather's back.

It bounced off harmlessly. Jack had never tried throwing a big knife before, he realized. Now he was without a weapon, and his grandfather turned again and ran toward the boy. At that very instant the moon was blotted out by the sun's shadow. It was completely black!

Herman von Himmel cackled in a crazed laugh as he made a wicked charge at his grandson. The length of the spear gave the old man some advantage in the fight, but Jack had the speed and quickness of youth. Herman's blade came fast in a swooping motion as his grandson dodged. The spear nicked Jack on his right side, mid-rib high, then sliced through and carried the blade and the lunging grandfather past the boy.

Jack staggered, his mind in turmoil from the sharp pain of the blade and the fog of struggle. Sara wailed helplessly, biting to loosen more of the bindings over her mouth and jaw.

"Jack!" she screamed— "look out!" and the warning was just enough.

Jack ducked low and to his left this time, and from deep within himself drew his last reserves of courage. As Herman's second lunge carried the old man to the boy, Jack stuck out his right leg and tripped von Himmel. The old man went head-over-heels into the same kind of brush and rock that Jack had used to hide.

In the few seconds he had while the old man recovered, the boy rushed to Sara and tore at the bedsheet ropes which held her to the stake.

"No!" she screamed and only the reflexes of the young gave Jack a nano-second of time to swing his head out of the way of the oncoming man and his spear. It slid across his left ear lobe and buried itself in the wooden pole holding Sara.

There was nothing left to do. Nowhere to go. As Herman struggled to pull the spear out of the creosoted wood of the Irminsul's center pole, Jack threw himself up the statue in a desperate climb for his life.

The boy knew he would die rather than concede. Herman's pause to raise the spear gave the boy a split second. With it, he leaped to the highest rung on the shrine's center pole and frantically clawed his way to the rock eagle's head.

"*Ja!*" shouted von Himmel. "Now all you got is a good place to watch me make the God-man in your girlfriend's womb!" and holding the spear in his left hand, he used his right to drop his pants and lift Sara's dress. "Odin be praised!" he roared.

"Never! Never!" screamed Jack, and with all the might and force within him, he rocked the Nazi eagle's head forward once, backward once, and with the last ounce of his strength pushed it off its perch, straight down to kiss his grandfather upturned face.

Herman von Himmel only had time to drop his spear and raise his hands in a futile attempt to stop the massive stone eagle before it flattened him and his useless weapon into a bloody puddle of flesh and twisted metal. The spear tip was thrown free from the shattered shaft. The golden scabbard was split apart and broken into pieces large and small. The fury of the fight gave up its ghost. The north wind off the Granite River exhaled a slow, wistful sigh announcing Herman von Himmel was no more. He died without a weapon in his hand. The bonfire simply simmered and then winked out.

It was finished.

Jack climbed down the shrine's pole. Sara quietly sobbed as he released her bindings. He gently put his head on her shoulder and cried too. Minutes passed in exhausted silence.

When Sara herself found enough strength to speak, she turned her face to Jack, stroked his face and whispered, "Oh, Jack—in the end, how did you know what to do? He had the spear!"

Jack lifted his face to hers, smiled a lover's smile and replied— "Rock crushes scissors!"

KKK Attorney Found Dead; Millions Donated to Family

-by Irma Lee, Hamot Journal News Staff-

Yesterday a bizarre twist of fate brought a fatal conclusion to the bombing of a local cranberry marsh and the kidnapping of local teenager Jack von Himmel.

Last week Karl von Himmel, the boy's uncle, died in a shootout with the Wisconsin State Patrol after he shot and killed Hamot Chief of Police Dewey Lassiter.

Jack's father Gunther was next to die. He was gunned down by a partner in crime, one of two agents of the Ku Klux Klan who showed up to find the boy once he escaped from the kidnapping. One of the KKK agents killed Peter Koleski, owner of the cranberry operation the von Himmels bombed in early September. Later, both Klan killers died in separate gunfights with War Chief Gully Hanging Moon and two deputies of the Ho-Chunk tribe.

The head of the family, Herman von Himmel, an acknowledged Nazi leader in Wisconsin kidnapped Sara Koleski and died in a fight over her with his grandson, Jack.

At trial Adolf von Himmel (a.k.a. Ade) had a guilty plea entered for him for murdering two Nazis who tried to swindle money from the family. Last night Adolf was pronounced dead at Hamot Memorial Hospital due to a massive gangrene infection from a wound received in an exchange of gunfire with Sheriff Josiah Grey Fox of the Black River Ho-Chunk Nation.

Finally, Ku Klux Klan lead attorney N.B. Forrester's corpse was found at the von Himmel trailer shortly after the trial yesterday afternoon. His fingernail marks on the stone supports used to level the trailer revealed Forrester had discovered that the undercarriage bricks were gold bars in disguise.

When an FBI crime lab expert, Lucille Mountain Wolf arrived at the trailer with State Patrol Commander Frederick Post, they found that some large predator had been feeding off the corpse of the attorney. The unidentified animal apparently had cornered the attorney against the trailer and devoured Forrester's posterior before disappearing into the bog.

The gold bars have been appraised at approximately ten million dollars. Jack von Himmel, the only surviving heir, announced he is reimbursing the money to the Koleski family as restitution to rehabilitate their cranberry marsh.

Chapter 76

IT WAS JACK'S first night in his new home. Police Chief Dewey Lassiter's widow generously stepped forward to be the boy's foster mother. Betty Lassiter allowed she was old enough to be his grandmother, but age she told the welfare department had nothing to do with the amount of comfort, love, and protection two lonely people could share. None of Jack's distant relatives had shown any interest in taking him in.

When bedtime arrived, Jack discovered what the woman meant about safety and comfort. As he sat down on the edge of his bed, the boy found himself marveling at the crisp feel of starched white sheets and the welcoming bright red and blue checkered comforter that made up his bed. Nothing in the universe of the von Himmel double-wide trailer prepared him for such luxury. It wasn't until he was falling asleep that Jack's memories conjured images of his dead Nazi kin, the KKK assassins who had failed to kill him, and most of all, his family's constant rants spouting irrational hatred for anyone different. Another being also recalled in vivid detail its return to the original scene of the crime.

As he was beginning the last, critical steps of his stalk, the sleek, brindle brown, black and white timber wolf sensed something again wasn't right. But this time he had a different target. His pack leader's experiences alerted him to the fact his prey was paying no attention to safety. This human, a tall, angular male, instead was furiously clawing at the underpinnings of the old mobile home the wolf and his pack occasionally visited still, despite the fact his brother wolf died there. So typical of all the human species, this food source was completely involved in an unsafe situation without any means of escape or thought of protection.

Yes, the von Himmel pack that had lived in the trailer had been shot, had run away or had been forced to leave. The human who shot his brother wolf died in a firestorm of lead; he was the first of two human pack members who had provided warm blood for tasting and satisfaction for where it came from. True, this target was not a trailer pack member, but his occasional visits made it clear this prey did run with them. And, of course, retribution was always on the agenda.

A voice within him had announced it was time to restore a semblance of order when his regular visit to the mobile home turned into a hunting opportunity, and the wolf had hurried to obey. Besides, the mountain wolf looked forward to protecting the boy who had fed his pack. Perhaps, somewhere in his long genetic history, man had tamed one of his forebearers with food. Perhaps not. But this was a chance to defend a friend.

. . . When the wolf reached the last strands of marsh grass hiding his presence, he discovered his adult prey was laser-focused on scratching loose some small, dark rectangular stones from beneath it. Then, curiously enough, the man bathed them in a bucket before the wiping off process revealed their bright, flashy gold surface. Even when the wolf made its final rush, no alarm, no scent of fear erupted from the human like it would have from a rabbit or whitetail deer. Instead, even in its last nanosecond of life, the pre-occupied human exuded the perfume of overripe flowers and fruit—the sugary stench almost disgusting enough to turn the attack aside.

Almost.

The pack leader lunged. The adult human crouching against the trailer's foundation had just enough time to half-turn and try to speak . . . as if words would provide a defense. The mere idea of prey arguing its way out of a trap rebelled against natural law. The mountain wolf simply snapped its jaws shut around the human's face to stop his noise, and when the target stopped thrashing, the bite stopped his breath. Nature this day would have the last word.

Afterwards, on the way back to his den high in hill country, the leader of the Big Stony Lonesome pack had to pause and smile his broad wolf smile. Wide and fierce, the grin's manufacture was the result of a belly full of red meat. His pups, he realized, would yip and howl in ecstasy upon his return. In fulfilling his role as a consummate leader, a protecter and, most importantly, a provider, he understood his family would welcome him home. All of them together now would be safe from fear, from want, and from hate because of him.

The next morning Jack thought he would be too.

-THE END-

Discussion Questions for Murder on Big Stony Lonesome

1. What kind of story did you expect when you first saw the book cover and title?

2. After finishing the story, how close did the novel come to meeting your expectations?

3. Which character did you feel most closely connected to? Which ones were offensive and why?

4. What comparisons and descriptions from the story did you find effective?

5. What surprises did you discover in the story?

6. Was this story hard or easy to read? Why?

7. What were some of your favorite lines in the story? Why did you like them?

8. Which characters seemed the most believable and the least believable? Why?

9. What details of the story setting taught you something or helped to make the scenes come alive?

10. Along with the murder of several people, what else is murdered in the story?

11. If you could tell the author one thing about the story, what would it be?

12 What roles and purposes does the wolf play and serve in the story?